THE
END OF
THE LINE

Edited by
Jonathan Oliver

THE
END OF
THE LINE

New horror stories set on and around
the Underground, the subway, the Metro
and other places deep below

Edited by
Jonathan Oliver

Nineteen stories by:

Paul Meloy
John L. Probert
Nicholas Royle
Rebecca Levene
Jasper Bark
Simon Bestwick
Al Ewing
Conrad Williams
Pat Cadigan
Adam L. G. Nevill
Mark Morris
Stephen Volk
Ramsey Campbell
Michael Marshall Smith
James Lovegrove
Gary McMahon
Natasha Rhodes
Joel Lane
Christopher Fowler

SOLARIS

First published 2010 by Solaris
an imprint of Rebellion Publishing Ltd,
Riverside House, Osney Mead,
Oxford, OX2 0ES, UK

www.solarisbooks.com

ISBN 978-1-907519-32-1

Cover by Luke Preece

Printed in the UK

CONTENTS

INTRODUCTION

FOR ME, THE London Underground is as evocative as any gothic pile or mist-shrouded graveyard when it comes to horror. I don't live in London, but I used to regularly visit when I performed stand-up comedy. Late night gigs would mean that I had to catch the last Tube back and I often found myself standing on an empty platform, praying that whatever was roaring towards me from the dark of the tunnel was a train, and not something worse. (Weirdly, one of my reoccurring dreams finds me trapped in vast, cathedral-like Underground stations.) It's surprising, then, that there haven't been more horror stories set in this subterranean world. There are, of course, classics of the genre such as *Death Line*, starring Donald Pleasence, and Neil Gaiman's brilliant fantasy, *Neverwhere*. But, in my opinion, the Underground is still a source relatively un-mined when it comes to horror fiction. This, then, is what prompted me to bring together some of the finest writers in the field to explore the world beneath our feet.

Of course, the London Underground – that iconic grandfather of all subterranean transport systems – is well represented here, but in my brief I encouraged authors to also look further afield. Hence we have stories set on the LA metro (the heavy-metal inspired 'Crazy Train' by Natasha Rhodes), the New York subway (Pat Cadigan's brilliant and moving 'Funny Things'), the Paris Metro (the sexually charged 'The Lure' by Nicholas Royle), and Liverpool's underground system (Ramsey Campbell's challenging story of paranoia, 'The Rounds'). There are also a handful of tales set on invented underground systems. Simon Bestwick reveals the secret history of the doomed Manchester underground in 'The Sons of The City',

Mark Morris takes us on a journey into a Cornish tin mine in 'Fallen Boys' and Gary McMahon's strange and Lovecraftian story 'Diving Deep' finds us in an iceberg in Antarctica.

It is to London, however, that many of our writers gravitated. Somewhat inevitable with a collection mainly populated by Brits, but it's incredible how thematically diverse these stories set in the UK's capital are. Stephen Volk asks just who is watching us as we take our journeys 'In The Colosseum' while the common fears of the commuter are explored in such breathlessly nightmarish stories as Adam L.G. Nevill's 'On All London Underground Lines' and James Lovegrove's darkly comic 'Siding 13'. There are also journeys into loss here with such powerful tales as 'Bullroarer' by Paul Meloy, 'Exit Sounds' by Conrad Williams and 'All Dead Years' by Joel Lane. Fans of sophisticated chills will find much to please them in Jasper Barke's Rod Serling-inspired 'End of The Line', John L. Probert's terrifically entertaining 'The Girl in The Glass', Michael Marshall Smith's cautionary tale 'Missed Connection', Al Ewing's garish, but brilliant, 'The Roses That Bloom Underground' and Rebecca Levene's creepy-as-hell tale, '23:45 Morden (via Bank)'.

And we end with a love-letter to London and the Underground, in Christopher Fowler's moving tale, 'Down.'

As you journey down into the worlds of these stories, just remember: depart from the correct side of the train and do check that your ticket takes you to somewhere you want to go…

Jonathan Oliver
Oxford
August 9th 2010

BULLROARER

Paul Meloy

Paul Meloy has that amazing knack of making the reader laugh out loud as well as delivering an emotional punch with his prose. His stories are beautifully rich and strange and have an intensity to them that makes him easily one of the most exciting new genre writers around. I remember being blown away when reading his story 'The Last Great Paladin of Idle Conceit' in an issue of The Third Alternative, *and every story I read after that from Paul made the writer in me green with envy. It's a great pleasure then to have Paul in* The End of The Line *and after reading the extraordinary story that follows, you could do no better than seek out Paul's remarkable collection* Islington Crocodiles.

NOEL BUCK HAD fallen into a stuporous doze on the train down from Manchester, and when he woke up, as the train was pulling into Euston station, he was dispirited to discover that his throat was raw, his head throbbed and every muscle ached like he'd been beaten with rubber hoses. Even his fingers hurt. His *skin* hurt. He had been incubating a 'flu bug for the past week and now it had arrived in force.

He grabbed his rucksack from beneath his seat and stumbled, bleary-eyed, down the aisle as the train pulled alongside the platform. His throat was so dry and painful it felt like his tonsils had enlarged to the size of fat, noxious plums; their presence at the back of his throat filled his world and every time he tried to swallow they ground together and made Noel want to be somewhere very far away from his own neck. He needed a cold drink. Coke. *Coke!* His tongue cramped with anticipation. He felt feverish, light-headed and weak. *How did this come on so fast?* Noel thought. But it wasn't much of a surprise. He was run-down, had been on the piss for six weeks solid and hadn't had a good night's sleep for roughly a year. His concept of five-a-day was units of alcohol consumed before lunch and nothing at all to do with portions of fruit and veg.

While he waited for the train to come to a standstill, Noel calculated the duration of the rest of his journey home. He reckoned he could make it to the Tube, take the southbound to Moorgate and then change for the Northern line to Morden just about without dying. He would then get a cab to Sutton and collapse in bed for a week. No more booze. Just lots of vitamins, Coke and cold and 'flu remedy. Then, when he'd emerged from his sickbed, weak and detoxified, he'd start rebuilding his life with a bit more dignity and focus.

He'd already started the ball rolling. He was on his way back from visiting his son at university. The reason he'd travelled up there was to break the news to Alan about his divorce from Alan's mother, Erica. To his surprise, Alan had shrugged and said, "I know, dad. Mum told me she was leaving you before I came up here."

That night, in the student bar, Noel had taken full advantage of the subsidised prices and got drunk. He remembered sitting in a booth talking with depleting eloquence to Alan and Alan's boyfriend – a scrawny little blonde student of dance called Ryan who spent the entire evening making grabs at Alan's knob beneath the table and grinning at Noel with tiny little sharp white teeth while his son snorted and slammed his knees against the underside of the table again and again in involuntary spasms – about how shit his life had become since Erica had left him.

To make matters worse, at some point in the evening a very overweight Indian girl called Niloufa had taken a liking to him and had begun a terrifying process of seduction which ended with ultimate disappointment following a quickie in the ladies toilet towards the end of the night. It had been, Noel reflected with tedious self-loathing, like trying to hang a manatee on a coat hook.

The problem with further education, Noel had decided when he woke up on the floor of Alan's room in the halls of residence, was that it gave people an unrealistic perspective on their course of life. It gave them a sense of control that was illusive if not downright delusional. Poncing around with their worthless fucking degrees with it all planned out. Noel's view had been that you got a job, worked hard to pay off your mortgage early, and then spent a long and happy retirement with the fucking *wife*. So much for that, but it wasn't lack of education that had destroyed his marriage, nor was it his innate distrust of those that pursued it. Not really.

Irritable and densely hung-over, Noel had gathered up his sleeping bag, stuffed it in his rucksack and let himself out. He'd stopped at the communal bathroom to be morosely sick, and then he'd left for the station without saying goodbye to his self-seeking, over-educated son.

Well, that was a start, he told himself. He knew where he stood. A week in bed with a high temperature might be just what he needed to sweat himself clear-headed again. Noel stepped off the train and made his way along the platform to the concourse leading to the escalators.

He stopped at a booth and bought a plastic bottle of Coke and a croissant the shape and texture of well-wrung chamois leather for about a tenner. Then he went to another kiosk that seemed to sell everything and bought a paper bag full of seedless red grapes and a carton of honey and lemon cold and flu sachets. Stocked up, Noel unscrewed the cap on the bottle of Coke and guzzled half of it down in one chug. He wiped his mouth, eyes shut in momentary bliss as his raging tonsils were sluiced with the lukewarm cola. He looked at the croissant and decided he'd pocket it just in case he got hungry on the Tube, or stuck in a tunnel, or something. He didn't like Tube journeys at the best of times. Crashing through those Victorian caves in a big electric cart wasn't his idea of travelling in style.

He traipsed across the concourse and descended to the Underground by escalator. His back ached beneath the weight of his rucksack and he shrugged it off for a moment and rested it on the descending metal step between his feet. He wobbled slightly, his leg muscles suddenly watery, and he had to grab onto the grimy, gouged rubber handrail running alongside the escalator. His brain felt like it had been given a coating of warm, slightly soiled fat. His sinuses felt full of gallons of yellow air and constricted with pressure and bad warmth; it was the kind of bad warmth you might encounter beneath an old hat worn by a pensioner who had died sitting next to a gas fire.

He swallowed some more Coke and watched as posters framed behind sheets of clear plastic affixed to the wall sailed past him. Most of these were defaced or had bits of chewing gum or, oddly, bits of what looked like sandwiches, smeared onto them. They advertised shows and sightseeing opportunities. Noel saw a poster advertising *The Woman in Black* and remembered how Erica had nearly cacked herself when they had gone to see that play. Good old-fashioned fun in those days. Now it was *The Thesmophoriazusae* and *The Bacchae* and other old Greek shit like that for Erica and her new man, Dion.

Dion was an artist, a sculptor. He was one of Erica's lecturers at college. Erica had taken a course on Art History, of all the pointless subjects to study, and Dion had mesmerised her with his knowledge and enthusiasm for his subject. It may have been instrumental somewhat in the triumph of his seduction, however, that his many self portraits and sculptures, arranged artfully around the borders of the classroom, depicted Dion naked and hung like the leg of a milking stool.

Noel remembered a time a month and a half ago when he had decided to surprise Erica at college by pitching up there to take her for a drink after class. She had been complaining that he wasn't spontaneous any more, so he thought he'd address that misapprehension with an unplanned visit. He'd been held up in traffic so arrived just as the college was closing up. Erica's orange Volkswagen Beetle was still in the car park so Noel slotted in beside it and hurried into the college foyer. He looked around for directions and saw a sign for the art department. The corridors were utilitarian and unadorned, pathways through mental endeavour that Noel had imagined would be filled with posters and pottery; but then again, he had to remind himself that this was adult learning and not a fucking infant school.

A notice on a classroom door to his right informed him that this was the art room. Noel stopped outside. There was a small rectangular window in the door, through which Noel ascertained that the room was empty. Then he heard a stifled giggle. It was unmistakeably Erica's and one that she so rarely let out these days. Noel thought of it as her fuck-chuckle, an irrepressible sound she made when she was getting turned on.

Well, he'd walked into the empty classroom to find Erica and a shirtless Dion standing behind a yucca plant in the corner of the room, Erica supporting Dion's cock on the palm of her hand like the belly of a juvenile stoat.

"Oh fucking *hell*!" Noel said, his mind unable to properly comprehend the spectacle before him. He tore his eyes from the sight of Dion's lustrous cockhead dropping against his fly like a gavel as Erica, startled, released it and reached up to re-button her blouse. Aghast, Noel took in the sculptures and paintings of Dion that stood around the perimeter of the classroom; the godlike aspect, Bellerophon chest and epic loins. In the flesh he was just as magnificent.

Noel had a moment to register Dion standing with his hands on his hips, head thrown back, waves of thick black hair rolling around his slender throat and across his huge, muscular shoulders, as he laughed. His laugh was like the roar of a lion.

Unmanned, Noel had turned and stumbled away.

Erica hadn't come home that night. Noel had sat up in a hateful state of rage and impotence necking the entire crate of stubby bottled lagers he had been saving for an early summer barbecue. Eventually he dozed and came to on the sofa with a hangover of Withnailian proportions – a proper bastard behind the eyes – just as the front door opened and Erica walked in.

She came into the lounge and looked down at Noel. Noel moaned and tried to sit up. He reached out a hand but Erica pushed it away. Noel tried to focus on his wife but all he could see was an image of her naked, her long slender legs glossy with ardent sweat, shafting herself onto a wang of sapling dimensions. Over and over again, and in high definition. He covered his face.

"I'm sorry you had to see that, Noel." Erica had said.

"Mmmf," Noel said into his cupped palms.

"It's been going on for months. I'm just surprised you haven't found out before."

"Aw, *Ghod*," Noel mumbled.

"Yes," said Erica, her tone smoothing into one of great admiration, and even with his senses smothered within the humid, breathy cavity of his palms, Noel could discern the change in her attitude. "He is."

Noel looked up at his wife, bemused. He stared at her as she stood amongst the discarded beer bottles as if she'd just appeared, genie-like, from one of them. Her eyes were glazed and her lips were upturned in a smile of saintly radiance. She looked ecstatic.

"Erica?" said Noel.

And then Erica went, "*Oooh*," and her legs wobbled and she clutched at her breasts with spasming fingers while a warm, pink flush suffused her throat and cheeks, and Noel realised, with growing astonishment, that his wife had just come quite robustly right there in front of him.

He sat back on the sofa and blinked. His headache pounded with pressure the approximate magnitude to that of an oceanic trench. The room was suddenly saturated with the cloying odour of musk. Erica gasped and stumbled backwards through the bottles. They clanked with hollow good cheer.

Erica looked embarrassed. She stepped over the bottles and stood, still trembling slightly, at the door.

"I – I'm going now, Noel," she said. "I'm going to get some of my things and move out. I think it's best."

Noel had said nothing more to Erica; he had just nodded and watched her go. He sat for a while bathed in what still remained of Erica's gamey aroma and listened to the sounds of her packing upstairs. It wasn't until the front door closed about twenty minutes later that the thought occurred to him that Dion might have been fucking his wife right here in his own house. And what about Alan? Had he known? Little shit. It wouldn't have surprised Noel at all. Alan had changed so much since he'd 'come out' a couple of months before. All those years playing rugby and bringing home pretty girls, and as gay as a Romanian folksong all along. What a disappointment. He just couldn't imagine... no, his mind closed down at the thought of his son doing those things, just couldn't face it. Not at the moment.

All this replayed through Noel's mind as the escalator descended. When he reached the bottom, he pulled his rucksack back on and stumbled towards the corridor leading to the eastbound platform. What horrible memories he had of that time.

He tottered onto the platform just as the train was pulling in. The carriages were moderately full but Noel managed to bundle onto the train and find a seat. He sat with his rucksack jammed between his knees next to a man reading an Arabic broadsheet to his right and a petite Chinese girl carrying a stack of books on psychology to his left. Noel felt hemmed in by erudition. He sank further down into his jacket and squinted with hot, congested eyes at the row of companion travellers who sat opposite. They looked propped up; they looked like the ill in some prefabricated waiting room, dull-eyed and resigned, all about to get the news that things were terminal and that there was no hope.

Something about the quality of the light on Tube trains makes everyone look ugly, renders them waxen and pallid, distorts features and blunts expressions. It enhances blemishes and flaws and makes people appear nervy, disheartened or cruel. Once, Noel had sat opposite a young woman in a business suit and watched as huge tears had rolled down her cheeks while she stared with a lifeless expression at a point somewhere above his left shoulder and a thousand miles away. Noel had been shocked at such a manifestation of unhappiness. He'd felt the need to make a gesture, show some empathy with a nod or a reassuring smile, and let her know she wasn't totally alone in this clattering transport burrowing beneath the city, but he couldn't even catch her eye. Noel supposed she might have been quite pretty and maybe when she got off the train and ascended into natural daylight then she might blossom into something lovely, but down there in the rocking yellow light her brow was too shiny and round, and blackheads darkened the pores around her glistening nostrils like welling pinpricks of anguish.

Thinking about this, and trying not to look at the polished, glabrous head of a fat man sitting opposite, and feeling like absolute shit, Noel fell into an aching, clammy doze.

He was jolted to wakefulness some time later. He opened his eyes and groaned at the pains in his head and joints. His rucksack had toppled across the centre aisle and the bag of grapes he had stuffed into one of the shallow side pockets had spilled open. Sprigs of grapes had been trodden into the floor.

"You bastards," Noel muttered. He leaned forward, wincing, and gathered his rucksack to him, pressing it back between his knees. He scooped up the little paper bag and inspected it. There were a few dark red grapes rattling around at the bottom, still intact.

Only then did he begin to register the rest of his surroundings. At some point during his nap the carriage had emptied of all passengers but Noel. He looked left and right to confirm that he was alone.

And he noticed that the train had stopped in the tunnel between stations.

Noel slumped back into his seat and rested the back of his head against the dark glass of the window behind him. His mouth and throat were dry again so he took a couple of the remaining grapes from the bag and chewed on them while he waited for the train to start.

He waited. He had a few more grapes. Even chewed to a pulp, they hurt his throat on the way down. He wasn't going near that croissant unless he was starving to death. He ruminated. *Alan*, he thought. His *son*, taking it up the Hovis. He couldn't believe it. What a dreadful disappointment.

The doors to his right slid open with a hiss.

Noel jumped and clutched at the top of his rucksack. The breeze that ran like a cold, desultory river through the Underground, pushed and buffeted by the constant passage of trains, gusted into the carriage. It had a gloomy, particulate smell, like cinders from a dead furnace. It rose up into the carriage and filled Noel's nostrils like a sensory extension of the blackened walls that encased the train.

Then he heard a sound. It was a strange, high vibrato, rising and falling in pitch as it became louder. Noel panicked for a moment, and imagined another train hurtling towards them through the tunnel, but the modulation of the sound and its volume made him reconsider after a minute, and so he relaxed a little. He remained curious – or at least *vigilant* – though, despite his weakened state and he got up from his seat and went to the open doors.

He was in the front carriage and so, when he looked out, the top of his head nearly touching the curving, tiled tunnel wall, and peered along the carriage, he could see that the train had stopped only about thirty or so yards from the entrance to the next station. He could see light, and he could see, silhouetted against that light, someone walking towards him along the tracks.

The figure was tall and well built, and appeared to be swinging something around his head as he walked with a wide lassoing motion. The unusual roaring sound Noel could hear, and had attributed to the passage of another train, seemed to be coming from the approaching figure, the sound driven towards the idle train by the narrowness of the tunnel.

Noel took a step back, away from the open doors. He shivered, aware of his aching muscles. He wondered for a moment whether he was hallucinating. He ran a palm across his brow. He was sweaty. He had a temperature. He paused and realised that the sound had stopped. He felt relived, and reassured himself that he was probably having a flu-induced – and stress related, to be fair – moment of delirium, and half turned to go back to his seat and wait for the journey to recommence.

But then someone said, "Hello, Noel," and a tall, naked figure slid out from the tunnel alongside the carriage and stepped up onto the train.

"Christ," Noel said, and stumbled backwards. He reached for a vertical steel grab rail to his right and used it to swing himself away from the figure mounting the train. He collapsed into a seat and stared up at the man who stood smiling at him; he was composed and magnificent, his head slightly bowed to accommodate the curvature of the carriage, and he carried two things: a piece of wood carved in to a spatula shape wound on a length of ancient-looking brown rope which was now looped round his muscular forearm, and in his left hand what could only be described as a large wooden dildo.

"Christ," whispered Noel. "Dion."

Dion stepped forward and raised the wooden spatula as if in greeting. Noel looked at it; it was pitted and engraved with curlicues and arcane-looking runes. He recognised it from books he had read as a boy, books about ancient history. It was a bullroarer.

He pressed back into his seat. Dion stepped closer and stood before him. He wasn't entirely naked. He was wearing what appeared to be a large fig leaf. It clung to his groin, held there by a tangle of tendrils that were twined through his pubic hair. It didn't quite cover everything, Noel noticed. He had no choice but to notice; it was at eye-level and Noel had a very good view. He groaned and averted his eyes.

Dion threw back his head and roared with manly good humour. His eyes flashed and his fig leaf lifted and fell. Then it lifted and stayed a bit lifted. Noel groaned again and tried to edge away along the seat.

"Noel," Dion said. His voice was melodious, enriched with a profound sensuality. Noel flinched. "Your wife is a *goddess*," Dion said. "She is a woman of great curiosity, beauty and ecstatic awareness. And for two decades you have repressed her creativity and desires with your narrow-minded and prejudiced outlook on life. Your only success is your underachievement, which alone is pitiable, but to attempt to drive the passions from your family with your affectless, monotonous reservations is *grotesque*."

"What are you talking about?" Noel asked. He peered up into Dion's broad, glowing face. Dion sported a shaggy 'V' of hair beneath his bottom lip – a soul-patch – which was an affectation that never failed to create hostility in Noel whenever he saw one.

"Don't stand there telling me what I have and haven't done," he rasped, trying to adjust his posture into something more poised than a subordinate cringe. He still felt awful and his throat was killing him. "Not with *Barbie*'s bush stuck to your chops."

Dion frowned, momentarily irritated by Noel's retort.

"Noel," Dion began, but Noel interrupted him.

"No, you listen to me, you smug bastard," he said. "I don't know what you're doing following me and trying to fuck with my head. Don't you think you've hurt me and my family enough? All I've ever done –"

But now it was Dion's turn to interrupt. He lashed out with the bullroarer and clouted Noel around the side of the head.

"OW!" Noel cried, and slumped sideways in his seat. He reached up and felt blood trickle from his ear. "You vicious cunt," he muttered. His vision blurred with both pain and emotion.

"I'm not trying to hurt any of you," Dion said. He leaned over and put his hands under Noel's armpits and lifted him upright again. His large, lambent eyes smoked with concern. "I'm trying to *free* you."

The side of Noel's head throbbed. Tears leaked from the corners of his eyes. "Free me from what?" he asked. Passivity rippled through his body like a pressure wave; all attempts to resist Dion fled before it leaving him trembling and spent. Fully in the grip of his sickness, Noel decided to let his delusions have their way with him. Thus, clear headed to a degree and almost comforted by the full-body encapsulation of his dull aches, he closed his eyes against the vision before him and allowed himself to become a channel for whatever Dion's liberation entailed.

MUCH TO HIS parents' surprise and delight, Noel had been selected for a grammar school. They had all been expecting him to go to the local mixed-sex Comprehensive but he had achieved high scores in his eleven-plus and had come in as one of the top three most intelligent children in his year. Noel was staggered. He had always considered himself to be a bit of a clown.

His parents had been so excited for him. Noel remembered how they had been glowing with a pride and a hope that had nothing to do with smug self-congratulation but everything to do with bright, surprised joy in the unexpected possibilities now open to their son. This was thirty-two years ago. Punk was dead and Thatcher was embarking on her medieval purge of the working classes. London buses ran with sluggish and unpredictable truculence and you could buy pulp paperback horrors for just 25p. You could smoke on buses and trains, even on the Underground. You could pretty much park anywhere you liked for free. Most cars were shit but you could drive them as fast as you could get them to go; there were no speed cameras and the eclectic profusion of humps and bollards that now clog pretty suburban back streets like traffic calming cholesterol had yet to spring up.

Noel had been popular at school for the first two years. He'd made friends; he could be a laugh in class without becoming a fool, and was skilful at tennis ball soccer in the playground. He wasn't the brightest child in his year but he wasn't the daftest either and had a raw, languid intelligence that struggled to focus itself academically but would see him through life well enough if he worked hard. He discovered he liked English and Biology but little else. Maths was like trying to pry apart the substance of the universe. Rows of numbers made him anxious and breathless. When the syllabus introduced geometry he was able to relax a little because the shapes that were drawn on the old chalkboards let his eyes focus on something concrete, less metaphysical. He still didn't really get it, though. He liked the Biology labs; large, airy classrooms at the top of the school, their walls lined with long, dark benches displaying murky glass tanks filled with stick insects static as mimes, and clusters of fluttering, stinking locusts.

And so it had been fine at first; Noel actually believed he might make it in this red brick and marble, rigorously uniformed, Dickensian-desked, chalky, covertly brutal world. He squeezed through corridors at break time and between classes with boys who were, to him, as big as adults – fourth- and fifth-years bulging out of blazers with blue chins and terrible broad backs – and endured bundles in stairwells that took dusty, beery teachers who still commanded a modicum of indulgent respect the best part of a quarter of an hour to unscramble with roars and wading, swinging arms.

He sat at desks stuck tight with chewing gum, looked down between his legs in wide-eyed, silent apprehension at the plump cocks drawn in pen on the seats of the rugged, greasy chairs upon which he sat, the bollocks always sporting a few slashes of cartoon pubes like a cat's whiskers, the fat, bisected glans chucking out a weatherman's snowstorm of correction-fluid jism.

It was a scary place, with teachers swirling about like huge ravens in their university capes in search of intellectual carrion, and science teachers called 'doctor' this, and 'professor' that; gone were the sweet little mums who had taught him the time not six months ago in classrooms full of Lilliputian desks and twinkling milk-bottle top collages.

But Noel thought he might survive; home after a bus journey spent head-down to avoid the attention of the marauding boys and girls from the comprehensive, Noel was greeted with a fuss and a fascination from his parents that filled him with both guilt and a drifting sense of midget superiority – borne of his social advantage and the fact that he had started swearing in coarse torrents of libertarian vernacular during football matches at break-time.

And then, with a suddenness that left him bewildered, hurt and afraid, the bullying started. It was a fat little cunt called Stuart Kale; envious of Noel's developing wit and popularity both with his classmates and with some of the more moderate teachers, Kale began a sustained and vindictive campaign of slander and belittlement designed to undermine Noel's self-esteem and leave him isolated and friendless. It worked.

Short and ugly, Kale used the sharpness of his tongue and an outstanding ability to hit every button dead-on when it came to the put-down to destroy Noel's life. In fear of reprisals and in part delighted by the sight of a wounded victim that was specifically *not* one of them, Noel's classmates turned on him with savage vigour. Noel found himself sitting alone in classes suffering the awful, dense humiliation of watching every chair fill up except the one next to him, the burning shame of seeing eyes dart away from contact with his own. Breathless with the dishonour of it, each of Noel's lessons seemed to drag on for days, the back of his head swelling, reddening, neck muscles tense and immovable for fear that he might draw attention to himself and his terrible, blighted unpopularity.

He travelled home alone, sometimes getting off the bus miles from his own stop in order to dawdle via the back streets. He became morose and withdrawn, curled up on his bed cramped by pangs of loneliness he could hardly stand. What hurt Noel more than anything was the undeserved nature of the harassment. It had come upon him like a curse, visited by that venomous but charismatic little demi-god, Kale.

Noel spent break times alone in the biology labs. He pottered and read, stared down from on high with dull-eyed distraction and watched the other children playing in the quad. He was left alone.

After a long year of emotional and verbal abuse, Noel had become accustomed to his new lonely lifestyle. He was rarely bullied now, Kale having done such a thorough job of brutalising him that everyone shunned him with callous and unconscious atavism. He found consolation in his routines, and a vague psychosis played around the margins of his developing mind, never becoming florid but occasionally enlightening his forlorn imagination. He hid-out in the unconverted loft rooms at the top of the school. They were tiny, antique, and plank-floored, the low walls hidden behind shelves packed full of small dusty books. In these little rooms ascetic old teachers bestowed upon a select few a Classical education. Rarefied prefects crept up back stairs and spent shaded afternoons learning Latin and Ancient Greek. Noel felt comforted amongst the books and fancied himself a curator of sorts. At breaks and in between lessons, he sat on a bench beneath a narrow dormer window and read peppery chapters describing pantheons and primordial monsters, odysseys, campaigns, Titans and Heroes.

And then, the following summer, a miracle of sorts.

A new boy joined his class. His name was Pascal. His mother was Italian and he had moved up from Brighton with her when she had divorced his dad. Pascal was diminutive, delicate and olive-skinned. He had large brown eyes endowed with long, feathery lashes. His teeth were bright and white, his lips cute and pouty. He was the prettiest thing Noel had ever seen.

And because he was new, and because the seats next to Noel remained vacant in classes, and because Pascal brought with him a gentle serenity and confidence that enabled him to fit into the society of the cohort without any of the unease and suspicion normally experienced by children joining an established school year, he walked into double History (truly, the longest day of Noel's life), saw the empty seat in the middle of the room and came straight over and sat down next to Noel.

Noel froze, his eyes wide and his mouth dry. The rest of the class was silent. All eyes seemed to be on Pascal.

Pascal opened his textbook. He looked at Noel and smiled. "Hi," he said.

And that was all it had taken. One shy smile and unforeseen, blessed proximity to this new and remarkable boy.

Noel had fallen in love

WITH THE PROXIMITY came healing. It was fragile, and Noel didn't question it; he was too infatuated with Pascal to analyse the process, but he was aware that the other boys were viewing him with less contempt than usual. Pascal had had junior trials for Brighton Football Club and his delicate skills and light touch with a tennis ball added extra dimensions to his popularity in the playground. Now Noel found that he was picked for games again, and rediscovered his own touch. The classes they shared, they sat together; those they attended separately didn't worry

Noel now. Boys sat next to him again. It was that simple. It was as though a patina of disease had sloughed off him, drawing off any unpalatable residue and brightening his aura, making him attractive by virtue of Pascal's simple acceptance of him.

But it wasn't a *friendship* exactly. Noel, who had become a reserved and introspective boy over the last year, was too aware of the tenderness of his feelings towards Pascal to form a robust familiarity; and Pascal, who seemed in favour with everyone, was just too distant in his novelty and popularity for Noel to try and monopolise or limit him. Noel was happy just to bathe in the gradual, remedial course of his renewal.

But Noel began to notice something else. When he awoke in the morning, warm and snug beneath his blankets, his dick hard and full of sizzling, fuming magnitude, he would roll onto his belly, half-asleep and comfortable, and press his groin into the mattress with dreamy fantasies flourishing behind his eyes, and find that he was thinking of Pascal.

Noel decided these weren't sexual thoughts. He didn't have a lot of experience with girls but he could summon up the faces and imaginary bodies of the girls from the comprehensive well enough, and replace Pascal's image with the innocent glimpses of thighs and warm mouths that passed for eroticism for a young teenage boy, more than adequate for his immediate, perplexing needs.

But the power of Pascal's *physical* presence was less easy to deny. If Pascal touched him, or nudged him with a knee beneath the desk, Noel would feel his heart rate double and his stomach tingle. And once, feigning tiredness in Sociology, Pascal had rested his head on his desk, it was all that Noel could do not to reach out and stroke the tanned nape of Pascal's neck where it ran in a smooth furrow into the soft dark hair at the base of his skull.

Noel started taking himself up to the loft rooms again during breaks. There was a small toilet, walled with large rectangular green tiles and smelling of rusty water and carbolic soap. Noel sat on the toilet seat and had weird, confused wanks.

He extruded fat, congested blobs into a cupped palm with the careful, breathless placement of a master cake decorator, followed always by an immediate feeling of emptiness and a pinched ache in his rectum from the force of his release against the unyielding wooden surface of the bog seat.

Then one day, noticing his now regular absences, Pascal asked Noel where he went during breaks. Noel felt a brief stab of guilt and stammered that he liked to take himself off to do some reading in the cool of the loft. Pascal was intrigued. He hadn't realised that there was a secret area at the top of the school and he asked Noel to show him during lunch break. Noel looked into Pascal's pretty, enquiring eyes and smelt rusty water and carbolic soap and said, yes, he'd be happy to.

After the bell, Noel led Pascal up the back stairs. They were accessed by going through a narrow door at the side of the Art Department. Their footsteps creaked and clumped on the old wooden stairs. There were three small rooms up there, a tiny kitchen, and the institutionally tiled toilet.

Noel led Pascal into the room to the left of the stairwell. It was the room in which he had liked to sit beneath the window and read his arcane books. Pascal took some time looking at the books lining the walls and then came over and sat beside Noel on the narrow bench beneath the window.

"It's good up here," he said. Noel nodded. He could feel the warmth of Pascal's slender leg against his own.

Pascal sat back against the wall and looked around. "It's like a secret place. You could get up to all sorts of things up here and no one would know." He giggled and looked at Noel from beneath conspiratorially lowered lashes. "What do you do up here? Apart from read."

Noel gazed at Pascal. "What?" he said. He was light-headed and breathless; his eyes took in nothing but the movement of Pascal's mouth and the tantalizing hint of the tip of his tongue as it flicked against the back of his teeth.

Pascal turned his body towards Noel and rested his arm

against the back of the bench. Noel heard him say, "What do you want to do up here?"

But he might have misheard him.

Noel leant forward and kissed Pascal on the mouth.

IF NOEL HAD imagined the bullying at the hands of Kale had been awful before, it was now apparent to him that it had been merely a taster when compared to the orders of magnitude by which it increased following Pascal's divulgence to the other boys what Noel had done to him up in the quiet seclusion of the loft; how Noel had enticed him up there and then tried to bum him.

Noel considered the humiliation to be worse because this time he had contributed directly to its source. He felt shame now whereas before he had merely felt an alienated sense of hurt and bewilderment. He had been able to fill his solitude with fantasies and learning; now he brooded and cringed with the horror of having brought about his own downfall.

And then one day soon after, Pascal and a group of boys had cornered him in the playground. He had been walking back from the canteen having waited until it had emptied before buying his lunch, skirting the quad by cutting behind the prefabricated huts that held the language laboratories.

Five of them had jumped him from between two of the huts, four more followed him into the narrow area between the back of the huts and the fence that ran along the length of the yard. A couple of fifth formers were standing beneath the branches of a horse chestnut tree sharing a cigarette. They perked up when they saw the gang converge on Noel. They watched with eager, gloating expressions as Noel was surrounded. News of Noel's transgression had percolated not just across his own year but had travelled like wildfire throughout the whole school. First years gawped in naïve and open fascination at him; he was the subject of rank graffiti on the walls of the sixth form common room. Even teachers seemed to ponder his affliction with low regard and the jaded narrowness of expression that was the sole tenure of world-weary and educated men.

Noel felt panic drench his system. He began to sweat, his heart rate doubled and his legs began to shake. He looked around. Somehow, by way of the contagion that sweeps through a group of organic beings at the hint of a fight, it seemed that the entire school had piled between the huts and were surrounding him, name-calling, pushing, swinging punches. Noel tried to run but his legs wouldn't support him. He was buffeted by kicks and deafened by the screams and taunts.

And then, for a moment, Noel was granted a vision. Perhaps it was triggered by the horror of the moment or perhaps it was released at last like an abreaction following the years of stress and torment, but for a moment Noel's grip on reality slipped. Gone was the howling mob and in its place, prowling, snorting, reviled of aeons, the *Hecatonchires* surrounded him, the great primordial beasts of Greek mythology, each with fifty heads and a hundred mighty arms. Noel had read about them during his quiet lunchtimes in the loft, read of their brute strength and ferocity, of their siding with the Olympians in the war for supremacy against the Titans.

Noel summoned the last of his strength and drew a little dignity from those pungent afternoons of sweet escapism and roared a command of his own.

"Fuck the lot of you!" Noel screamed, and collapsed.

WHEN HE RETURNED from being off sick, a period of slow recovery that leached into the long summer holiday and gave him the extra six weeks needed for a recuperation of sorts, Noel had already decided what he was going to do with the education system. He spent the next year with his head down, did virtually no work and scraped four 'O' levels at the end of the fifth-form exams. His parents were distraught but Noel's heart was hardened. All that promise dissipated before his parents' eyes. There was to be no University education, no degrees, no proud career; Noel quit school and went out to work in a factory. Four years later he met Erica at a party. They got married and four years after that, Alan was born.

Hard physical work and a happy family enabled Noel to put the memories of his humiliation behind him. He was troubled by dreams, though. Dreams of being encircled by roiling many-headed torsos and buffeted by the blows of hundreds of fists. He awoke with shouts, entangled in sheets that felt as thin and damp as over-moistened Rizlas. And sometimes he dreamed of Pascal, that sweet and beastly boy who had broken his heart. And those dreams stayed with him all day as a dreary sense of failure and disgrace. And this, these unresolved feelings never spoken of, never counselled or acknowledged, was what had contributed most to his alienation from his wife and maturing son.

"YOU REMEMBER," DION said. It was a statement, not a question.

Noel was sobbing. "Yes," he spluttered, "Yes, I do." All those feelings and memories so long suppressed were raging through his head. He was shaking.

With great tenderness, Dion helped Noel stand up. Noel leaned against Dion's chest. It was like holding tight to the flank of a tiger; he could hear Dion's blood thudding through him, driven with the endless might of an immortal's heart. He wept.

Dion stepped away and picked up Noel's discarded rucksack. He rummaged through the pockets and came up with a handful of grapes and the box of honey and lemon cold and flu remedy. Noel stood swaying and watched through bleary eyes as Dion crushed the remaining grapes in his hand and smeared the juice across his chest.

"What are you doing?" Noel said, but Dion put a finger to Noel's mouth. Noel tasted grape juice. He licked his lips. He watched, a simple fascination expressed on his blotchy face, as Dion tore open the sachets of honey and lemon and tipped the powder over his chest and belly. He ran his palms across his flesh, smearing the powder into the grape juice, making pink and yellow patterns with his fingertips.

"An offering," Dion said. "To a god. For resolution."

Noel looked up into Dion's overwhelming face and smiled.

Dion smiled in return, and pressed something into Noel's hand. Noel looked down, frowned, unsure of the purpose of such a gift.

"Remember Prosymnus," Dion said, and again it was a statement and not a question. Noel nodded, and recalled the story of the young boy who had aided the god Dionysus and then died before he could collect his reward.

He stumbled, and Dion caught him.

The train had begun to move.

THE TRAIN PULLED into the station and the doors hissed open.

A man stood alone on the platform. He was dressed in an expensive tailored suit and had his dark hair cut in a short, salon style. He looked cultured and successful, and confident despite his slight, boyish stature. He worked in the city and had all the trappings of wealth and achievement.

This afternoon he was travelling a circuitous route home having been drinking in wine bars in Wimbledon to toast his success at negotiating a deal to provide his company's brand of champagne to the All England Tennis Club for this year's Grand Slam event, and he was quite drunk. The right education still afforded opportunities in circles such as these; it wasn't what you knew, the man confirmed to himself with intoxicated self-congratulation, it was *whom* you knew that really mattered. He tottered as the train doors opened and he stepped up into the empty carriage. It seemed he had been waiting ages for this train, but he had amused himself with his recollections. That huge guy with the little beard under his chin had certainly oiled the wheels at the business meeting. Apparently he'd been a lecturer at his old University. What were the chances of that? Economics and business studies. Boring, but he was sure he'd have remembered a lecturer as striking as that. Maybe he'd missed those lectures. He had, after all, sailed through the course with the minimum of effort. Life was like that for some, he knew.

And then, as the doors slid shut behind him, and the train began to move off in to the tunnel, and as he staggered trying to get to a seat, something clubbed him around the side of the head. He gasped, and fell into the aisle, his briefcase flying from his hand and sliding away along the length of the train.

He tried to get up but was struck again by what felt like a snooker ball in a sock. He rolled over onto his back, his arms raised to ward off further blows, but none came. Through tear-stained eyes, a black agony in the back of his head, the man looked up and tried to focus on his assailant. All he could see was a figure standing over him holding a weapon. A club of some sort. He whined in the back of his throat.

"I have money," he was able to say, but realised very quickly that this wasn't going to be a mugging. He tried to kick out as hands began pulling at his trousers but was dealt a further blow to the temple and went limp.

NOEL STOOD OVER the trembling figure and smiled. He held up the weapon he had been given by Dion. It was a large, carved fig-wood phallus. It had some blood and hair stuck to the round, smooth bulb at the top. Noel picked the hairs off and wiped his fingers on his trousers. He looked round, but Dion had gone. He frowned, and then returned his attention to the man at his feet. He smiled again, but this time there was no good will in it.

"Hello, Pascal," he said. He adjusted the phallus into a suitable position in his right hand and bent to roll him over.

THE GIRL IN THE GLASS

John Llewellyn Probert

John Probert and I share a love of old-school horror movies and by that I mean the productions of such studios as Hammer, Amicus or American International. Something of the gaudy thrills and Technicolor nightmares of that generation of film making find their way into Probert's style and rather than making his fiction seem old and creaky, it actually gives his tales of terror a refreshing edge. 'The Girl in The Glass' is no exception; all the elements are there – the ghost, the curse, the fiendish payoff – and all delivered with John's usual wit and finesse.

DR TOM NEWFIELD arrived in London on a Sunday afternoon. By Monday evening he had seen a ghost.

It happened under the most unremarkable of circumstances. But then Tom was hardly the sort of chap who went out of his way to visit haunted houses, cemeteries, or the kind of weird abandoned buildings favoured by the producers of low-budget cable television programmes that purported to contact the deceased. So if he was ever going to encounter the weird, he reasoned later, it was likely to be in the most mundane of settings.

Tom had come to the city to attend a course at the Royal College of Surgeons, and encountering something that as far as he was concerned only existed on the pages of dusty old books read by even older people with too much time on their hands was the last thing he was expecting. No, he had thought afterwards. A rational, reasonable, newly qualified doctor just out of medical school was not the sort of person who saw spectres on the London Underground. He was yet to realise that coming to terms with the supernatural would give him the only chance of saving his soul.

Tom had arranged to stay with his anaesthetist friend Mike, who worked at the Hammersmith Hospital and lived near Ealing Common. To get from the Royal College at Lincoln's Inn to Mike's flat meant catching the Tube at Holborn and staying on the Central line until Tom reached his destination. On the Monday that he first saw the ghost his final lecture had finished at 6:30pm, which meant that while he had still had to deal with the tail end of the rush hour commuters, by the time the train had left White City the carriage he was in was almost empty. After East Acton he was by himself.

Except for the girl whose reflection he could see in the window opposite.

The girl who wasn't actually in the carriage with him.

When Tom thought about it, he realised he had first noticed her much earlier in his journey. In fact he seemed to remember seeing that heart-shaped face framed by a bob of dark brown hair as far back as Oxford Circus. Having no newspaper to distract him, and the thought of reading his lecture notes making him even queasier than the claustrophobic atmosphere of the compartment already had, his eyes had searched for some form of distraction.

And alighted upon the reflection of an attractive girl in her early twenties who appeared to be searching for something. From the desperation in her eyes and the frantic movements of her head his first thought had been that whatever she had lost it must be very important – perhaps her handbag or an item of jewellery. Or perhaps, he thought with a pang of concern, she had lost a child. Every time he had looked up there she was, her furtive attempts to recover whatever was missing obviously still unsuccessful.

She still appeared to be searching once the train was empty except for Tom, who looked back and forth from the glass to the carriage several times before he was able to convince himself that she wasn't in the compartment with him. Whatever he was seeing must be some form of optical illusion, he thought – perhaps a trick of the light playing on a poster that had been put up in every station. Then her eyes locked on his, and that lost, wan, appealing expression changed into something frightening; her lips drawn back over her teeth to reveal a smile that was anything but enticing or alluring. In fact there was only one word he could think of to describe it.

Hungry.

When he looked again she was still there, staring at him from the black glass in the way someone starving might view a potential meal. Or, he thought with a shudder, how someone close to death might view their only hope of a cure.

He had never been so happy to see Ealing Broadway station in his life, and by the time he was indoors he had almost forgotten the entire episode.

Until he saw the girl's photograph in Mike's flat.

"YOU LOOK AS thought you've seen a ghost!"

Tom looked up at his friend and then back at the copy of the two-week old newspaper that he had found lying on Mike's couch. 'Girl Critical After Near-Fatal Tube Accident!' screamed the headline, followed by the tragic story of twenty-three year old Emily Phillips who, despite the best efforts of the 'expert team at the Hammersmith' was still close to death. Tom didn't know which to do first – tell Mike what he thought he had seen on the Underground, or query the unusual behaviour of a friend both renowned and ridiculed at medical school for keeping his place meticulously tidy. In the end he went for the easier option.

"Why have you still got this? It's not like you to keep old newspapers."

Mike Parsons reached over and plucked the crumpled issue

from Tom's fingers, folded it neatly, and laid it on the coffee table next to the wine he had poured for both of them.

"Call it morbid fascination if you like," Mike said with a grin as he picked up his glass. "She fell under a train on the Central line and because they didn't have beds anywhere else she ended up being brought to the ITU at the Hammersmith."

Tom sipped his wine but it tasted bitter and he put his glass down.

"Did someone push her?" he asked.

"No," said Mike, "and before you ask she wasn't a jumper either. They mostly tend to go for that stretch of the Circle line west of St James' Park. No, apparently she came running onto the platform and would have been fine but some kid had spilled something and she slipped on the tiles and went flying. Even then she would have been okay but a train was just leaving and somehow she got dragged underneath it. Her arms and legs were crushed so the orthopods put on external fixators to try and hold all the broken bits of her limbs together. Her bowel was ruptured in three places but the general surgeons managed to repair all of that. The train just missed her head which is really the only reason she's still alive."

So, Tom thought, whatever it was he had seen, or thought he had seen, it wasn't a ghost in the traditional sense of the word. Somehow that didn't make him feel any better.

"And she's still on intensive care?" he asked.

"She's been there since the accident. We had to put her on a ventilator when she came in because of her injuries and now we can't get her off it. She's almost completely unresponsive."

"You mean she's in a coma?"

Mike nodded.

"We're not calling it that clinically but yes. For a while we were worried she was brain dead but caloric testing and other responses are positive, so she's definitely still with us, we just can't bring her back to consciousness."

Tom gestured at the paper.

"That still doesn't explain why you've got that."

His friend gave him a sheepish grin.

"I know. Ridiculous isn't it? Good thing when they interviewed me for the job they didn't ask if I was superstitious. I just haven't been able to shake off the feeling that if I threw it away that might mean the end of her. Anyway, you looked pretty shook up when you saw her picture. Do you know her?"

Tom shook his head.

"I thought I did," he said. "But obviously not."

HE SAW HER again the next day, and this time there could be no doubt. The face staring at him from the glass was that of Emily Phillips. The girl in the newspaper, the one who had been in a terrible accident on the very rail line on which he was travelling. The one who was currently in a coma in intensive care, hovering between life and death, with her spirit (or whatever it was) trapped on the Underground.

And she was looking at him right now.

But today she seemed different. Gone was the frantic searching. This time her eyes stayed fixed on Tom during his entire journey, and she seemed distressed when he left.

Once he was at the college Tom found himself unable to concentrate on what he was being taught, and he spent the entire day wrestling with the concept that what he was seeing was not an illusion, nor an hallucination, but the image of a person currently lying comatose on an intensive care unit.

On the way home it was even worse. Nothing he did – looking away, changing seats, changing carriages, even changing trains and waiting fifteen minutes at Notting Hill Gate – made any difference. Every time he picked a different seat the girl was there, staring back at him from the dirty glass opposite.

By the time the train pulled into Ealing Broadway that evening Tom had been doing his best to ignore her, but as he got up to leave he could not help but look to see what her reaction would be to him leaving the train for good.

The girl had vanished.

Thank heaven, he thought. Whatever she was she obviously must have realised there was no point in persecuting him from beyond the grave, or rather from beyond the intensive care unit, which was hopefully where her spirit or whatever it was had gone back to.

He was stepping out of the train when he felt something ice-cold grip his right ankle and yank it downwards. He tried to shake himself free but it was hopeless. Whatever had hold of him began to drag his leg down through the gap between the train and the platform. Tom took hold of the doors for support, but before he knew it he had been pulled onto his backside, his left leg splayed out in front of him, his right swiftly disappearing beneath the carriage.

It was only when he felt something bite into the flesh of his calf that he screamed.

And then he was being dragged free amidst a hail of abuse from two employees of the London Underground who, once they had him safe on the platform, told him to "be more fucking careful in the future."

Tom limped back to the flat, wary of every breath of cold air that laid itself upon him. Twice he was convinced that something with a hand of ice tried to push him into the traffic. Each time he turned to see no-one near him, still hoping that he could attribute the sensations to the rush-hour population of Ealing rather than a vengeful spirit.

But she was still alive, Tom kept reminding himself as he pulled his coat around him and did his best to steer clear of anything that might cause him injury. According to Mike she was still on his intensive care unit, paralysed, ventilated, as incapable of lifting a finger to harm him as—

Someone dead?

He halted beneath the streetlamp outside Mike's flat. He didn't want to go in. Not just yet, not after the shock he'd had and the ludicrous thoughts filling his mind that had plagued him all day and that, try as he might, he couldn't ignore. Was that how ghosts were created? Were they formed when a person was still alive but incapable of physical acts, their mind a prisoner in a body so useless that perhaps the frustration that ensued might be sufficient to lever their soul free? Even if all of that were somehow true that still didn't explain the really important question.

Why was she coming after *him*?

The cold wind had picked up and began to buffet him. As he ran inside Tom tried hard to ignore the feeling that it was trying to push him into the road, towards the dark shape he felt sure he could see moving across the common in his direction.

TOM RANG THE college the next day to explain that he was ill and would not be attending the day's lectures. The lady on the phone did her best to sound concerned and hoped he would be better soon. It was only once he had put down the receiver and immediately wondered if he should have asked her if she knew anything about ghosts that he realised how desperate he was becoming.

Once Mike had left for work Tom succumbed to the lure of the internet. As he might have predicted even before tapping the words 'ghost specialist' into a search engine, the phrase yielded more hits than he could possibly look through. He ignored the shopping sites, and the video downloads where somehow the word 'ghost' had found its way into a randomly put together assortment of pornographic references, and decided that as he had developed a severe aversion to the Tube and had no wish to go traipsing all over London he might start by limiting his search closer to home. Nearly all the telephone calls he made that morning were unsuccessful, as he found himself talking to a mixture of academics who "studied the phenomenon but didn't actually believe in ghosts per se", psychics who told him his dead mother was happy – even though Tom knew she was still alive and living in Abergavenny – and the out and out loonies, including one who promised to help him provided Tom came round to their flat as they were too scared to go out anywhere because they were being pursued by a giant invisible tortoise.

Just when he was about to give up his eye caught on a name that he was sure he hadn't seen before despite not having refreshed the screen. It hardly seemed worth it but Tom knew he had to do something, and so it was with some sense of relief that his telephone call to 'Eleanor's Alchemy' was answered by a young woman whose calm measured response to his plea for help made her his best option. Plus, the shop was only about half an hour's walk away. Tom pulled on his overcoat, stuffed the newspaper into the inside pocket and made his way down the stairs very carefully.

'ELEANOR'S ALCHEMY' WAS situated in a tiny side street off the Uxbridge Road. A Starbucks to its left and a clothing boutique to its right seemed to be trying to squeeze the life out of the tiny building, whose glass front displayed a variety of different coloured powders in large storage jars crowned with stoppers of thick brown rubber, dried plants sealed in little plastic packets, and crystal balls of varying sizes and colours. At first the door resisted his hand and he eventually ended up having to push hard to open it. A bell tinkled somewhere in the shop's dark recesses. Precariously positioned candles added some light to the gloom, as well as providing a fire hazard, Tom thought with a wry smile. A scent of herbs as thick and as acrid as dust caught Tom at the back of his throat. He tried to suppress a cough, but failed.

"You get used to it with time," said a soft voice from the shadows. Tom peered past what looked like bones hanging beneath a tatty stuffed animal to see a slim girl approach him from the darkness. She was probably only about five feet tall but the mass of frizzy dark hair that was failing to be held in check by a gold-threaded black lace hair band made her look taller. "I am Eleanor," she said, "and you are the one who rang, yes?"

Tom nodded.

"Is that one of your special powers or did you just guess?" he said with a nervous grin.

"I don't have any special powers," she said, coming into the dull light that shone through the shop window and regarding him with eyes Tom could have sworn possessed copper coloured irises. "I merely possess knowledge that may be of use when combined with some of the items I have for sale here."

Tom groaned inwardly. He might have guessed. It was just a shop selling rubbish to gullible tourists.

"Neither tourists nor the gullible come here," she said, smiling that she had his attention. "This is not the kind of place that is stumbled across by just anyone. The mere fact you are here means you were guided to this place."

She paused expectantly, but Tom wasn't ready to tell her of his predicament, not just yet, and so instead he gestured round the tiny cramped space.

"What kind of things do you have for sale, then?"

Seemingly happy to play along with his stalling tactics for the moment, Eleanor picked up a tiny phial and held it up to the light. Outside it had begun to brighten up, but the morning sunshine seemed somehow dulled by its passage through the liquid.

"Tears," she said.

"Tears?"

"And not just any tears." She handed him the bottle to inspect. "The tears of the broken-hearted. Very potent, even though you might be surprised how easy they are to come by."

The next jar she handed him appeared to be empty. Tom gave it a shake. Nothing.

"Solitude," she said.

"Is that one of your curses or one of your blessings?" he asked, surprised the question had even occurred to him.

"Both of course. Depending on what sort of person opens it."

Tom reached up to take down a small bottle that appeared to be filled to the brim with some black, tarry substance.

"What about this one?"

Eleanor's hand closed over his, and he took in the softness of her palm, the length of her fingernails that had been filed into points as her fingertips curled into a grip that was insistent as it pulled his hand away.

"You don't want to go touching that," she hissed.

"Why? What is it?"

She gripped his hand, presumably to prevent him from reaching up for the bottle again.

"It's a jar of darkness," she whispered as a passing cloud caused the sunlight to leave the shop.

He looked at it again. Whereas the flickering candlelight glinted off the other bottles and containers that cluttered up the shop, that one seemed to absorb it, and yet somehow remain empty-looking, as if whatever it contained was more of an absence than a presence.

"Well to use your style of describing things," he said, "it almost looks to me like a jar of emptiness."

"No," she said. "If you were to open it you would find it anything but empty. Now," and suddenly she was more businesslike, "tell me why someone such as yourself should need to come here."

Tom licked his lips and felt the same reluctance he had experienced before entering the shop. But Eleanor had put him at ease, and if anyone was going to take him seriously, even if it was just for the sake of a quick sale, it might be her.

"Ghosts," he said. She raised an eyebrow. "Or rather a ghost." What else could he say? "I think I'm being haunted by one," he finally spluttered.

There was a pause as she appeared to be mulling over what he had said before she eventually spoke.

"And is this ghost with you now?"

"Oh no. I only see it in one particular place."

"In that case my advice is simple. Avoid it. Most spirits are tied to the location they haunt. If it's where you live, move. If it's somewhere you visit, make your excuses and never go there again. Believe me, avoidance is the best policy. Anything else can become complicated." She moved close to him and laid a hand on his arm. "Very complicated indeed."

"It's on the Central Line of the London Underground," Tom said, knowing it sounded ridiculous.

His words did not have the effect he was expecting. In fact from the way she responded he wondered if he had just told her he had contracted some extremely contagious, and extremely unpleasant, disease. Eleanor recoiled and turned away from him, hugging her arms about her.

"Is that bad, then?" he said. When she failed to respond he repeated the question but louder. When there was still no answer he grabbed her shoulders and turned her to face him.

And was shocked to see she had begun to cry.

"I can see that you have been sent to me not for your own benefit, but as a cruel reminder of my own powerlessness," she said.

"What on earth's the matter? Is there nothing you can do for me?"

She turned away from him again and stared out of the window at the passers by, none of whom seemed to notice either the shop or the weeping girl in its window.

"What else can one do for a sacrifice but shed tears?" she said.

Her words filled him with horror.

"What do you mean, 'sacrifice'?"

She moved away from him again, and as he didn't want to risk distressing her any further he kept his distance.

"This ghost," she said. "Tell me more about it."

"It's a girl," he said, taking the newspaper from his coat pocket. "She's twenty-three years old. It even has her name in here if you need that – Emily Phillips. In fact when I said she was a ghost I wasn't exactly telling the truth, you see she's—"

"Still alive. Of course she is. That's why she's trying to find you."

"That doesn't make any sense," said Tom. "Why is she after me if she's not actually dead?"

Eleanor looked at him as if he was being exceptionally stupid.

"Why, to get you to take her place of course. I presume she was in an accident on the Underground line you mentioned?"

"A couple of weeks ago, yes," said Tom. "But what do you mean, 'take her place'?"

Eleanor sighed.

"The Gods of this country are cruel," she said as if it was something Tom must have heard a hundred times before. "They demand payment for the use of their highways."

"I don't understand," said Tom, starting to feel that he was getting way out of his depth.

Eleanor spoke slowly, as if she were addressing a rather slow child.

"Have you never paid a toll to cross a bridge? Had to gain permission to use a private road, perhaps sometimes for a fee?" Tom nodded. "Well, those to whom this land belongs demand such a toll from time to time. And I mean those who truly own it, not the petty cash mongers who have laid down money in the mistaken belief that lucre allows them to own a small part of this country. Powers far greater and more incomprehensible than we are capable of fully understanding truly own this soil, this earth, the rock beneath, and they demand payment for its use. And so, from time to time, sacrifices must be made. Those who die in car accidents allow the rest of us to use the roads, and those whose blood is shed onto the metal and concrete of the rail tracks allow the rest to commute to and from their dreary city existences. But the Gods are not entirely without mercy, or without a cruel sense of humour in your case. It is said that if an intended sacrifice does not die in the accident arranged for them, then that person has the chance to find someone to take their place." Eleanor took the newspaper from Tom and pointed at the photograph. "This girl has selected you."

It was ridiculous of course, but enough had happened to Tom in the last couple of days for him to believe what she was saying.

"And if she succeeds?" he said.

"When you die, Emily will undergo a miraculous recovery, following which she will remember very little of the entire affair, except perhaps for a few scraps of memory that she will attribute to a dream."

Tom looked bewildered, but figured he had a right to.

"What can I do?" he said, gesturing once more to the myriad tiny bottles that sat on the shelves of the shop. "Can't any of these help?"

Eleanor took down the bottle filled with the black tarry substance, pondered a while, and then shook her head.

"Even if I were to give you this there would be no guarantee that it would make any difference at all."

That was a chance Tom was prepared to take.

"How much?"

Eleanor shrugged.

"It is best you do not take it. Opening that bottle may lead to worse things than if you had never used it."

"I can't think of anything worse than being dead," said Tom, handing her all the twenty pound notes he had in his wallet. Eleanor shook her head.

"Take it if you want. But you would be better off doing something else."

"Which is?"

The girl's voice was surprisingly calm as she spoke the words that chilled Tom with their implication.

"Only one of you has to die."

TOM STUMBLED OUT of the shop, and when he turned to make a mental note of the address he wasn't really surprised to discover that it had vanished, the space between the coffee shop and the clothing store now nothing more than a memory. He could still feel the jar in his pocket, though, and he held onto it as he made his way back to Mike's flat.

He was halfway across the main road when he felt a hand of ice grab him and hold him fast before the path of an oncoming bus. Tom knew what was happening, just as he knew that as he struggled with nothing but himself his attempts to escape would appear to any onlookers as if he was having a fit or possibly a heart attack. As the bus blew its horn and applied brakes that would be too slow in taking effect Tom thrust his hand into his pocket and managed to get the cap off the jar the girl had given him before he was hit with the force of a battering ram and everything went black.

"WELL I SAID you could stay in my flat but the invitation wasn't meant to extend to my hospital!"

Tom came round to see Mike's face staring down at him. He tried to speak but his throat was so dry all he could manage was a croak.

"You'll be able to talk again soon enough," said Mike with a grin. "Although it's going to take a bit longer for that to start working again." Tom looked over at his left arm as Mike tapped its new plaster of Paris casing with his ballpoint. "You had a really nasty knock but nothing else seems to be too damaged. The general surgeons want to keep you in overnight just to watch for any insidious bleeding but you should be able to go home tomorrow. The nurses will be able to get you anything you need." Mike chuckled. "Believe it or not the ICU's just round the corner, so I thought I'd pop in to say hello on my way home. Anyway – you get some sleep and I'll see you tomorrow!"

And with that his friend was gone, leaving Tom to mull over everything.

First, and most importantly, he was alive, and not even badly injured. He wondered how much of that was down to the strange substance the girl had given him, the one that must have somehow protected him. But that was gone now, and he wouldn't be so lucky a second time, not when Emily tried again.

Emily, the girl in the intensive care unit.

The intensive care unit that Mike had said was just round the corner from the ward Tom was in right at that moment.

He remembered what Eleanor had said and closed his eyes tight at the thought. Only one of them had to die, only one of them had to appease the gods Eleanor had spoken of, and only one was capable of getting out of bed and going to the other who was still in a coma.

And killing her.

Tom shook his head. It was unthinkable. And yet the girl had tried to kill him twice now, and if it had not been for the intervention of others Tom's soul would already be damned. He owed it to those who had already tried to help him to take matters into his own hands. Or at least that was the only way he could think of justifying what he was planning to do.

He waited until two in the morning.

He passed the time up to then experimenting to see how well he could move, and even tried a practice trip to the toilet at midnight. His joints ached a bit and there was a nagging pain in his lower abdomen but a quick self-examination with his good hand satisfied him that there wasn't anything urgent to worry about. At just after 2am the sole nurse on duty on his ward was called away to check drugs with her colleague next door and Tom took that as his sign to act.

He made his way out of the ward, into the dimly lit corridor, and followed the signs to intensive care. When he got there he pushed the door open a crack.

From where he was standing he could see that the unit was a hive of activity. They must have just had a new admission. According to the whiteboard near the door Emily Phillips was in the first side room. With luck he should be able to slip inside without anyone noticing him. He held his breath and pushed the door open.

In the end Tom needn't have worried. The staff were far too busy with whatever disaster had just been brought in, and the next thing Tom knew he was in the same room as the girl who had been tormenting him for the last few days.

He made sure the door was wedged shut and then looked down at her. Could it really be true? Was the lifeless form in this hospital bed, surrounded by beeping machines, enmeshed in plastic tubing delivering drugs, nutrients and oxygen, the person who had been trying to kill him? A beeping from above her bed caused Tom to look up at the monitors to see the measurements of the girl's pulse, blood pressure and arterial oxygen levels being traced out in green, red and blue lines respectively.

And to see a now familiar face staring back at him from the glass of the screen. A face contorted with hatred and fear. He began to feel icy claws pick at his dressings to get to the freshly bleeding wounds beneath.

That was enough. Someone would be coming in here soon so this could be the only chance he might have. Tom held his breath as he reached over and grasped the cables that ran to the life-giving equipment around her.

Then he pulled.

The ventilator that had been filling and emptying her lungs ceased its regular rhythm, the carefully graduated syringe drivers that had been delivering minute but essential doses of medication to her heart stopped working, and the pump that had been delivering a nutrient feed to her stomach via her nasogastric tube beeped once to indicate there was a problem and then was silent. Tom watched as the coloured lines on the monitor went flat. Alarms should have sounded but he had pulled those cables out at the same time. For a moment he stood there, regarding the body of the girl he had just killed, unable to accept the full implication of his actions. In fact, so appalled was he at the realisation of what he had just done, that when her eyes flicked open Tom almost felt relieved, right up to the point where she turned her head and glared at him.

When she began to pull herself out of the bed, Tom urged himself to run but found himself powerless to do so. All he could do was stand there, helpless, as the girl who by all rights should now be dead hobbled towards him, the coiled plastic intravenous tubes still in her veins leaving spattered patterns of her own blood on the white floor tiles.

When she was almost upon him, she pulled the endotracheal tube from her throat, gripped his shoulder with blood encrusted fingernails, and brought her mouth close to his ear. Her words were a choked whisper from a throat inflamed and torn by the multiple repeated attempts by the intensive care staff to wean her off the ventilator. But there could be no doubt what she said.

"Now we're... both... lost."

And as the girl fell into his arms and her life left her Tom realised with sickening horror that he had not saved himself at all. He had not listened closely enough to what Eleanor had said and in doing so had damned both of them. Emily had needed to die from her accident, Eleanor had said. But now she hadn't. Now he had killed her, and therefore had not altered his fate at all. Perhaps it was what had been predestined for him all along, he thought, as the icy claws began once more to pluck at his dressings and scratch at his skin.

As Tom turned to leave the room he realised that there were only two things of which he could now be certain. That very soon now he would meet with an accident he would not survive, and that until that time he would be haunted by the soul of his victim, of the girl he had perhaps always been fated to kill.

The girl in the glass.

THE LURE

Nicholas Royle

I've always thought that the Paris métro would make a great setting for a horror story. Knowing that Nicholas Royle has more than a passing knowledge of the city, I suggested it as the background for his contribution to The End of The Line. *Nick has managed to capture the essence of that European capital in a story that has a powerful and dangerous erotic charge. There's something of the feel of a Robert Aickman tale here and, like Aickman, Royle is a master of suggestion.*

As A YOUNG man I lived in Paris for a year, in the north-eastern corner of the city, the 19th *arrondissement*. My nearest métro station was Bolivar but I almost never used it. Jaurès may have been further away, but it was a pleasant walk down avenue Secrétan, past the *boulangerie*, the *épicerie*, the *charcuterie*. Past the cheap supermarket – Monoprix or Franprix. I can't remember. It was a long time ago.

I was teaching English in a school on rue de Seine in the 6th, so I used to take line 5, *direction* Place d'Italie, from Jaurès to Gare du Nord and then change to line 4, *direction* Porte d'Orléans. I would get off at Odéon, then walk up boulevard St Germain and turn right up rue de Seine. I used to enjoy the various colours of the different times of day. In the morning everything seemed golden, the polished brass and gilt of the shop fronts, the windows full of *pains* and *baguettes*, the early autumn sun flashing on the flanks of passing trains on the elevated métro line at Jaurès – line 2. By late afternoon, when I left the school to walk back down rue de Seine, everything had turned red. Giant hams and sausages, the scarlet faces of pheasants hanging by their feet. Beaujolais sloshing into glasses at pavement cafés. As I descended into the métro at Odéon, the sun would be suspended in the sky behind me like half a blood orange. By the time I emerged from underground at Jaurès, the sun would have set.

I first saw him on the final leg of my homeward journey one Friday afternoon in October. He sat with his guide dog at his feet. He wore glasses – an old, unfashionable frame with smeary, fingerprinted lenses. There was something about his eyes. They weren't right, somehow. He was sitting diagonally across from me, on the other side of the aisle, so my view was not the best, but I couldn't tear my eyes from him. He alighted, as I did, at Jaurès, but while I made for the exit, he veered off to change to line 7b, *direction* Pré-St-Germais.

He was of average height and appeared to be in his late fifties, the same age as my father. Iron-grey hair, stiff as wire wool. A crumpled, resigned look to his jowly features. But the eyes…

I poured myself a glass of wine before dinner and sat at the round table in the centre of my tiny studio apartment. The brown wallpaper featured large pale-coloured flowers with dark centres that thrived in the damp conditions. Yellowish artificial light filtered through the lace curtains covering the tall windows giving on to the courtyard. In the kitchen, I kept the radio permanently tuned to a jazz station. I could barely hear it, but it was the only place where I managed to get any reception at all. The shower room was located just off the kitchen and late at night I would run the hose until the shower tray was full and then sit in it listening to the radio. I missed being able to have a bath.

My single bed was pushed into a corner. There was a nightstand with a bedside light that I kept switched on at all times to try to create a little cosiness. In addition, I had Blu-tacked some postcards to the wall to give me something to look at other than the sickly flowers. On the wall facing my bed I had put up a couple of large film posters. At the foot of the bed was a door that the landlord had advised me would remain locked. It was partly glazed, like an interior door, but both the glass and the wooden panel below it were papered over with the same extravagant blooms.

I lifted my wine glass to my lips and thought about the man on the métro. It was not uncommon to see blind people wearing glasses, of course. He could be partially sighted. But the odd thing, I realised as I got a *demi-baguette* from the kitchen and took a knife to the Boursin, was his fixed stare. I couldn't remember seeing him blink.

I saw him again a couple of weeks later. It was a Sunday and I had gone to have lunch at the apartment of a colleague, an older woman whom I knew only as Madame Villemain. On my originally taking up my duties at the school at the beginning of the autumn term, my fellow English teachers, all of them French, had not been overly friendly. I had put this down to what I regarded as excessive French formality.

Madame Villemain was one of the older English teachers, in her early fifties like my mother. She commanded a certain fearful respect from the rest of the staff, smiling rarely, but she had favoured me with a flash of slightly gappy teeth on several occasions. I would smile back, taking pleasure in the illusion of complicity. She stopped me in the corridor and asked me how I was getting on. She didn't condescend to me by speaking in English. Instead, she stood very close and held my gaze with her ice-blue eyes. I was peripherally aware of a strip of lacy white undergarment visible at the open neck of her blouse. The combined aroma of coffee and cigarettes mingled with her strong body scent to produce a powerful cocktail. I felt myself start to blush and automatically lifted a hand to the side of my face. She smiled at me then but continued to speak in a low, fast voice. I was close to fluent and my understanding was better than my spoken French, but I had difficulty following her. Was she inviting me to lunch? Just me or would other people be ·

present? Obviously I couldn't ask. She scribbled her address and phone number on a scrap of paper torn from a student's homework and handed it to me before turning to go. Suddenly I was alone in the corridor, unsure what had just taken place, my face burning. I felt, somehow, as if her eyes were still on me.

Madame Villemain's home was a large apartment in an ancient building on the Isle St Louis. Out of breath from my climb to the fourth floor, I was taken aback when the door to the apartment was opened by a tall, gaunt man with a wide forehead and shoulder-length black hair streaked with grey. He failed to introduce himself beyond shaking my hand and issuing a grunt. He retreated into a book-lined study while Madame Villemain ushered me out on to a little balcony. While I stared at the view over the river, Madame Villemain's blue eyes seemed to bore into the side of my head. I asked about Monsieur Villemain and briefly turned to look at her, to catch a flare of irritation in her eye. She used her hands to make a dismissive gesture and muttered something about Freud, Jacques Lacan and the Université de Paris.

Over a lunch of salad and cold meats, she watched me while her husband pushed his plate to one side and lit a cigarette. He had been talking about his work; his wife's apparent lack of interest must have been as obvious to him as it was to me, but he seemed indifferent in turn. When he had finished his cigarette, he pushed back his chair and left the room. Madame Villemain and I then discussed the Luc Besson film, *Subway*, which we had both seen, separately, the week before. I confessed to having most enjoyed the look of the film, its fluorescent glimmer, while Madame Villemain gave a dark smile and made a remark about the film's star, Christophe Lambert. She used an idiomatic expression that was unknown to me, but its general tenor was clear and I looked down at my empty plate, embarrassed. She immediately apologised and placed her hand on my arm. I transferred my gaze from my plate to her hand: tanned from a summer spent in the Midi, it was marked by spots of sun damage that revealed her age. I imagined her long, tapering fingers pressing into the flesh of my bare back.

Monsieur Villemain could be heard opening the door of his study. I looked at Madame Villemain, waiting for her to release my arm before her husband entered the room. She did so only at the last moment, but continued to hold my gaze while Monsieur Villemain rooted about for something in a bureau at the far side of the room. I expected him to sense the tension in the air, but he paid neither of us the slightest heed. I left shortly afterwards, when Madame Villemain said she wanted to have a lie down. I half-imagined that it was intended as an invitation, even with her husband in the apartment.

I crossed the river via the Pont Marie and instead of descending into the métro continued walking. If you had asked me, I would have said I was wandering at random, but as Dr Freud understood, a man walking in a city is controlled by forces he may not even be aware of. I soon found myself walking up rue St Denis. At the lower end of the street, the young, lithe girls in their 20s and 30s in their bustiers and suspenders were of no interest to me. Regulation erotica for sexual conformists. Each to their own. It wasn't until I had crossed rue Réaumur that my responses began to remind me of Madame Villemain's apartment on the Isle St Louis – without the tension provided by the presence of Monsieur Villemain, perhaps, but then the absence of touch began to create another, very particular tension. I looked at each woman in every doorway and as my gaze slithered over exposed flesh and plunged into areas of shadow, I felt as if my eyes were an extension of my sense of touch. As on previous visits to this part of town, it was on rue Blondel that I came closest to surrendering control and crossing a threshhold I had never crossed.

On the north side of rue Blondel, a tall, well-built woman in black stood in an open doorway at the top of a short series of steps. Statuesque, she towered over me. As I walked past, I tried to make sense of what she was wearing. It revealed a certain amount and yet still contrived to leave much to the imagination. Mostly she seemed to be covered by a filmy veil, or veils, a fine mesh, offering a partial view of a magnificent décolletage and long, strong, powerful legs. When I reached boulevard de Sébastopol, I crossed over and walked back along rue Blondel on the other side. After a third pass, I felt a familiar combination of intense desire and self-loathing. I hurried towards the métro at Strasbourg St Denis, but on reaching the top of the steps realised it would make more sense to keep walking up boulevard de Strasbourg to the Gare de l'Est, which would obviate the need to change lines.

I saw him as soon as I entered the over-crowded carriage. The guide dog, the old-fashioned glasses. I was going to take a seat opposite him, but yielded to a determined-looking middle-aged woman. She said nothing, didn't even glance at me.

"*Je vous en prie, Madame*," I said with heavy sarcasm, standing with my legs apart in the middle of the carriage.

The woman dismissed me with a glare.

The guide dog lifted its head and sniffed the air. The *signal sonore* announcing the closure of the doors rang out and the dog allowed its head to sink back down to the floor. The man's eyes did not blink and now that I was closer to him I could see why. He was wearing a mask – a rubber eye mask similar to a sleep mask but with eyes painted on to it. I couldn't tell if they were hand painted or if the mask had been imprinted by a machine. Now I understood why he wore the glasses – to obscure the outline of the mask and soften the intensity of the painted stare – though of course now that I had seen that he *was* wearing a mask, the presence of the glasses seemed even more bizarre.

Closer to, he looked a little older than I had first thought – early sixties perhaps – though it was hard to be sure without seeing his eyes.

The train pulled into the platform at Gare du Nord, the *signal sonore* was heard and the doors sprang open. The blind man leaned forward and patted his dog. A large number of people got off, the woman among them, and I took her place. An Arab sat down next to the blind man, who checked on his dog again, making sure it was lying down between his feet and not blocking the way. The train was very soon back in the darkness of the tunnel. By the interior lights of the carriage I could make out the round edge of the mask at the side of the blind man's face. In fact, the mask had a slight curl on it, just above the elastic that secured it to his head, leaving a narrow black gap between rubber and skin. It wouldn't matter how long he stood in front of a mirror with his painted-on eyes, he wouldn't see that, and it would be hard to detect by touch.

The Arab got off at Stalingrad. There were now no other passengers in our immediate vicinity. I wondered if the blind man knew that someone was sitting opposite him. I imagined so. I raised my arm and waved it in the air between us. The dog stirred and the man patted the dog, murmuring reassurance. He sat back in his seat. I wanted to know what lay behind the mask. Did he have eyes at all? Were they open or closed? (Closed, surely.) What did they look like? Did they look anything like the ones painted on the mask? Had they ever worked or had he been born blind? Was it preferable to have been born blind and therefore never known what he was missing? Or to have lost his sight and therefore understand what it meant to see and have memories to draw on? Would that be a source of comfort or anguish?

At Jaurès, he got up, the dog preceding him as he headed towards the doors. I followed. When he went to change to line 7b, I still followed. I stood ten yards away on the platform. I watched him while we waited. After a couple of minutes, he turned his face towards the stillness and silence of the tunnel, and seconds later I heard the first rumblings of the approaching train. There was no doubt in my mind that he had sensed it before I did, whether he'd heard it or felt the slightest draught on his face. We were alone on the platform, and when the train arrived, the nearest carriage was empty. I followed him through the doors and remained standing while he went to sit down, led by the dog.

To my surprise he got to his feet as the train entered the next station – Bolivar. I maintained a careful distance between us as we ascended to street level. He crossed the road and walked a little way up avenue Secrétan before turning left into a doorway between a café and a *patisserie*. While he was inserting his key into the lock, I drew level. I stood on the pavement and watched as he opened the door. The dog was leading him into the hallway, but he stopped and looked back. His protuberant painted eyes found mine among the passing crowds and watched me for a moment before he turned back and followed his dog into the hallway. As the door started to close, I saw his hand reach up to open his *boîte à lettres*.

MADAME VILLEMAIN INVITED me to go with her to the Bois de Vincennes. Again, it wasn't clear to me who or how many people would be going. Part of me hoped it would be just me and Madame Villemain, and part of me didn't. She proposed that we meet at Bastille, which meant I could get line 5 from Jaurès, *direction* Place d'Italie, and stay on it past Gare du Nord and Gare de l'Est. I felt jumpy on the métro and I wasn't sure if it was the prospect of spending the day with Madame Villemain or the fact that I now half-expected to see the blind man whenever I descended below street level.

At Bastille I made my way to line 8, *direction* Créteil-Préfecture.

I spotted her as soon as I stepped on to the platform. She was wearing a long green woollen overcoat and had tied a gold silk scarf around her neck. I approached tentatively, but as soon as she saw me, she caught hold of my arms and offered me first one cheek and then the other. She started talking excitedly – in French – about what we were going to see or do at the Bois de Vincennes, but I was lacking key bits of vocabulary and I was distracted by her hand on my arm. Her left hand had remained attached to my right forearm, her long ringless fingers curled around it. To emphasise certain points, she would squeeze my arm lightly. I wasn't sure if even she was aware she was doing it. There was a naturalness about it that I found exciting.

The métro arrived and its metallic doors rumbled open. It was busy and we stood leaning against the back of one of the blue-upholstered seats. Our hands touched on the vertical steel pole and neither of us hurried to reposition our fingers or apologise for the touch.

"*J'aime beaucoup le métro,*" she said. "*C'est comme si on était déscendu à un autre niveau de la réalité.*"

"I don't know about another level of reality," I said, "but I sometimes think of it as representing our subconscious."

"*Exactement!*"

We got off at Liberté and crossed into the park. Madame Villemain was walking quickly and I almost had to break into a trot to keep up. It was entirely possible that I was imagining something that was not happening. Madame Villemain was nothing more than a friendly colleague who had gone out of her way to make me feel a little less isolated and lonely. The fact that she and her husband appeared rather tired of each other was not unusual and it certainly didn't mean she was about to have an affair with a callow Englishman young enough to be her son.

A horseshoe-shaped crowd had gathered between the velodrome and the lake. At its centre a man in old-fashioned dress wearing a sturdy gauntlet on his left hand used his right hand to twirl a lure on the end of a long line. Suddenly, the crowd gasped and people ducked as a large bird appeared, arrowing in low and catching the baited lure in mid-air. Madame Villemain clapped her hands together in excitement and then pointed at the bird, some kind of falcon or hawk, as it settled on the grass some metres away. It held down the lure with one claw and tugged at its meaty cargo – the reward – with its large, fearsome-looking beak.

"It is an 'arris' 'awk," she told me, in English.

The falconer whistled and the bird, still clutching its prize, flew the short distance to his glove, settled and folded its magnificent wings. Deftly, like a magician, the falconer removed the lure from the hawk's grip while allowing it to keep the reward.

"Named," Madame Villemain went on, leaning towards me conspiratorially, "by Audubon after his great friend Edward 'arris."

I wanted to tell Madame Villemain that I liked the way she dropped her aitches. I looked at the hawk's yellow feet gripping the falconer's gauntlet. I could feel Madame Villemain's fingers on my arm again. The hawk adopted an upright posture on the glove. The slight overhang of its brow gave it a stern expression; its eyes were the same chestnut shade as the leading edges of its wings, while the body was a darker, muddier brown. Now that it had consumed the meat, the bird was constantly switching its gaze between the falconer and the crowd, reacting to the slightest movement. Its flexible neck allowed it to turn its head almost all the way around while its body remained still.

"Look," said Madame Villemain.

The falconer had produced a little leather hood, which he now slipped on to the bird's head from behind. The hawk accepted the imposition of the hood without protest and instantly became still.

"*La nuit est tombée*," said Madame Villemain in my ear, adding in English, "It thinks it is night-time. It immediately becomes compliant."

I turned to look at her but she was watching the hawk. A smile crept on to her lips.

AT THE END of the display – it continued with an eagle owl and a peregrine falcon, but it was the Harris' hawk that had impressed me most deeply with its docile acceptance of temporary blindness – Madame Villemain smoked a cigarette while we walked back to the métro. Our train rattled through the tunnels and I watched the tendons in Madame Villemain's neck as she followed the toing and froing of other passengers. At one point she looked at me and I raised my eyes, too slowly. I lifted my hand to the side of my face and Madame Villemain's own hand went to the scarf at her neck, but instead of tightening it, she loosened the knot.

"I am 'ungry," she said. "Where do you like to eat? Take me where you like."

I decided to take her to Chartier – or to Le Drouot. That was the problem. I knew they were two restaurants under the same ownership, but in my mind they had become one. I had eaten in both a number of times, but I didn't know which was which or how to get to either. Instead of owning up to this, I allowed Madame Villemain to think I was confident and in charge. As a result, we got off the métro at least two stops early at Strasbourg St Denis and before I knew where we were we were walking south down boulevard de Sébastopol. We had already passed one turning on the right, which meant that rue Blondel would be next. I knew I had made a mistake and that we needed to head west, whichever of the two restaurants was our goal, since they were located close to each other either side of boulevard Montmartre. I couldn't suggest that we turn back, and to go straight on would only lead us further from our destination.

We turned into rue Blondel.

"Are we going the right way?" Madame Villemain asked me.

"Yes," I said without looking at her.

Women stood in doorways up and down the street. Many of them were about the age of Madame Villemain. I looked, because not looking seemed too obvious somehow. I never liked to do what was expected of me. I felt my skin prickling inside my clothing. I looked across the street. The tall woman in black was in her usual spot. She looked down at me and I looked away. Madame Villemain walked closer to me. I felt her arm bump softly against mine.

"It's OK," she said, but I couldn't look at her.

We turned right at the end of the street and moments later we were walking west along boulevard de Bonne Nouvelle.

"I think I took us the wrong way," I said.

"It doesn't matter," she said as she linked her arm through mine.

When we were finally sitting at a table in Le Drouot, I realised I had probably made a mistake in the choice of restaurant also. The reason I liked the place – and its sister restaurant – was because the prices were cheap and I enjoyed the legendary rudeness of the waiters. Bad wine didn't matter to me. I always drank Beaujolais and didn't know any better. But Madame Villemain would be accustomed to a better class of restaurant. To combat my nervousness, I drank quickly, and Madame Villemain matched my pace. Soon it didn't matter that the wine was a bit rough and the veal rather thin. It wasn't really about the food and drink.

We talked about school and Madame Villemain was indiscreet about colleagues. She propped her head in her hand, elbow on the table. Her shoes had been slipped off and her legs were crossed, one stockinged foot sticking out into the aisle, reminding me of my mother, who would often take off her shoes in restaurants, on the few occasions we ate out, and always wore nylons. If Madame Villemain didn't retrieve it quickly enough, the waiter would catch the stray foot as he strode by. I felt certain that if I were to suggest we leave and take the métro to Jaurès, Madame Villemain would agree, but the very thought brought into my head an unwelcome image of the blind man sitting in the middle of an otherwise empty carriage, his dog at his feet.

I heard myself asking about Monsieur Villemain.

"What does he do in that study of his?" I asked. "What's he into?"

By now we were speaking a mixture of French and English.

"Freud, mainly. The Oedipus complex," she said, lighting a

cigarette. "Also Lacan. His theory of the Gaze. Laura Mulvey and the Male Gaze."

"It means nothing to me," I said, laughing.

She asked me why I had laughed and I explained that if I had said that line back home, among friends, one of them would have responded, "Oh Vienna."

She didn't get it. It meant nothing to her.

"You mean because of Freud?" she asked, smiling and frowning simultaneously.

"No," I said, laughing again and dropping my hand on to hers for the first time. "It's a line from a song."

"So," she said, "are you going to take me 'ome?"

I looked at her, aware that my mouth was hanging slightly open.

"Or I can just get the métro myself," she added.

The penny dropped. "*Non, non. Je vous accompagne.*"

Outside it was just beginning to get dark. We went down into the métro at Rue Montmartre, then changed at Strasbourg St Denis, *direction* Porte d'Orléans. We didn't talk much, just rocked with the motion of the train and watched other passengers. I asked her if she wanted to change at Châtelet, but she shook her head.

"I'll walk from the Île de la Cité," she said.

The Seine at dusk, Notre Dame floodlit by passing Bateaux Mouches – I had heard it said that if Rome was the City of Love, Paris was the City of Lovers. As we crossed the Pont St Louis I had to fight an urge to blurt out some romantic foolishness. I shoved my hands in my pockets so that they couldn't grab Madame Villemain and press her up against the stone embankment. We stopped outside her building. She removed her shoes and held them in one hand, then offered her cheek and was gone, the heavy door clicking shut after her.

At Pont Marie I skipped down the steps into the métro. I watched the other passengers through an alcoholic haze. For some reason, I wasn't at all surprised when I changed to line

5 at Gare de l'Est and found myself in the same almost empty carriage as the blind man.

I was surprised, however, when he opened his mouth and spoke: "How are you this evening?" he said, across the space between us, in heavily accented English.

I felt as if the métro tunnel had become a lift shaft. "What?" I stared at his unblinking eyes, which were pointed straight at me. I moved closer to him, took a seat opposite. "You can see," I said, shaking my head in disbelief.

He didn't bother to answer that.

I stared at him but his face gave nothing away.

"Why did you speak to me in English?" I asked.

"Because you are English."

The whites of his painted eyes glimmered. I looked at him, but felt as if I was seeing someone else. I tried to think of another context in which a man might speak to me from behind a mask. There was nothing sinister about the surgical mask a doctor or dentist might wear out of courtesy for you, for your benefit. You could see the eyes and the movement of the jaw, maybe even the push and pull of the fabric of the mask as words were spoken. This, though, was like speaking to an automaton or doll, although the lips moved with a naturalness that was denied by the mask. It was bewildering, alienating.

"How did you even know I was here? On this train, in this carriage?"

"I can smell you. I can smell your fear."

I got up and looked down at him, feeling nauseous, full of violence and chaos. The dog immediately rose to its feet, a low growl building in its throat. The man reached out a hand and the dog sat back down again, but kept a wary eye on me.

"How did you know I was English?" I asked, my jaw clenched.

"You spoke. You let a woman have your seat and she didn't thank you and you said, '*Je vous en prie*.' A Frenchman would never say that. A Frenchman would not be so sarcastic. Ironic, yes, perhaps, but not sarcastic. Your sarcasm was very English. Actually," he went on, "your accent is quite good. It was your mentality that gave you away."

I moved across and stood by the doors.

"This is not your stop," he said.

I needed some air. I needed to be above ground.

The doors opened and I stepped off the train. In the brief silence before the *signal sonore* I heard him mutter, ironically, "*Bonsoir, Monsieur.*"

OVER THE NEXT ten days, I spent more time in my apartment than I had during recent weeks. Some evenings I got through two bottles of Beaujolais instead of my customary one. I had a lot of 'baths', listened to a fair amount of jazz.

I didn't see much of Madame Villemain. If our paths crossed, it always seemed that one of us was in a rush to do something or be somewhere. She smiled at me and I stored those smiles up. I walked the length of rue Blondel a couple of times but I didn't climb any steps or cross any threshholds. For a few days I used different routes to get to work. I walked down rue de Meaux to Colonel Fabien and took line 2 to Nation, then changed. Or I wandered over to Louis Blanc and took a roundabout journey on line 7, *direction* Mairie d'Ivry, getting out at Châtelet and crossing the river on foot to reach rue de Seine. The unpredictability of these routes meant that either I was late for work, or I sat on the métro worrying that I would be late for work. And if I knew I had plenty of time I experienced non-specific anxiety instead, only it wasn't really all that non-specific.

Gingerly, I returned to line 5, changing at Gare du Nord. I did see him in the distance on one occasion, but he was at the other end of the carriage and there were enough people between us that I doubted even his sense of smell was acute enough to alert him to my presence.

I had just reached the end of a seemingly endless lesson with a class of 14-year-olds, none of whom had any interest in learning English, when I noticed Madame Villemain coming towards me in the corridor.

"Are you finished?" she asked.

So many of her questions or statements could be interpreted in a number of ways, it seemed to me. I said that I was and she demanded that I take her for a drink. We went up the road to La Palette, a few doors down from La Galerie 55, the so-called English theatre of Paris.

"Have you seen that?" she asked me, pointing with an unlit cigarette to the poster in the window advertising the theatre's latest production, *The Pink Thunderbird*.

I shook my head.

"*C'est nul*," she said.

"I'll cross it off my list," I said.

I remarked that she seemed agitated. She told me that Monsieur Villemain – she used his Christian name, Bernard, for the first time in my presence – was spending the evening with one of his students. The French for this – "*une de ses étudiantes*" – included more information than the same line in English would have done. Madame Villemain was jealous, but I didn't mind being used.

"*Je veux aller au cinéma*," she said.

"*Qu'est-ce que tu veux voir?*"

"*Un orange mécanique.*"

"*Ça se joue où?*"

Madame Villemain abandoned her cigarette in the ashtray and took that week's *Pariscope* from her bag, turning to the cinema pages. *A Clockwork Orange* was playing at Studio Galande, a short walk down boulevard St-Germain. There was a screening in three-quarters of an hour. Madame Villemain said she would prefer to walk by the river. I paid and we left, walking up rue Guénégaud to the *quai* and turning right. She asked me if I had seen the film and I said I had been to see it in my first week in Paris. I explained about its having been withdrawn from public exhibition in England and assured her that I was more than willing to see it again. She had seen it many times, she said. It was her favourite film.

During the rape scene, she took hold of my hand.

As we left the cinema, she said she did not want to go home. In fact, what she actually said – "*Je ne veux pas rentrer chez moi*" – arguably contained a double meaning.

Emboldened by the spirit of Malcolm McDowell's portrayal of Alex DeLarge, I said, "*Vous préférez rentrer chez moi?*"

She nodded, linked my arm and we walked toward the métro at St Michel. Between Etienne Marcel and Réaumur Sébastopol, she kissed me. We changed at Gare de l'Est and on the platform for line 5, *direction* Eglise de Pantin, I kissed her back. I kept my eyes closed, partly because that was the normal thing to do and partly because I was afraid of whom I might see further down the platform if I opened them. We walked up avenue Secrétan arm in arm. I apologised for my apartment because I felt I had to.

"*Vous êtes jeune*," she said once we were inside, as if this explained – or excused – the lamentable standard of my accommodation.

I went to switch off the bedside light, but Madame Villemain requested that I leave it on.

Her hands were soft.

Afterwards, we lay together in silence. Suddenly self-conscious, I picked up my crumpled shirt from the floor and put it on, fastening a couple of buttons.

Madame Villemain lit a cigarette and looked around for an ashtray. I went and got her a side plate from the kitchen. She smoked for a few moments, then asked me to make her a coffee. I said I only had wine and she said that would do. I fetched the bottle and filled two glasses. A claw-like hand shot out to grasp one of them and she swallowed half of its contents in one go. She pointed to the half-glazed door at the foot of the bed.

"What is beyond the door?" she asked.

"Nothing. I mean I don't know. It's locked. It's got wallpaper on it."

"I can see that. You should decorate."

"I'm not allowed to. The landlord was very clear. The apartment stays as it is."

"Did the school find it for you?" she asked.

I nodded.

"I have to go," she said.

"I'll take you back," I said.

"There is no need."

I protested, but she insisted. She would get a taxi.

I watched her get dressed.

"This will probably not 'appen again," she said. "My zip, please."

Overcome by a terrible weariness, I struggled to an upright position and helped her with her zip.

After Madame Villemain had gone, I lay awake for a long time staring at the half-glazed door at the foot of the bed. Thoughts of the falconer and his Harris' hawk became jumbled up with images of Monsieur and Madame Villemain in their apartment, and of Madame Villemain in my apartment, indeed, in my bed. I slept badly, dreaming that strange noises were keeping me awake. In the morning the apartment smelt of cigarette smoke.

I STOPPED USING the métro. I found I could no longer take the stairs down without expecting to bump into the blind man. I felt his painted eyes on me as I walked along the platform. Every time the *signal sonore* rang out and the doors snapped open, I expected to see his dog leading him into the carriage.

I discovered that I could get at least half way to the river by walking along the Canal St Martin and then there were a hundred different routes to the Left Bank that didn't go anywhere near rue Blondel.

At school, Madame Villemain still smiled at me, but it was a kindly, motherly smile, now, more than anything. I wondered if perhaps it always had been, if what had happened had been some kind of accident, a mistake. I didn't feel any pressing need to question Madame Villemain about it.

Then one night I went to the kitchen to open a second bottle of wine and happened to notice, just in time, the two empty bottles on the worktop. I put the corkscrew back in the drawer and pushed the third, unopened bottle away. I walked into the shower room and leaned my hands on the sink. I had avoided mirrors for a few days after reading up on Lacan and the Gaze. I looked exactly like someone who had got through two bottles of wine in three hours. Behind me the radio played Thelonious Monk.

I left the shower room, passed through the kitchen and re-entered the bed-sitting room. I sat on the edge of the bed, thinking. I looked at the walls, at the flowers on the wallpaper, pale petals and dark centres. I looked at my film posters. I looked at the half-glazed door with its own plastering of wallpaper. I looked at the bed itself and remembered Madame Villemain lying there.

I sighed deeply and got to my feet. Putting a jacket on, I left the apartment. I turned left into the street and then left again into rue Baste, and left once more into avenue Secrétan. When I reached the doorway between the café and the *patisserie*, I had to wait ten or fifteen minutes before someone eventually exited the building. I let them get a few metres away before grabbing the door and slipping inside. I looked at the bank of *boîtes aux lettres* mounted on the wall. I had not forgotten which one was his. The second one from the left on the bottom row. Number seven, I saw. There was a name written on a piece of card in that strangely illegible handwriting that all French people seemed to have, but I wasn't particularly curious.

I passed apartments 1, 2 and 3. A door to the courtyard stood ajar. On the far side were numbers 4 and 5. I heard music coming from one of them. Another door led to a dark passageway. I pressed the timer switch, but the bulb was not working. I delayed to allow my eyes to become accustomed to the dark, then proceeded. There was a door on the right – number 6 – and a short way after that I found number 7 on the left.

I stood in front of the door for a moment listening, but no sound came from within. I knocked once. Twice. There was no answer. All I could hear was the faint music I'd heard in the courtyard. I knocked again. Once I had decided there was no one in, I barged the door with my shoulder. With a splintering of wood, a narrow gap appeared. I gave the door another shove and it yielded. I entered and pushed the door to behind me, waiting to see if anyone would come to see what all the noise was about. No one did.

The apartment was a similar size to mine, but the layout was different. I had entered directly into the kitchen. There were some dirty pots and cutlery both in the sink and on the work surface. They had not been left to soak: the food on them was congealed and would be difficult to remove. There was a head of garlic on top of the fridge. It was dried out, little more than a husk. Some over-ripe tomatoes sat in a chipped bowl on a shelf. At the left-hand end of the kitchen, behind a plastic curtain, was the shower room, which was no better appointed than mine.

A doorway led from the kitchen into the bed-sitting room. Under the skylight, which was the only window in the apartment, there was a small desk with a chair tucked beneath it. On the desk was a spiralbound notebook with a number of pages missing (otherwise empty), a couple of cheap ballpoints, and a small, neat pile of three books – one of Simenon's Maigret stories, a Série Noire translation of a Robin Cook novel and *Djinn* by Alain Robbe-Grillet. They were standard paperback editions, not Braille. Elsewhere in the room there was a single bed, a dog basket, a free-standing radiator, a small chest of drawers and an armchair that needed re-covering. Behind the armchair was another door, glazed at the top, wooden panel at the bottom. The glass was covered over, but only on the other side. I dragged the armchair out of the way and tried the door handle. The door appeared to be locked. I inspected the top half more closely. There was small hole in the covering on the other side of the glass. The hole was more or less at eye level. I approached the hole and peered through into my apartment – the bed, the nightstand, the round table in the middle of the room. You could see just about everything. It offered a very good view of the bed.

I pictured the half-glazed door from my side. The wallpaper on the glass. The hole must have been cut in the dark centre of one of the flowers.

I moved away from the door and repositioned the armchair. I sat down in the armchair. Faintly, I could hear the radio in my apartment. I looked around the room from where I sat. I wasn't looking for anything in particular. I noticed something I hadn't seen before, a little bedside table with something resting on it. I got up and walked across the room. From the bedside table I picked up the rubber eye mask. I turned it over in my hands. It had been hand-painted. There were little holes in the centre of the pupils that looked as if they had been made with a large-bore needle. I held the mask at arm's length and decided I could only see the holes now because I knew they were there. Besides, I had only ever seen the mask behind a pair of glasses.

I went to put the mask back down on the bedside table and saw that it had been resting on a piece of paper. I picked it up. It was a photocopied notice giving advance warning of a talk by Bernard Villemain at Université Paris V. The title of the talk appeared at the top of the page: 'Falconry and the Oedipus Complex: the Psychology of the Lure'. It was in French; the translation is mine. There was a bit of blurb, which mentioned names and theories that were familiar to me: Freud, Lacan and the Gaze, Laura Mulvey and the Male Gaze.

The date was two weeks hence.

I replaced the notice on the bedside table and positioned the mask on top of it.

I stood in the middle of the apartment, thinking.

I knelt on the arm of the armchair and had another look through the spy hole into my apartment.

I walked into the kitchen and opened various drawers and closed them again.

I inspected the damage to the door.

I took a glass from a cupboard and filled it from the cold tap. I drank the water and placed the glass on the worktop next to a dirty knife.

I went back into the other room and sat down in the armchair to wait.

23:45 MORDEN (VIA BANK)

Rebecca Levene

Rebecca Levene is one of those authors who seems to be able to turn her hand to anything. That is not to say, however, that she is not a stylish and complex writer, as can be seen from the haunting story that follows. It's clear that Rebecca knows London intimately and something of that love/hate relationship can be seen here. Described in beautiful detail is a geography of the damned, a place where lines cross, leading us into dark journeys and to horrifying destinations.

THE PUB HAD shut and the alcohol had started to turn from buzz to piss inside him. Adam leaned against the brick wall and knew he needed to go home. Drinking on a Sunday night, never a good idea. The air was claustrophobic with traffic fumes and a light, dirty drizzle. Hoxton was grubby and crowded and shabby.

"You all right, mate?" Rich slung an arm over his shoulder and breathed beer fumes into his face. His sandy hair was plastered against his skull by the wet and his usually handsome face looked bony and a little unwell.

"I'm fine," Adam said. "When's the last Tube?"

"About eleven thirty. You're gonna have to get a cab."

But he didn't have the money for a cab. He sprinted towards Old Street station, lurking beneath the ugly roundabout at the end of the road. His head cleared in that odd drunken way that found running easier than walking and he felt a pleasant burn in his lungs. He really needed to go to the gym next week. He'd left it nearly a month.

The underpass leading to the station was gloomy. Adam could

see a homeless man at the end of it, stubbled face raised to the few stragglers who passed him by. He fumbled in his pocket for change from the last round he'd bought and dropped it into the man's hands. "Take care, mate," he mumbled and the man smiled at him and touched a finger to his hair like something out of fucking Dickens.

There were people coming out, a post-train wave breaking against the gates, but no one seemed to be going in. Adam saw a TFL employee lounging, eyes drooping, by the luggage exit. "Scuse me," Adam said. "When's the last tube?"

"In about thirty seconds," the woman said. "If you run..."

Adam swore and slapped his Oyster card against the reader. The gate stuck half-open and he squeezed through anyway then pelted for the escalator. That was broken too. The grooved metal treads felt awkward beneath his feet as he trotted down. His footsteps echoed in the empty tunnels as he sprinted to the southbound platform, ricocheting from the walls with drunken clumsiness.

The train sighed as he reached the platform and the doors shut just as he reached them. The couple in the carriage looked at him as he banged his fist against the glass. The woman smiled and shrugged and the man just looked blank as the train groaned and drew away.

"Fuck," Adam said. He looked at the display above the platform, but nothing was showing. A business-suited Asian guy ran onto the platform behind him, stared after the retreating backside of the train and said "fuck" too before swivelling on his heel and leaving.

Adam tried to figure out how many miles it was from Old Street to Stockwell. Two? Ten? He could walk it in a couple of hours, couldn't he? There was a rumble of agreement from the tunnel behind him and he breathed in the stale fumes which brushed past his face for a few seconds before he realised it was another train approaching.

Ha! So the woman at the ticket barrier had lied to him. Then he heard the loud hoot blasting from the tunnel and his heart sunk. It must be one of those out-of-service trains, the ones that slow down as they pass straight through the station as if to give commuters the maximum possible time to be pissed off that they weren't actually stopping.

Except this one slowed steadily and then stopped. Adam rested his hand against the closed doors and peered in. Empty. It was one of the older trains, letters and random squiggles scored into the glass of the windows and the material of the seats shiny with the grease from thousands of sweaty thighs. The lights flickered off, then on, and he saw that the floor was spattered with vomit.

The doors finally creaked open and he got on anyway, picking his way through the congealed lumps on the floor to a seat at the far side of the carriage. A high, steady screech came from the tannoy. A mumble of static beneath it might have been a route announcement but Adam couldn't make out the words.

The train jolted then pushed forward. He braced his feet as it swayed from side to side and took what felt like a 90-degree corner as it entered the tunnel. A crumpled *Metro* brushed his neck as it fell from the shelf behind him. It landed on his lap, the headline 'Dad Laughs As Children Burn' staring up at him in bold type for a second before it fluttered the rest of the way to the floor.

There was another jolt, another sharp swerve to the right, and Adam felt his heart speed as the lights flicked out. What the fuck was wrong with the driver? Was he drunk or something? Maybe there wasn't *meant* to be a train now. Maybe some mad bastard was just taking it out for a joyride.

Then the lights flicked on and the train slowed as it drew in to Moorgate. The platform was deserted and Adam half rose from his seat. Should he leave? He peered out of the open doors to the tunnel leading out and saw that there was a grating across them. The station had shut for the night. Jesus. He really was stuck on here. He considered getting out of the train anyway, waving at the

CCTV cameras until someone came to let him out. But what if no one was watching? He imaged spending the night on the platform, upright in one of the hard plastic seats or on the floor where the dirty black mice could run all over him, and sat back down again.

The doors closed and the train accelerated. He was braced this time and he started to enjoy the swerves as it took corners he didn't remember between Morden and Bank, then Bank to London Bridge. The rattling was almost soothing. He let his eyes drift shut in the pleasantly alcoholic haze that would turn into a burning headache at four in the morning.

When he opened them again what felt like thirty seconds later, the train was already in Stockwell. The beeping of the door pierced his stupor and he leapt up and out of them before he was properly awake. He was tense as he walked the length of the platform, not sure if he'd find the exit shut off, but it was open and the escalator was still running as he reached its foot. He could see another man at the top, a straggler from the previous train. Adam smiled and leaned against the side of the escalator as it took him up to the street and home.

HE WOKE THE next morning with his alarm buzzing in his ear. He grunted and blinked at the time. *Shit. Eight-thirty.* The alarm must have been going off for an hour without waking him. He rolled out of bed, tangled in the duvet and surprising a meow from Pickles, who had been curled asleep between his legs.

There was no time for a shower. He sprayed extra deodorant under his arms and pulled yesterday's clothes on over it then pelted out of the door

The train was delayed – of course it was – signal failure at Chalk Farm, and how the hell did that affect the service all the way down here, anyway? It was crowded too and the people already on the carriage glared and muttered as he elbowed his way on. He was squeezed in too tight to pull out a book, so he read the ads instead, three-times over, idly considering switching his broadband provider and knowing he wouldn't.

As they drew nearer to Warren Street he felt the sensation of watching eyes prickling between his shoulder blades. He glanced around and saw a flicker of movement as if someone had quickly looked away. But when he looked at one young woman she glared back with a sneer and he blushed, realising she must think he was hitting on her.

The escalator was broken and his back and armpits were damp with sweat after he'd taken the steps two at a time. The office was round the corner from the station, in a square around a dingy basketball court that looked New York by way of Dalston. A group of teenagers who should have been at school were throwing a ball backwards and forwards, but they stopped when Adam approached and turned to watch him walk by. The look wasn't quite hostile but it wasn't friendly, either, and his pace picked up as he crossed the square.

The smell hit him before he saw it, a round turd curled on the doorstep like a snake. Probably one of the smack addicts who loitered in the shadows by the buildings. Twenty other people must have passed the doorstep already and stepped over the thing without bothering to clear it up. He stepped over it too and climbed the three flights of stairs to the office.

Matt tapped his watch and raised his bushy eyebrows when Adam slid into his seat at the desk opposite. "Yeah, yeah," Adam said. "It's not like I've got anything to do today. "

Matt's eyebrows raised further and his eyes tracked behind Adam's head. He swivelled in his chair to find the MD leaning over him. "Nice to see you're earning that four per cent pay rise I just gave you," Reynolds said, peering over his thin rectangular glasses. "There's a backlog of filing I was going to ask Angela to tackle, but since you've got nothing to do..."

"Shit," Adam said, when Reynolds had left. Matt grinned at him, not quite sympathetically.

When he returned to his desk two hours later, his eyes were dry and gritty with the dust from a thousand unfiled folders.

He flopped into the chair then frowned as he felt a patch of dampness beneath his left buttock. "What the fuck?" He tried to peer round at his arse before he realised it made him look as daft as a cat chasing its own tail and stopped.

Matt made a face that seemed to be the result of an amused smirk trying to masquerade as an apologetic grimace. "Sorry – spilled some coffee on there earlier. Meant to clear it up but I forgot."

Adam glared at him as he sat back down. *Mate*, he typed to Jon, who worked in accounts two floors down. *What a fucking shit day. Matt's being a tosser and Reynolds is even more of an arsehole than usual. Made me do the bloody filing. What do I look like – his secretary?*

The reply came about a minute later. He read it with a twinge of unplaceable unease which hardened into panic when his eyes scanned back up the message and he saw the long, long list of CCs. Why? Why? Why on god's good earth would Jon copy the entire fucking company into the message?

When Reynolds' bulbous head appeared round the cubicle wall a minute later, it was almost a relief. The MD raised an eyebrow before heading back to his office and Adam knew he was meant to follow.

Ten minutes later he walked out with a written warning on his record. He would have preferred it if the bastard had shouted, but he'd done the whole more-in-sorrow-than-anger thing. Adam was absolutely sure he'd enjoyed it.

As he scooped up his jacket from the back of his chair he was horrified to realise he was close to crying. He sat and swallowed a few times until he could be sure he wasn't going to humiliate himself. Something must have showed in his face, though, because when he walked past reception Angela sprung from behind her desk and threw her arms around him.

"Totally unfair," she said, wide, moist lips close to his ear. "Everyone knew you were just joking."

He nodded, because her words had put a lump in his throat and the press of her breasts against his chest was threatening to put one somewhere lower. He pressed his face against her apple-scented hair. When he lifted it, he saw Reynolds standing in the doorway, glowering at him. He pulled away, blushing, and left.

HE WOKE TO a Tuesday so grey and cold that he fell straight back asleep, convinced it must be earlier than his alarm was claiming. He woke again with 10 minutes to spare before he had to leave, threw some dry food into Pickles' bowl and dashed out of the door, his coat hanging off one arm.

Stockwell station was packed. When the first train drew in it looked like some mediaeval painting of hell, white faces pressed flat against the glass of the doors. They opened and people popped out like the cork in a shaken bottle of champagne, only to force their way back on again before those waiting on the platform could board. There was a collective sigh from those who'd been waiting and a groan from the ones squashed inside the carriage before the doors closed and the train pulled away.

The next one was just as bad and the one after. When the fourth train clunked to a halt, Adam sucked in a breath of air then pushed himself against the solid wall of humanity at the doors until he'd forced a square inch of floor for him to stand on. People around him tutted and he travelled the rest of the way to work surrounded by their BO and their irritation.

The tramp had shat on the doorstep of the office again. Someone had trodden in it this time and the smell was pungent. Adam tiptoed through the muck and into the building. He smiled at Angela when he reached reception, remembering last night's hug, but she crossed her arms over her full chest and frowned at him. "Reynolds wants to see you," she said. "Right away."

Yeah. Of course he did. The MD's office was on the top floor, with a view towards UCL and the massive dome of its library. Reynolds stood when Adam entered, gathering himself up to make the most of his three-inch height advantage. His wide mouth and bulging eyes made him look like a disapproving frog.

"I'm going to come straight to the point," he said. "That kind of behaviour isn't tolerated in this company."

"Er..." Adam said.

"Angela was very upset. Very upset. And frankly, in this day and age, it's pretty shocking you could think that was an acceptable way to act."

"But –" Adam said.

"Don't tell me she was asking for it!" Reynolds roared.

Adam snapped his mouth shut, then opened it and tried again. "It wasn't what it looked like. She just knew I was upset after... you know... after yesterday."

"And how do you explain the previous seven times you made inappropriate advances to her? She was on the point of resigning before she plucked up the courage to complain. She tells me you've been sexually harassing her for months."

That wasn't true. It wasn't even a little true. Angela had nice tits but he didn't fancy her and he certainly hadn't come on to her. Not even at the office Christmas party when he'd knocked back ten butterscotch vodkas in an hour and thrown up on his own shoes.

"I've really got no choice," Reynolds said. "I want you to take some gardening leave while I investigate this properly. You might want to look around for an employment lawyer, or you might not want to waste your money. I don't really see any way you'll be keeping your job."

Adam felt like all the air had been punched out of him. He found himself nodding mechanically and backing out of the office, as if he was in the presence of the Queen.

People stared as he walked past and he wondered what they'd been told. Angela looked up as he passed reception and he couldn't leave it alone. "What the fuck was that all about?" he rasped. "I mean... what the fuck?"

She rose and circled the desk and he was surprised to see tears in her eyes. "I'm so, so sorry," she said. "I didn't mean it to end up like this." She flung her arms around him and he was too shocked to retreat, his body rigid as he endured the hug. Her breath was warm and moist against his ear as she leaned closer. "Nobody wants you here," she whispered. "Why don't you just go away?"

He stumbled back as she released him, staring at her face for some kind of explanation. But she just smiled blandly and sat back down and when he saw Reynolds oozing down the corridor towards him, he turned and left.

HE WAS WOKEN at seven on Wednesday morning by an alarm he'd forgotten to switch off. Its shrill buzzing sawed against his skull and he fumbled to switch it off and knocked it onto the floor instead. Pickles stared at him wide-eyed for a moment, then rubbed his face against Adam's and purred. Adam stroked his cheek and the purring got louder.

He didn't remember much about the night before. When he'd left the office he'd just wandered around for a while, numb with shock. Eventually he'd found himself at some ill-lit pub near Marble Arch that seemed to be filled entirely with elderly men and rent boys. He'd bought a beer anyway and then another, and the next thing he remembered was waking up here with – he looked in the bathroom mirror – a love bite on his neck and stubble burn around his mouth.

A uniquely hungover combination of nausea and hunger drove him down the road to a greasy spoon. He shovelled beans and sausage into his mouth until he at least no longer felt hungry, then went back to the flat because he didn't have anything else to do. He knew he ought to call his mum but he couldn't quite face telling her he'd lost his job, especially if he had to tell her *why*. He called Rich instead.

"Mate!" Rich said. "Where the fuck were you last night? I called you ten times. We were wasted. I'm still off my face this morning."

Adam sighed and told him what had happened.

"Jesus, mate" Rich said when he'd finished. "Look, we're gonna have a laugh tonight. Come along. Get mullered and forget about it. Seven-thirty, Hampstead station."

He ended the call before Adam could protest that the last thing he needed was more booze or ask what exactly they'd be doing in Hampstead.

He set off at seven anyway, after a day that had somehow passed without anything meaningful having happened in it. The walk to the Tube seemed longer than usual and he realised that he felt oddly reluctant to see his friends. It was probably just his hangover, that odd sort of gloom that lingered with the last of the alcoholic poisons, souring his view of the world. Rich and the others would cheer him up.

A beggar had settled himself at the bottom of the escalator, hand out and head down. He had a torn scrap of cardboard at his feet, but it must have been rained on and whatever claims it had once made on the man's behalf were now blurred beyond reading. Adam dropped a pound into his hand anyway, feeling virtuous when he might soon need every penny.

"There you go, mate," he muttered.

The beggar raised his head and glared with bloodshot eyes. Adam noticed for the first time the track marks down his arms and the weeping sore in the crook of his elbow. "I'm not your fucking mate," he hissed. "You ain't no one's mate."

Passers-by stared and Adam blushed as he hurried to the platform. A train ground into the station and he climbed on, leaning against the door between carriages when he couldn't find a seat. The window was jammed open and the unclean wind from the tunnels tangled his hair. He ran his fingers through the knots as he waited for the lift at Hampstead station and realised from the greasy feel that he'd forgotten to wash it again that morning.

Rich was outside the station, along with Jasper and Lee. Jasper's arm was slung loosely over Lee's shoulders as he lifted a lazy hand to wave at Adam. They both had dark hollows under their eyes and their skin looked mottled and unhealthy, the legacy of too many nights taking too many drugs. Rich's expression couldn't seem to decide if it was aiming to be sympathetic or cheering. "Mate," he said. "You up for it?"

"Always," Adam said, and was forced to trot at Rich's heels as the others made a swift move up Heath Street before he could ask what exactly it was he was up for.

It was full dark by the time they made it onto the Heath itself. The grass brushed against his legs, damp from an earlier rain. "What –?" he said.

"Not so loud, mate," Rich whispered. "They'll hear us."

"Who'll hear us?" Adam whispered back.

Rich smiled and dropped to his hands and knees to crawl forward through the grass, the other two behind him. After a few seconds they were almost lost in the shadows. Adam's gut clenched with unease but he ignored it and crawled after them.

His thighs and back were aching with the strain when they finally stopped. His night vision was working by then and he saw the figures ahead of them clearly: two men, one pressed up against a tree trunk by the other as they kissed.

"Fucking queers," Rich said. "I'd like to shove their disgusting cocks right up their own arses."

Adam stared at him open-mouthed, then at Jasper. Jasper *was* gay, but Jasper was just grinning and nodding. They were playing a joke on him – they must be. He smiled uncertainly back, the smile sliding into open-mouthed shock as Rich leaped to his feet and launched himself at the two men with a raw yell.

The sound of fists hitting flesh was loud and meaty and shocking in the silence of the Heath. For a second longer, Adam *still* didn't believe what he was seeing. Then there was another wet thump, Rich laughed and one of the two men screamed and Adam scrambled to his feet and fled through the thigh-high grass.

An hour later he lay in bed, shivering and wondering if he

could possibly have imagined that. Losing his job was a huge stress; maybe he'd had some kind of breakdown. Maybe he'd never left the house. Perhaps he'd just dreamed that thing on the Heath. He *must* have dreamed it. He hugged a squirming Pickles as he tried to fall asleep and draw some kind of line, a thick black indelible line, under the day.

ON THURSDAY MORNING, he woke to find Pickles gone. A quick circuit of the flat revealed he'd left the living room window open, even though it hadn't been hot last night. Why had he done that? But he couldn't remember. Most of the details of the evening had been blurred by shock.

The fat old tabby cat had always lived indoors. The road outside was too dangerous and, besides, Adam didn't fancy his chances against foxes or bull terriers. He didn't want to believe that Pickles had run out now, after all these year being lazy and content and indulged, but after the third time he'd looked behind the bath, he knew it must have happened. His gut churned at the thought of the half-senile animal wandering South Lambeth Road as he pulled on his jeans and T-shirt without washing or brushing his teeth and went outside to search.

He told himself he was looking for Pickles, but he knew he was looking for his corpse. He peered between parked cars on side streets and into garages. After a while, a light rain fell and raised a metallic smell from the pavement. It soaked him as he wandered past dingy terraces and grim council estates that were almost certainly too far for the elderly cat to have reached.

After two hours, he bought himself a wilting sandwich from Costco and headed back to the flat. He'd try again after lunch – maybe put up a few posters with Pickles' picture on them, ask if anyone had seen him. He'd always found them pitiful when he'd seen other people's missing cat posters before, a self-deceiving failure to admit the creature was already dead. But you had to hope, didn't you?

When he turned into his street, he noticed a figure waiting outside his flat, small and hunched. It was wearing a red raincoat and he shuddered, reminded of *Don't Look Now*. But when he drew closer he saw that it was just old Mrs Matthews from the house next door.

She leant against the wall, a pencil clutched in one arthritic hand as she laboriously wrote out a note. A bag rested on the pavement at her feet. There was a dark patch beside it and for a moment he thought it was its shadow. But the sun was hidden behind clouds and the dark patch was spreading. A coppery smell drifted from it and he felt his gorge rise.

"Oh, hello dear," Mrs Matthews said.

He nodded as he looked down at the bag. He could see now that the stain on the pavement beside it was red. "You found Pickles, didn't you?"

"That's right." She smiled, revealing teeth so perfect they could only be false. "Just as well you came back. Saved me the effort of finishing the note."

He nodded again, still staring at the bloodstain on the pavement. "Where did you find him?"

"Eating my rosemary. Luckily I had a hammer to hand. If you get another pet, do try and keep him away from my window boxes, dear. Took me all day to get them the way I like and then that little bugger dug them all up."

He stared at her and she smiled at him again, over-white false teeth shining in a sudden shaft of sun. He looked down at the bag again, its floral pattern smeared with blood. He paused a moment, then unzipped it. Pickles was inside, his fur matted and white brain matter showing around his ears where the hammer had caved in his skull. He looked back up at Mrs Matthews.

"What's the matter?" she said. "Cat got your tongue?" She was still laughing as she shuffled to her red front door and disappeared inside.

* * *

HE STAYED IN bed till three o'clock on Friday. In the end it was the smell which forced him out. It wafted rankly from the bag at the foot of the bed. Pickles lay curled inside, gently decaying. Adam knew he ought to bury the cat, but he didn't want to. He wondered if he could take it to the police and ask them to arrest Mrs Matthews.

When he finally got up it was only to hunch in front of the television in boxers and a T-shirt watching *Countdown*. Just like being a student again. At five-thirty he grudgingly acknowledged that he had to get dressed. He hadn't done any washing all week, so the shirt he picked had been worn once before and the socks three times. They didn't look too dirty.

The walk to Stockwell should have taken him past Mrs Matthews' front door, but he went the long way round, walking three sides of a square to avoid it. It was rush hour at the station again. A burble of chatter spilled from the carriage when the doors opened. When Adam stepped in, squeezing himself between a thin, mixed-race teenager in baggy jeans and an Asian woman in a sari, the noise cut out. He felt scores of eyes on him, but he looked at the floor and didn't meet them.

After a few moments, the conversations began again. There was a hostile buzz to the noise and he was sure they were all talking about him. He fumbled for the earphones on his iPod and turned the volume up loud enough to drown the talk and hurt his ears.

Outside Golders Green station, he turned from the busy, charmless Finchley Road into the leafy streets which circled the Heath extension. His mum's place was only a ten minute walk away, but the time seemed to drag, or extend, so that he felt exhausted by the time he got there.

His brother and sisters were there already. They grinned at him and he saw the echo of Mrs Matthews smile in their faces.

"What's the matter?" Simon asked.

Adam shrugged and walked over to give his mum a hug. Her

body felt stiff and bony in his arms and he released her after only a second. When he kissed her cheek it was cold beneath his lips. She stared at him, frowning, her thin face seeming skeletal in the harsh overhead lighting. He just shrugged again and took his place at the table.

As the eldest, it was his job to say the kiddush over the wine. The Hebrew words felt awkward on his tongue and Simon and Jess talked through the whole thing. He found himself suddenly and burningly angry. They *always* did this together, one of their few remaining family rituals, a kind of sacred relic of their childhood. *How dare you?* he wanted to shout. But when he met Simon's eye, the sly amusement in his brother's face chilled his anger into unease.

It was roast chicken for dinner. The meat had been overcooked and seemed to suck the saliva out of his cheeks as he chewed it. His mum had given him breast meat, too, when she knew he'd always preferred dark. The beans looked like they'd been cooked almost as long as the chicken. They disintegrated into a green mush on his fork. He took a swallow of roast potato to try to ease the rest of the food down his throat.

There was a momentary burst of flavour on his tongue, acrid and strong, and then all he could feel was the burning. He tried to scream, but only a muffled choking sound came out as tears poured from his eyes.

"Need a whack on the back to help it go down?" Paula asked, glancing up briefly from her own forkful of potato.

Adam jerked his arm out spastically and knocked her fork out of her hand. The lump of potato landed on the tablecloth, cream on white.

"Jesus, Ads," Simon said. "Get a grip."

"Burns," Adam said. "Potatoes." Then he was up and out of his chair, rushing to the bathroom. His mouth didn't feel like it was working properly as he spat and spat into the sink, then washed it round with water again until the burning had quietened to a painful throb. When he opened his mouth and looked in the mirror, he could see the blisters on his tongue and the insides of his cheeks, yellow and weeping.

As he approached the dining room, his brother's voice floated out – "Did you see his face?" – followed by laughter. It died as soon as he opened the door and his mother leapt from her chair to hug him.

"I'm so sorry, darling," she said. "I'm such an idiot. I must have put caustic soda on the potatoes instead of salt. Are you all right?"

"Caustic soda?" He looked around the table. There were half-eaten roast potatoes on every plate. "Just on *my* food, mum?"

She pulled away from him. "I honestly don't know how it happened."

"You did it deliberately," he said.

"What?" She looked shocked, but it was a bad actor's impersonation of the expression, designed to be read even at the back of a large theatre, the eyes too large and round and the mouth comically open.

"You're all in on it," he said. "All of you. Everyone."

Paula exchanged a raised eyebrow with Simon as Jess sunk back in her chair and pursed her small mouth, clearly finding the whole thing terribly awkward – or pretending to. Before Meir lowered his own head, Adam got a good look at the smirk on it, and Liz was pretending to cough but he knew that she was really laughing. She always used to cough to hide the giggles when they were kids.

"Why?" he said. "Why are you all treating me like this?"

"Well, darling," his mother said. "I find that when it seems like people are treating me badly, they generally have a reason. More potatoes?"

Now her smile was *exactly* the same as Mrs Matthews'. He tore the door open and fled the room and the house, the laughter of his family following behind him.

* * *

HE DIDN'T GET up at all on Saturday. Pickles' corpse was reeking horribly and the stench seeped into his dreams and darkened them, but the waking world felt no lighter. He went over the week again and again in his mind until he knew the exact moment when everything had gone wrong. That journey home, when he'd caught the train after the last train. He should never have got on it. Something had happened, the world had... slipped a track. It wasn't him, whatever his mum said. *He* hadn't done anything wrong. Except get on that train. If only he could undo that. If there was a way *not* to have got on it. If there was a way to reverse it.

There *was* a way to reverse it.

After sleeping till midday it should have been easy to stay awake past midnight, but his eyelids felt weighed down. He forced them to stay open as he lay on his side and watched the numbers on his alarm clock tick over, one by one by one. Three in the morning, Three fifteen. Three thirty. Three fifty. Four.

When it was quarter to five, he finally rolled out of bed. He made himself take a shower. He hoped it would refresh him but it just left him feeling cold and weak. He dressed anyway, carefully picking out the clothes he'd worn last Sunday, or at least the ones he thought he'd worn, it was hard to remember. At ten past five he started the walk to the Tube station. The first train was due at 5:31, he'd checked on the internet.

There were no other passengers at the station when he arrived, but the gates were working. A blue-clothed TFL worker glared at him as he went through. The escalators hadn't been switched on yet, so he took the stairs. He held on to the railing, walking slowly. He knew that if he could slip, he would.

But he didn't. He made it to the bottom and onto the platform by 5:25. He was shivering, so he wrapped his arms around himself, stamping his feet and rubbing his fingers up and down his sleeves as if he was standing in a snowstorm.

The train came in at 5:30 – exactly one minute before the first was due. He smiled. This was going to work.

The carriage was empty. He climbed on and sat, hugging his knees to his chest and resting the tips of his toes on the seat. He grabbed the arm as it departed, remembering the way that train a week ago had flung him about. This one was far smoother, though. Smooth and silent. If it hadn't been for the shadowy pipes and cables flicking by outside the windows he wouldn't have been able to tell he was moving.

He didn't know how far he needed to travel, but he thought reversing the entire journey would probably be best. Kennington went past, and then Borough and Bank, the stations dark and empty.

He got off at Old Street as another passenger got on at the far end of the platform. Adam caught a brief glimpse of his dark hair and blue T-shirt and felt a lurch in his stomach he couldn't explain. Just as he boarded the train the other man turned to look at him, raising his arm to wave, and for one baffling moment Adam found himself looking at his own face. Then the man was gone and the train pulled out and he told himself that it was all his imagination. Too much shit happening, too little sleep.

The escalator was working here and he stood still as it rose, drawing deep, calming breaths. When he reached the top, he pressed his oyster card against the reader and strode through the gate. He hesitated only a moment, then walked down the tunnel that led out. There was a homeless man at the far end, huddled in his sleeping bag. He'd been dozing as Adam approached but he woke at his footsteps and blinked blearily at him.

"It's you," he said and suddenly smiled. His gums were bleeding and they'd stained his teeth red. "I've got a message for you."

Adam felt the beginning of a fear so profound it seemed to melt his bones. "What message?" he said.

"Thanks for the loan of your life, it's been a fun week." He said the words slowly, as if it took his fuddled brain some effort to remember them, but he wanted to get them right. "That was all it was. Thanks for the loan of your life." The beggar winked conspiratorially, as if they were both in on the joke, and his eyes dropped to his collecting cup, where a £50 note nestled amongst the 10 and 20 pence pieces.

"Who told you that?" Adam whispered. "Who gave you the message?"

"You did," the man said. "Don't you remember, guv'nor? It was you."

Adam shook as he climbed the stairs from the station. The streets above were spotted with the residue of the same rain that had fallen before he got on at Stockwell. Red and blue lights flashed on the puddles and his neck felt stiff as he turned his head to find the source. Police cars crouched behind yellow tape blocking the road ahead of him, the black beetles of rain-jacketed policemen beside them. A series of clicks echoed loud in the early morning silence and he realised with a sick shock that it was the sound of guns being cocked.

They told him to drop on his face and he did, hands splayed against the pavement, his cheek pressed against the tarmac until they were on top of him, a whole herd of them holding him down as they cuffed his hands behind his back and dragged him to his feet while they read him his rights.

The cop facing him looked drawn, almost ill. "You sick fuck," he said. "Your whole family."

"What about them?" Adam said. He remembered the family he'd left in that other, twisted world, who had hated him with an inexplicable urgency. And he thought about his real family, left for a week at the mercy of the other him, the one who belonged in that hateful world.

"What happened to my family?" he whispered.

But they didn't answer. They thought he already knew – and maybe he did.

END OF THE LINE

Jasper Bark

*With 'End of The Line', Jasper has built a nightmare worthy of
The Twilight Zone's Rod Serling. But there's more to this story
than a twist or shock-ending. Instead there's so much going
on here that it's kind of hard to pin down. There's a sense of
psychogeography and magical thinking at work that shows us
that the Tube map can easily be read as an arcane chart. Once
you come to realize this, you may never think of the Circle Line
the same way again...*

He woke on the platform in a pool of blood.

It was congealing round the side of his face. He peeled his
cheek off the ground and blinked the blood out of his eyes.

It was dark and quiet. His eyes took a while to get used to the
gloom. He was in a Tube station, but not one he recognised.

His legs shook as he stood. He put a hand against the wall to
stop himself falling. His fingers met ancient fraying paper. He
peered at it as his eyes became accustomed to the dark. It was a
poster for Ovaltine. 'Isn't it 'licious Mummy?' said a cherubic
little girl clutching a golliwog and holding up a glass of murky
brown liquid. It was obvious the station hadn't been used for
a very long time.

Everything smelled dank and musty. The air hadn't been
disturbed in ages. His footsteps echoed around the space as he
stumbled along the platform. Off in the distance he could hear
rats skittering in the tunnels.

He had no idea what he was doing here or why he was
covered in blood. It had soaked into both his shirt and trousers.

He felt himself for injuries but couldn't find any. He tried to recall his name and where he lived but drew a blank. He had no memories at all.

He could feel the panic rising. He stopped for a moment beside an old wooden door. Its paint was peeling and distressed. It probably led to a store cupboard. There was a rank smell like rotting meat coming from behind it.

He stepped back and his foot skidded. There was a puddle coming from underneath the door. A thick, viscous fluid that might be blood or pus, he couldn't tell in the dark.

He could hear rats behind the door. No, not rats, it was something else. It sounded like someone stirring in their sleep. Was that breathing he heard? No, not breathing – voices, whispering voices. The voices called out to him.

"Open the door. Open the door,"

"You want answers?"

"Open the door."

He backed away. Part of him desperately wanted to open the door, but he wasn't ready to go there. A grinding, scraping noise came from the tracks. It was followed by a clattering inside the tunnel.

Three pre-war carriages emerged from the pitch black and pulled up at the platform. Only the middle carriage was lit. A single bulb flickered inside an art deco light fitting. The central doors slid open with a hiss.

"Don't get on the train. Don't get on the train."

"Stay here."

"Open the door."

That was enough to make him board. The doors shut behind him and the train started with a jolt. He caught a chipped bakelite grab handle to stop himself falling. The patterned seat covers were worn and fraying, showing the horsehair and springs beneath. The wooden floors were riddled with scuffs and scratches, the polish long gone.

He checked the overhead line diagram. He didn't recognise

the line. It was dark crimson and called simply JOHN SANGER. The stops had names like CHRONONAUT'S FIRST EXCURSION, TUNNEL PREMONITIONS and POLICE VISIT. Rather ominously the final stop was called END OF THE LINE.

Had he stumbled on some disused line? Why were they running services? There was something about the line diagram that was incredibly familiar. He felt as though he'd ridden it before. No, not ridden, lived it. He was John Sanger. This was a timeline of the last six months of his life. He didn't know why but he was certain of it, even if he couldn't recall any of the names or events.

He stared at the timeline as the carriages rattled along in the dark. What did it mean? Could the train really take him to these points in time? If it could, then would he be able to change things so he didn't end up back on the platform in a pool of blood? Was that the purpose of the train?

Even if it was, how would he know what things to change or how to change them? With no memories all he could do was guess.

The carriages stopped and the doors wheezed open. The platform outside looked as old and unused as the last one. A rusting tin sign said BRIEF SINCLAIR. This was the last stop before END OF THE LINE. Whatever happened to leave him on that platform must have occurred at this stop. If he could alter things here he might just save himself.

He stepped out onto the platform. A single overhead light lit a small section of the station. The rest was in total darkness. The carriages pulled away and left him.

A 'Way Out' sign pointed to a spiral staircase. There was a sharp turn at the top. He stepped round it and found himself on a pavement at night. In the street lights he saw that the blood stains were gone and he was wearing a freshly washed shirt and trousers.

A woman pushed past him on her way into the station. He turned round to warn her and saw that all trace of the station he'd just left had vanished. In its place stood Leicester Square Tube station.

A tap on the shoulder made him start. "Day dreaming as usual?" said a tall man, wearing a tweed jacket with elbow patches. He had sandy brown hair that was greying at the temples. "We're going to be late if we don't get a move on."

The man led him into a maze of Soho backstreets. He'd lost all sense of direction by the time they entered a discreet gentleman's club. "Can you tell Mr Sinclair that Daniel Brown and John Sanger are here to see him?" the tall man said to the person on reception.

So his name *was* John Sanger. He was here to brief a man called Sinclair. The names on the station and the timeline were becoming clear. A member of staff showed them to a private room where Sinclair was waiting.

Sinclair stood up when they entered and shook both their hands. He was as tall as Daniel but more thick set. His bald pate was ringed with close cropped grey hair and he wore an expensive suit. The minute John saw Sinclair he felt a strange but intense familiarity. "I took the liberty of ordering a little wine," Sinclair said, steering them into plush leather armchairs. "It's a '95 Chateau Margaux, well worth trying."

John sipped the dark, fragrant wine and hoped no-one asked him a direct question. Luckily Sinclair fixed Daniel with his fierce blue eyes. "So, how are my Chrononauts?" he said.

Daniel became agitated. "Not too good actually, that's what I wanted to talk about. I need you to have a word with the university faculty, they've gotten jumpy and they might try and take our offices away."

"Are they still sceptical about the existence of past life consciousness?"

"No, we've amassed an impressive amount of evidence, under laboratory conditions, that prove the existence of past life consciousness. And we've made contact with three. We've even been able to sustain the connection for up to twenty minutes experiencing everything they experience. That means seeing, hearing and feeling what it was like to be alive hundreds of years ago. We've even identified some landmarks that are still visible today."

"So what's the faculty's problem, I thought they were impressed by your findings on group minds."

"Some of them are, others are determined to close their minds to parapsychology. Even though we've demonstrated how effective our programme of telepathic exercises are. All the project members can synchronise their thoughts now. It doesn't give you much room for privacy though. The gossip is horrendous."

"I have to say we were all concerned when you suspended the project for a week. This sub-dimension you say you encountered, you're sure it's more than just a theory?"

"Oh it's real enough, and we've encountered it again. John can verify that."

Both of them turned their gaze on John who nodded to hide the fact that he had no idea what they were talking about.

"I just can't understand where it's coming from," said Daniel. "I've checked every stage of the procedure. We slowly built up the group mind, just like we always do. Then when everyone was synched we sent Michael into a deep regression."

"This is Michael Sayles," Sinclair said. "The one who was a middle-eastern shepherd two hundred years ago?"

"That's right, he's been making direct contact with this past life consciousness for two months. This was the second time the group had attempted mass contact. Once Michael was inside the mind of his past life he opened the door to the rest of the group. We were all looking out of the shepherd's eyes and sharing a direct experience of the past when it happened."

"What triggered it this time?"

"We were searching for a lamb in a mountain cave. Suddenly we all had this feeling of incredible vertigo and this fissure opened up."

"In the cave?"

"In time itself. We all saw it. It was like looking into a tunnel that ran beneath space and time."

"Is that even possible?"

"Theoretically, yes it is. If you think of time as the fourth dimension, it's like a huge plateau where the past, present and future occur simultaneously. It intersects many dimensions other than space and this creates sub-dimensions, hidden sub-terranes that no human mind is supposed to explore."

"Why not?"

"It's too much for the human mind to take in. The shock was so immense we had to drop the connection and splinter the group mind. One member went into catatonic shock and two others entered a fugue state following premonitions of violent death."

Sinclair looked concerned. "This is what made the faculty jumpy?"

"The police are what made the faculty jumpy. They came to see me yesterday after two of our group members – Joanna and Michael – went missing. Full of innuendo they were too."

"Do you think their disappearance is linked to this sub-dimension?"

"Days before it happened both Michael and Joanna told me they'd been having dreams about falling into the tunnel we saw."

"Is that where they've gone? Can someone physically enter this sub-dimension and leave time all together, or explore it from below?"

"I don't even know if that's possible. We only encountered the sub-dimension by accident. How would you open a doorway?"

"Murder perhaps. I hear the ancient Druids used to practice ritual sacrifice for similar ends."

A look of shock, or was it panic, ran across Daniel's face. He put down his wine glass and stood up. "Yes, well anyway, I know you're busy so I won't keep you any longer. If you could have a word with the faculty like I asked I'd be very grateful."

"Won't you stay for another glass?"

"No, no you're very generous but John and I have far too

many things to be getting on with."

Daniel dragged John out of his chair and propelled him towards the door. "Before you go John," Sinclair said. "I ought to let you know that I've sorted out that little offer I made. Let me know when you want to take me up on it." Daniel pushed John out of the door before he could answer.

"You'll forget all about that little offer if you know what's good for you," said Daniel when they were outside the club. He gripped John's arm and leaned in close. The look in Daniel's eyes unnerved him. "We need to talk, but not here, there's something I need to check out first. Meet me at Leicester Square station in an hour, we can go back to my place."

Daniel let go of him and charged off. John tried to retrace the route they'd taken. There was so much to take in and he wasn't sure he entirely trusted Daniel. Why had he panicked when Sinclair mentioned ritual sacrifice? Was he afraid Sinclair had found something out? Why had he threatened John about Sinclair's offer, what did he think Sinclair was going to tell him?

Could this sub-dimension that ran beneath time explain what was happening? Was that how he was able to travel back to past events? This was the last stop on the timeline before END OF THE LINE. Whatever caused him to wind up on a platform in a pool of blood was just about to happen.

It had to be Daniel. Seeing the sub-dimension must have sent Daniel over the edge and now he was murdering the other members of the project. That's why the police had been to see him.

John turned a corner and found himself on Oxford Street. He could see Tottenham Court Road station. He had no idea where he was going. He couldn't even remember where he lived. He just knew that if he wanted to stay alive he had to get as far away from Daniel as possible.

The platform was crowded with late night commuters. John stared at the Tube map, trying to remember what route he took home. He was hoping one would just spring out at him, but it didn't. Oddly Sinclair appeared in the crowd and nodded to him.

At that moment a complete silence settled on the platform. John heard a familiar grinding and screeching from the tracks and the three pre-war carriages trundled into view. Lights began to go off on either side of the platform, plunging both ends into darkness.

The overhead display read: 'Please board immediately.' A voice on the tannoy said: "Passengers are advised to board while the station is still in existence." More lights went out and John realised it wasn't darkness creeping along the platform so much as an all encompassing nothingness that was swallowing everything in its path. He knew that if the nothingness touched him he would cease to exist like everything else it consumed.

The doors hissed and made to close. He leaped through them in a panic. The carriage shuddered and started to move. He didn't dare look at what happened to the platform. He glanced at the diagram of the timeline. Nothing had changed. He was still heading back to END OF THE LINE.

He didn't understand. Hadn't he evaded Daniel and avoided being murdered? Why hadn't he altered the timeline?

His stomach began to itch with an uncomfortable ferocity. He hitched up his shirt and saw a huge scar forming. He was certain it hadn't been there before. It was made up of three ragged slashes, that traced the perimeter of his stomach wall. The itching got worse and began to sting. The tissue was getting redder by the second.

The skin on his throat started to sting. He put his hand to it and felt a thick scar appearing down the length of his artery. The wounds seemed to be un-healing themselves. The particles of his skin felt like they were unknitting and pulling away from each other.

The pain got worse as tiny scabs began to form in the scar tissue, like crystals in a petri dish. As the scabs spread and replaced the scars the pain became unbearable. He sunk to his knees and howled with agony as the carriages came to halt.

He got to his feet and staggered onto the platform holding his stomach. The scabs on the wounds became fresher and fresher and eventually started to dissolve into blood. What started as a trickle became a thick red gush and the wounds opened up completely.

He could barely stay upright as the severed section of his stomach wall collapsed and his lower intestines spilled out in a great torrent of blood. They slipped through his fingers and hit platform with a wet slap. He gave up trying to hold them in as the scab on his throat opened into a vicious gash and a fierce geyser of blood pumped out.

His arms and legs became cold and numb as the blood drained from them. Multi coloured blotches burst in front of his eyes. Everything went black and he felt himself falling

falling

falling without end...

HE WOKE ON the platform in a pool of blood.

He peeled his cheek off the ground and blinked the blood out of his eyes. His footsteps echoed around the space as he stumbled along the platform. He stopped for a moment beside an old wooden door. The whispering voices called out to him.

"Open the door. Open the door,"

"That's where the answers are."

"Open the door. Open it now."

The urge to open it was stronger this time and, before he realised, he was gripping the handle. He couldn't bring himself to turn it though. He was too afraid. It felt too much like defeat and he wasn't ready to admit that yet.

A grinding, scraping noise came from the tracks. Three prewar carriages emerged from the pitch black and pulled up at the platform. The central doors slid open with a hiss. The whispers became frantic and shrill.

"Don't board the train."

"Stay here and open the door."

"You won't change anything, you never do."

He stepped onto the train and the doors slid shut behind him. He checked the dark crimson timeline once again. How was he going to change it this time and make sure he didn't end up back at the END OF THE LINE? Maybe he needed to travel further along the line and try to alter things earlier on, when events had yet to be set in motion.

The first three stops on the timeline were JOB INTERVIEW, START POST and MEETS SINCLAIR. He felt strongly drawn to Sinclair. The third stop must be the first time they met. If he got off at that stop and found a way to warn Sinclair about Daniel then maybe things would turn out differently.

At the top of the spiral staircase he found he was wearing chinos and a polo shirt. He also had a folder of documents under his arm.

Around the sharp corner at the end of the staircase John stumbled onto a pavement. The bright sunlight dazzled him and he walked straight into someone. "Sorry. I wasn't looking where I was going."

"S'alright mate," said the man. He offered John a tattered magazine. "*Big Issue?* It's me last one."

"Sorry, I've err... got that one already," John lied. He saw a sign that said 'New Cross Station.'

"Can I 'ave your travel card if you you're done with it?"

John gave it to the man who added it to a pile in his pocket. John flicked through the papers in his folder to see if they held a clue to what he was doing. He found a print out of an e-mail:

From: Daniel Brown <daniel.brown345@camford.ac.uk>
To: John Sanger <j.c.sanger@undergroundswell.co.uk>

John,

Sorry to call you in on your day off but Mr Sinclair, our project sponsor, is coming in tomorrow to 'inspect our premises', and he'd really like to meet you. Without his donation to the university our project wouldn't even be up and running, so I'm keen to keep him 'on-side' as they say.

He's due to arrive around ten thirty so I'd appreciate it if you could be here by ten.

many thanks

Daniel

John glanced at his watch and saw it was already ten thirty. The *Big Issue* seller gave him directions to the university but he had a hell of a time finding where he was going on campus. Twenty minutes later he burst into Daniel's office.

Sinclair was chatting with Daniel when John arrived. They both stood up. John was struck by the same feeling of intense familiarity as soon as he saw Sinclair. "This is my newly appointed assistant John Sanger," said Daniel. "You'll have to excuse his late arrival, we've all been working very hard to get things up and running."

"Not at all," said Sinclair. "So, did you major in parapsychology too John?"

John had no idea. Daniel came to his rescue. "John's currently doing his PHD on the history of poster art on the Tube. I hired him because he's actually a highly talented telepath and administrator."

"Poster art on the Tube," Sinclair said. "Is that right? I know of something that might interest you then. I imagine Daniel's told you that I run the UK's leading Electrical Installation and Maintenance group. We do a lot of work for the Underground so I have access to several disused stations on the Metropolitan line. They haven't changed since before the war, old posters on the wall and everything. You'll have to come and have a look sometime."

"I'd love to," said John.

Before he could give any more thought to Sinclair's disused stations Daniel said: "I've just been telling Mr Sinclair about the plans for our little group of time travelers, or 'Chrononauts' as we like to call them."

"Fascinating stuff," said Sinclair. "As soon as I came across Daniel's paper on Group Minds and Past Life Consciousnesses I knew I had to give him the funding for this project."

"I'm pleased to say Mr Sinclair's as passionate about our research as we are," said Daniel.

"I'm obsessed with time travel," said Sinclair. "I've read all the scientific and occult theories on the subject. This project is the closest thing I've seen to making it a reality. Looking out at the world of the past, or the future, through the eyes of someone who actually lives there. I'm not a telepath myself, but I envy you that opportunity."

"Do you mind me asking what's behind your interest in this field?" said John.

"No I don't mind at all. It's my legacy to future generations. I'm afraid I won't be around to see the fruits of your research. A few months ago they found a tumour in my intestines. It's not operable. I have about a year left."

"I'm so sorry. I didn't realise or I..."

"That's alright, you weren't to know. The worst part is the feeling that you're trapped by some inescapable fate that you can do nothing to alter. That's why I'm interested in time travel. To conquer time is to master our own destinies. To transcend the boundaries of space and time so that no-one has to feel trapped by their fate again. Today I'm dying from a condition they'll be able to cure in the future. If we had time travel I'd be able to travel forward and save myself. When you think of the lives that your research might eventually save, you begin to see how important this work is."

"That's quite humbling," said John. "I can see you've given this a lot of thought."

"Mr Sinclair's extremely well informed in this area," said

Daniel. "He was telling me before you came that time travel has a longer history than we realise."

"Many ancient civilisations believed there were hidden paths beneath time," Sinclair said. "That's why they built underground labyrinths and catacombs. They were a key to understanding these paths and a way of opening them. The druids practiced ritual disembowelment deep underground for just that purpose."

"Well I'm not sure the faculty will let us disembowel anyone," Daniel laughed. "Unless the Bursar's in a particularly bad mood." Sinclair laughed too and slapped Daniel on the back. It seemed like a friendly gesture but for a second a predatory look passed across Sinclair's face.

In that moment everything fell into place. John knew now why Daniel had panicked when they went to Sinclair's club. He'd worked out what Sinclair was doing. He hadn't threatened John outside the club, he was trying to warn him. Daniel wasn't the killer, Sinclair was.

Sinclair knew they were going to encounter a sub-dimension that ran beneath time. He planned to use it to travel to the future and save his life. He was going to sacrifice all of them to do so, down in his disused Underground stations. John had to find a way to stop this.

"I'm sorry," John said. "But I can't be a part of this any longer. I'd like to tender my resignation." He picked up his folder and left the room.

Daniel caught up with him in the corridor. "What on earth is going on?"

"It's Sinclair, you've no idea how dangerous he is. He's going to kill us."

"You're not making any sense. Look John, you've obviously been working harder than I realised and I think the strain is beginning to show. Why don't you take a few days off and just rest up? We'll talk about this later."

John realised that nothing he said would convince Daniel. It all sounded too preposterous. He didn't have any proof, because nothing had happened yet. He suddenly felt powerless. He turned and ran from Daniel without saying another thing.

He got lost in the building again and ended up in the underground car park. He spotted the exit and made for it. He had to get out of the city and hide. Then he could try and expose Sinclair. It was the only way to stop it all happening again.

Complete silence settled on the car park. The lights at either end started to go out. John went cold. "No, not here," he said. "It shouldn't happen here. I haven't had enough time."

Rail tracks appeared in front of him and he heard the familiar screech and grind of the carriages. He pulled a piece of paper out of the folder and tried to write himself a note of warning about Sinclair, but the dark nothingness was eating up everything around him.

The doors opened and he boarded the middle carriage. The folder disappeared and he was back in a blood stained shirt and trousers. He glanced at the timeline. Nothing at all had changed. The futility of his efforts began to dawn on him. As soon as he climbed back on the carriage his old unwitting self would be back in charge of his life.

If he *had* left the city he would only have turned around and come back to his old life. If he *had* written a note he wouldn't have understood it. He would probably have put it all down to a temporary lapse of sanity.

He stared at the timeline and considered each of the stops with dismay. He could visit every one without significantly changing a thing. He would still end up stuck on this train speeding towards END OF THE LINE. He was trapped by an inescapable fate that he could do nothing to alter.

The walls of the carriage moved in on him. A vein throbbed in his temple and sweat soaked his blood stained shirt. He tore the front of his shirt open, scattering the buttons. He roared and kicked the scuffed seats then punched the windows. If he could just shatter the glass he could at least try and jump off, but the glass wouldn't break and his knuckles were too sore.

"Stop the train," he shouted. "Do you hear me? I said stop it you fucking bastards STOP! Stop... stop it... please... please stop it please..." Tears spilled out of his eyes and his chest started to heave with sobs. "Just tell me what I have to do... please... just tell me..."

His stomach began to itch with an uncomfortable ferocity. He looked down and saw a huge scar forming.

HE WOKE ON the platform in a pool of blood.

He peeled his cheek off the ground and stumbled along the platform. He stopped beside the old wooden door. The whispering voices called out to him.

"You couldn't do it could you?"

"You tried and tried but nothing changed."

"You're trapped here and you can't do anything about it."

"Open the door."

"Open the door it's the only way out."

He took hold of the handle and the fear overcame him again. Fear of failure, of being unable to set things right, of having to admit this to his peers. But he was too tired and too beaten to fight the voices. The door opened inward with a screech of rusted hinges.

The stench made him gag, spoiled meat and blood wafted up. His eyes took a while to adjust to the dark and he didn't make out the corpses at first.

There were six of them piled up against the far wall. Each one had its stomach torn open and its intestines pulled out. He peered through the gloom and saw that the intestines were all hanging from metal pegs hammered into the wall.

The thick pink tubes were stretched out into lines that occasionally curved back on themselves, formed loops or crossed one another diagonally. In places the glistening flesh was torn and leaked blood or pus. Something about the shape they made was familiar. Then it hit him. The intestines were forming a crude replica of the Tube map.

He looked down at the corpses and there, in the middle of them, he saw the body of John Sanger wearing a blood stained shirt and torn trousers.

But that didn't make any sense. How could he be looking at his own corpse?

"You aren't," said John's corpse. "You're not John Sanger and you never have been."

"Then who am I?"

"Isn't it obvious," said a corpse he recognised as Michael Sayles. "You're the one who's responsible for all this."

Wait, he was Sinclair? Yes of course he was. It was all coming back to him. He was Sinclair and the corpses...

"... are your handiwork," said John's corpse. "Your first attempt at time travel. But it didn't go so well. You knew you needed a group mind to find the sub-dimension and a group sacrifice to open it. What you didn't know is that the tunnel won't lead anywhere without the group mind to guide you. You didn't transcend time and space, you erased yourself from them. You're trapped and you killed the only people that could save you."

"Not that you'd listen to us anyway," said Daniel's corpse. "You never do. Even now you're trying to use the spell to go back into our lives and change them so you can alter the outcome and get to the future."

"It won't work," said John. "It never does. As soon as you get inside our lives you lose all perspective. You forget who you are and what you're doing. You make the same mistakes over and over again."

"You didn't conquer time, Sinclair," said Daniel. "You're not the master of your own destiny. You're trapped by the fates of your victims and all you can do is relive them time and time again."

Sinclair ignored their prattling and concentrated on the intestinal tube map. He didn't need their guidance to fix this.

He'd already proven how superior he was to all of them. The map was a key to the sub-dimension. He remembered now. It was also part of the spell that kept the corpses reanimated. Sadly he needed them in this state and he hadn't found a way to silence them yet.

He just needed to change the right moment in the right victim's life to change the working and get to the future. Sinclair studied the intestines and picked another victim. He focused his will on entering the victim's life and slipped into a trance.

He let go of his consciousness. He let go of his identity and found himself falling

falling

falling without end...

HE WOKE ON the platform in a pool of blood.

THE SONS OF THE CITY

Simon Bestwick

Simon Bestwick is easily one of the most prolific writers I know. He seems to produce words at an astonishing rate. Even if you were to cut off all his limbs he'd probably bang out a couple of novels a year, using only a Bic and his teeth. But not only is Simon incredibly prolific, he's also a bloody good writer. I've been an admirer of Simon's short fiction for quite a few years and when I finally got the chance to compile an anthology, I knew that he had to be in it. This then is an offering from Manchester's master of horror, a cautionary tale of the grisly price that must be paid in the name of progress.

1. Knightley

I CROUCHED BY the barbed-wire fence and squinted through the telephoto lens at the old farmhouse below me.

It wasn't much to look at. There were slates missing from the roof and a window was smashed, the hole patched with cardboard. Paint flaked from the brickwork and the wooden window frames were crumbling. A gutted, rusty shell of a Morris Minor was up on bricks in one corner of the potholed farmyard.

Christ, he's come down in the world.

If he *was* here. I was having trouble believing that part. Jolley was well-known for liking the finer things in life. Among other things, obviously, but down on his luck or not it'd be a cold day in hell before he'd live in a shithole like this.

Still, I'd got my information from someone who'd been close

to Jolley; they hadn't let me down yet, so I kept watching. Waiting for some sign of –

Click.

Not for some sign of that. I didn't like that click. I had a pretty good idea of what it was. I'd covered enough crime scenes, enough stories on gun crime, to have heard sounds like it before.

Of course, I liked it even less when cold metal touched the back of my neck and a hoarse voice whispered: "Don't move."

2. Finch

WHAT CAME NEXT was pretty undignified. The camera was taken off me and I was made to lie face-down in the mud – face inches from a pile of sheep-shit – while a large rough hand frisked me so thoroughly I thought it'd finish with a cavity search. Thankfully it didn't go that far.

"Hands behind your back." The metal was still pressed to the nape of my neck. I did as I was told. I couldn't see him – when I tried to turn my head, he jabbed me with the gun – but I could smell him. Stale sweat and piss, old cow shit and gun oil.

Something bit into my wrist and I let out a gasp. The gun barrel jabbed the back of my neck again. "Fucking quiet, pal."

It was thin, whatever he'd put on me, and bit into the skin like wire. Cable tie, I was guessing.

"Right. Up, pal. *Now.*"

Not easy standing up from a prone position in a patch of mud, especially with your hands tied behind your back. But I managed when he hauled me up by the collar, even if he damn near garrotted me in the process.

He shoved me against the fence-post, still keeping the pistol on me. Big guy, early forties; thickening round the middle but still in good shape. Thick greying hair and beard. Eyes like chips of dirty ice. Wax jacket, an old sweater, combat trousers and army boots.

"Look," I said, "I'm –"

"Shut up," he said, and pointed the gun at my face. It was an old army Browning and the muzzle looked very big. "You don't speak till you're told to. Clear? Nod if you get it."

Ex-squaddie, maybe a Para. He doesn't just know how to use that thing, he has *done. This fucker's killed. Don't test him.*

I nodded.

"Walk," the man said, and prodded me down the footpath to the farmhouse. He rapped at the front door – two short, three long. Another man answered; long, thin, hatchet-faced, permanent smirk. "Hey Finch. What you found?"

"Snooper. Better get His Nibs. He'll want to take a look."

The thin man nodded and wandered off. Didn't look in a hurry. Finch prodded me at gunpoint into a grimy, stone-flagged kitchen with about a fortnight's worth of dirty pots piled up in the sink. There was a big wooden table with a couple of old phone books wedged under one rickety leg, but I didn't get an invite to sit down. My shoulders ached from the angle my arms were pulled back at. I wondered how long before the cable ties cut off the circulation to my hands.

Of course, Finch's Browning would speed up the schedule if I did anything he didn't like, so I stayed standing upright and didn't say anything

Above, the stairs creaked. Someone was coming slowly down.

Whoever it was, it couldn't be who I was looking for. They sounded ancient. Or very, very ill.

The kitchen door opened.

"Knightley," he said.

I blinked, staring. "Jolley?"

3. Jolley

WHEN I'D LAST seen Mike Jolley, about six months earlier, he'd been, not to put too fine a point on it, a fat bastard. Not anymore. He must have shed five or six stone, easily. He wore army boots the same as the other two, plus a ragged old sweater and a pair of cords. His grey hair was matted and his pocked flabby face hung slack on his skull. His eyes hadn't changed, though; still two little studs of burnished metal stuck in the mottled pudding of his face.

Cancer? Maybe AIDS?

"Should've known you'd find me." His voice was weak but gravelly. He glanced at Finch. "Sit him down."

Finch pulled a chair out and shoved me into it. I winced.

"Cut him free," Jolley said. "He's only a fucking journo. Can't do fuck-all."

Sod you too.

Finch sawed through the cable tie with a combat knife. I rubbed blood back into my wrists and Jolley sat down facing me.

"Why can't you fuckers just leave me alone?" I'd heard him bluster, shout, threaten and bully; heard him smarm and charm and smirk, delivering some pre-packaged soundbite to the congregation, but I'd never heard him whine. "I left, I jacked it in. I've lost everything. What else do you want? Why can't you just leave me in peace?"

I glanced at Finch, who'd leant back against the kitchen counter, arms folded, the Browning shoved through his belt.

"A lot of people died that day," I said.

I was nearly one of them.

"And that's all my fault, is it?" Jolley bared yellow teeth. "Why don't you blame Rawlinson? He was head of the company. He's to blame if there was anything sub-standard."

"You were the one made it all happen," I said, remembering.

4. Flashback

I WAS RUNNING late that day. Caught in traffic on the East Lancs, cursing through my teeth as I drove.

Today was the day, you see. The ceremony. The first stone of the first station platform was about to be laid.

Richard Rawlinson, your classic local boy made good – best not to ask how – owned TubeCo Limited. TubeCo had put forward a proposal to finally give Manchester its own Underground, replacing the Metrolink tram system. A proposal forced through by the might and main of none other than Council Leader Mike Jolley.

Never mind that the Metrolink had had a full and very pricey overhaul only two years earlier, or the price-tag on the new Underground. Or the number of locals up in arms. Money had changed hands, palms had been greased, the fat cats were going to make out like bandits (again) and sod the rest of us. And my editor says I have a chip on my shoulder.

I knew I was walking a line with him. The *Evening News* wasn't the place if you wanted to expose corruption in high places. Harry, the editor, played golf with Mike Jolley; if you'd read the paper you'd never have known anyone but a few well-picked nutters were against the Underground.

I had my brief. Take a few snaps, lob some soft, easy questions Jolley's way and take down the soundbites he'd mouth back. He'd smile his shark's grin at me, but his eyes'd be like bullets. He'd already complained to Harry once. Harry, to be fair, liked me. He'd known my Dad. I didn't like getting cut extra slack because of that, but then again I didn't like dole queues either.

Just get down there and do it. Dig on your own time, don't tip him your hand.

Not that I had much of one, but I could put two and two together. Jolley had got his way but it'd cost him, both with his colleagues and the public. He'd every chance of being booted out by his own party if the voters didn't do it for them. That meant:

a) Rawlinson was bunging him some *serious* cash to make it worth his while;

b) Rawlinson was blackmailing him – they'd grown up together and it wasn't hard to imagine Rawlinson knowing where a few bodies were buried; or

c) Both. Stick and carrot.

Personally, I favoured c) – no amount of money or blackmail on its own would make Jolley buck a gravy train like the one he was riding. But there was no evidence. If I could find any, I could sell the story to one of the big nationals and piggy-back from that to London, the journo's Mecca.

Meantime, though, I had to make the ceremony. I was running late and there was no signal on my mobile.

Fucked.

I cut down the A6, onto Chapel Street, pulled down New Bailey Street and into the NCP there, then legged it up Bridge Street towards Deansgate, where the first station platform was to be – and *that* had made Jolley popular, shutting down one of the main streets in the city centre while they dug it up. I'd come out right next to the dig, maybe just in time to snap Jolley. I could call in enough favours off the other hacks to cobble some copy together from theirs. Not that Jolley'd miss the chance to let Harry know I'd fucked up –

I was out of breath, heart thumping. Out of condition. Get down the gym. I stopped for breath on the bridge over the Irwell and put a hand on the parapet.

It vibrated.

The fuck?

Felt almost like a train was passing underneath. Which was ironic.

Earthquake, maybe? We'd had a couple of mild tremors a few years back. But we didn't get shocks *that* bad in the UK. No excuse for not trying to make it. I started running again.

Besides, anything bad happens you want to make sure you get pic –

THUMP.

The ground yanked itself out from under like a pulled rug. I yelped, did a sort of quickstep on the pavement as I flailed to stay upright, then failed and landed on my arse.

I wasn't the only one. Other people hit the ground too. Four cars went into the back of one another; the lead one slammed into a traffic light. The driver went headfirst through the windscreen.

Fuck.

A bus coming down from Deansgate slewed, mounted the pavement and ploughed into the front of the Masonic Hall.

Screams. Yells. Shouts. Wails. And then a voice, rising over the howls and the drilling shriek of car alarms: "Oh fucking god it's a bomb look they've blown it up–"

And seeing the thick black mushroom cloud billow up over Deansgate.

Did I forget my job? Did I muck in and start pulling the dead from the wreckage? Did I help administer first-aid and CPR?

I did not.

I snapped photos of crashed cars and the guy wearing his windscreen like a hula skirt with his face hanging off the bone.

I snapped photos of the trashed Masonic Hall and the concertina'd bus and the red glop oozing out the front end.

A good dozen shots of each, PDQ.

And then I pelted on up Bridge Street towards Deansgate.

A BIG CHUNK of Deansgate was now a hole in the ground. A fucking *crater*.

The dig had been in the middle of the road, between Waterstone's on one side and Kendal's on the other. My granddad'd taken me to Kendal's for my birthday one year when I was a kid. It'd had a great toy section back then; for months afterward I'd called it, much to my parents' amusement, 'Toy Kendals.'

Now the department store was gone. Five, six storeys. A great big bite taken out of it. The back wall was left, and a few yards of each floor. The rest – gone.

It looked like a fist had punched straight down from the sky to drive road, buildings, cars and people forty or fifty feet down into the ground.

I could see rubble clogging the hole, and billowing clouds of smoke and dust. I could see smashed red things.

I could hear the whoop and wail of police and ambulance sirens approaching.

I could see people trying to climb into the crater. I could hear screams rising out.

I raised my camera. I took my pictures.

Around the edge of the pit, like blood crusted round a wound, were survivors. Some were only dusty and shocked, others had been mangled by falling debris. I saw missing limbs and faces. Guts ballooning outward through a bloody weave of hands.

I raised my camera. I took my pictures.

Richard Rawlinson was not among the survivors. Neither money, minders nor blackmail leverage had saved him, and when they dug up the rubble his was one of the surprising number of bodies that they never found.

But most of the local councillors attending had made it out, huddled together in shrouds of clinging dust like bedraggled ghosts. I was glad to see Samantha Redgrave was one of them. She was maybe the only councillor I rated as having anything close to integrity. She'd been one of the leading opponents to the Underground, damn near losing her job over it. She'd made it out, and in the months to come she'd take over leadership of the Council and demand a full investigation. Heads would roll, all except the one that most needed to.

That afternoon he sat beside her; pale and empty-eyed, head hanging down and hands dangling slack – Mike Jolley, knowing the end of his world had come.

And I raised my camera and I took my pictures.

* * *

IT WASN'T A bomb. The ground had just, pure and simple, caved in. There were screams then about corruption, lack of proper safeguards, but surveys showed the ground should've been fine.

"I remember, just before it started to shake," one survivor told me, one of the few workmen to make it out alive, "there was this noise. It's hard to explain. It sounded a bit like soldiers marching on gravel. A kind of *crunching* sound. Almost like *digging*, but going on underneath us, d'you know what I mean? And then the shaking started, and then–" He broke off and took a few deep breaths. He was still getting flashbacks. "But I've no idea what it was. Might not even have been there, really. None of it seems real now. You know?"

That bit never made the published article.

So, the cause was never established. But Mike Jolley – AKA 'Teflon Mike' – finally came well and truly unstuck. Within a month he was off the Council and within a week of *that* he'd vanished, leaving his wife a garbled note, the night before the police showed up with a search warrant. My guess was someone who still reckoned they owed him a favour or two had tipped him off.

They found his car abandoned on the Fylde coast, door ajar. A lot of people put two and together from that, but by then I *knew* Jolley. He wouldn't kill himself. He had two, three bank accounts under false names stuffed with his bribes and backhanders. He'd clear out, leave the country, start up somewhere else with a new name.

Thanks to the pictures and copy I'd brought back from the Deansgate holocaust I was now Harry's star reporter. Harry, meanwhile, was doing his best to pretend he'd never even known Jolley, so he was quite happy to give me a free hand hunting the bastard down.

In all modesty, I'm good at my job. I had various clever ideas which all helped, but what it boiled down to was this: I found him.

Jolley was lying low, waiting for things to cool off. He'd been just a little slow and by the time he'd thought of flitting abroad they were watching for him at every air and ferry port. He was hiding a long way north of Manchester, right up near the Scottish border. Pity; I'd've enjoyed blagging an overseas jaunt off Harry.

I drove up and carefully picked my way over open ground and craggy hills to the little valley where his farmhouse stood. Thinking I was so bloody clever, sharp and subtle, right up until Finch put the Browning to the back of my neck.

5. The Picture

JOLLEY OPENED HIS mouth to bluster some more, and then he sagged. "I didn't have any choice," he said at last.

What I'd figured all along. I gave it a few seconds, then asked, as gently as I thought I could get away with, "What did Rawlinson have on you?"

He let out a sigh like air escaping a punctured tyre. "Does it matter?" When he looked up at me, he looked tired, beaten. "He had... something. That's all that matters, innit? And of course he'd cut me in on the profits if it went through."

"Stick and carrot."

"But I suppose you already knew that."

"I guessed it."

"Yeah, well, you were right." His top lip pulled back from his teeth in a sneer. "Sorry I haven't got any gold stars to give you." Then his jaw clenched. "You did alright out of it, though, didn't you, you little bastard? Like a pig in shit. Should've done you over when I had the chance."

He did now, of course, but I wasn't going to remind him. "I was just in the right place at the right time. Could've been anybody who –"

"Yeah, but it was fucking *you*. You and that *bitch* Redgrave. Well, I hope you've enjoyed yourselves, the pair of you, cos you'll both be laughing on the other sides of your *fucking* faces soon enough. *All* of you fuckers will." He was shouting, half-on his feet. Then the air went out of him again and he slumped back into the chair. "All fucking Rawlinson's fault," he muttered at last. "If it wasn't for him I'd still be in charge. I told him about Them."

"About who?"

He didn't answer; didn't hear me, I don't think. "*Had* to. Couldn't think of anything else that'd make him give up. Didn't believe me, till I showed him. But even *then* he wouldn't give it up. 'It's the twenty-first century, Mike,' he kept saying. 'We can sort the fuckers out if they try anything. We've got the technology.' That's what he'd keep saying. 'We have the technology.' All the time with that *stupid fucking smile on his stupid fucking chops –*"

He slammed his fist down onto the table, hard. Things rattled. I'd pulled as far back in my chair as I could from him. Finch leant back against the kitchen counter, obviously used to it. Jolley blinked, breathing hard, mouth pressed to his clenched fist. Then his eyes rolled up to fix on me again, and his hand dropped. "Seddon!"

The thin man came back in. This time I could see he wasn't smirking; there was a scar on his cheek that pulled up the corner of his mouth. "Yes, O Lord and Master?"

"Get the folder from my room." Seddon rolled his eyes and went out; his footsteps creaked on the stairs.

"Might as well tell you the lot now," Jolley said. I didn't particularly like the sound of that, but there wasn't much I could do about it just yet. *Keep your eyes and ears open*, I told myself.

Seddon's footsteps plodded back down the stairs. He came back in with a plain manila folder. Without looking away from me, Jolley held out a hand for it. Seddon gave a low deep bow, flourished the folder and put it in Jolley's hand.

"Here," Jolley said, "take a look."

He dug a photograph out of the folder and flicked it over to me. It lay upside-down; I turned it the right way up.

For a good few seconds I sat there thinking *what am I looking at here, exactly?* Not that there was anything complicated about the image itself. It just took those few seconds for my brain to accept what I was seeing.

A man stood in some kind of underground chamber. He was tall, in his forties or thereabouts, with thinning black side-parted hair and a drooping moustache, and he wore a suit, a silver watchchain and a pair of round-lensed spectacles. He looked stiff and upright and if he wasn't comfortable being there he hid it very well. Very Victorian; very Age Of Empire. Back straight, chin up, unruffled – a soldier, maybe.

Beside him squatted something white, naked and eyeless, with long arms and wide flat hands. Its mouth was huge and open, a long tongue hanging over sharp teeth. They were not alone in the cave, but their companions were huddled near the back of it; thankfully the shadows mostly hid them.

There were bones on the cavern floor. Long bones. Hopefully animal. On the cave wall behind were crude pictures, paintings and charcoal sketches.

"The man was called Bryant Fossington," said Jolley. "Ex-Colonial Service. They brought him in for negotiations with *them.*"

"What…"

"What are they?" Jolley smiled bitterly. "They call themselves the *Marakh Shehn.* Roughly translated, I'm told, it means 'the Sons of the City'. They're the reason I'm in this fucking mess."

6. *Marakh Shehn*

"Do you know how many attempts there've been, over the years, to give Manchester an underground railway?" asked Jolley. "About fifteen, since 1839. Now that's quite a lot."

I nodded. I didn't know what else to do.

"The last attempt – before mine, I mean – was back in the seventies. They got quite a long way with that one. When they built the Arndale Centre they even had space allocated for an Underground Station – Royal Exchange, it was gonna be called. Some people reckon they even got as far as building platforms. But, never happened. Same as with all the other times. Guessed why yet?"

I nodded at the photo. "That?"

Jolley clapped slowly. "Well spotted. Another gold star. Oh, they passed it off as economic reasons – cutbacks, too expensive, all that bollocks. Same as all the other times, they came up with some excuse. But the *real* reason was not pissing the *Marakh Shehn* off."

I looked at the pale thing in the photo. "What are they?"

"Believe it or not, they used to be human. We think. Beyond that, it's all guesswork. I mean, Manchester as a city's not that old, as cities go, but there've been people living round here a long time."

"Since the Romans."

"Go to the top of the class," said Jolley. "You've seen the old fort at Castlefield. That'd be another gold star, only I've not got any. Now shut up and listen, you stupid little cunt."

Something gritted underfoot as Finch shifted position. I shut up and listened.

"Have another look at the photograph. The wall there. See anything?"

"Drawings?"

"Yeah. Drawings. Like cavemen used to do."

Jolley lit up a cigarette from a crumpled packet of Dunhill. His fingers twitched and shook. "They might go back to Roman times, maybe even further. Or they might only go back to the Middle Ages. That's one interpretation they've made of the drawings. Anyway, back when the Black Death came to this little corner of Blighty, bunch of victims got buried in a mass grave. Only, not all of them were actually dead. What do they call it?"

"Catalepsy?"

"Gold stars a-fucking-go-go. Anyway, they woke, these ones, under the earth, buried alive, no way back. Even if they could dig 'emselves out, they'd have probably been staked – either through the heart or bloody burned at one, coming back from the grave like that. And anyway, state things were in up top, would *you* wanna go back up there? Bear in mind people thought it was the end of the world. So they stayed down there. Because it was actually better. Learned to tunnel. Dug out chambers for themselves. I don't even want to *know* what they ate. Found caves, water. Made all of that into their home. And then they had children."

Jolley blew smoke in my face across the table. I normally hated cigarette smoke, having quit three years ago, but right then I found myself craving a smoke. "That's one version, anyway. There's others. Bottom line, though, it's all the same idea – somewhere back in the day, a bunch of folk ending up going underground. Maybe they chose, maybe they didn't. Whichever it was doesn't matter. How long did people live, back then? Thirty, forty years? If they were lucky? Even less if they were living like that. But they kept going. Probably shagged like rabbits. Big families, so a few kids'd survive. Just a few. Just enough. How many generations you reckon that musta bin? They'd've stayed down there. There were rats and the like to feed on. If they got lucky, they'd rob a grave. Underground streams for water. Didn't need eyes, so they lost 'em. Learned to do it all by touch and hearing, smell and taste. Now and again, they might go up top. At night when it was quiet. If they needed food. Or something else. They could home in on what they were looking for, dig right under it and –"

The inch of ash at the end of his Dunhill fell on the table; Jolley didn't notice. "Nobody even *knew* about 'em till two, three hundred years ago. Back when Manchester started turning into a proper city. How long'd they bin down there by then? Hundreds of years. There were a lot of them, and under the ground was *their* territory. Oh, and they didn't like trespassers. But of course, what did we do? We were building mills, digging canals, sewers, *tunnels*. Oh, I mean, compared to them, we were a right bunch of fucking amateurs. But we were still trespassing."

Jolley chuckled. "You would not – believe me – believe how much stuff's bin hidden away. How many records are missing – maybe even from your own newspaper's files. We made damn sure it got kept quiet over the years. That's the Corporation and all that, back in the early days. We were building a city. There were fortunes at stake. The people who built Manchester weren't gonna let anyone get in the way of that. So anyone who wasn't going to play along... well, it was a lot easier to fit someone up back then, and there were about two hundred hanging offences. Not to mention how easy it was to get someone banged up in a loony-bin. Or the equivalent. And then they could bang on about underground monsters till the cows came home. No fucker'd believe them.

"See?" said Jolley. "But for all that, they had a fight on their hands, and it just got stepped up and up as the years went by and the city started taking shape. Bottom line was, the *Marakh Shehn* didn't want anyone on their patch. I can understand that. What you have you hold." He chuckled, puffed his cigarette, tapped ash on the floor. "Lot of workmen going missing, lot of accidents, lot of people seeing stuff down there in the dark. Sooner or later, it was gonna get out. First off they tried killing them. Obviously. But how were they gonna do that? The *Marakh Shehn* belong in the earth like fish belong in water. They burrowed like the clappers, and they could just fill burrows in behind them as they went. By the time you'd even started to dig after them, they were that far away you'd never find which way they'd gone. It was like they'd never been. Can't kill the fuckers if you can't get near them. They sent yeomen down there, the local militia. Even dragoons a few times, and they were the crack troops back then, like the Paras or the SAS. Right, Finchy?"

Finch just blinked and eyed Jolley's Dunhills. Jolley sighed and flicked one over. Finch caught it one-handed, put it in his mouth and lit it. The Browning, now, was in his belt, but it wouldn't take him a second to draw or fire if I made a move. Jolley trod his fag out on the kitchen floor, lit up another, speaking between puffs.

"So in the end," he said, "they made a deal."

7. The Pact

"OBVIOUSLY, NEXT TO no-one knew about it. That's how they wanted to keep things. There'd be a few people in the Corporation kept in the know, later the Council.

They made a deal. A *pact*. It was that or all-out war and don't forget, back in those days, the cutting edge of technology was the fucking flintlock rifle. Not much cop if you can't see your enemy to shoot at. Specially not when they can burrow right under your gaff and make it fall in – *What was that?*"

"Nothing, boss." It was the first thing Finch had said since Jolley had appeared. "Mouse."

Jolley was breathing quickly. His face was the colour of dry slate and he'd crushed his cigarette out of shape. He dropped it on the floor and trod it out, licked his lips and lit up one of the few remaining Dunhills. "The *Marakh Shehn* could wipe Manchester off the map, like *that*. So, we couldn't take 'em on in a fight – these men were businessmen. They wanted what they wanted, so it was just a case of which way they got it. We wanted to dig our canals, later our sewers, build our mills and our factories... we had to negotiate with them. Find out what kind of stuff *they* wanted, and give it to them."

"What sort of stuff *did* they want?" I asked. I could've *murdered* one of those cigs, but I was fucked if I was going to ask. Jolley shrugged.

"Varied. Could be anything. Wasn't usually owt *expensive*,

mind you. Sometimes they'd maybe want food animals – pigs, cows, chickens. Lot easier than burrowing up into some farmer's yard for them. Same with milk. Well, why go out hunting when you can get free delivery? Kids' toys, too, sometimes, believe it or not. Suppose even blind mutant monster kids are still kids. Course," Jolley blew a smoke ring, "sometimes they'd want *other* things."

"Like?"

"Bodies."

"What, dead ones?"

"Usually."

"Usually?"

Jolley shrugged. "They'd got quite partial to human flesh over the years. Specially by then. All those workmen and soldiers they'd taken – lot of fresh meat there. Be stupid letting it go to waste. But we're not talking a big gene pool here, are we? Needed some new blood from time to time. Breeding stock. I'm guessing in the old days they'd nip up top and hang around looking for a bird out on her jack they could drag downstairs. But like I said, if you can get free delivery…"

I blinked. It took a few seconds to sink in and Jolley sat there letting me process it all. "Are you telling me you rounded women up to… give to… *them*?"

Another shrug. "Not *that* often. Look, they didn't get what they wanted off us, the *Marakh Shehn* would just come out and take it. Not like there weren't ones we could spare. We're not exactly short of council estate slags these days. Open their legs for fucking dogs, there was a packet of B&H in it."

I just stared at him. When I'd said *you*, I'd just meant the Council, generally. As in, back in the distant past. Not here, not now.

"Don't you fucking look at me like that, pal," he snapped. "If you'd seen what I'd seen…"

"But you tried to screw them, didn't you?" I said. Bang me over the head with a four-by-two often enough and I'll get anything in the end. "That's what you meant. Rawlinson blackmailed you to make you go along, so you showed him, what, that picture?"

"Among other things." Jolley's little eyes were narrowed tight.

"But even that wasn't enough, was it? He wanted his railway no matter what. Wouldn't believe they couldn't be beaten with modern weapons. Modern technology."

"'We have the technology.'" Jolley said it through his teeth. "He just didn't get it. Wouldn't. We've been dealing with those little fuckers for years. *Centuries*. And they've just got this fucking thing about trains. They don't even like having them overground. The noise, the vibration – they can feel it, hate it. Took a hell of a lot of sweetening just to make them swallow that. But underground? Forget it. Cold day in hell. Nothing'll shift them on that. No way round it. And believe me, it's been tried. About fifteen fucking times. And if you can't get them to agree, you can forget it. The *Marakh Shehn* take it fucking seriously when someone else breaks their precious *pact*."

"Then why did you?"

"I didn't have a choice!"

"Why didn't you turn 'em loose on Rawlinson?"

Jolley's face went slack and he stared at me. "You what?" He blinked. "Say that again."

"Rawlinson was the threat – to them, I mean. Why not just sic the…" I stumbled over the words "… *Marakh Shehn* onto him?"

Jolley snorted. "Be your age. Rawlinson knew I wasn't above trying something. Anything happened to him, it'd all come out. You ask Harry, it's probably in his safe. Least he kept that much out of the paper. Then again, he had enough material to go to town on anyway."

He trod out his cigarette. "You know the rest of the story. Except for the last bit. And I like this bit, but you won't. Nor will Harry. Or Redgrave. Don't think anyone much round Manchester way will either. See – think about it. That bitch

Redgrave had a damn good go at fucking up the deal for me but she couldn't, and you wanna know why? Because when they set up their little arrangement, they had to have a line of communication with the *Marakh Shehn*. There's a place you have to go, things you have to do once you get there..." he waved a hand. "The details don't matter. What matters is that only one person knew how to get in touch with them. And that person was the Leader of the City Council, just to make sure none of his juniors tried anything smart with the *Marakh Shehn*. Obviously, there were instructions on what to do, in case anything... sudden happened to the current Leader. But I destroyed them."

"You what?"

"And that fucking Redgrave bitch *hasn't a fucking clue*. She knows she'll never find me. She's spending all her time trying to find a way to contact the *Marakh Shehn* and put things right." He sniggered. "But she'll never make it. And if they think the pact's broken, *really* broken, for good and all... well, that's when it'll *really* kick off. Because when that happens it *will* be all-out war." He was shaking with laughter now. "Don't you get it? The *whole city* only exists *because they let it*. And a little bit of digging and they'll rip it all down, tear it all apart."

... hope you've enjoyed yourselves, the pair of you, cos you'll both be laughing on the other sides of your fucking faces soon enough. All of you fuckers will.

Dog in the manger, that's what they call it. *If I can't have it, no-one else will.* I remembered a case I'd covered a while back, few years earlier; a businessman who'd gone bust. I could understand him killing himself – but not only that, and not only had he burned his house down, he'd shot his wife and their teenage daughter too before blowing his own brains out. *That* part I found unforgivable. Even evil.

But none of that had anything on Mike Jolley.

"You pathetic bastard," I said.

Jolley stopped giggling, like I'd thrown a switch. The smile dimmed and faded. When it was gone, his mouth puckered and twisted like he'd just chewed a whole lime. Muscles jumped in his cheeks. Then he turned and looked at Finch and said, "Take him out and shoot him."

8. A Place Of Execution

FINCH GRABBED MY collar and yanked me to my feet. I could have kicked or struggled or fought, I suppose, but I didn't. Why? Maybe because the bastard was too big to fight. Maybe because I hoped to try and talk him out of it once we were outside. Maybe because I couldn't really believe I was about to die.

Outside, Finch planted a hand in my back and shoved. In a corner of the yard was a slurry pit, a deep place full of foul water where they dumped all the pigshit and the filth. I was guessing that was planned as my final resting place. Someone might find me eventually, but I was guessing that by then Jolley planned to be long gone.

Talk, Terry. You're a persuasive fucker when you want to be. Talk to him.

"You don't want to do this," I tried. Great start, not even remotely original. I got another shove in the back.

"Shut up. Keep walking."

"He's mad," I said. "You can see he's fucking mad. Why are you doing what he tells you to d–"

Another shove sent me staggering. "Cos he fucking pays me, that's why. Couldn't give a shit. Now –"

A final shove and I almost went into the slurry pit head-first. I landed with my head just over the edge and the reek was foul. I rolled over, twisted away, and saw Finch above me, aiming the Browning down at me.

"See ya," he said.

And then the ground began to shake.

Like there was a train passing under it.

9. The Fall Of The House Of Jolley

FINCH BLINKED, LOOKED round, then snapped back into focus and got his mind back on the job. His finger was tightening on the trigger again, but I was already moving.

I'd found a fistful of grit and I flung it in his eyes as I dived forward. I heard the gun go off as I hurled myself at his shins, hard as I could. Finch pitched forward, bellowing. His boot clipped my head, but I got on my feet and ran.

I'd interviewed a couple of old soldiers for some article on the anniversary of World War Two and something one of them had said came back to me. He'd been in a situation like this one, legging it across open ground followed by some nutcase with a gun. *Weave*. That's what he'd said you had to do. Everything screams at you to run straight, get clear of the fucker fast as you can. But it just makes you an easier target. While if you zig-zag as you go...

Something went past my ear with a loud angry buzz. The crack of the actual gunshot followed a split-second later. 'Like hornets', that's what the soldier had said bullets sounded like when they zipped past. So far, he'd definitely known what he was talking about.

And then my feet went out from under me.

I hit the ground. *Vibrating*. It was vibrating.

The same as the bridge had, that day.

Another shot, then another, spanging off the dusty ground. I rolled over. Finch was approaching. He was running in but didn't fire, not yet. He wanted to get close. Finish the job.

Behind him Seddon was coming out of the house, clutching a gun of his own. Slates were falling off the roof. One hit Seddon as he ran. He screamed and spun, blood spraying from what was left of his face. Half of it had been sheared clean off the bone. He dropped his gun and fell to his knees, screaming through bloody hands.

Finch didn't even look at him. He was one focused bastard. He wasn't going to look away or give me the slightest chance this time.

Seddon had started crawling, the hand that wasn't trying to hold his face together feeling his way over the ground.

Glass shattered in the house.

And then, with a grinding, splintering rip, the ground split open.

A rent shot across the farmyard surface, arrowing in towards the house. And another, and another. One opened right between Finch's feet. It was like the cut a sharp knife makes. At first you hardly see it, then it gapes, widens. In a couple of seconds it was two feet across and growing; Finch swayed for balance. Then he lost it and fell, dropping the gun.

I jumped up and ran. I looked round just in time to see Finch clinging on to the edge of the crevasse he'd dropped into, trying to haul himself out. Then suddenly he screamed. His mouth and eyes gaped wide – more expression than they'd ever shown – and then he was gone. *Taken*. I couldn't help myself thinking that.

I pelted across the farmyard, making for the footpath to the ground above. A crack slashed the earth ahead of me and started to widen. I leapt it, just making it. Then I made the footpath and went up it on all fours.

At the top, I heard another scream and I looked back. I couldn't see Seddon anywhere. I guessed it'd been him who screamed. The cracks in the earth were getting wider and wider. The valley floor seemed to be sagging in the middle, where the farmhouse was. The house sank and listed, shed all the slates on one side in a splintering crash. The wall facing me fell in.

A moment later it all went.

Dust puffed up out of the cracks like smoke and the house, the farmyard – everything in the little valley – just dropped, almost gracefully, into the swirling billow of dust with a massive, terminal *THUMP*. A jarring convulsion of the earth sent me flying into the fence post at the top of the path. I narrowly missed tumbling back down into the pit revealed when the debris belching upward in a great black column cleared.

In that moment I saw:

Mike Jolley scrambling out through the front door, screaming. I don't know if he saw me or not. I doubt it. And I doubt he'd have made it to safety in time anyway. But what gets me is how he screamed just before the house fell in.

I can't be sure, but I think he shot back inside the house. As if he'd been pulled.

And I can't be sure, but I may – only *may* – have seen a large, pale hand come out and cover his face in that last instant before the hungry ground claimed him for its own.

10. Coda

MANCHESTER'S STILL STANDING. It hasn't all caved in. Yet. Of course, the *Marakh Shehn* might have been concentrating first and foremost on tracking Mike Jolley down and getting their revenge on him. Demolishing a whole city would be a bigger, longer project. Take time to set up. Or maybe Sam Redgrave managed to communicate with the *Marakh Shehn* and patch things up.

I wouldn't know. Not long after that I got a job offer from one of the big London papers and I headed south. It's a long way from home but that's the way I like it these days. I haven't gone back. I just can't look at my home town again, knowing what's under there. London's already got its own Underground and plenty more besides. I'm guessing it doesn't have any surprises like Manchester does. Or maybe the sons of my new city are just better hidden.

THE ROSES THAT BLOOM UNDERGROUND

Al Ewing

Al Ewing is mental, but in a good way. I've edited four novels by this mountain of a man and each has been surprising and slightly unhinged. You never know quite where you are with a story from Al, and that's as true for his superb comic work as it is for his prose. Al, then, was one of the very first people I asked to submit a story for The End of The Line *and this is the result. There is something of the splatterpunk in 'The Roses That Bloom Underground,' but it by no means relies on gore for its impact. Instead Al's story is disturbing and darkly comic. A cautionary tale about what the Underground could one day become...*

IF YOU BREATHED in, you could smell roses.

And the trains *whispered* into place, sleek and silver and smooth, and the doors breathed open in perfect silence. No pushing, no shoving, no crowding, and the very warmest of smiles on the faces of the commuters as they each carefully took their seats in carriages that were so sparkling clean, with not a trace of graffiti, not even a speck of dirt. Just three weeks into the new system and already this was the norm. Passengers were even starting to look each other in the eye, exchange pleasant little items of chit-chat about the weather or the football. The new Tube system seemed to encourage it, somehow.

And if you breathed in, you could smell roses.

And when the doors breathed gently shut again, and the train sprang back to life and whispered down the tunnel, another took its place with barely a beat between them. And once again, the doors sighed softly open, as if in the pleasure of service, and all those who'd waited patiently on the platform for their turn took their places on their own comfortable, modern, graffiti-free seats. Everyone was happy. Everyone was on time. Everything was perfect. Everything smelled of roses.

Not everyone was smiling, not everyone could be. That would be too much to ask. But those who frowned and cursed and muttered under their breath did it because of the grim office full of fake smiles and machine coffee that waited for them, the marriage that had turned cold over too many years, the ugly scene over breakfast that morning. Not because of the trains.

Never the trains.

Dexter slouched along the platform, giving a sour look to the beautiful silver tubes with their rich red decals, veering away from the open doors at the last moment, as if getting on would diminish him somehow. Instead, he turned left, up a corridor – the tiles on the wall shining healthy and white, the steel floor clean and gleaming, no sign of litter or even dust – and felt the bile turn in his stomach. There was something about the shining, gleaming clean, the terrible *efficiency* of it all, that made him want to pour petrol over the whole thing and set it alight.

But even then, it wasn't really about the trains. Never the trains.

It was about the press conference. It was about the Mayor.

THREE WEEKS IN the past, head full of the minutiae of his re-election, the Mayor smiled down from the podium and waved his hand benevolently over the sea of cameras, even as he steeled himself to say That Bloody Catchphrase.

"London Underground has evolved, ladies and gentlemen. Live Tube – the Tube lives for you!"

Oh God. Awful. Like ashes in the mouth. *Live Tube,* what did that even mean? Just an ugly collection of nonsense words, not that that made a difference to anyone – he'd kicked and screamed at it like a two-year-old and poor Philip had tied himself in knots trying to work it into the speech, but those damnable marketing johnnies had simply refused to give in. It had synergy, or some such thing. And he had to admit, it fit awfully well with the... well, with the improvements. Jeremy's little re-election scheme.

He coughed, swallowed once again and concentrated fully on the moment, on the rest of the speech. New Underground. New trains, new track, new décor. No more engineering works, no more rush hour crowds. No more rats nesting under the tracks. All gone forever. Efficiency was the new watchword – efficient, clean and green, sleek and silver, perfect and smelling literally of roses. The Tube remade, recreated, a luxury service in place for the benefit of all, from the highest to the lowest.

"... and I rather think you'll agree that London Transport is out of the tunnel and into the light at long last." Not one of Phillip's better endings, but serviceable if invested with just the right touch of gravitas. "Are there any questions?"

He'd wanted to be the one to take the questions. He wanted to own this. This new, gleaming, shining system, these perfect trains that smelt of rose petals and whispered into place and arrived just when you needed them – this, all this, was going to belong to him. He was the bloody Mayor, he had a right to it. He'd answer the questions, and speak to the reporters, and talk on the radio and the breakfast shows and the evening news programmes until his fat face was inextricably branded on everything to do with this New Tube, saying *yes, this is a new London, a clean London, a bright and gleaming and shining and perfect London, and I gave it to you. Vote for it. Vote for me. Me, me, me, I'm the bloody Mayor and this is MINE.*

Of course, it was Jeremy who'd thought of the improvements, Jeremy's chums who'd carried them out. A good man to know, Jeremy, and a jolly good advisor, despite his little eccentricities. All the Mayor had done was ease the way for Jeremy's... well, for his thoughts on how the Underground could be improved.

That and be in power at the right time to capitalise on it all.

But people have voted for less.

He signaled to a man in a grey suit, ash-blonde with severe blue eyes that were looking for something to disapprove of. One of us, by the look of him, but of course that didn't mean an easy ride. A lot of his sort of people still blamed him for the Tube being re-nationalised, which was jolly unfair, even if he'd somehow ended up in charge of the whole thing. That was mostly Jeremy's doing, or one of Jeremy's chums. Jeremy had rather a lot of friends in high places.

"Clive Barrett, *Evening Clarion*. How much can the taxpayer expect to pay for this, Mister Mayor?"

"Not a penny. All the, ah... improvements... were carried out within the current London Transport budget." He ignored the look of disbelief of the fellow's face. He was telling the truth – the improvements had been free, at least in terms of money. That was the beauty of Jeremy's methods.

Wonderfully handy chap, Jeremy.

"In fact, the new system is far cheaper and more efficient, and we'll be passing those savings on to you, as it were." That got a chuckle. "Next question."

A fat, angry-looking chap with a comb-over. One of those awful far-left rags, the Mayor seemed to remember. Best to get it out of the way now, he supposed.

"Nigel Bright, *Working Socialist*. Is it true the new trains don't have drivers?"

The Mayor smiled genially and answered the real question. "All drivers are being retrained and employed elsewhere within the London Transport network. We're not putting anyone on the scrapheap, believe me." Bright didn't, judging by the scowl – presumably the frightful man was already writing his next blistering front page in his head. Oh well, no-one would bother reading it. Tiresome little oik. "Next question, please – you, sir."

A sour-looking man in a dark blue coat. Looked like he'd been sucking a lemon. Wanted to start a fight of some kind, by the look of him. Well, one more tough question wouldn't hurt, and after that he could start picking some smilers. All part of his press conference strategy. The Mayor was rather an old hand at these by now.

"Michael Dexter, *Daily Herald*. How was this done, Mister Mayor?"

The Mayor smiled. "Well, obviously it took a lot of jolly hard work –"

Dexter spoke over him. "With respect, Mister Mayor, it would've taken more than hard work. We're talking refurbishing the entire Tube system inside three weeks, with some brand-new driverless system and a full refit of every station out to Zone Six – and all inside the current transport budget? There wasn't enough in that budget for a packet of crisps."

The Mayor's smile grew thin-lipped. Hard questions were one thing, but there was such a thing as going too far. "I think you'll find there was rather more than that, once we trimmed some of the fat that had –"

The rude little blighter simply refused to let him finish a sentence. "It doesn't matter how much you trimmed. It wouldn't matter if you had a budget of infinity. It could not, physically, be done –"

The Mayor had had quite enough. He had a reputation for speaking his mind and he was going to jolly well let this chap have both barrels. "*Mister* Dexter – it *was* done. Now I'm afraid I've had enough of your attempts to denigrate the hard work of others and I have no idea what point you think you are making, so I'm going to take another question... you, Madam."

He picked one of the smiling faces – a fortyish woman with a blonde bob and glasses.

"Fiona Hughes, *Wow Magazine*. Apparently you've become a devotee of astrology and psychic phenomena –"

The Mayor winced, shuddering. A couple of unguarded remarks over a sherry really could follow one into the bloody grave. Bad enough everyone thought of him as a brainless posho without thinking he was doolally into the bargain.

The smiling woman continued on, breathlessly. "– I was wondering if you'd let *Wow*'s astrological expert, Astral Annie, do a full election work-up of your charts for you?"

The Mayor perked up. Well, that was harmless enough. He'd play the duffer a little, get some laughs, move on to the next one. "Well, it's true I rather enjoy that sort of thing – just as a lark, mind you – but I'm afraid I've rather got someone handling that whole astral side of things for me already."

He smiled again, guilelessly.

"But if Jeremy's busy, I'll certainly give your people a call."

THREE WEEKS ON and Dexter was prowling the shining, gleaming, clean and sterile corridors of the New Tube, face sour, head pounding with ugly thoughts about the schoolboy Mayor and his stupid damned press conference. He stubbornly bumped against the crowds as they swarmed towards the platform, staring down anyone who looked up.

Dexter was in a foul mood, and the Mayor and his New Tube were to blame. They'd taken his story away.

After that bloody joke of a press conference, he'd done his best to look into it. He'd burnt through his contacts, trying to dig into the mechanics of the new system, into how they'd managed to refurbish the whole network in so short a time. Oh, they were bending over backwards to tell him about it – vague explanations, nonsensical press releases, a diagram purporting to explain exactly how the driverless trains ran which amounted to no more than brightly-coloured arrows chasing each other around a page. He'd walked away with that diagram and immediately shown it to the smartest computer scientist he could find.

"Got no idea what that's meant to be." Bobby, with his Comp. Sci. Phd and his cardigan, had shaken his head and chewed some more on his sandwich like a ruminating cow. "I mean, It looks nice and it's got a lot of nice big technical words on it, but it's not explaining anything. It's like... asking what makes a boat float and getting told that it floats by not sinking. And then when you ask what makes it not sink you get given a diagram with a little down arrow saying 'not sinking' underneath a boat." He'd laughed, bits of food tumbling out of his beard. "Bloody hell, I've seen shampoo ads with more science than this..."

It was the same with the question of how the improvements had been made so quickly. A few anecdotes of workers going above and beyond the call of duty, but no names, no photos. Press releases praising the hard work of the engineers without actually saying what they'd worked on. 'Jolly hard work' was as good as he was going to get.

He'd tried talking to actual Tube engineers. Mostly, they just refused to speak to him, citing non-disclosure agreements if they gave any reason at all. One went so far as to tell him it was the easiest job he'd ever done, and laughed before putting the phone down.

One sounded terrified. "It's not right. I saw what was happening. It's not right." Silence, then the sound of vomiting. Dial tone.

What was that about?

Dexter had kept looking, dead end after dead end, and there were other stories that needed telling. Youth gang stab pensioner in Hackney, bee populations on the wane, MPs in expenses uproar, could your child be a paedo, the situation in Iran, Barrowman's Big Brother bombshell, Queen's Park Rangers in drug test shame... Every day, fifty new things that needed covering, and all more important to his editor than 'reporter has bad feeling about Tube.'

And now, here he was, and he should have been riding in one of those carriages, those silver sleek bullets, breathing in the roses on the way to Cockfosters to interview a family of four whose dog had dug up an unexploded bomb. An important story. Vital news.

And instead of covering it, he was standing in a bustling

corridor, looking at a section of tiled wall; white tiles alternating with a very light blue in a pattern like the wing of a moth, with an advertising poster under clear, untouched glass. LIVE TUBE – THE TUBE LIVES FOR YOU.

He wanted to smash the glass, and spray paint on the tile, and piss on the steel floor. He wanted to fill this inhumanly clean and efficient station with human filth and grime and dirt, make it how it was before. He rammed his hands deep in his pockets, staring at the circle-slash symbol of the Underground, watching it stare back at him like an unblinking eye. Then he pulled a couple of crumpled receipts out of his pockets and scattered them on the ground, feeling foolish, feeling triumphant, happy to have spoiled all that pristine purity. The people walking past him didn't notice or care. A metaphor for something.

He stared back at the unblinking eye. The brand. Far away, he heard the rumble of a Tube train roaring through a tunnel.

He was imagining it, obviously.

The trains whispered now.

He reached out and touched the white tile, feeling the surface, cool and slick and unearthly. On impulse, he glanced down at the floor.

The receipts he'd dropped had vanished. The steel floor was gleaming, fresh, pristine. There was nothing there at all.

Not even dust.

How could anything be *that* clean? He shook his head, crouching, gently sliding his fingertip along the walkway – then flinched as a pound coin suddenly hit the metal flooring next to his hand, clinking loudly. He stood, looking around for who'd dropped it. Had they thought he was begging for change? When was the last time he'd seen a beggar on the Tube? – but there was no telling who it was. The mass of humanity walked on, ignoring him. He turned his attention back to the impossibly clean floor.

The pound coin was no longer there.

Feeling his stomach lurch, Dexter resumed his course, but

this time the rushing river of people was banging into him, pushing him around. On impulse, he took a left turn, randomly moving down a short flight of steps into a quieter, almost deserted tunnel, away from the main crush of humanity. That faint taint of rose petals in the air seemed more noticeable now. Dexter wondered if he should find a way out, up into the fresh air, into the dirt and smog and smell of London, away from these white tiles, white as bone, this gleaming metal floor, so supernaturally spick and span and achingly clean...

He almost didn't notice the door.

The sign read Authorised Personnel Only, in an unassuming font. Dexter blinked at it for a moment. What was behind there? Probably nothing. A store cupboard, maybe. A break room. Maybe the system that was running the driverless trains, guiding them so perfectly that as soon as one left, another arrived. Maybe a records room, filing cabinets full of schedules, work orders, timesheets, documents that would explain how you could refurbish the whole Underground in three weeks. Maybe nothing at all.

Without thinking, Dexter reached to try the handle, only mildly surprised to feel it turn and the door open slightly. Unlocked, then.

Quietly, without giving himself time to consider it, he pushed the door open and stepped through.

There was light on the other side, revealing the same white-and-blue tiles, the same brushed steel flooring, the same sterile cleanliness. A set of steps, leading down, then turning around a corner.

Dexter let the door close behind him and began to slowly walk down, still not really thinking about what he was doing. That disquiet in his stomach was gone, and so was the anger of earlier. In their place, he felt a strange, deep calm.

He'd likely be found by security and escorted gently out of the station. Fined for trespass, maybe. There would be a response that he understood, that would place him back in the framework of the world, that would quiet that restless twitching in the pit of his belly. His editor would shout at him. Some disciplinary action, maybe. Everything would be predictable. Everything would be normal.

Instinctively he reached out for the metal railing that ran alongside the stairs.

It was wet.

Oily – almost slippery. Dexter yanked his hand away, startled by the unexpected sensation. Part of him was almost giddy – spilled oil, grease, some evidence of human mess, some normal honest human dirt and grime – but when he raised his fingers closer to his face, the pungent stench of rose petals almost made him gag. Some sort of cleaning fluid, strong enough to make his head reel. He wiped the gunk onto his jeans, making a mental note to wash his hands before he put any fingers in his mouth.

Still, he felt better. Cleaning fluid meant cleaners, which meant that strange sterility was being maintained by someone. That thought made him shake his head, laughing internally at himself – what was the alternative? That the Underground was cleaning itself? Don't be daft.

Eventually, the stairwell leveled out into a long corridor, lit by the strong light of the translucent ceiling tiles overhead. The light had developed a slightly sickly pinkish quality, and the smell of roses was stronger – strong enough to be unpleasant. Dexter turned a corner and found himself facing a dead end.

Lining the corridor up until it ended in a blank tiled wall were a series of doors, equally spaced, marked with the same AUTHORISED PERSONNEL ONLY signs. Dexter tried the handles. Unlike the one he'd come through, these were firmly locked, and the handles were slippery and slightly sticky with the same rose-scented gunk he'd found on the rail, leaving a thin thread of slime as he took his hand away. He wiped his hand on his jeans again, and as a result they clung to his leg, a constant sticky reminder of something not quite right. Even the walls seemed to be glistening now.

Dexter suddenly felt a deep need to talk to someone in

charge, to get some explanation, to get some human contact. Tentatively, he knocked on the nearest door. There seemed to be more give than there should be, and the sound echoed in the silence, muffled somehow, as if there was a thin layer of sponge between his knuckles and the wood. The sound only seemed to highlight the stillness. There was no answer.

Nobody there.

For some reason, Dexter couldn't help thinking of the driverless trains.

He swallowed, shaking his head, rationalising, thinking of all the ways that this would make perfect sense – and then he noticed something at the end of the corridor, right in the centre of that dead-end wall, that blank canvas of tile.

A bulge.

Dexter walked towards it, looking closer. Definitely a slight bulge in the wall, forcing the glistening tiles outward, just a little. He wondered for a moment whether he should feel relieved. Another imperfection, another sign of humanity, like the cleaning fluid on the handrail.

It *was* cleaning fluid.

It must have been.

As he stared, the bulge in the wall shifted slightly, and a thin trickle of something slippery, glistening and pink began to ooze from between the tiles. Something that smelled strongly of roses.

Somewhere, far away, Dexter heard the screech of a train braking in a tunnel. A thin scream of metal on metal.

The kind of sound the new trains didn't make.

A wave of nausea washed through him and he was suddenly very aware of the way his jeans clung, sticky and wet, against his leg. He had to get out of there, retrace his steps, head up out of this place, out of the station, away from this pink artificial glow and up to real sunlight –

– the door opened.

It didn't creak, or groan. There was simply the soft sound of it unlatching and swinging open, gentle as a sigh. "Hello?"

called Dexter, his voice sounding hollow and unnatural, as the knock had. There was no reply. Nobody was there.

Beyond the open door, there was another empty corridor, done up in the same white and blue tile, the same steel flooring, glistening softly in the pinkish light. The corridor continued for a few metres before becoming another stairwell, leading further down.

Dexter stepped through. "Is anyone there? Hello?" His voice sounded thin, unnatural, distorted by the acoustics. His throat was dry. Again the thought crossed his mind that he should walk away, or better still, he should run. Run and never stop.

Instead, he took a few paces forward, the sickly scent of roses clinging to the inside of his nostrils, treading carefully so as not to skid on the slippery-sticky ooze that glistened on the floor.

The door closed noiselessly behind him.

Dexter began to descend the stairs, watching where he trod on the slick metal, moving carefully to avoid slipping and falling. He was beyond rationalising now, although part of him still desperately hoped to see a stern human face at the bottom of the stairwell, to hear some explanation for it all, something he could laugh at himself for not thinking of right away. Something that would let the world make sense again.

He didn't find anything at the bottom of those stairs that made sense.

At the bottom of the stairwell was another corridor, and this one was different from the others.

This one had things growing out of the walls.

Terrible things.

Dexter's first instinct was to turn and run, but the soles of his shoes wouldn't grip on the floor suddenly, and even when he tried to climb back up the stairs hand-over-hand, he couldn't get a grip, only succeeding in coating his shirt and the front of his jeans with the slimy rose-scented secretions that seemed to be everywhere now. His hands slid over the steel flooring, that now felt almost like sponge, or rubber, or flesh. He couldn't get any traction with his hands or his feet. He couldn't clamber up the stairs, no matter what he tried. He couldn't get away.

Eventually, he realised he didn't have a choice.

He was going to have to look.

The tiles on the walls splayed out obscenely, forming a vertical slit between, as wide as a human head. On either side, the grotesque curving tiles shifted organically, so that the walls seemed to breathe, and from the slit bulged what looked like a huge balloon, a membrane filled with the same shifting, translucent ooze that now coated his hands and the soles of his feet.

In the centre of the bulging, sagging sac of fluid was a rat – one of the tube-rats that had vanished from under the rails. It floated, the small body covered in whitish lumps that looked like tumours. It looked quite dead.

Dexter put his hand on the metal floor to steady himself and felt himself sink slightly, the metal impossibly giving way like sponge. It pulsed beneath his fingers, and his hand jerked up and away as if he'd laid it on a burning stove. He looked down, and saw the solid-seeming metal bending impossibly under his weight. A slick of pinkish fluid welled up around his knees, where they pressed against the floor.

The smell of roses was everywhere, thick and cloying, clogging his nostrils and his throat, making his eyes water. He didn't dare to wipe the tears from them in case he got the sticky syrup that clung to his fingers into his eyes. He imagined being blind in this terrible place, his eyes replaced by two fat, white, pulsing tumours...

There were similar sacs of fluid stretching ahead of him down the corridor, each with its own dead rat floating inside. The corridor seemed to stretch on and on, losing its sharp angles and defined corners as it went, the tile looking more and more like bone, the harsh pink light looking like the inside of a body. Occasionally, he heard the rumble of a train, sounding closer now, and it sounded like some huge, trapped animal, some massive leviathan that had found its home at last.

Dexter wanted to vomit, but couldn't. He hung his head, crouching on his hands and knees, feeling the metal-that-wasn't pulsing and shifting underneath him. Suddenly, his head jerked up, and he looked at the nearest rat, eyes wide, taking in the suppurating mass that was its body. He thought he'd seen it move.

The rat opened its eyes.

Its mouth and nose and lungs must have been filled with that semi-transparent pinkish slime, and yet it tried to squeal, twitching, tortured muscles trying to thrash against its liquid prison. One of the larger tumours was shifting, and as Dexter watched, the skin that stretched over the white mass began to crack and split.

Something small, long and thin emerged, like a silver worm. It coiled lazily, then swam around the inside of the bulging membrane – inside the egg – as if it was running smoothly and quickly around a track. Then, with a flick of a silver tail, it burrowed into the rat's open eye.

Dexter tried to scream, and he couldn't.

Even when he looked down and saw that his hand had sunk fully into the slimy, sticky, spongy metal mass that was the floor, he couldn't scream.

EIGHT MONTHS ON, the Mayor – and he was the Mayor, as if there had ever been any doubt he would be – relaxed as best he could in the cramped confines of the studio. The disc jockey carried on speaking, chattering away like a budgie.

"Now a lot of people are attributing your landslide victory to your involvement with the Tube refurbishments and the introduction of the new driverless system, Mister Mayor, and some people – and I'm not saying there's any sour grapes here – some people are accusing you of being a bit of a one-note candidate. Any comment on that?" The disc jockey smiled obsequiously over a cup of coffee, while the producer absent-mindedly cued up some Howard Jones for after the interview.

"I believe the exact quote was that I was all Tube and no trousers..." The Mayor chuckled gently, imagining various housewives and lorry drivers doing the same. Nothing better than turning an opponent's joke into one of your own. "I will admit that had been my biggest success, but that doesn't mean I'm not concerned with all of London, you understand. The whole city, not just the parts under our feet." Although he was growing very concerned indeed about the parts under his feet. "For example, I'm consulting with the Chief Commissioner of the Met about the sharp rise in missing persons cases–"

"A fifty per cent rise from this time last year! Makes you think!" The disc jockey's crinkled face collapsed into a pantomime of faked concern, even as the producer made a brief hand gesture – *wrap it up*.

"Oh, absolutely, and it's something that, as Mayor, I will be very deeply involved in." Well, he already was deeply involved in it, really. He had no illusions about where those missing men had gone.

Occasionally he wondered if he'd been right to listen to Jeremy. To let him and his chums... call in their little favour, so to speak. Bring the new Tube system into the world. Give birth to it, so to speak.

Well, it wasn't like he used it himself.

"It's been a real pleasure to have you on the show. One of my best mates, everyone, my absolute best friends – the Lord Mayor of London!" He pressed a button on the desk and the air filled with pre-recorded cheers. "And now we're going to head back to the eighties with an old song... called 'New Song'! Take it away, Howard!"

As the song droned gently over the speakers, the disc jockey stood to shake the Mayor's hand, grasping it in a sweaty clasp that reeked of need. "Wonderful to see you again, Mister Mayor. Come back anytime at all. I suppose you'll be taking the Tube now, eh?"

The Mayor smiled warmly, shook his head – *no, never* – and muttered some pleasantry. Then he extricated himself and walked outside, where his chauffeur was waiting to take him to the TV studios. He took a single deep breath, savouring the warm afternoon, and then frowned, a slight twinge of worry passing up from the base of his spine.

The air smelled of roses.

EXIT SOUNDS

Conrad Williams

When it comes to supernatural fiction, for me Conrad Williams has the edge on many other writers. I remember reading his superb debut novel – Head Injuries – for the first time and being very taken with the way he uses the figure of the ghost to talk of tragedy and loss and the dislocation from reality that these states bring. 'Exit Sounds' is as scary as hell, using two distinct settings to great effect. But there are much more than shivers here; the melancholy and yearning in this story brings you to the heart of the protagonist as he travels underground.

IT WAS OLD recording equipment, but it was where it needed to be on time, every time. Saul Waxler didn't care much for the new digital technology. It didn't seem right, somehow, to commit important work to a chip in something as fragile as a recorder the size of a tie clip. He wanted to see the tape turning on its spool, to see the signal light burning green, the levels needle twitching like an insect's leg. His clients did not want to know about hard drive failures and corrupt files. Until such things had been eradicated, he would stick resolutely to the traditional means of recording sound.

The only problem with that, he considered now, as he climbed the third set of stairs to the balcony seats, was that it was so damned heavy. In his shoulder bag he had a tape machine and a back-up, a battery pack, a fresh pack of chrome C90s, a pair of Sennheisers and a couple of microphones. By the time he reached the booth, sweat was trembling on his brow and his breath formed its own peculiar soundtrack. Waxler imagined recording it. *Sounds of exertion, 2:14.*

He dumped his bag and stretched, then leaned on the handrails and took in the view while his breathing steadied. He could just make out the hardwood edges of the seat-backs under a neon purple mood strip that edged the top of the vast, ghostly cinema screen. The lights had not yet been activated, despite Waxler's request. There had been a look of mild incredulity on the manager's face, as if Waxler ought to be able to do his job in the dark; after all, it was about sound, not vision. Waxler had to patiently explain that he needed a rough idea of the auditorium's size and its visible acoustic set-up so that he could adjust his recording controls accordingly. He also had to wait for security to arrive and deposit the No Entry bollards outside this particular booth. He must not be disturbed: all it took was for the doors to be opened, a whispered *Oh, sorry, wrong section* and thirty minutes of prep and recording would be ruined. He'd have to come back another day, and that would be his budget screwed. It was all about attention to detail, this job. Get the background and surroundings right, legislate for the random hazards, and the rest took care of itself.

What also helped was an original take on old, old material. The serious sound effects collectors could get the sounds they wanted from any library. You could buy BBC 45s on ebay for less than a fiver a pop these days. All kinds of stuff. Aircraft powering up, taxiing, taking off; wind chimes; busy restaurant kitchens. Where Waxler made his killing, however, was in specifics. His clients knew that if one of his tapes was labelled *007 (Goldeneye-Brosnan) BMW ZX engine cooling, 3.27*, or *Crowd tension, pre-penalty shoot-out, Liverpool v AC Milan, Champions League Final 2005, 2.13*, then that was what they were listening to.

So it would be tonight.

Once he was certain that his booth was barred, he set up his microphones and, making sure the gold-plated jacks were free of dust, plugged them into the recording machine. He checked the levels and positioning, then switched everything off and went down to the foyer where he ordered a large, black coffee. The audience was trickling in. He watched them as they milled around, snatching a quick half of lager from the bar, perusing the leaflet of coming attractions, nipping to the toilets or buying overpriced chocolates and ice creams. He watched them gradually head towards the auditorium, registering the dull murmur of their discussions, the rhythms and cadences, the shape of it all, and, when most of them had filed through and the staff were readying to close the door behind them, he returned to the stairs and trudged up to the gods.

This was the cinema his father had visited, with Waxler's grandfather, many years previously. Waxler knew neither of the men. Both had died when he was a baby. His mother had been a quiet woman who would not utter a word about who they were, or what they had been like. But she had sat him down when he was sixteen and explained that they had died together in a car accident. She had taken him to see the grave that they shared, in case he might wish to visit it himself, but she had never referred to them, or the incident, again. Occasionally he tried to engage her in conversations that would swing around to his father, but she gently deflected him when his vague overtures became more focused. "That's passed now, Saul," she would say. "That is all yesterday."

He had learned to cope with his frustration, with a strange, dislocated sense of loss. It wasn't so much his father and grandfather that he missed, rather it was the grief. How could he properly say good-bye when he had barely had chance to say hello?

He did what he usually did and shrugged it away, replaced it with the routine of work. He sat in the dark and monitored the pre-performance hubbub. The green and red LEDs on the unit fascia flickered like the scales of some iridescent sea creature. Although he had not triggered the record switch, he kept an eye on the levels, trying to gauge the way the audience would drift. Every audience, every crowd, he knew from experience, was unique and their voice depended on a number of factors: demographics, time of day, material consumed, pre- or post-prandial performance, type of event... it was a long list, but Waxler's study of it over the years meant that he could anticipate the slightest timbre change of a reaction and set his equipment accordingly. Rhythms. Ripples. Moods. What mattered to his client were the noises made by patrons leaving. Boden Heel wanted at least four minutes of an audience exiting an auditorium after a performance was over. He had not stipulated what kind of performance he wanted this dispersal to follow, but he had insisted that there be no residual echoes or hums or encores. For practicality's sake, Waxler had chosen the cinema. Concerts of any kind caused problems. Usually the venue was too large to trap the kind of intimate aftershocks that were expected. Orchestral gatherings usually vacated the premises in respectful or awed silence, with a smattering of coughs from those who were looking to be able to identify themselves on Radio 3 at a later date. Rock concerts were liable to be infected by the overkill of the PA system: feedback hell. Either that or coarse, drunken louts over-excited by too many power chords. No, the cinema it had to be. And not just any old Odeon or CineWorld. Multiplexes were out. It had to be a discerning crowd, and it had to be an intense film. Heel had specified that there must not be any children.

He was only faintly aware of the film starting. His interests lay outside cinema, although he had read a few technical texts on the craft of sound in movies through the ages. What mattered was that it was not a comedy, and not overly long; this film wasn't, although Waxler had not realised how difficult it was to find a cinema showing anything less than two hours long. But there was one film on general release that came in at a comfortable 112 minutes. Past 120 minutes people were less chatty when they vacated spaces. It was as if they were re-adjusting to new light and sounds forgotten during their marathon viewing session, coming awake again, to a certain degree. Comedies and glossy, loud thrillers sent people the other way. They were too noisy; the audience were too engrossed in the experiences to allow any ambient fragments through. It was all brash, brassy surface. Too shrill: Waxler had an ear for what he was chasing. The audience, the surroundings, the medium, the technology; he could almost imagine the tonal warmth of what was to be recorded. Crowds contained their own moods and manners. They were macrocosmic, unpredictable. A saying Waxler had picked up over the years – he could not remember who had coined it – was *You cannot plan success, but you can prepare for it*. Groundwork. It was all about setting out one's stall.

Shhh, shhh, tok-tok-tok, shhh, shhh...

Warm in the cinema; comfortable chair in this booth. Did they still use the stalls these days? He had not seen anybody else up here; only heard the faint scrapes and scratches of staff as they went about their duties. The audience had been shepherded into the lower circle. Maybe height skewed the picture quality; he was too drowsy to lean over the balcony to check. An old building like this would have been used to house theatre productions in the past, opera, maybe, music hall, ballet. He had not read up on the building's history, but he would. It was part of the job. It was his way of paying respect.

He realised he was on the edge of a dream but he could not emerge from sleep. He was far too comfortable: maybe that was why they stopped using these booths. Too many complaints from too many punters who had drifted off and missed the feature.

Confusion fell upon him: a gunshot, a scream. This was a peaceful town. It did not appear on the front pages. Another gunshot. Echoes opened within him. He wiped and re-wiped his cheek as if something wet had dropped upon him, but he was quite dry. There was a rising swell of music and, for a moment, as he rose too, out of sleep, out of a fury of frustration and panic that he had no image to blame upon that he could remember, he thought the music was his own, personal soundtrack. But then sense returned with a thud, like a tape slotted into a deck and he understood where he was. He groped his way upright, horrified. The audience was leaving. He heard a hundred seats spring erect to their backs. He punched out an arm and depressed the record button, already thinking of Heel and what he might say were Waxler to miss some crucial part of this event. But then, as Waxler saw now, it wasn't too bad. The hiss of the loudspeakers was still just audible; yes, there was the crackle as the circuit was broken. Heel would not have wanted that anyway. Waxler would cut it later. For now he silently blew out his cheeks in relief at how close he had come to ruining his entire contract.

Stealthily he leaned over the balcony and watched the audience depart. The lights had come up a little and the aisle was a milling mass of heads, hair ringed with light. The thrum of conversation they created was almost palpable; it was a thing of beauty, better than he had expected. He could not discern a single word, yet the patterns of it suggested excitement; almost, had Waxler not known better, of anticipation, rather than this retrospective release, a mulling over of things only just gone by. Waxler grew envious of it. He might point his microphone at a couple talking candidly but it was something that did not come readily to him. It wasn't that he could not socialise; he had no trouble chatting about work or current affairs if he were approached at a party or a sound effects convention. He was at a loss when it came to volunteering private information about himself. He could not emote. There was no special person in his life. He could not give of himself enough to secure the release of the essential part of another to make him feel whole. He worked so hard that he lost himself to it. Even when he wasn't actually recording material, he was plotting maps with possible sites of aural interest, reading up on a location or cataloguing his enormous collection. His library, he called it. He had devoted most of his adult life, some twenty years, to documenting everything that could produce sound. It didn't matter how strange, or unlikely the source, if it produced some degree of vibration in the air to get his recorder's sensors quivering, then down on tape it must go.

Waxler disconnected, gathered together and packed his things with the assured pace of a man who has done such a task many, many times before. He hoisted the bag on to his shoulder and took the steps down to the foyer. The lights were out. The bar and the ticket booths were vacant. Light from the street, piercing the locked doors, gleamed on the chrome barriers. The sounds of feet scuffing on tiles continued, as did the hubbub of contented people with its pockets of laughter. Where were they, though? Why weren't they exiting here?

Waxler stood in the centre of the foyer, all feeling sucking out of him, as if he were a potted plant positioned too close to a raging radiator. The noise of people leaving the cinema was all around him, but the area where there ought to have been the densest human traffic was deserted, apart from him. He turned to peer along the corridor leading to the toilets. There was a fire escape there. Maybe everyone had left through that. Maybe staff had redirected them because there was a fault with these main doors. In which case, why had he not been re-routed too?

He hurried after the tail of the noise. He noticed how the sound of his feet was cut off as he entered the carpeted corridor, the walls severing the distance the vibrations could travel, killing all immediate echoes. He heard the breath charging from his lungs. He heard the descent of leather upon concrete. He arrowed after it, panicky and hot, suddenly bloated with a childhood fear of being left behind. He barged through the fire doors into a dimly lit stairwell, painted ochre. He thought he glimpsed the last thin shadows of heads jerking and tottering down the steps to the next storey, but wouldn't that take them below street level? Was there an underground car park down there? He hurried after the audience, keeping his eyes on his feet as they skipped from one riser to the next, until the gloom deepened and he stuttered in his pursuit. He looked up at the light. The bulb was still working, bright enough to make him wince. It was its reflection off the walls that had been dulled. And now he saw why, as he drew his gaze down level with the streaks and spatters of blood that proscribed any number of high-velocity arcs across the paintwork. Something had died, violently and fast, down here, jetting its life as if in some unspeakable race to be free of it. He didn't know what to do. To go on was to expose himself to a group of people that had blithely tramped past this crime scene without a thought: he could hear women laughing, no doubt as the blood on their soles smeared a trail for him to follow. His crazed thoughts suggested they might have had something to do with this. He imagined a scrum of people carrying the rag doll remains of whatever they had drained. Waxler faltered, momentum causing him to descend a little further, but his heart was no longer in it, especially when he saw the security gates barring his progress. A smell came to him, of diesel and undigested alcohol and sour aftershave. He felt sudden pain in his neck and raised a hand, believing himself to have been struck. He checked behind him: nobody there. He pulled his hand away and found it to be dry. His fingertips tingled where he had felt the keen drum of his own pulse in the thick artery pressing against the underside of his jaw. *Fear sounds, 40 years and counting*.

He retreated.

He didn't remember returning to his room at the hotel. The next thing he was aware of, through the haze of a headache, was the view through a window opaque with steam as his bath filled. He had poured himself a drink from the mini-bar and clutched it in fingers turning white against the glass. The spirit had managed to chase away much of the shock and confusion of what had happened at the cinema, but it had been replaced with something equally puzzling. He was thinking of his father, or of the projection he had formed of him, via photographs and third-person testimonies. He hadn't thought of Dad, not in any depth, since he was a teenager. How much time can you spend thinking of someone you never knew? He tried now, in vain, to recall the way his father moved, or spoke, or laughed, but it was like trying to evoke character from a 2-D image. There was a gap in him, a Dad-shaped gap. There had been all that love that was meant for him, and where did it go instead? Into his work. On to his tapes.

Remembering the purpose of his visit, he set his drink down and slotted the tape into the player. He depressed the play button and watched through the little window as the capstan turned the pinch roller and the tape was fed to the heads. Waxler cued past the leader to the magnetic tape proper and listened.

Nothing.

He checked the tape counter and the levels indicator. Both were functioning normally; the tape was spooling through the machine. He kept his equipment scrupulously clean, toting with him a little emergency kit of cotton buds and denatured alcohol. It couldn't be any negligence on his part. The wrong tape, then. But even as he reached to eject the tape, he knew this was not the case. He had recorded on *that* tape. He had marked *that* tape: *Audience Leaving, Coronet, Seven Sisters, 4.32.* All of the other tapes were still in their shrink-wrapped packing.

Waxler turned the volume up; maybe it had been knocked low during his hasty journey back to the hotel. But of course it hadn't. Even when he felt under threat, the professional in him kicked in. The gear was padded, protected. The buttons and switches couldn't be knocked so easily. His fingers shook as he turned the volume higher: all that happened was an increase in hiss. He swallowed the contents of his glass and went to turn off the bath water. He would have to return to the cinema and re-record the people vacating it again. And that he did not want to do. He couldn't nail why, but he felt on his last visit that he had averted some catastrophic event, that if he had chased those people down he would not have come back, not easily, anyway.

The nature of the hiss altered. He stared at the speakers as if they might offer some explanation for the madness that was leaking from them.

Shhh, shhh, tok-tok-tok, shhh, shhh...

That was it? That was the sum total of what he had picked up during his hours on duty? Now he felt panic plucking at the centre of him. What would Heel say? There would be no payment, and no invitation to work for him again. His name would be besmirched. He would have to build up confidence among his clients again and to reach this level, that might take him years. He'd be finished. He took the tape out and cleaned the mechanism. He tried the tape again. Long, long, passages of hiss and then that funny little hiccup of sound. *Something* had been recorded. But it wouldn't pay his rent.

He took a shower and gathered his things together, then he checked out of the hotel and caught a taxi straight to the cinema. It was shrouded in darkness. It couldn't have been more still if he was viewing it on a photograph. The cabbie tried to crack a joke about underground films, but Waxler wasn't listening. His eyes were intent on the upper storey windows. He realised he had paid the exterior scant attention earlier in the day, his work obliterating all other thought. The cinema was an art deco building, a tribute to streamlined modernity, from a time when palaces really did exist outside of Westminster. The frontage consisted of a geometric pattern of ivory faience tiles that glowed green-blue in the ambient light. Pebbles of glass glinted on the forecourt. His determination faltered: the ground floor windows were boarded up.

He accepted his change from the cab driver, who was winding up his window.

"This cinema," Waxler said.

"You want to go somewhere else? Only this place has been shut for donkeys, mate. The only people using this place are ghosts and gangsters. Drug den. Nasty bastards knocking around. Take you somewhere else?"

He might have said no. He was only aware that he was walking away from the taxi, his shoes gritting on the glass, his hands digging into the padded walls of his equipment bag. The entrance was padlocked and it had been so for many, many years. The links ground against each other when he tested it; flakes of rust fell. There was the blood taste of old iron at the back of his throat. The wind dragged the corpses of a hundred leaves across the pavement; he thought of broken nails scratching at the inside of a coffin lid.

I need sleep. I need coffee.

He heard, or imagined, the muffled cry of a tannoy informing passengers of a change of platform, or a body on the tracks. The red and blue light of an Underground station burned in the near distance. He blinked at it. He wondered if the gate he had reached at the bottom of the stairwell might be connected to the Tube network. It would explain where the audience had vanished to. Perhaps there was some kind of short cut to the platforms that they knew about. He decided to check for himself, as much to get him away from the impossible façade of the cinema where only hours earlier he had mingled with staff and patrons as he went about his work. Was all that a dream?

He counted steps until he was standing outside the entrance hall.

The ticket barriers were empty. A member of staff moved sluggishly away from a service hatch obscured by reflected light. Waxler bought a ticket from the automated machine and allowed himself to be transported south by the escalators. He heard a train thunder into the station. Before he reached the foot of the escalator he remembered why he chose to go everywhere by taxi, or by foot. He found it very hard to accept that the system of supports down here were strong enough to keep all those millions of tons of earth off his back. Breathing more shallowly, more quickly, he scurried through to the platform as the train began gathering pace, a rising cry as if it was bemoaning the prospect of returning to all those miles of black, sooty tunnels. The last train. He felt in missing it that he had missed an opportunity, a last chance, even. Despite his never using this form of transport, there was something about it that seemed familiar, comforting almost.

Waxler oriented himself, gauging quickly where he was standing in relation to the cinema. He must turn left, and follow the tunnel north, a hundred or so steps to take him to what he hoped would be the metal grille where he had lost the audience earlier that evening. But the blackness seemed so dense, like something he might actually have to wade through, that he hesitated. It was oppressive. It was a wall. He glanced behind him once more as he heard the noise of the station shutting down. Metal squealed and clattered as the gates were dragged across the entrance. He heard voices approaching. Maybe he had been picked up on CCTV and was to be escorted out. That decided him. He dropped down to the tracks and headed into the dark.

HE ALMOST MISSED it.

The dark was tangible, after all. The stirred-up dust of a century of to-and-fro furred his skin, tickled his sinuses, irritated his eyes. His feet kicked through what seemed like inches of matter, all of it soft as ash. Echoes came to him through the tunnels and at first he flinched from them, shuttling back against the wall in the belief that he was about to be discovered, but he soon came to learn that the sounds were far away, many miles, perhaps. It was like being inside an immense whispering gallery. The voice of the Tube carried far; it was trapped down here, even across centuries he thought, with a shudder.

Lost in this fantasy, he bypassed a sudden area of cool air. He'd travelled another half dozen steps – 150 now – when he thought it might indicate a change of wall scenery. He was right. Recessed in the black tiles of the tunnel was a gap. He stared at it, trying to assimilate its shape, its purpose, with the rest of the underground geography. Was this a planned exit, a fire escape? If so, then where were the relevant signs? He touched the wall, feeling for the edges of a warning cartouche, but all he could feel was the near-animal pelt of dust clinging to the stone. He squinted through the gap and saw the grille that earlier had blocked his progress from the other side. Its padlock was unclasped, hanging from one of the links like a tease.

He pushed through and rose to the ground floor, ignoring the arcs and spatters of old blood – *paint, let's think of it as paint; paint from a decorator who was too unprofessional to complete a proper job* – until he was standing, foyer-side of the fire escape door, staring at the broad sweep of stairs that would take him to the booths at the top of the building. Sodium light from the street lamps picked through the boards in the windows. Everything was dulled by dust and time and mould. An astonishing bulge of fungus blistered the counter where once popcorn and drinks had been served. The apron was warped by decades of moisture. Cracks in the glass display cabinets were green with lichen. A deep, autumnal smell. Mushrooms and seed cases and age. He climbed to the upper floor and found the bollards that had guarded his territory while he worked that afternoon. They were matted with cobwebs. Up ahead was a door for staff only. Its positioning suggested access to the projection room. With a heavy tread, Waxler approached it. Heel was going to do his nut. There would be no more performances here. There hadn't been, for decades.

He opened the door and turned his face away from the breath of rot that tumbled down the steps to greet him. He pressed a handkerchief to his nose and mouth and ascended into utter blackness. Out of habit he fumbled for the light switch and blinked, astonished, as the bulb sprang to life. The projectors were gone, stripped from their housings. Wires snaked over a table occupied by a plastic container of bleach and a telephone directory obliterated by mould. Throw switches for the lights and curtains were frozen into position by rust. Old vinyl records lay shattered on the floor. Some enchanted evening. I could have danced all night. A couple of projector lenses gathered dust on a table, their once sparkling eyes blinded by filth. Coiled lengths of film reel cringed as if in pain. He picked one up and scanned the frames, but they were opaque, ruined. In one he thought he could see the barrel of a shotgun, emerging from the mist as in some murky noir crime flick, but it was not replicated in any of its neighbours. He put a small section in his pocket, to keep as a memento, and returned to the corridor.

He was in time to see a pair of shadows slide across the far wall. The snick of a door opening. Waxler tore after them and slowed only when he saw that they had entered the booth where he had sat and recorded – thought he had recorded – the afternoon performance. The door swung slowly on its hinges. He caught it before it met the jamb. Inside, the booth was empty. The seats were rising with mould, the carpets they were bolted into bloated and discoloured by the soft insistence of water. What light there was in here dimmed further. The torn purple velvet faltered on its runners as it drew back from a screen wounded with mould and tears.

Shhh, shhh, tok-tok-tok, shhh, shhh…

A sudden shaft of light splashed into it from the aperture in the back wall. A kaleidoscopic image. A voice that took him back 30 years: "Now it's time for ice cream… a cool glass of orange… why not try a hot dog? Or the real thing, a cool, refreshing Coca Cola, from the sales staff or in the foyer."

King Cone. Kia Ora. Fry's Turkish Delight. May we remind you that for the convenience of those Patrons who prefer not to smoke… OUR NEXT PRESENTATION. SHOWING TODAY.

Even through the horror of it, the impossibility of it, he remembered the tingle of excitement he would feel whenever he came to this place as a child. The queue would reach out of the door some days. Mum would buy him a box of caramel Poppets, or they'd share a bag of Opal Fruits. Or an ice cream from the girl with the tray in the intermission.

He felt something wet fall against his cheek and realised he was crying.

A 'fade in' on a busy Underground platform. People smoking, holding cumbersome broadsheet newspapers the size of Ordnance Survey maps. People wearing trilby hats and tweed jackets; umbrellas tucked under their arms. Shiny black shoes. A flurry of movement. Staff helping a woman and an old man carry a Silver Cross pram from the stairs to the platform. The woman crying. The old man trying to placate her. A tiny hand reaching from the pram.

Waxler's breath caught in his throat. He didn't know who to hail first, his mother or his grandfather. He was so wrapped up in what he was seeing, he believed either might turn to acknowledge him.

The twin spots of a distant train in the tunnel, coming on, coming on. The rails hissing like the writhing of snakes in a disturbed nest. Another ripple of movement in the crowd. This time edged by panic. A shout of indignation. A scream.

The mother's head snapping around. The old man stepping back. Space clearing on a crowded platform. Bad things. The cry of a baby needing reassurance. A shadow breasting the arch. People falling off the edge and on to the rails. A long coat being shrugged away. A levelled shotgun. A face ruined by pain and grief. A clenched bar of white teeth. Determination.

He clearly heard the younger man – his father – say: "No, Dad. Come on. Put the gun down. Think of Saul."

Waxler's breath rattled out of him. He leaned forward to rest his shaking arms on the balcony and was granted a wider view of the auditorium. The seats down there were packed out. And every single person was gazing up at him with ash-black eyes.

The squeal of brakes as the train thundered into the station. Staff shouting for people to get back. Shouting for the electricity to be turned off, for God's sake, there are people on the track.

Waxler's father backing away. His grandfather, stoic, destiny bowing his shoulders, closing in, waiting for the moment. The shot. His mother screaming. Waxler was screaming too: then and now.

His father dropping in front of the astonished driver, his grandfather dropping to his knees, placing the muzzle of the gun against his chest and destroying his own heart.

But now his father rose, his hands wrapped around his neck, and it was as if he had pulled on a pair of crimson gloves. Was his face always that pale, or was it the blood, creating some ghastly contrast? He gazed at his wife, at his baby, at the ruination of his own father for a second or two, and then he took off into the gloom as Waxler himself had done earlier.

The stairwell.

Waxler dropped his equipment bag and hurried out into the corridor. Madness filled his mind. *If I can get to him before he reaches the stairs.* There might have been nothing else to him but this feverish thought, the bestial thrash of his heart, his unblinking eyes. The great escalator of time had collapsed to the point where he believed he could intervene, save his life, love his father. The desire to meet the person that ought to have shaped him more completely erased all rational thought. He must get to the stairwell now. He must do what he could.

He descended. He regressed. He heard a howl of anguish and the cocking of barrels, like the sound of a bone breaking in this cathedral space. The shadows on the walls must be those of the men he had never had near him, but desperately needed in his life.

His entire span, since then, had been about capturing the present so that, as it instantly became the past, it might be cherished in the future. He felt momentarily naked without the weight and bulk of his recording equipment knocking against his leg but it was also a curious source of liberty. He was more than the confluence of tape and magnets. He tried not to, but it suddenly struck him like an epiphany, as he piled through the fire door and into the cold, stone stairwell, that he was so wound up in the preservation of history – of dead things – that *the moment* was always lost to him.

"Dad?" he called out, but his voice crumbled under the simple force of the word. He had never uttered it. Whenever he had tried to winkle information from his mother, he always referred to him formally. Now his excitement burst within him and he called out again, this time joyous and loud, until his throat threatened to crack. He saw the shadows shifting. He was dying down there. But he could make a difference.

"Dad!" he cried. The air was filled with the sour tang of fear. Violence, or the threat of it, filled every available space so that, combined with the entangled limbs of the men wrestling at the foot of the stairs, Waxler felt that there were a great many more people squeezed into this space. But in the end it was just the three of them. Did it become two just because this man, this boy, with the jogging top and the expensive trainers plunged a knife into the chest of his opponent? The other – wiry, black, no older than fifteen – dropped as if a switch had been turned off inside him. He rolled huge white eyes in their sockets, fixing Waxler: the last person he would see alive.

"Fucking lesson learned, prick," his killer spat. "And as for you..." He seemed almost bored as he bent to pick up the shotgun that had been dropped in the scuffle. Waxler craned his neck to see if his father were behind him. Adrenaline was draining from him; he felt weak, his joints stiffening. Sense was coming back, but he didn't have the wit to match it with action.

Jogging top checked the safety was off, brought the muzzle up and shot Waxler at point-blank range.

Waxler was aware of a body stepping over him and coolly ascending the steps, but he was too busy trying to hold his neck closed. Blood was leaping from him, making a curiously soothing sound, but he was irritated by his foot, which would not stop twitching, and kept tapping against the wall: a profane Morse code. The slack face of the youth was not what he wanted to spend his final seconds staring at. A gargantuan effort took him over on to his other side. From here he could look down the steps to the security gates, and to his father, who was coming up to collect him.

FUNNY THINGS

Pat Cadigan

Pat Cadigan is all over the place. This is a good thing. 'Funny Things' takes you on a journey through many different stations, some of them physical and some of them emotional. Her ideas and themes rapidly branch off from one another, and though this may seem, at first, an unruly approach, when you realize just where she is taking you, you come to the understanding that you are in the hands of a master. This is a story about lives intersecting, chances taken and the darkness that may be behind the scenes, controlling the directions which we take and the choices we make. More importantly, 'Funny Thing's is a deeply powerful story about a journey into grief.

MY HUSBAND USED to say his affinity to subterranean mass transit systems in general came from the fact that he'd been born in the Underground, on a Circle Line train as it had been rounding the bend between Gloucester Road and High Street Kensington. Maybe it was true; plenty of babies have been born in the carriages or on platforms, although if there were really as many as claimed all the drivers would be midwifes. But it was a charming story, very Tommy.

He had lots of stories and I loved listening to them. In the first flush of our romance, over licorice and a pine-tar liqueur called *terve* from Finland – the land of his ancestors and where his parents had chosen to spend their retirement – Tommy had given me a long account of how the first computer hackers at MIT had emerged from a primordial ooze composed of model railroads, which was why computer programs shared a lot of train characteristics, including vocabulary.

Okay, it was romantic the way Tommy told it. To my ex-pat American ears, his British accent made everything he said sound significant. But I was also charmed that someone who had been a one-man computer build-and-repair business since his teens would know so much about the human angle. He wasn't obsessive enough to be a full-blown anorak-wearing train-spotter, but if we went on holiday to a city with an underground transit system, we had to check it out before we did anything else.

Together, we'd taken the U-Bahn and the S-Bahn in Berlin (I'd snapped Tommy's photo next to the Wittenbergplatz sign), the Paris Metro, and the Moscow Metro. Before we'd met, Tommy had been to Barcelona; I never had. We talked about going there, and to Prague, to Japan, to Greece, to Australia, and Hong Kong and Singapore. The only other UK system I'd been on was Liverpool. I figured Tommy must have ridden all of them.

But the one place I had experience with that he didn't was the Manhattan subway system. He'd taken the T in Boston (he even knew the old Kingston Trio song about that man who never returned) and BART in San Francisco but he had yet to do more than change planes in New York. I told him I thought he would find Manhattan's subway rather tame next to the London Underground, which used almost twice as many colours to differentiate its various lines.

"New York may not use as many colours but it looks trickier to me. You can't just get on a green line, for example – you have to make sure it's the right letter or number. And look, all the way down at the bottom, where they all go under the East River to – what is that, Brooklyn? They come out and go every which way. Take the wrong one and you'll end up who knows where – Chicago, Tokyo. Maybe even in some other dimension. The Underground doesn't do that south of the Thames."

"That's because there's barely any Underground there at all,"

I said. "It might as well be a cab driver. 'Sorry, don't go sarf of the river, mite.'"

"But all New York taxis go everywhere. 'Toity-toid and toid, and step on it, buddy.'"

From there, the discussion degenerated into a wrestling match we both won.

Funny, the things that stick in your mind, as if caught on some mental hook. This one came back to me when we finally went on holiday to New York. I thought of it when we were figuring out when to go and when we took a Yellow Cab to our Times Square hotel. Also when we took the wrong train on our way to the Ground Zero memorial.

And again, when I got *that* call on *that* morning, four days before we were supposed to fly home, just as I reached Union Square where Tommy and I were supposed to meet. When the police took me down into the station but wouldn't let me go through the turnstiles. When they waited until an ambulance arrived and there was a paramedic with me before they showed me Tommy's passport.

THEY WOULDN'T LET me touch it. Hell, they wouldn't even take it out of the plastic bag. They held it in front of my face, folded to show only the page with Tommy's photo. I'd seen his passport a million times but that wasn't the picture I remembered.

The paramedic said things always looked funny in an evidence bag.

They wouldn't bring me his jacket, even wrapped in plastic. It was Tommy's favourite: black with silver-coloured buttons and two inside breast pockets, one on top of the other so he could keep his passport separate from his wallet. They said it was mostly still intact because he had been carrying it, not wearing it, as he'd stepped off the train and walked along the platform before it happened. Still, they wouldn't let me see it.

I overheard someone saying that they could have brought me

his shoes, there was nothing wrong with those. They'd been sitting neatly on either side of the track as if he had deliberately taken them off and put them there before the train headed uptown had flattened him. One pointing east and one pointing west, laces still tied. Funny things happened when someone got hit by a train.

The paramedic decided I'd be better off in the back of the ambulance. I didn't want to move. I was picturing Tommy's shoes sitting on either side of the track and wondering if loafers miraculously acquiring laces was another of those funny things. But when she pulled me to my feet, I went up as if I weighed nothing at all. So this was shock, I marveled as she steered me toward the exit. But why would I be in shock? I wasn't injured, I was all in one piece and safe for anyone to look at. Except now I was weightless. Funny things really did happen when someone got hit by a train. Who knew?

Not me. I'd had no idea when I'd gotten up this morning and Tommy had said he would rather sleep in than explore Soho with me. I'd had no idea when I'd kissed Tommy goodbye before leaving our hotel, or when I'd boarded the right train from the right platform and ridden it to my chosen destination.

Tommy wouldn't have been going *uptown* to Union Square. He would have been going *downtown*. Tommy had been in the wrong place.

Which meant I was in the wrong place. How did I get to the right one?

I needed a map. Did I have one in my shoulder bag? It was on the floor of the ambulance by my feet and as I reached down, I turned toward the back door the paramedic had left open ("You need air, let me know if you feel faint") and I saw *her*.

The sight was so clear, so sharp, so unmistakable. I'd bought that shirt in a deep rich blue; she'd bought it in pink. My shirt was being dry-cleaned after a spaghetti incident. Either she wasn't as messy or she hadn't had the spaghetti.

It wasn't just *where*, I realized – it was also *when*.

"I got here too early," I said aloud. "I should have had

another coffee. Or a mocha thing. I should have walked slower. No, if I'd stayed in the room, slept late instead of going out, it wouldn't have been *my* phone."

Magical thinking was part of being in shock, the paramedic said sympathetically. It was tempting to believe that if we'd only done this instead of that or that instead of this or nothing instead of something, everything would be OK but one person couldn't control the universe and make it turn on a dime, and blah and blah and after a while her soft, kind voice was a faraway hum and I could hear myself think.

I shouldn't have been *there*, not *then*; *my* phone had intercepted *her* call. *I* should have been where *she* was *right now*. Then *she* would have been *here*, where *I* wasn't supposed to be and *I* would have been *there*, listening to the call *she* was now taking on *her* phone. The one *I* was supposed to get.

"There's been a mix-up," I said. *She* was smiling, happy, talking on her phone, The longer I stared, the better I could see her, *perceive* her. I could practically read her lips: *They closed the station at Union Square, something must have happened. Let's meet at that big used bookstore instead –*

Did she know it was a wrong number?

Would she have cared?

I tried to get to my feet and found I was no longer weightless; the paramedic had injected me with something that made me too heavy to move.

"What mix-up?" she asked in a too-kindly tone, pushing the syringe through the top of a bright yellow plastic box marked 'Hazard'.

"Wrong plat. Form." Even my tongue was too heavy to lift.

"Lie down, everything'll get straightened out."

"Tommy. Wrong. Platform." It took all my strength to force the words out and make them distinct. "Uptown. Coming down. Town. But. Found going. Up."

The paramedic told me not to worry about going uptown or anywhere else. I tried but my thoughts were too heavy to think.

* * *

TWO OF MY sisters and my youngest brother came down from upstate New York and tried to get me to extend my stay even more than I already had for the sake of the police investigation. I should stay, they said, and I should have had Tommy buried in the family plot rather than letting the coroner deal with the remains. I tuned them out so I wouldn't have to listen to them ask me, for the millionth time, why we couldn't have made a side-trip to Niskayuna.

Who were they, I wondered. Mine? Or *hers*?

I honestly wasn't sure. While there wasn't anything really wrong about them, they didn't seem quite right to me, either. But then, nothing did. The counselor Victim Services provided – or more accurately, forced on me – said this wasn't unusual. He went on to tell me about a boy who had complained his favourite foods tasted like 'sour metal' after losing his mother, and a woman who couldn't taste or smell anything at all for over a year after her husband's death.

"Those are extreme examples, of course. Your experience is more common. Memory lapses – the way you forgot you were checked into the downtown Hyatt, not the one in Times Square, for example. And the way familiar things look strange. That's the most common of all, actually. You know déjà-vu? This is the exact opposite. It's called jamais-vu. Grief does funny things to people."

'PERSONAL EFFECTS' WAS what it said on the box, not 'Funny Things'. Two women police officers brought it to me at the Brooklyn apartment of a cousin my siblings had descended on for emergency hospitality in the name of family, and whom I'd never met. I'm not sure they had, either. Faces respectfully sad, the officers explained that since it was an open case, some things had to be kept as evidence. There were photographs so I would know what they were. They were very sorry if this caused me any further emotional pain.

I locked myself in one of the cousin's three freshly-scented bathrooms so I could look through the box in private. I wasn't sure I wanted to, because I knew it would be wrong but I forced myself to cut the tape and remove the lid. Everything was in its own labeled plastic bag and all the photos were in separate sleeves, also labeled, as if the box had been packed by the OCD employee of the month.

Some things weren't wrong – his key-ring, his watch, his wedding ring. The bank cards, loyalty cards, and foreign currency debit card from the post office were right but I didn't recognize some of the business cards or the wallet. The small black address book was right – or rather, it would have been except Tommy had decided at the last minute not to take it; as well, some addresses were missing. The Swiss Army knife – Tommy had talked about getting one. Would he have bought one here or waited till we were home? I couldn't make up my mind so I called it Schrödinger's Swiss Army knife and put it aside.

The shoes were a punch in the stomach. Smooth black leather with laces (still tied), brand new, barely any wear on the soles. *These* were sitting on either side of the tracks, one pointing east and one pointing west? Where were his loafers? I had found only a pair of trainers in the luggage the hotel had sent over. When would Tommy have had a chance to buy shoes, and why these? They looked like the ones he'd described having to wear with his uniform in secondary school. Nostalgia? A joke? I took a corner of each plastic bag between thumb and forefinger and tossed them into the bathtub.

Then I found the camera. Not our digital camera – I'd had that with me in my shoulder bag. I had already paged through the shots on the memory card. There were some of Tommy, some of me, and one of us together at the Italian restaurant courtesy of the waiter, taken before the spaghetti incident. This was a single-use film camera. Its cardboard housing was a bit crumpled but otherwise intact; the counter on the bottom showed half the roll of twenty-four had been used.

There was a peculiar dropping sensation in my chest as the hair on the back of my neck stood up. If this was an open case, shouldn't the police have developed these as evidence?

Oh, sure. Right after the commercial break. The last photo would be the image of the killer, whose *epithelials* would be all over the victim's jacket. Later, his widow would listen to the killer *allocute* in the courtroom and find comfort in justice done.

But since this wasn't a TV show, I'd just go home with the 'Personal Effects' and a piece of paper with a case number on it.

I was putting everything back in the box except those awful shoes when the thought came to me.

Home?

I searched the box for something with an address on it. No such luck.

THE HOUSE LOOKED the same, at least from the outside. I made the cab driver wait while I tried my key in the door. I don't know what I expected him to do if my key hadn't worked, or if the door opened and I found myself face-to-face with *her*. But my key did work and the door opened into what I remembered as home. At first glance, anyway.

I changed the locks before I took a second glance. It cost extra to get a locksmith on such short notice and it was probably as unnecessary as it was expensive. *She* had already been home with him for a week and a half, assuming her departure date was the same as our original one. That was plenty of time to… to figure out how to…

Well, what? Keep Tommy where he didn't belong or keep herself where she didn't belong? Or maneuver them both into a different place altogether?

If it had been me, I thought, I'd have gone for door number three.

And then I remembered it *was* me.

* * *

AT LEAST I didn't have to worry about employers. I'd been working temp jobs sporadically since my most recent lay-off; Tommy had cleared his calendar before we'd left for the States. I left his answer-phone messages as they were and emptied his voice mailbox whenever it got full. If all his old customers went elsewhere, there would always be others. Computer repairmen were seldom short of work.

Our social life was a different matter. As half of a couple, I had three groups of friends to deal with: his, mine, and ours. Except I *couldn't* deal. What was I supposed to say when someone asked me where Tommy was?

Oh, Tommy got on the wrong train at Times Square and now he's living with a woman who's actually supposed to be his widow. Well, not his widow, exactly – the Manhattan subway lines are a lot more complicated than they look and the stations all have multiple exits.

A trial-separation fib was also out of the question – my friends would be all over me offering support while the rest chose sides for the divorce. Finally, I hit on the secret-project white lie: Tommy was off looking into something and if it worked out we'd be telling everybody and if it didn't, we'd tell everybody anyway but right now we agreed that we didn't want to say anything to jinx it.

It was just silly-married-couple enough to work. Even Tommy's best friend bought it. Some impulse made me tell Martin to think good thoughts for Tommy so everything would come out right. As soon as the words were out of my mouth, however, I was sorry. Martin was especially hard-headed and I'd already pushed it with the jinx bit. But I guess even the hardest of hard-heads has a soft place for a best friend. He told me to tell Tommy he'd said good luck out there in the wild whatever.

Tommy. Out there in the wild whatever –

* * *

EVERY MOMENT OF every day, I wondered not just how I could find him but also what was going on with him. Did he notice any differences when *she* had gone back to the Times Square Hyatt with him? No doubt fitting herself into his life made for a much smoother start than trying to fit him into hers. She'd had another four days in New York with him before going home.

But where was home? Obviously not here. Now *she* was fitting him into *her* life. Had it really been so easy after only four days? Had she only had to take him to wherever she lived and announce they were home for Tommy to go along with it?

What would have made him do that. Drugs? Brainwashing? Torture?

Or had she just rubbed off on him somehow?

Rubbed off... She and her life just rubbed off on him. Like dust, or paint, or make-up. The idea should have been stupid, absurd, crazy.

Except they'd been away from home – excuse me, *we'd* been away from home, all of us, away from the familiar and the routine, in unfamiliar territory, with only each other as known quantities, and even known quantities will seem different in a strange place. She'd had my Tommy to herself in a strange place long enough to become his known quantity. His brain – or self? Soul? – had readjusted, re-set itself. Maybe when the cab from the airport had pulled up in front of her house, *maybe* he had hesitated because it looked unfamiliar. And then he'd told himself it was only jetlag doing funny things to him.

Did he know that was called jamais-vu?

DID SHE THINK she could now live happily ever after, I wondered. Or was she still a little nervous? Maybe she was a lot nervous. Maybe she was walking on tiptoe, peeking around corners, looking both ways and then not crossing the street after all.

No, she'd have everything figured out, I decided, because *I* would have. That would have been the first thing I'd have done, mapped out all the old roads not taken – well, not all of them, just the major ones – and started plotting a new course, or as new a course as Tommy would accept.

Everybody has a multitude of roads not taken and even if you consider only the most unusual, that's still a lot. There was little chance of finding which one she and Tommy were on now unless I could outsmart myself.

Could I actually do that?

Without my head exploding?

YES, I DID wonder if I'd lost my mind, but not very often. I couldn't see where it would have made any difference, anyway.

ALL MY ROADS converged at a single point – the northbound green line platform in the Union Square subway station – and they all went on from there.

For a while, I tried plotting courses in all kinds of ways – deduction based on hard facts, second-guessing old second guesses, flipping a coin, reading horoscopes. But something kept pulling my thoughts back to the subway. I couldn't imagine why. Going back to New York was pointless. They weren't there anymore and probably never would be again. Still, it nagged at me, and nagged, and nagged until my brain hurt. Until my *hair* hurt.

That's another of those funny things: you can think and wonder and concentrate on a problem and never get anywhere. But then, when you're so drained you waffle over the simplest decisions – like, say, which line to take to Leicester Square, the Northern or the Piccadilly – everything is clear.

She was taking the road but, as all city-dwellers know, the Underground is faster.

* * *

IF TOMMY COULD see me, he'd laugh, I thought as I pored over all the transit-system maps I'd printed out. I pushed all the living room furniture back against the walls so I could spread the papers out more easily. Sometimes I grouped them together by how similar they were – Berlin and London, Washington, DC and Tunis (if you cut off some DC lines), Montreal and BART (if one of them were upside-down), Budapest and part of Boston. Then I'd rearrange them according to what colours they had assigned their longest or shortest lines, or the number of stops going north-south, east-west, or some other combination. I traced some in coloured-marker and super-imposed them to see how congruent they were. Then I tried laying them end to end.

That was good for a laugh. Around the world in eighty stops – oh, sure. Not any world I knew. I couldn't think of anything less likely.

Could *she?*

I went straight to the stash of credit cards Tommy and I kept in the freezer (Tommy's idea). We had sworn to each other that they were for dire emergencies only – to raise bail, to bribe our way out of a foreign prison (we never discussed how we'd do that with them in the freezer), to flee the country in the event of a minor apocalypse. I'd thought there had been half a dozen cards the last time I looked; now there were nine. Had I misremembered how many there were or had Tommy forgotten to tell me he'd taken out three more?

Didn't matter, I told myself firmly, and called all the providers to report them lost, asking for replacements as soon as possible. Family emergency, I had to fly out yesterday.

I HADN'T TOUCHED her suitcase or the over-sized duffle-bag that was supposed to be Tommy's except to roll them into the house. The duffle was expandable, with all kinds of compartments and pockets inside and out. Not exactly made for traveling light but taking only a carry-on bag would attract the attention of airport security. I could pack light and maybe all those pockets would come in handy.

The first thing I saw when I unzipped the main part of the bag was the 'Personal Effects' box.

Not that it was really a box any more. I'd forced it in, squashing it to make it fit while my horrified sister danced around me asking why I didn't just take all the stuff out of the box, I didn't need the box, what the hell did I think I was doing? Airline baggage handlers had had their usual fun with it and now it was thoroughly mashed.

I tore it apart and dumped everything out on the floor. Plastic bags slid all over the place. I was pushing them into a more compact heap when I spotted the disposable camera. I had actually forgotten all about it, which made me feel like an idiot. How could I have forgotten something like that?

I took it out of the bag and examined it for further damage; nothing. I could drop it at a one-hour photo place, then, and see what Tommy – that Tommy – had photographed.

Only I didn't want to. I told myself I had to.

No. Don't look.

It wasn't like a voice in my head or even a coherent thought – more like a reflex, the way you'd stay back from the crumbling edge of a cliff or not stick your hand into an open fire. It felt like that. Then I'd look at the slightly-crumpled camera and feel stupid.

Don't look. Don't. Don't.

I went back and forth, arguing with myself. Finally, I decided I wouldn't have the film developed yet. I'd just keep the camera and either I'd think of a reason compelling enough to over-rule my weird anxiety and get the film developed before it was so far past its expiration date that it rotted away on its sprockets, or I wouldn't.

Did film rot? I could only hope. Or not.

*   *   *

SOMETHING ELSE OCCURRED to me: pack my own things, or hers?

I still hadn't opened her suitcase. I nudged it out of the corner with my foot so I could open it and suddenly found myself kicking it downstairs and out the front door. I kept on kicking it, sending it off the front step, down the walk and onto the curb where it could sit until it was stolen, which I hoped wouldn't take long. I didn't want to touch her stuff and I didn't want any of it loose in my house. I got queasy just thinking about it.

My feelings about his things weren't quite as strong but I decided to get rid of them anyway. I stuffed his clothing into a black garbage bag and then added all the 'Personal Effects' I knew were wrong. I meant to put it out in the wheelie bin as trash and instead dropped it on the sidewalk next to the suitcase.

IF YOU WANT to make enemies and alienate people on the London Underground, travel with an inconveniently large suitcase during rush hour, when the trains are sardine cans. I waited till after nine a.m. before I headed for the Underground with the duffle bag. After half a block, I was sorry I hadn't tossed it out on the sidewalk, too. The wheels squeaked and rattled like they were going to come apart at any moment and the bag itself was always off-balance somehow, veering one way or another as if it actually wanted to go in a different direction.

Getting on the bus for the short ride to the tube station was a struggle. No one offered to help me on or off – some days were like that. By the time a scowling Underground employee opened the handicapped gate for me in the ticket hall (checking that my travel card was valid both before and after I went through), I decided to ditch the thing and buy something at Heathrow.

As it turned out, I was thinking much too far ahead. Two very tall, beefy men in Transport Police uniforms stepped into the carriage at King's Cross and stepped off with me between them, the one on my left carrying the bag as if it weighed nothing at all.

*   *   *

"I'M SURPRISED YOU got as far as you did with that thing." The woman on the other side of the table in the small, bare room might have been a mature twenty-seven or a youthful fifty. Her uniform was similar to that of the men who had removed me from the train at King's Cross; a patch on her shoulder said TRANSPORT AUTHORITY X-RAIL. "You're lucky you didn't fall under a bus with it."

I thought about the very annoyed bus driver and the passengers. "In retrospect, I can see it was a near miss."

She didn't ask me to explain. "We'll have to dispose of it. Sorry."

"What about my things?"

Her brow puckered a little. "We can give you a bag for whatever you want to keep. Provided it actually belongs with you."

The wording wasn't lost on me. "Why?"

"You know why." She jerked her chin at the duffle propped up in the corner to my left. "It's out of place. It needs to be put back before someone gets hurt."

"Someone already got hurt."

"Before someone else gets hurt, then."

"What about –" I searched for the right words. "What about how I got it?"

She was silent for a few seconds. "That's a different area. We're only responsible for objects. Things."

That made sense; you didn't report a missing person to Lost and Found. "So who do I see about a person out of place?"

"Well." Her ageless face took on a pained expression. "There isn't anyone."

I felt my mouth drop open. "Why not? Why would a *thing* out of place be a big deal but not a *person?*"

"I didn't say that wasn't a big deal," she said apologetically. "I said there's no one to do anything about it."

"Why not?"

"Free will."

I wasn't sure I'd heard her correctly. "Say again?"

"Free will. People have it. Objects don't." She shrugged.

"That's – that's –" I couldn't think of anything bad enough. "I want to talk to your supervisor."

The way she nodded told me I wasn't the first person who'd made that request. "She's not available right now but you can leave a note. Or I can give you an email address."

"Where's her office?"

She looked at her watch and then at the clock on the wall behind me. "Right now, I'd say it's either between Leicester Square and Charing Cross or..."

I waited but she didn't go on. "*Or?*" I prodded.

"Or it's somewhere else."

I was about to tell her what I thought of her bullshit when I had a sudden memory of something I'd seen one morning about a year before Tommy and I had met. I'd gotten up indecently early for some reason and while I was waiting on the Underground platform, a short train, just two cars, had come through without stopping. Inside I saw not the usual arrangement of seats but an office – filing cabinets, printer/ fax, several laptops, and a whole bank of monitors. I barely caught a glimpse of any of the displays; my impression was of the usual CCTV scenes of the underground.

"OK," I said and nodded at the duffle. "When can I sort through my things?"

SHE HAD ME spread everything out on the table and took less than half a minute to decide that only the duffle itself had to be confiscated. I told her how thrilled I was.

"Don't worry, we can give you a replacement," she replied, ignoring my sarcasm, and stood up. "We're done here."

The door opened and one of the men who had taken me into custody at King's Cross appeared with an overnighter on wheels. She took it from him and rolled it over to me.

"Everything should fit in there," she said, pushing the handle at me.

I frowned down at it. The case was brand new, better-made than what I usually bought from street-vendors, and a shade of fuchsia that could only be described as audible.

"Did someone lose this or was there a sale?" I asked as I re-packed my things.

"We have a supplier who specializes in neutral contingency goods. Of course, now that it's yours, it's yours. Not neutral."

"Of course." I was about to add a smart remark about being careful not to lose it and then shut up. Some things you can never keep track of and some things you never lose. I had a feeling this fuchsia horror belonged to the latter group, not just for me personally but also in general. I'd be hard to miss, wheeling this thing around.

THE TWO TRANSIT officers took me back to the entry hall and deposited me on the other side of the turnstiles. If I wanted to get back in, it would cost me another fare and possibly a penalty for not swiping my card when I'd exited.

Maybe I could persuade a sympathetic ticket-seller I'd just made a mistake. Joining a queue for one of the windows, I reached into the back pocket of my jeans for my travel card; the small vinyl wallet came up nestled between the pages of Tommy's passport.

For a moment, I could only stare, dumbfounded. Then I retreated to a spot against a far wall to ponder this new development. I didn't remember putting Tommy's passport in my back pocket. It was the sort of absentminded thing I might do with my own passport – I checked my other back pocket and found my travel card. My own passport was still in my shoulder bag, but not Tommy's. I didn't even remember taking it out of the plastic bag but apparently I had. Good thing I hadn't put it in the duffel or it would have been confiscated.

I took another look in my shoulder bag, where I'd stashed the cardboard camera. To prevent any more damage, not to hide it. Not really. Good thing they had only searched the duffel. Apparently they hadn't thought to search anything else, or maybe they couldn't without just cause. Not wanting to provide some now, I put both passport and camera out of sight quickly before I got back into the line for the ticket window.

The woman behind the counter nodded wearily as I told her I wasn't sure I swiped my travel card properly. She held it against a sensor and then frowned at something on a monitor. She took it out of the vinyl wallet and tried again, touching the sensor with the front and then the back. The result made her frown deepen.

"Is something wrong?" I asked, getting nervous.

She shook her head. "How long've you had this card?"

"I'm not sure," I said, bracing myself for another walk between two large transit cops. "Is there something wrong with it?"

"Sometimes funny things happen with these cards. Computers, you know? What do you want to put on it?"

"Twenty pounds," I said without thinking as I fished a note out of my left-hand pocket.

"Don't forget to swipe in *and* out." She smiled cheerfully as she slipped the card into the well below the bottom of the window along with my receipt and the wallet.

I thanked her and all but ran for the turnstiles.

I WAS SO nervous thinking transit cops were going to descend on me again at any moment that I didn't realize I was on the wrong train until I heard the recorded voice announce I was bound for Uxbridge – *after* the doors had closed, of course. Not a problem; the Piccadilly Line didn't divide until Acton Town. I looked up at the Tube map above the windows to check the number of stops between there and King's Cross and was startled to see that every station between Russell Square and Hyde Park Square was marked as closed for repairs.

When had *that* happened and how had I missed it? Well, I knew how I'd missed it. I'd been more than a little pre-occupied. And I'd taken a cab home from the airport. Since then –

Since then, I hadn't been in the Underground. I hadn't taken the Tube for any reason since before Tommy and I had left on holiday. I stood up to take a closer look at the closed stations.

They had all been carefully stickered-over; each one had a notice in small capital letters giving the estimated re-opening as November 2014. Except for Covent Garden which said, CLOSURE PERMANENT.

I could actually feel the blood draining out of my face. I fell into my seat and leaned forward, resting my elbows on my knees.

"Are you all right?" asked the woman sitting opposite me.

"Fine." I raised my head slightly to look at her. "Just got up too fast."

Not the most believable excuse but neither she nor any of the few other people nearby said anything else.

WHEN A TUBE station is closed for any reason, Tommy had told me, the trains pass through without stopping but at reduced speed. I'd asked why.

A train whooshing through an empty station at top speed would create a vacuum, he'd said. Solemn but with a twinkle in his eye. *And that would suck.*

The memory coupled with the sight of the empty platform at Holborn sent an intense, aching loneliness through me. There was nothing else to see – the track is pretty far removed from the rest of the station. As we came to Covent Garden, I got up to peer through the doors, hands cupped on either side of my head.

A wood hoarding took up most of the platform, all the way to the yellow safety line. Through a few small square cut-outs, I caught brief glimpses of shelving, electronic equipment, and someone in a jumpsuit holding up what might have been an iPad (a tablet computer, anyway) and talking to someone I couldn't see.

Leicester Square was being re-tiled by a squad of people too busy to look as the train went through; likewise Piccadilly Circus.

The brightly-lit platform at Green Park was empty and the walls had been stripped of any and all decoration. The train slowed to a crawl and then came to a complete stop. I waited for the usual recording about a short delay. Instead, the doors opened.

"This train terminates here," a cheerful male voice said politely. "Service is suspended. All change."

NONE OF THE forty or so other people on the platform with me seemed surprised or put out as the train closed its doors and left. Maybe this station wasn't closed after all, I thought and looked for the familiar WAY OUT sign.

There wasn't one. I walked the length of the platform twice, just to make sure but there was no WAY OUT or EXIT or THIS WAY TO THE EGRESS. The one opening off the platform had an iron gate drawn across it. I gave it a shake just to make sure it was really locked before wandering down to the far end of the platform, dragging my fuchsia horror behind me.

"Something wrong?"

The young guy who had spoken was probably in his twenties, although he looked about fifteen to me. His head was shaved except at the crown and in front, leaving a longish, slightly floppy shock of dyed black hair. There was a silver ring through his left eyebrow, his right nostril, and the centre of his lower lip; quite a contrast to the expensive-looking, possibly bespoke three-piece grey suit, not to mention the *Financial Times* folded up under his arm. Ten years from now, I thought, this would be the dress code for bank presidents.

"What are we supposed to do now?" I asked. "Just wait?"

He nodded.

"But what if someone doesn't want to wait?"

"Then someone could take an alternative route."

"What alternative? There's no way off this platform," I said. "Unless there's an invisible emergency exit –"

He smiled faintly as his gaze moved from me to something behind me. I turned to see what was so interesting. Another gate, only waist high; the sign on it said, DANGER – NO PASSENGERS BEYOND THIS POINT. I slung my shoulder bag diagonally across my body and clambered over the barrier.

As I leaned over to lift my suitcase, he pulled the gate open for me. "It's not locked. And you shouldn't bend over to pick things up," he added, rolling the suitcase around to me. "Lift from your knees." He did a small plié to demonstrate.

"Thanks." I peered down the dark tunnel, then turned back to him. "You wouldn't happen to have a flashlight, would you?"

He gave a small, silent laugh and ambled away, unfolding the *Financial Times*. None of the other people on the platform so much as glanced in my direction. I decided not to push my luck, in case one of them suddenly decided to be hallway – excuse me, tubeway – monitor, and hurried down a small flight of steps to track level.

A few feet in, I found a recessed area in the tunnel wall with a walkway just wide enough for one person. Built for maintenance workers, I figured, so they wouldn't get smeared the length of the Underground by a passing train while on the job. The fuchsia horror was almost too wide, however. I had to push it ahead of me to keep the outer wheel from falling off the edge, and even then it wasn't easy. It was also dark. Small blue lights set into the walls on either side at semi-regular intervals showed only where the tunnel curved to one side or the other, or slanted up or down, but provided no real illumination. By the time I began to seriously consider turning back, the opening to the platform behind me was out of sight.

Going back would be easy, I told myself, just a matter of following the lights and putting one foot in front of the other.

But if I couldn't see the platform I had left, I might as well go on. Somewhere up ahead was another platform and I had to come to it eventually. I might even get there before a train came along –

As if on cue, I felt the walkway vibrate under my feet.

My heart simultaneously tried to leap into my throat and dive for my stomach. I had to stop and lean against the wall, which I thought was probably what I ought to do while the train passed: hug the wall, remain still, keep my balance.

A train whooshing through an empty station at top speed would create a vacuum, said Tommy's voice in my head. Solemn but with a twinkle in his eye. *And that would suck.*

You know what also sucks? demanded another voice in my head, this one my own. *Dying because you're too stupid to live!*

Almost directly over my head, a green light lit up, blinked, and then changed to yellow. Twenty feet ahead, another yellow light appeared above a flashing green arrow pointing to the right. Now I could hear the train; the sound was getting louder *very* quickly and the whole tunnel seemed to be shaking. With nothing to lose, I started to run toward the flashing arrow, pushing the suitcase ahead of me.

The fuchsia horror immediately rolled off the walkway. I let it go.

Abruptly, the tunnel flooded with light. I saw the tracks, the gleaming metal of the rails, some sections looking almost unused, thick black cables strung along the walls and finally the opening in the wall below the flashing arrow. I ran faster, thinking I felt the push of air at my back and the walkway moving under my feet as if it were folding against the wall.

That was exactly what it was doing. In the train headlight, I could see how sections were snapping up flush with the wall, the progression coming toward me while sections lifted quickly enough under my feet to scrape my shoes.

I made it to the opening barely a second ahead of the train and threw myself sideways, hoping there'd be something to hold onto so I wouldn't get sucked out again.

The full-blast roar of the train damped down sharply to a muffled thumping. Lights flickered on; a panel had slid closed behind me. Pretty good sound-proofing, I thought as I got to my feet and brushed myself off. Just as I turned around and saw the panel of numbered buttons, there was the slight unmistakable jolt of an elevator stopping. The door in front of me slid back to show a blank, windowless outer door.

I hesitated, looking at the buttons. They went from 0 to 8. Impulsively, I pressed 8; nothing happened. Pressing all the other buttons had the same effect. I finally gave up and tried the outer door.

It opened into a low-ceilinged hall full of people, their voices and footsteps echoing as they got on or off the escalators I could see several yards opposite of where I stood. There were three escalators but only two were working. The one on the left was blocked by a small barricade with a sign that said, *Nepoužívejte*. Not a language I knew but it seemed vaguely familiar. Then, over the heads of the people moving in and out of an archway on my left, I saw the dull metallic gleam of a curved wall covered with a metallic pattern of large, round indentations – or were they bubbles?

I felt that dropping sensation in my middle again and had to lean against the wall. This was Prague. Tommy and I had talked about spending a week or two here a few years back and we had looked at videos online.

Only it couldn't be. It wasn't possible to walk into an Underground tunnel in London and emerge in Prague.

Of course, it also wasn't possible to steal your husband from yourself and go off to live an alternate life, either.

I tried to open the door I had just come out of but it wouldn't budge, as if it had been cemented shut behind me.

Tommy's passport and the travel card were still in my back pocket, along with my own passport. And the fuchsia horror was probably confetti. And –

Was *she* here with Tommy? Was that why I was here? I needed a guide. I wasn't even sure what day it was, any more.

I was still wondering what to do when a train arrived at the platform on my left. Before I was even aware of my intention, I joined the flow of people and boarded the red, white, and silver train. As it pulled out, the name Staroměstská slid past the windows.

Two stops later, I got off at a station called Muzeum for no other reason than I could pronounce it easily. This station was much larger, the platforms open; no metallic décor, just tiling. Even the train itself looked different. No, it *was* different – red and silver, with dark grey, almost black sliding doors. Apparently, my powers of observation were starting to fail me. If Tommy had been with me –

All at once, I was on the verge of bursting into tears. I was in the middle of a strange city with no idea how I'd gotten there or how to get back and I was no closer to finding Tommy.

And what would I do if I did find him? What would I say? *Darling, you've been living with my evil twin. I'm here to rescue you and take you back to your* real *life.* Yeah, that sounded completely plausible.

Maybe I could show him the passport, the one that belonged to the man who had died in New York. He'd see that it was a real passport, not a forgery. That would get his attention. That was assuming I could actually find him, of course. If he was even in Prague.

He must be. Not only that, there must still be some kind of connection between us. Why else would I have emerged here instead of Barcelona or Tokyo or Stockholm or anywhere else in the world?

Barcelona. Tokyo. Stockholm. The names echoed in my head. Like Prague, these were all places Tommy and I had never been to together. And she would know that, I thought, just by looking at his passport. Or by asking an innocent-sounding question like, *Where would you like to go that we've never been before?* And now she was going to take him to those places, one by one, forging a new, stronger connection between the two of them. I had to find him soon before my bond with him withered away.

A shadow fell over me. I looked up to see one of the beefy transit cops who had taken me off the train at King's Cross. My heart skipped a beat, then stumbled, as if it had forgotten its own rhythm. Instead of dragging me off, however, the man sat down next to me.

"Relax. I'm off duty." His voice was low both in tone and volume but still full; *solid* is the only word I can think of to describe it.

I frowned. "You're still in uniform."

"I haven't been home yet." He let out a long breath that wasn't quite a sigh. "And neither have you. Am I right?"

"How did you find me?"

"Your travel card."

"I didn't use *my* travel card."

He gave me a Look. "The card you used. You're on CCTV, swiping it to gain entry."

"I should be on CCTV putting twenty quid on it, too," I said.

He shrugged. "That transaction was legal. It didn't raise any flags."

"But my using it did?"

He chuckled a little. "You're out of place. And you know it."

"My travel card worked just fine. Besides, people out of place aren't your department. Or so I was told."

He smiled, leaning his elbows on his knees and lowering his head so we were closer to being eye-to-eye. "All right, the card's out of place. You're outside the zones that card is good for."

"I haven't tried to leave the station," I said. "As long as I stay on this side of the turnstiles, no one'll know the difference."

"You and your boyfriend do that a lot – ride out to zone six on a card good only as far as zone three and hang around inside the station, feeling smug?"

"He's not my boyfriend, he's my husband. And if we'd wanted to leave the station, we could have paid the difference at a window by the gate. But we didn't break any rules so why would we feel smug?"

The cop frowned thoughtfully. "Hmph. Then maybe it's just him."

I didn't like the sound of that; neither did the hair on the back of my neck. "What do you mean?"

"Your boyfriend – excuse me, husband – has been fooling around with this sort of thing for a while. Testing the limits. Stepping out of bounds just a little bit here and there where nothing showed or not enough so anyone would notice, anyway But then he got a little bolder, or needed a bigger thrill. People started noticing funny things –"

"What kind of funny things?" I asked. "Give me some examples."

"OK. You get on a train up front thinking that's closest to the way out at whatever stop you're getting off at you find out the exit's all the way at the other end of the platform. Or you notice someone getting on at one stop and then the same person gets on again three stops later and you put it down to déjà-vu."

"Or a glitch in the you-know-what," I said chuckling.

His frown deepened. "What?"

"You guys don't get to the movies much, do you? Never mind," I added, "it's not important. Those examples you gave me have simple and very ordinary explanations. And even if they didn't, I don't see how they could be connected to anything Tommy did. Whatever he did. If he even did anything, which I don't think he did."

"You know how everything has an equal and opposite reaction?" he asked, sounding a bit weary. "Well, reactions have other reactions, which have other reactions, and so on and so forth. And sometimes, those reactions lead up to some kind of very undesirable event so someone makes an adjustment to compensate. The idea is to steer the chain of reactions away from catastrophe and, ideally, back into the sequence of events the original was supposed to occur in. Follow?"

"I don't know," I said, wishing I didn't.

"The compensating mechanism is pretty much automated but we have to keep an eye on it anyway because you never know for sure where something will lead. With some disturbances, you have to compensate for compensations to a dozen levels before everything comes out right."

"And Tommy's been causing disturbances?"

"For some time now."

"Can't be my Tommy. It must have been the one who got hit by the train in New York."

The cop chuckled again. "What makes you think that wasn't your Tommy?"

"The clothes. The shoes. The –"

"Ever think he might be trading off with the other guy?"

My jaw dropped.

"Other *guys*, I should say. His field's computers, right? He's experimenting with the program, trying out all kinds of alternatives to see the different outcomes. I'm sorry, I can see it's a blow. I wasn't supposed to tell you. If anybody knew, I'd get written up, maybe even suspended."

"Why did you tell me?" I asked him, feeling nauseated.

"Because the guy's trouble and you had that look in your eye."

"What look?"

"The one that says you're not gonna let go of this until you get some answers or fix it or both. I hate to see clever people wasting their time on something they can't do anything about."

"He's my husband."

"I'm sorry to say you ended up with the one that fell under a train."

"But I wasn't supposed to –"

He shrugged. "It wasn't out of the realm of possibilities. So technically, yeah, you're supposed to have a live one. But who's to say he wasn't going to fall under a train at some point?"

"If that happens, I'll deal with it. But I want the one I started out with."

The cop straightened up and let out a sigh. "Of course you do. And you're not giving up, are you?"

I shook my head.

"Well, I tried. If you can get him while he's still Underground, you might have a chance. Once he leaves the station aboveground, he's out of your reach."

"Why?"

"Different department. They've got all their own rules out there and nobody understands them. Which means this station is out of the question. He's already come through here with y – *her*."

"What if he comes back in?"

"Doesn't matter. If he left a station and you stayed behind, that station's out of play. You'll have to catch him at another one. If you can." He pushed himself to his feet. "Sure you wouldn't rather come have a beer with me? Pilsner-Urqell on tap is really nice. Or maybe you're a wine person. Wine's good, too."

My jaw dropped again. This had all been a roundabout way of picking me up?

"Hey, I don't make a habit of this," he added, his face reddening. "I told you, I hate to see people wasting their time on lost causes."

"I'm flattered but I'll decide if my cause is lost or not, thanks all the same." I said.

"Well, if you ever do…" He spread his hands.

"I'll hang onto the travel card."

"I tried," he said again and walked off, disappearing down an escalator a few yards away.

I really was flattered but I was more concerned with what he'd told me about Tommy and underground stations. Which stations in Prague, I wondered, had he stayed in without exiting?

The ones he had only passed through, of course. But which

ones were those? I looked around and caught sight of the signs hanging from the ceiling showing all the stops on the line with Muzeum highlighted.

When we had talked about going to Prague, Tommy and I had looked into staying in or near the old city. So we'd have gotten on the Metro at Staroměstská or the one before it Malostranskà. But we wouldn't have gotten off at Müstek.

So what could I do now – hang around the Müstek station watching the trains, looking for them? I'd be pioneering an entirely new form of train-spotting. Too bad I didn't have an anorak.

Some impulse made me look in my shoulder bag as if I were making sure one hadn't suddenly materialized in there and I saw the camera.

I pulled it out, holding it tightly. It felt important but I had no idea why or how. It was just a disposable film camera, half the roll exposed with photos Tommy had taken. I started to choke up and then stopped. No, not Tommy, not exactly. Tommy but not my Tommy. As long as they didn't rub off on me like *she* had rubbed off on Tommy –

Unbidden, the idea sprang up fully formed in my mind. The camera and the passport were really her property. She had taken nothing with her when she had slipped into my life with Tommy except whatever had been on her person that day. By the time she and Tommy had gone home – to her home – had she rubbed off on our belongings the way she had on Tommy? Or had the airline conveniently lost their luggage? That would have left her with fewer things that didn't belong in her life, small things easy to dispose of and easy to replace. No muss, no fuss, and no embarrassing moments with bus drivers or transit cops.

She'd done this before, I realized. Swapped out her husband for a different model. She must have. It was working too well to be sheer dumb luck.

My stomach did another slow forward roll and then twisted sharply. Migod, *was it always because hers died?*

Was Tommy that accident-prone in her life? Or was she killing him?

I hugged myself, trying to control my trembling. In a small part of my mind, the rational explanation was forming line by line as if it were coming out of a mental printer: widow unable to accept the reality of her husband's death, delusions, hallucinations, memory loss, black-outs, fugue states, episodes of jamais-vu, in need of serious professional help even hospitalization grief does funny things to people grief does funny things to people grief does funny things funny things funny things funny funny things –

She was in such a hurry, I almost missed her. As it was, seeing her running across the platform alone surprised me so much I almost missed getting on the train with her. Where was Tommy? I wondered, watching her from the far end of the metro car. Surely she couldn't have gotten rid of him already?

Maybe she hadn't meant to. Maybe the ones she stole kept dying on her because she was supposed to be a widow? Crazy idea but crazy was the standard I lived by now. Crazy was the new sane. Grief did funny things to people and funny things happened when someone got hit by a train and when you thought about it, life itself was really just a whole series of funny things, one right after another, ready or not.

I looked down to find I had one hand in my shoulder bag, holding onto the disposable camera. I took it out and held it up to look at her through the viewfinder.

She was looking at her phone, for no good reason I could think of. It was fancier than mine but not fancy enough for service down here. Checking her calendar, then, or she might have a lot of tourist information loaded –

GPS. Or something like it. That was how she'd found him. She probably knew where the nearest one was at any time.

A plan was trying to take shape in my mind. Still holding the camera, I moved a bit closer to where she was standing, hoping I wouldn't somehow draw her attention. She seemed to be unaware of me. And why not? She probably figured I was back home in London wearing black and crying myself to sleep every night.

I got within half a carriage-length of her before the train pulled into Müstek. Only a few people got off but, to my dismay, she was one of them. I trotted along several feet behind her, trying to think of what to do. Was she meeting Tommy here? Inside the station or outside? Or were they staying nearby?

She stepped onto an escalator and, scared I would lose her, I got on almost directly behind her. Just as we reached the top, there was a blast of live music as a rather unlikely five-piece band – saxophone, accordion, clarinet, and flute, led by a trumpet-player – launched into something I couldn't identify but which sounded complex and more than a little frenzied. A crowd started to gather and I narrowly missed bumping into her when she decided to stop and listen, instead crushing the toes of an older man and dropping that stupid camera. He picked it up and gave it back to me with a good-natured smile, waving away my apologies and assuring me in perfect, elegant English that I hadn't crippled him.

Keeping my back to her, I moved toward the outer edge of the crowd and found a couple of tall tourists to hide behind. She was still there, applauding with everyone else as the trumpet player did a few dance steps. If the collection of instruments was unusual, the band was even more so. The woman on saxophone was in full traditional Indian dress, including bindi; the accordion-player was at least eighty, the boy playing clarinet must have been cutting elementary school and the flute-player had apparently just come from her ballet class.

And their trumpet-playing leader, I realized, bore a strong resemblance to a certain transit cop.

I looked around but saw only Czech police and none of them resembled anyone I knew. If they were enjoying the music, they weren't giving anything away, but then it was probably inappropriate to smile while holding an automatic weapon. Terrorism had apparently spoiled things everywhere. I was glad I didn't have that suitcase to worry about. Abruptly, I pushed forward into the crowd again until there were only a few people between her and me and tapped a young student-type guy on the shoulder.

"Excuse me, do you speak English?" When he nodded, I pushed the camera at him with one hand while pointing her out with the other. "That lady right there – yes, her, next to the man in the tan jacket – she dropped this just as she got off the train. Can you pass it over to her, please?"

Smiling, he did so without asking why I couldn't manage this rather simple task myself. I should have walked off immediately without looking back but I was too curious. I wanted to see if she would recognize it and how she would react if she did.

She had it in her hands before she quite realized it and I could see she knew exactly what she was holding. Her face went pale and took on a pinched expression as she looked around frantically. I ducked down, pretended to tie my shoe for a few seconds and stayed bent over as if I were searching my shoulder bag for something as I pushed my way out of the crowd. The music had stopped and people were applauding, cheering and whistling. It took every bit of willpower I had not to turn around and see what she was doing now.

I had almost passed the Czech police officer men when I had another idea.

"Excuse me, sir," I said, putting on a pained expression, "do you speak English? Oh, good. I saw an American tourist do an awful thing on the train just now and I'm not sure who to tell about it. She knocked down an older lady on the train and took her bag. The older lady couldn't get off the train to catch her." I described her and the purse she was carrying in detail and pointed toward the crowd.

He told me to wait. I didn't. I had no idea whether he'd arrest her on the spot or simply question her for a few minutes, then let her go when he saw I had skipped. Either way, I would get out of the station before she did, which meant I could use my phone first.

It rang as I was taking it out of my shoulder bag. Tommy. *OK, now let's see what kind of 'funny things' happen to you, bitch,* I thought, grinning as I flipped the phone open. "Hello, darling," I sang.

For a moment, there was silence. Then a male voice, strangely familiar in spite of the heavy Czech accent said, "It is urgent that I speak with a friend or family member of the man whose phone this is. There has been... an incident..."

ON ALL LONDON UNDERGROUND LINES

Adam L. G. Nevill

Adam L.G. Nevill is a writer whose star is very much in the ascendant. Already he has two highly regarded novels to his name – Banquet for The Damned and Apartment 16 – and is being lauded as a strong new voice in horror. What's always impressed me about Adam's writing is that while he undoubtedly brings something new to the feast, his work is very much rooted in the traditions and tropes of supernatural fiction. Rather than going for the shock and gore methods of modern Hollywood horror, Adam will lure you in with whispered promises of dark delicacies. 'On All London Underground Lines' shows Nevill at his very best, exploring the familiar through a glass darkly.

"THERE IS A good service running on all London Underground lines."

There are too many of us down here.

"Scuse me. Scuse me," a voice cracked by age says to my left. A face with yellowish teeth is turned towards me.

No. Not now. Please. Can't you see I'm in a hurry.

The smile I turn to the woman is too tight, and has become a grimace. I think I'm showing too many teeth, like her.

"I was wondering if you could tell me which way to the Piccadilly Line," she says. Her hair is brittle; the perm a carapace of dead coral that could be snapped off. The face is deeply lined, like it's gone through a pane of glass. But I doubt there is any blood in that head. No make-up on it either. She's really let herself go. This London lifestyle is hard on women: all this rushing about underground with long hours of pressure and stress between journeys; their impossible aspirations for professional advancement in this recession; their ambition to find the right man and start a family; the need for peer approval, status, glamour, fulfilment. It makes them mad, then mummifies them. Once the hair's gone all wiry like this, with tufts of grey and odd patches of orange mixed in, sprouting like the trees on a model railway, it's all over. And then they're just slow nuisances down here, asking for directions.

I'm too thick-headed with dehydration to think of anything to say to her, let alone form any words into a sentence. Inside I'm dry, my joints are stiff and my muscles ache. I need to sleep more. I forget what it was she asked of me. Thoughts of bottled water I can buy from a concession at Victoria Station spur me on, toward the end of the platform.

A page from a free newspaper catches on my shin, clings and flaps at the same time, makes me kick that leg out. It won't come off. I have to turn around and let it slide down and over my shoe.

The woman speaks to another man. "Scuse me, scuse me." He is sitting down, bent over his lap, on a bench at the back of the platform. He doesn't move. Maybe he's asleep. I suddenly remember her question.

"Central Line, eastbound," I call to the woman. "To Holborn. Change there."

All I can see in her face is incomprehension. She wants to tell me something. Her question was just a ruse. How can a face be so grey? She returns to her position beside the intercom where passengers are invited to call for assistance. She depresses the green button. No one answers. I don't think the service is working. I have a vague memory of depressing that green button myself, a long time ago, but no one answered.

"Scuse me. Scuse me," she says into it.

From my position on the Central Line eastbound platform,

at Oxford Circus, I can see the queue for the Victoria Line Southbound has already begun in the distance. The delay on the Victoria Line must be colossal if they're all waiting on this platform. I could just fall to my knees and weep.

When I get closer to the queue, I am confronted by a wall of slumped shoulders. Are the people all standing still or are they shuffling forward, one step at a time, to reach the distant platform promised to them on the stained direction board above their bowed heads? It's hard to tell. And how long have they been waiting to ascend anyway?

I'll have to take the Bakerloo Line to Embankment and then pick up the Circle Line to Victoria. If I don't, at this rate, I'll be hopelessly late for work. Again.

I can just squeeze up the side of the staircase. None of the pale faces in the crush even turn to look at me; they are committed to their immobile futile yearning upwards. A smell hangs about the crowd, like old clothes left in airless spaces, and something else: the sweetish hormoney smell of meat just spoiling.

At the top of the staircase, I duck into the tunnel forking left and head for the next staircase that should lead to the Bakerloo Line. I follow the curved roof, discoloured like a long empty swimming pool, arching over a scattering of figures that appear to have come to a halt under the flickering strip lights. They are moving, but not progressing, as if lost. Confused perhaps. No time to find out. Fuck them; I have a train to catch.

I duck to miss the wires that hang through an aluminium mesh. Surely that is not safe? I wipe the face of my watch and check the time: 9:15am.

"Shit. Damn."

I have fifteen minutes to be at my desk. Not going to happen. I have at least twenty minutes underground ahead of me, and then a fifteen minute walk from Victoria to the office. At this rate, I'll be lucky if I'm in by ten. My chest is tight with so much frustration I've given myself indigestion, or heartburn. I feel weak. When did I last eat?

The air is hot and thin in the tunnel housing the second staircase. I can smell sweat in it, and something like an old pair of curtains ruined by damp in a garage I once investigated as a child. At the foot of the stairs a small woman gets in my way and brings me to a sighing halt. She is trying to lift a suitcase on wheels up to the next step. The terrible smell is coming out of her case. Ordinarily I would stop and help, but I am in a rush and can't waste a moment.

I climb the second flight of stairs on my tight thighs and enter a connecting tunnel that will lead to the Bakerloo Line platforms.

The lights are so dim in the tunnel I bump into someone coming the other way. Neither of us apologises and we both rush on, but I can still feel the impression of his bony elbow against my ribs, as he can feel mine in his.

Temporarily bewildered by the collision and bad light, I tread on something that crunches under my foot. Looking down into the silty shadows around my feet, I see a shape huddled into itself against the wall. I've stepped on its leg. I can see a flip-flop and some kind of robe extending across the floor from the side of the tunnel. But whatever I stepped my entire weight onto made the sound of a handful of breadsticks being snapped in half. I look down. Wince. "Sorry."

Does the head wrapped so tightly in the dirty scarf look up at me, or is it not bothered? In the thin light I'm reminded of a balloon I once covered in wallpaper paste and strips of newspaper at school, before painting it. Within days the balloon was punctured and removed, leaving a dry and hollow head behind that I didn't want to take home with me, and was glad to see crushed into a bin that smelled of orange peel and pencil shavings. This head doesn't have defined eyes either. They look papery and flat in their sharp-edged sockets. But something moves under the robes. An arm extends, I think, and then drops to the grubby tiles upon which the figure sits. The hand clatters as if it is holding dice.

At the end of the tunnel, the platform marked Bakerloo Eastbound is thick with commuters, who don't seem to be making much progress into the waiting train. I assume they waiting for people to alight from the carriages first.

Between their motionless bodies I can see the vanilla light inside the stationary train carriages. Against the grimy windows, I can also see the back of the heads of those passengers lucky enough to be seated at this time of the morning. Some of the heads are dipped to read newspapers and books, or to just look down and away from all of those crammed around them. Who wants the sudden glare of a stranger's eyes in the enforced cohabitation of a Tube carriage?

I shuffle into a gap on the outside of the crowd on the platform, and make my way around the edges hoping to see a chink in the bodies through which I can get closer to an open carriage door. But I can't get near the train because each open door is encircled by a ring of immobile people looking for an opportunity to get on board themselves. No one seems to be alighting and there is no room on board for anymore bodies. The passengers inside the train, stood before the open doors, all look out in silence. No one meets anyone else's eye.

"Passengers are reminded to keep their belongings with them at all times."

The announcement is repeated twice, before I lose patience and ask the man closest to me, "What's up?"

But then I see the trickle of a white wire trailing from his ear and disappearing inside his overcoat. iPod. His overcoat has seen better days and I wonder why he doesn't brush the dandruff from the shoulders.

"Due to a person under a train the Jubilee Line is suspended in both directions."

Maybe there is a knock-on effect to the Bakerloo Line; I know how that terrible momentum of malfunction spreads down here.

I turn around and catch the eye of a young woman. I raise my eyebrows, and shake my head – the familiar sign of the thwarted London Underground passenger. But her face remains blank. And her skin is in a bad way, and it would be rude to stare for any longer than I already have. She wants no parlay anyway. Just wants to get going again and is standing still, with all of the others, quietly willing the Bakerloo Line trains to start moving again.

I look up at the digital display to see what that has to impart. It reads NO SMOKING AT ALL IN ANY PART OF THE STATION. Then it changes to inform us that the next train bound for Elephant and Castle is 7 MINS away.

Oh enough of this; I can't stand here for hours staring at a stationary train. This one will have to go and when the next train arrives, everyone already clustered at the edge of the platform will get on first. I'll have no chance.

I bump and sidle and squeeze my way back through the silent fixated crowd on the platform and go back into the tunnel to check progress on the Victoria Line. Maybe the crush will have cleared by now.

Back inside the darkened connecting tunnel three indistinct figures are walking very slowly in front of me, and abreast of each other so no one can pass in either direction. Tourists no doubt. No etiquette. Ambling in rush hour, unsure of where they are going. Just blithely unaware of the needs of those who actually work in the city. Walk on the left for fuck's sake, in single file. The whole system would fail if we all took this attitude.

I try to step around them, but end up on my toes, overbalancing and clipping the heels of the figure on the left. She must be infirm or elderly because the merest touch of my toe against her heel makes her stumble forward, raising her arms on either side of her hunched body, like she's trying to keep her feet on ice.

Have I hurt her? Her? Is it a woman, with those thin legs ending in some kind of white sports shoe? She's wearing a skirt too, I think. It's hard to see. The other two stop and turn their heads to the side to watch their companion totter like a child taking baby steps away from a parent's hands. They say nothing.

"Sorry. Please. Excuse me," I say, but the two upright figures don't react beyond turning their faces, that I cannot see properly, toward me. I sense animosity within the silhouettes of their heads, or defiance, and possibly outrage at being rushed.

Am I being inconsiderate, or unnecessarily aggressive? I pause to examine my behaviour. But then they all start milling about on the spot as if the interruption or change in direction is disorientating for them. One of them looks at the ceiling as if trying to remember a distant event in its life, and sighs. With slow and deliberate movements, they seem to spread further apart, while still leaving no easy way through. I reach out to help the figure I have knocked aside.

"Sorry," I say again.

But I quickly retrieve my hand when my fingers encircle what I take to be something hard, but no thicker than a flute, inside the thin sleeve of a blouse. And even though the tunnel is only illumined by the ambient light spilling down from the Bakerloo line platform, I am sure the figure I have touched has just bent forward at the waist and tried to bite my retreating hand. I hear the sound of something clacking, like two domino pieces in a wooden box. I take a step back and away.

All three of them have turned to watch me now.

"You're walking three abreast in rush hour. Jesus."

I push through them and continue on. Behind me, there is a moan, a shuffle of clothing and then a slapping sound like the palm of a hand on a ceramic surface. Back there someone is moaning now too. I turn around at the end of the short tunnel and peer back, guiltily, into the darkness I have emerged from. Against the distant semi-circle of white light at the far end of the tunnel, I can only see one of the figures standing upright now, its head tatty, like an old man with unkempt hair grown long at the sides.

I go past the squat woman with the big suitcase on wheels; it's still on the first step and she is just staring at it now.

Tough shit. Why bring something that size down here? I'm supposed to put my back out heaving it up the stairs? Those cases are always heavy enough to be carrying an anchor or an anvil inside. You might be on holiday, but some of us have to get to work, dear.

The crowd eager to get on the Victoria Line Southbound are still as they were when I passed them minutes before. Still huddled together, with their heads lowered, the wedge of bodies stretches from one side of the staircase to the other. The only difference I can infer now, is that they are packed even tighter together and the sense of brittle impatience has risen to the point when someone will soon start shoving. Those at the back all look as if their hair could do with a good wash and comb.

Maybe I should go back to the Bakerloo Line East platform and walk to its farthest end. Why didn't I think of that before? At the far end of that platform I will be able to cut through to the Victoria Line Southbound, and then arrive on the opposite end of the platform to the crush on the stairs here.

I turn about and re-enter the darkened tunnel. Mercifully, there is no sign of the three old figures I confronted. And anyway, in the lightless tunnel, they will not recognise me as I pass. But half way along the tunnel, I become aware of voices close to the floor. A muttering. I look down and in the thin light I see the suggestion of a group of bodies huddled together and moving slowly. They are pressed into the wall and on all fours, groping forward as if searching for something that has been dropped.

Nothing has changed back on the Bakerloo Line platform either. The crowd of thwarted commuters standing about the open doors of the stationary train has not moved, and those I brush past at the rear of the platform mumble and totter. Inside the carriages, I catch sight of the same indifferent faces staring out of the same open doors; arrogant as if they are members of a superior social class because they are actually inside the train, while those on the platform can only look in at them with envious eyes. No one inside the train moves at all. They are perfectly motionless but still expectant, like manikins; dishevelled parodies of people in formal working attire, standing under the dusty yellow lights of a warehouse.

All of the benches at the rear of the platform are full of those tired of standing. Some lean into their neighbours, mouths open, eyes vacant. With no room on the seats I am soon stepping over those who have just sat down on the dirty tiled floor. Men in two-piece suits sit with their legs thrust out, socks showing, laces undone. They have such thin ankles. Scuffed briefcases are clutched by white fingers.

Up ahead I can hear the monotonous beat of some kind of drum. It makes a sound that is too hollow and feeble, like something old and cheap and worn in the music room of an impoverished school.

It is a busker making the noise, standing in the mouth of the interconnecting tunnel from the Bakerloo Line South to the Victoria Line South, no doubt getting in every one's way.

He is elderly and stooped over. He wears a black overcoat that once complimented a smart suit. His feet are wrapped in dirty bandages and he steps from one foot to the other as he beats a stained tambourine with a wooden peg. His hands look like cold chicken with see-through skin. The knuckles are so swollen I doubt he could do anything but the hopeless banging of the wooden stick against the tambourine. What I can see of his head is the same purple colour of a hairless baby mammal, save for a crown of white wisps at the base of his skull that trail over the collar of his overcoat. It must be the light that discolours his skin, or alcohol. An enamelled mug is positioned before his shuffling, side-to-side stepping feet. I peek inside and see the dull brass of a two pence coin.

Ahead of me in the connecting tunnel, a dozen or more scruffy people all seem to be walking from side to side too, but barely moving forward as if caught up in the primitive rhythm of the busker. I fall into the same rhythmic pattern of steps, and then wrench myself out of it, feeling hateful.

I strike out for the end of the tunnel and pick up my pace

until I am nearly running to the Victoria Line Platform. The sound of the drum follows me.

Under the arch to the Victoria Line platform, a figure is slumped on the floor. Looks like a woman has fainted. I can't see much beside a hand, liver-spotted with age, that trembles. Her body seems to be shivering, or is she crying? I don't have time to stop and check, and there are two people bent over her anyway, talking to her, so she is being looked after. But as I rush past they sound as if they are making the cooing sounds people make when feeding their pets.

"Passengers are reminded to stand behind the yellow line."

The Victoria Line Southbound platform is crammed with commuters at this end too. Every one of them has turned their head to the left and is staring into the dark tunnel from which the train will come. Their mouths hang open and are as dark inside as the tunnel they watch. They must all be hoping to see the distant headlights of the train, and are desperate to feel that sudden unnatural wind against their unsmiling faces, and to hear the distant scream of the tracks while static snaps beneath their soles.

There are far too many people on this platform for it to be safe. As I squeeze down the rear of the platform, I get a sense that a few figures have dropped from the edge and on to the tracks. It must be an illusion because I hear no sound of them landing on the gravel and rails below, and those figures that appeared to topple didn't even flail or put their arms out.

Everyone here must be worn out by the wait because no one is talking at all for the entire length of the crowded platform. I look up in desperation at the electronic information board. It looks like it could do with a good clean, because the amber letters and digits are hard to make out under the dross. Eventually I figure out that it informs ALL STATIONS TO BRIXTON – 1 MIN.

I wait for a lot longer than one minute, with my head turned left with all of the others, staring at the black mouth of the empty tunnel. I wait long enough for my neck to ache and for someone to faint further down the platform, because I hear what sounds like a sack full of sticks rattling to the floor, and a brief commotion as if the fainter has taken at least three people down with them.

My eyes start to burn and smart and I have so little energy left I do wonder if I should just stand here for a while longer and try to regain some strength.

"Due to a signal failure at Blackfriars, the District Line is suspended in both directions. Passengers are advised to seek other forms of transport."

I close my eyes for a while. My chest goes hot, my teeth grind. I need to make a call to the office and tell them that I just can't get through.

I'll have to go up to street level to get a signal on my phone. And I'm getting nowhere here; it's time for a change of plan anyway. The Northern Line. I need to get out of this station and walk down Oxford Street to Tottenham Court Road Station. From there I can travel southbound on the Northern Line to Embankment and pick up the Circle Line to Victoria.

I bump my way from the Victoria Line platform, apologising quietly as I go, but no one acknowledges me, and I re-enter the tunnel between the Victoria and Bakerloo lines. The busker is still stepping from side to side on his dirty cloth feet and those in the tunnel seem unaware that they are performing basic imbecilic dance steps to the beat of his filthy tambourine.

I side-wind through them, and then rush through another arch that leads into another tunnel that also seems to have problems with its lights. These flicker, cut out, then sputter back to life for a few seconds. I look up and spot a sign that says WAY OUT.

A tall blonde woman strides out of the darkness toward me. She is wearing a tight-fitting suit. The tipped heels of her stilettos click-clack a staccato that fills the tunnel and seems to echo for miles underground. Even in the unstable light I can see the definition of her sharp bone structure, and the imperious cast of a face set with a purpose no greater than self-importance. Some eye-candy nonetheless and something to relieve this interminable search underground.

I get ready to quickly admire her before she passes me and strides away, but as she draws level and the flickering light strikes her, I see that under closer scrutiny she is not the young fire-fox I presumed she was. With that posture, that chin held so high, those cold beautiful eyes, that tight tapering skirt and those feet mounted on pedestals with heels like blades, how could I have been so wrong?

Her hair is not blonde, but white. The dead white of a pantomime wig. The haughty catwalk face is actually a skull with aged parchment stretched across it; a dry surface freshly painted with a palette more suited to the circus clown than the city girl. I also catch sight of a shrivelled ear and a neck loosely papered with a brownish skin. She must be some kind of drug addict or former vamp with an eating disorder, because I have never seen legs so thin and the way her bracelets clatter about her bony wrists is disquieting.

The suit she wears was once chic too, but is now a dirty relic and she must have recently sat in something foul, because the scent of things left forgotten in the damp spaces beneath old houses drifts from her stained clothing. And that wig, or whatever it is that she has upon her mottled head, smells of something recently burnt.

She teeters down to the drummer, and before I turn my head around to face forward, I suffer the illusion that she has suddenly thrown her thin arms into the air, as if with joy, and shaken that terrible head about.

I'm so tired now my breath is too loud about my own head and if I don't drink water soon I am sure I will hallucinate and then faint. I think of the shrivelled organs of Pharaohs inside canopic jars up at the British museum. That's what my insides must look like.

"Due to a security alert at Barons Court, the Piccadilly Line is suffering severe delays in both directions."

I follow the illuminated sign that reads WAY OUT all the way to the broken escalators. A loosely assembled crowd stands and stares upward in disbelief at the motionless iron stairs. Half way up I can see a seated figure, surrounded by bags. It seems to have either collapsed or sat down with exhaustion. It is not moving at all.

Beside the escalator, there is a temporary sign indicating that we should PLEASE USE THE STAIRS. It is referring to the adjacent spiral staircase ascending to street-level, that also warns us with a sign that 139 STEPS will have to be climbed to leave the Underground by this route.

I bend double and place my hands on my knees. Can my journey get any worse? And this is not the first time this has happened; I have lost count of how many times this scenario or similar has repeated itself. The infrastructure seems to have collapsed in this city. And yet we still pay these prices.

I begin my ascent, slowly, with one hand clutching the cold rail on the inside of the staircase. With a monotonous and solemn slap of foot, a stream of people descend from above. Others join in my ascent and stand too close behind me, as if to hurry me upward. Round and round we all go.

I mostly look down at my shoes that need a good clean and polish. The toes of my shoes are scuffed like the shoes of a school boy who kicks stones about a building site. Even when this exhausted and thirsty and tired I'm still able to feel shame at how I've let my footwear go. But with all of this travelling and the hours I work, I don't have the headspace to even engage with such chores.

And when I do look up, the grey and miserable faces and the expressions so long with worry, that solemnly bob down the spiral staircase toward me just lower my spirits even further. Why do we go through with this? Have we forgotten what quality of life is? No one is smiling on the stairs.

I have to stop a few times to get my breath and there are moans of irritation from those close on my heels. Inside my suit, my back is wet with sweat. It is the last of my body's moisture leaking out. Little white dots speckle my vision. I feel dizzy. It passes.

When I eventually reach the top of the staircase, I trip over my own scruffy feet and stumble into the gassy yellow light of the station entrance. Can I not even walk in a straight line anymore?

The ticket office is in darkness and I can't see any station assistants. On the other side of the turnstiles, a thin bald man feeds coins into the ticket machine. He watches the coins ejected into the refund slot and appears mesmerised by a sound that reminds me of a seaside amusement arcade. He feeds the coins in again. The shoes he is wearing are far too big for his feet. They are a tan colour and clash with his navy suit. They have either come from a different decade, or have been taken from another man's feet.

A long queue has formed behind him. A woman looks over his shoulder and bites at her bottom lip, as if impatient to see what it is he has won from the machine.

A thick huddle of commuters all stand at the foot of each of the two staircases leading up to street level. They are silent, but I can tell they are impatient by the way they stretch their necks upwards and by how their mouths hang open. I swipe myself through the turnstile and go and join the back of the crowd. "What now?" I say out loud and surprise myself with the volume of my own voice. No one appears to be listening.

At the top of the stairs I can see that the steel grill is down. This is a measure the station staff undertake if too many people are crowding into the station during rush hour. It is designed to regulate the flow and volume of crowds. And there is a large crowd up there too. Between a backdrop of dark sky and the people on the stairs queuing to leave the station, I can see the silhouette of many heads close together and pale fingers pressing through the grill from the other side, where the commuters who are trying to get into the station have raised their arms to hang on to the steel roller grill.

I pause to marvel at how dark it remains outside, long into these London winter mornings. I thought the sun would be up by now.

But this is just hopeless; no one can get in or out of this station through here. I march across to the ticket office. I can see little behind the glass of either counter. There might be someone in the chair, but I'm not sure. Maybe someone in the murk, slumped over or looking at the floor between their legs.

"Look. I need to get to Victoria. Is anything working today?"

But then I notice the sign for POSITION CLOSED at the foot of each of the glass screens. I turn and walk back to the turnstiles. In the free newspaper stand a few yellowing copies of the *Metro* remain. RECESSION ENTERS EIGHTEENTH YEAR shouts the headline, but those must be weeks old because I remember that headline a long time ago. Or do I? Maybe it was something very similar..

I swipe myself back through the turnstiles and then run to the broken escalators going down to the Victoria Line Southbound. I clatter down them, almost losing my balance just before the bottom, and I knock aside the sign informing people to use the stairs. I'm really going to have to find some water fast.

I take a different tunnel that promises to deliver me back to the Central Line platforms. I'll take the Central Line West and emerge at Marble Arch. I can get any number of buses from there down to Victoria Station.

Just inside this tunnel a cleaner, a tall spindly African in a luminous bib, is pushing a mop at something on the floor. He's cordoned off the affected area with a barrier that consists of a canvas tape stretched between four plastic poles.

It looks to me like someone has dumped a pile of rags in a London Underground tunnel. Or perhaps it is the nest of one of the cities homeless, recently abandoned. But the Tube mice are certainly active about it, so maybe some scraps of food have been left inside the rubbish. My mouth fills with saliva.

A woman in very high heels, leans over the barrier tape. Her head is bowed and the thin wrist that emerges from the sleeve of her suit jabs a bony hand at the grubby pile on the tiles as if she has spotted something of value.

I rush past them; who has the time to mess about like this on their way to work? The lack of urgency down here never ceases to amaze me. I just wish everyone would damn well step aside; their thoughts and movements seem as slow and interrupted as the transport service we've all come below to use. Like this fellow here, drunk at this time. On all fours and dragging that dirty sheet of cardboard behind him. Stand up straight man! Tuck your bloody shirt in!

The chap ahead of him is moving a lot faster, even faster than me, and he's on crutches. Swinging those wooden poles back and forth and moving like he's on stilts. But when a man has lost that much hair on top, he really should get his hair trimmed at the sides. The top of his head looks like a greasy eggshell with freckles, fringed with that wispy stuff that hangs off tree branches in swamps. It makes me shudder.

At the end of this passage the lights are out in the arch. Something rushes across the mouth of the exit and catches a bit of the flickering illumination from the one working strip-lights in this tunnel. I'm really starting to get dizzy and disoriented because whatever it was that I have just seen cross the arch, was moving on all fours, as quickly as a dog, and was as thin as a greyhound too. But it couldn't have been a dog, because I definitely saw a tie about its wizened throat and it was wearing a shirt.

By the time I reach the Central Line platform Eastbound, I'm exhausted. My feet are burning and my throat is so cracked I doubt I can speak. Quite a few others seem to be taking time out on this platform too. No one is standing up; they are all packed on to the benches. They've had enough. Anyone can see that. They can barely sit up straight, and those that are able to keep their spines upright are just resting their heads against the dirty walls, eyes closed, mouths open. In this dim brownish light, they look like the inhabitants of an ossuary under a cathedral, or something the allies found at the end of the war, piled behind barbed wire.

I put my briefcase on the floor beside a crowded bench and sit upon it. I'm too tired to feel shame at sitting on my arse on the floor like this, as if I'm some kind of crazy art student. I laugh out loud. It echoes.

My briefcase could do with being replaced too; the leather is worn down to the hide in most places and I can see the metal frame poking out of two corners. It was a present, when I moved on from the last job. A shoelace has come undone too. I don't have the strength to tie it. I just need to sit here and get my breath back for a while. Close my eyes. Calm down.

I snap awake when something brushes past my face. Whatever it was seems to have already gone by the time my sticky eyelids break apart. Must have been the hem of a coat when someone rose from that bench beside me? If it was, the coat needs a good dry clean, because it smells like it's come out of a dustbin that needs emptying. No one is standing up though, and I couldn't have seen a shape slipping over the edge of the platform on to the tracks. So whoever it was must have made off pretty quick down a side tunnel.

Did I miss an announcement? My head feels heavy and my neck aches.

"Due to overcrowding at Finsbury Park we have severe delays in both directions on the Victoria Line."

The directional board is still promising a train to Ealing Broadway in one minute, like it was when I got here. I'm pretty sure a train pulling up would have snapped me out of the doze. And no one has moved from the bench beside me either.

I get to my feet, and I'm reminded of how the suppleness has gone from my knee joints.

The billboard on the other side of the platform is advertising mineral water, and even though the giant bottle of water on the poster is so stained by soot it looks undrinkable, it still makes me groan at the thought of anything wet passing my lips. To my shame, I even shake an old can of Coca Cola that I spot under the bench. But it's as dry as the skin of the chap sitting above it, who seems to be just as puzzled by the same crossword clue he was staring at when I sat down a couple of minutes ago.

I pass through the short interconnecting tunnel between Central Line platforms Eastbound and Westbound.

"There is a good service running on all London Underground lines."

Oh at last. Maybe we'll all get somewhere now. Because this morning's service has been a damn disgrace. I pull back the sleeve of my overcoat. Jesus, I must have rubbed the cuff of my shirt sleeve against something really filthy down here. And I'm almost frightened to look beneath the grubby cuff at my watch.

But I wipe the face of my watch and check the time: 9:15am. "Shit. Damn." That gives me fifteen minutes to be at my desk. Not going to happen. No chance. I'll be bloody lucky if I get there for ten.

FALLEN BOYS

Mark Morris

When Mark sent me the idea for 'Fallen Boys' I leapt at the chance of having a traditional ghost story in The End of The Line. *Mark is a dab hand at supernatural fiction, you only have to check out his novels* The Immaculate *and* The Secret of Anatomy *to see what I mean, and I've been a fan of his work for a long time now. There is the thrill of the Ghost Train in the first part of this story, but it quickly becomes something much darker and more insidious. Mark's ghosts aren't mere bed-sheet phantoms and the horrors that he describes are very real indeed.*

WHEN THE CHILD screamed, Tess Morton felt guilty for having to repress the urge to snap at it. She was aware that it wasn't Matthew Bellings who should be punished, but his tormentors, and yet the boy's cry of pain or distress was so *whiny* that it grated on her nerves.

The reason she felt little compassion for the child was because she knew it took almost nothing to provoke a wail of complaint from him. Matthew would cry out whenever someone barged into him in the school corridor; whenever a football was kicked towards him in the playground; whenever a classmate flicked a paper pellet at him, or snatched a text book out of his hand, or pushed in front of him in the lunch queue. Indeed, the merest slight would cause Matthew's red-cheeked, strangely wizened face to crumple, his mouth to twist open and that familiar, toe-curling bleat to emerge.

Tess liked children; she truly did. Unlike many of her more world-weary colleagues, she was still young enough, and optimistic enough, to regard teaching as a noble and worthwhile profession. She looked back on her own school days fondly, and regarded many of her former teachers with great affection. And as such she liked the idea of feeding and enthusing young minds, of equipping her pupils for the trials of life that would inevitably lie ahead.

All of which made her feel doubly bad for the way she felt about Matthew. He wasn't a naughty boy. He wasn't disruptive or snide or cruel. He was just... unlikeable.

Physically, he was stick-thin and uncoordinated. When he ran his limbs resembled a collection of slender twigs loosely bound together. He had no real friends, and as far as Tess could tell had made no particular efforts to acquire any. Breaks and lunchtimes he could most commonly be found in the library, cowering behind an open book, as if hiding from pursuers. He was the sort of child whose parents – of whom Tess had only ever met his nervous, bird-like mother – did him no favours whatsoever. Whereas the other boys carried rucksacks or sports bags, Matthew had been provided with a satchel of gleaming, conker-brown leather. Additionally, his shoes were too shiny, his trousers too short, and his old-fashioned crew cut gave him the look of a child actor in a wartime drama series.

For a while Tess had taken pity on the boy. She had put herself out, spent extra time with him, in an effort to prise him from his shell. Matthew, however, had remained not only unresponsive, but so sulky and ungrateful that in the end she had given up. She still felt a bit ashamed of abandoning the cause, but she consoled herself with the thought that at least she wasn't as downright hostile towards Matthew as some of her colleagues. The other teacher on this year eight field trip, for instance, Yvonne Harrison, who most of the kids loved for her friendliness and good humour, frequently referred to Matthew Bellings as 'that snivelling little shit'.

Turning now, Tess saw that Jason Hayes, his back to her, was hopping from foot to foot, waving his arm in the air. Her immediate thought was that Jason had snatched something of Matthew's and was taunting him, holding whatever-it-was out of reach. Then she saw Jason lunge forward, lowering his arm in a thrusting motion, which made Matthew squeal again. Some of the other children, especially the girls, squealed too, though there was laughter in *their* voices.

"Eew, you are *so* gross!" one of the girls (Tess thought it might be Francesca Parks) shrieked delightedly.

Muttering at the child behind her to halt, Tess strode towards the knot of pupils at the back of the queue. "*What* is going on here?"

Jason Hayes looked over his shoulder guiltily, and then flicked his arm, tossing away whatever he'd been holding. Because of the other kids milling around, Tess couldn't tell what it was, though she got the impression of something black and ragged sailing over the edge of the metal walkway and disappearing into the scrubby bushes below.

"Nothing, miss," Jason said innocently, turning to face her.

"Nothing," Tess repeated. "Do you honestly think I'm stupid, Jason?"

Jason was a sporty, thick-set boy with spiky hair. Often cheeky and excitable, but essentially a good kid.

"No, miss. No way."

"I'm very glad to hear it. So perhaps you'd like to tell me what you were doing to Matthew?"

Tess still couldn't see the smaller boy. It was as if the other children were purposely shielding him from view.

"Nothing, miss," Jason said again, and then added quickly, "I was just showing him something."

Tess sighed inwardly. She knew that to get to the heart of the onion you had to patiently peel away the layers one by one. "I see. And *what* were you showing him?"

"Just something I found, miss."

Tess stared at him silently for a moment, and then very deliberately said, "Do you *want* to go on the Mine Railway, Jason?"

"Yes, miss."

"Because it's no skin off my nose to take you back to the coach. For all I care, you can sit there for the rest of the afternoon, writing an essay on how important it is to be a positive representative of the school. Would you like that?"

"No, miss."

Francesca Parks, a precocious thirteen year-old with a pierced navel, shrilled, "You can't do that, miss."

"Can't I, Francesca?" Tess said coolly. "And why's that?"

"You can't leave Jace on his own. It's against the law."

"He wouldn't be on his own," Tess said. "Mr Jakes would be there."

Mr Jakes was the school coach driver. He was a scrawny man in his early sixties who always stank of cigarettes. He had a collapsed cavern of a mouth and bad teeth.

Francesca's eyes, still bearing the trace of the eyeliner she applied every afternoon the instant she stepped out of the school gates, widened. "You can't leave him with that old perv."

Tess stared at her unblinkingly. "I beg your pardon?"

Francesca's eyelids flickered and she bowed her head. "Sorry, miss," she mumbled.

"I don't want to hear another word from you, Francesca. Not one. Do you understand me?"

Francesca's head jerked in a single, sullen nod.

Tess paused just long enough to allow her words to sink in and then she focused on Jason again. "Now, Jason," she said, "I want you to tell me exactly what you were tormenting Matthew with, and I want the truth. This is your one and only chance to explain. Don't blow it."

Jason braced himself. "It was a bird, miss."

"A bird?"

He nodded. "I found a bird on the path back there, miss. A dead one. It was a bit manky."

Tess could guess what had happened. Jason had picked up the bird, waved it in Matthew's general direction, and Matthew, as ever, had over-reacted. It wasn't much more than boyish high jinks, but Matthew's response – and the fact that Jason must have known from experience exactly how his classmate *would* respond – meant that she couldn't be seen to condone his behaviour.

Curtly she said, "What did I tell you before getting on the coach today, Jason?"

"You told us we were representing the school and we had to be on our best behaviour, miss," he replied dutifully.

"Correct," said Tess. "And would you say you've adhered to those stipulations?"

"No, miss."

"No," she confirmed. "You've let us all down, haven't you?"

"Yes, miss. Sorry, miss."

"I appreciate the apology, but it's not me you should be apologising to."

"No, miss."

Raising her voice, Tess said, "Step forward please, Matthew."

The gaggle of Jason's classmates, who had been hovering in the background, now half-turned, shuffling aside to create an aisle. Revealed at the end of the aisle, crouching against the chain-link fence which enclosed the metal walkway leading to the mine entrance, was Matthew Bellings.

Tess immediately saw that Matthew was trembling and that he had something dark on one cheek. She wondered whether the incident had been more serious than she had thought. Surely Jason hadn't *punched* Matthew, knocked him down, bruised his face? Despite the antipathy that the other children felt towards the boy, she couldn't believe that any of them would actually resort to violence. As Matthew shakily straightened up, Tess saw one of the girls – Charlotte McDonald – silently hold something out to him. Something small and white. A tissue. And immediately Tess realised what was really on Matthew's face.

It wasn't a bruise. It was blood.

It wasn't his own blood, though; she was sure of that. His face wasn't cut or swollen, and the blood was too thin and brownish to be fresh. As Tess looked at Matthew staring at the tissue but not taking it, her brain made another connection.

It wasn't human blood. It was the bird's blood. Jason must have swung the dead and rotting creature – whether intentionally or not – right into Matthew's face. The thought of it made her feel a little sick.

However, the fact that Matthew was doing nothing to help himself, that instead of taking the proffered tissue and cleaning himself up he was simply cowering against the fence, elicited in Tess a wave not only of revulsion, but of an almost contemptuous irritation towards the boy. Marching forward, she snatched the tissue from Charlotte's hand and brusquely applied it to Matthew's cheek. Matthew was so surprised that he half-twisted away, releasing another of his plaintive squeals.

"Oh, for God's sake," Tess muttered, "don't be a baby."

Instantly she knew she'd overstepped the mark, shown too much of her true feelings. She was aware of shrewd eyes on her, could almost hear the identical thoughts forming in half a dozen thirteen year old heads: *Miss doesn't like him either*.

"Jason," she snapped, trying to make amends, "didn't you have something to say?"

"Er... yeah. Sorry, Matthew," Jason said, but there was a smugness in his voice that left Tess in no doubt that the damage had already been done. Despite his behaviour, Jason *knew* he was still the popular choice, even with his teacher, and that could only mean more trouble for Matthew further down the line.

"Everything okay?"

Tess turned briskly and straightened up. Her friend and head of department, Yvonne, older and more experienced by five years, was standing behind her. Yvonne had returned from collecting their pre-booked group ticket from the kiosk at the foot of the walkway.

"Just a little incident with a dead bird," Tess said. "All sorted now."

She glanced at Matthew, who stared resentfully back at her.

The boy still had a faint brown stain on his red cheek. If she had been his mother she would have spat on the tissue and rubbed it until it was gone.

"I don't want to know," Yvonne said jovially. She was a large, rosy-faced woman with a mass of red hair. Raising her voice, she looked up and down the queue and called, "Right you lot, nice, straight line. No pushing or shoving. Who's looking forward to a terrifying plunge into the centre of the earth?"

Most of the kids cheered and raised their hands. A few of the girls looked gleefully terrified.

"Excellent!" Yvonne said. "Come on then."

For the next few minutes, Tess and Yvonne busied themselves handing out yellow hard hats and getting the children settled into the wooden seats of the open-sided train which would transport them underground. Aside from the bird incident, it had been a good day. Even the weather had held up, though the clouds were gathering now and a few spots of rain were beginning to patter on the plastic canopy of the walkway overhead.

They were at Porthellion Quay, a tin mining museum and visitor centre surrounded on three sides by towering Cornish cliffs. The museum was a sprawling affair, set in two hundred acres of hilly countryside, and consisting of a long-abandoned (though beautifully-preserved) mining village, and a small quayside and docks beside the fast-flowing River Tam. The children had been given a tour of the village and assay office, had had a lesson in the Victorian school (after first dressing up in period costume, much to their embarrassment and hilarity), had made rope on the 'rope walk', and had enjoyed a picnic lunch down by the quayside. Now it was the highlight of the trip – a journey on a rickety narrow-gauge railway into the tin mine itself.

"Everybody wearing their hard hats?" asked the driver, a grizzled, wiry man dressed in blue overalls and an old miner's helmet with a lamp on the front.

Tess glanced at Francesca. She was the only one who had protested about the headgear, but even she was now perched sullenly in her seat, the strap tightly fastened beneath her chin.

"All ready, Mr Hardacre!" shouted Yvonne, looking around and raising her eyebrows in gleeful anticipation.

"Let's be off then," Mr Hardacre called.

He gave an unnecessary double-blast on the whistle, which made several of the children jump, and then, to a smattering of cheers, the train chugged jerkily forward.

Tess settled back, enjoying the rattling motion and the feel of wind on her face. She knew that the train cut leisurely through half a mile of woodland before plunging downhill into the mine itself, and she half-closed her eyes, relishing the sensation of light flickering across her vision as it forced its way through the gaps in the passing trees and bushes.

Raising his voice above the noise of the train, Mr Hardacre began to deliver what was obviously a well-rehearsed spiel, providing them with various facts about mining and the mine itself. Tess listened as he told them how arsenic was a by-product of tin smelting, and how one of the often lethal jobs given to women and children was scraping the condensed arsenic off the walls of the calciners, which drew toxic fumes up from the smelting houses.

She phased out when he started to quote facts and figures relating to ore production and the length and depth of the mine's various shafts, and only knew that the mine entrance was coming up when several of the children sitting near the front of the train began to whoop. Opening her eyes, Tess saw the glinting thread of track, like a long zip, disappearing into the centre of an approaching black arch. Dazzled by the flickering sunlight, the arch seemed to her to be not quite there; it was like an absence of reality into which they were being inexorably drawn, its edges fuzzy, its heart of darkness utterly impenetrable.

She blinked fully awake just in time to be swallowed by blackness. A palpable ripple of fearful excitement ran through the group at the sudden claustrophobic chill emanating from the rocky walls, and at the way the light from Mr Hardacre's lamp slithered and fractured across the tunnel's myriad planes and surfaces. Tess swallowed to ease the sudden pressure in her head, but even after the silent pop in her eardrums the previously guttural rumble of the train's engine sounded thick and muffled. She imagined the thick, dusty air clogging her throat and had to make a conscious effort not to cough. After a couple of minutes of travelling downhill, Mr Hardacre eased back on the brake and brought the train to a grinding halt.

He gestured towards a tableau on their left. Illuminated by the light of a number of ersatz Davy lamps, fuelled not by oil but by electricity, was a family of mannequins. There was a father, a mother, a boy and a girl, all dressed in the drab clothes of a typical mid-nineteenth century mining family. The father's shiny, chipped face was streaked with black paint, evidently intended to represent subterranean grime. Like Mr Hardacre, he wore a mining helmet and was resting a pickaxe on his shoulder.

"They're well creepy," Tess heard one of the girls whisper. She glanced in the direction of the voice and placed a finger to her lips, though she couldn't disagree.

The wide, painted eyes of the family seemed to stare blankly at the newly-arrived group. The little girl was missing a chunk of plaster from the centre of her face, which gave the impression that some hideous skin disease had eaten away her nose and part of her mouth.

Mr Hardacre told them about life underground, about how the father would toil away for ten or twelve hours at a time in stifling conditions, while the children would sit waiting, often in pitch darkness, looking after his food and matches and whatever ever else he might bring down the mine with him. Meanwhile the women – if they weren't scraping arsenic off the walls of the calciners – would be at home, cleaning and washing and cooking the Cornish pasties that their husbands ate every day.

"Any questions?" Mr Hardacre asked finally.

For a long moment there was silence, and then Simon Lawson tentatively raised a hand.

"Is the mine haunted?"

The shadows occupying the wrinkles in Mr Hardacre's face deepened as he frowned. "Haunted?"

"Yes... I mean... well, people must have died down here. Accidents and that. So I just wondered whether there were any, like, stories or legends or anything..."

Tess glanced at the boy, but in the gloom he was nothing but a hunched shadow.

"Ghosts, eh?" Mr Hardacre said, and this time he smiled, the shadows flocking to his widening mouth. "Well, I don't know about that, but have you come across the story of the fallen boy on your travels today?"

There was a general shaking of heads.

"There's a bench with a plaque on it outside the sweet shop," Mr Hardacre said. "It's dedicated to Michael Rowan, who died at the age of thirteen on March 16th 1865. Did anyone see that?"

A few hands went up, though Tess herself had not noticed the plaque.

"Well, there's a strange little story associated with him," Mr Hardcastle said. "Not a ghost story exactly, but still... sad. And a bit creepy.

"The mine, as I told you earlier, was founded in 1832. However there's a secondary shaft, which we'll see in a few minutes, which was created in 1865. The reason for this was that after thirty years of mining, the seams on this level were all but exhausted. It was decided, therefore, to mine deeper – and so the secondary shaft was created, in the hope that further seams would be discovered on a lower level.

"One of the most prominent miners at that time – he was a sort of manager, answerable directly to the mine owner – was a man called William Rowan. By all accounts, Rowan was not popular. He was a bear of a man, and something of a bully, and he had a son, Michael, who was apparently much the same.

"One of the victims of Michael's bullying was a young lad called Luke Pellant. The story goes that Michael chased Luke into the mine one night and that in the darkness Michael ended up losing his way and falling down the secondary shaft. It was just a big hole in the ground at that point, and back in those days there were no safety barriers or anything like that. Anyway, when Luke told everyone what had happened, a rescue operation was mounted, but of course it was too late – the lad had fallen eighty feet or so onto solid rock and was pretty much smashed to pieces.

"Although Luke claimed that Michael had fallen, Michael's father, William Rowan, didn't believe him. He accused Luke of pushing his son down the shaft, of murdering him, and he swore he'd see the boy brought to trial and punished. The general view, however, was that Michael's death had been nothing but the result of a terrible accident, and one that he had brought on himself. When nothing came of Rowan's campaign to see Luke brought to justice, Rowan was furious.

"A few weeks later, Luke disappeared, and it seems that although Rowan was initially suspected of having had something to do with it, Rowan himself put it about that the boy had fled out of guilt or shame for what he had done. In any event, nothing ever came of the incident – until about twenty years ago, when they were excavating the ground down by the quayside to lay the foundations for the information centre. During the excavation some bones were found – an almost entire skeleton, in fact – which tests revealed were about a hundred and fifty years old, and were those of a boy somewhere between the ages of ten and fifteen." Mr Hardacre shrugged. "It's never been proven, but the general consensus is that William Rowan abducted and killed Luke Pellant and buried his remains down by the river. Of course, the Rowan family, who are still quite prominent in the area, refuse to accept it, and had the bench erected as a sort of... well, a sort of statement of defiance, I suppose."

"Are there any members of the Pellant family still about?" Tess asked.

Mr Hardacre shook his head. "Not that I know of. Not in these parts anyway."

"So the bad kid gets remembered and the good one gets forgotten," one of the girls piped up. "That is *so* not fair."

Mr Hardacre shrugged. "I don't think it makes much difference after all this time. Although if it's any consolation, Michael Rowan, despite the commemorative bench, is not regarded fondly around these parts. The locals call him the 'fallen boy', not only because he fell down the shaft, but also because, in their eyes, he – and his father – had fallen from grace."

"So does Michael Rowan's ghost haunt the mine then?" Simon Lawson asked.

Mr Hardacre smiled. "Not that I know of. Shall we carry on?"

He started the train up again and they went deeper, the engine creaking and grinding as they chugged downhill. The tunnel became narrower, the walls more jagged and uneven, and Tess had to suppress a wave of claustrophobia when she looked up at the black ceiling and got the impression that it was crushing down on them, closing them in.

She was relieved several minutes later when the tunnel abruptly widened and they found themselves in a natural arena-like cavern, the walls and ceiling sloping away on all sides, giving a sudden disorientating sense of space. Once again, Mr Hardacre eased back on the brake and the engine groaned to a halt.

"Right," he said, "who fancies a bit of mining?"

This time the response was not quite as enthusiastic. Tess and Yvonne ushered the children out of the train and ordered them to follow Mr Hardacre, who led them across to what looked like a huge, squared-off well, surrounded by a metre-high wall. The shaft of the 'well', a raft-sized square of impenetrable blackness, had been overlaid with a sheet of thick but rusty wire mesh.

"This is the secondary shaft I was telling you about," he said.

"The one that the boy fell down?" one of the girls asked.

"That's right. This shaft has been unused since the mine closed a hundred years ago. Even before then it was prone to floods and cave-ins."

"Are there any plans to open the shaft up again?" asked Yvonne.

Hardacre shook his head. "It would cost too much money. And there's nothing to see down there that you can't see up here." He raised a finger. "Now, remember I told you that children often used to sit down here for hours in the darkness, waiting for their fathers to finish work? Well, when I said darkness, I *meant* darkness. I was talking about the kind we don't usually experience in this modern age. The kind where you literally can't see your hand in front of your face. How many of you want to know what that kind of darkness is like?"

Tess glanced around. Most of the hands were going up, though some of the children looked nervous.

"All right then," Mr Hardacre said. "But when the lights go off, I want you all to stand absolutely still. We don't want any accidents. Okay?"

There was a murmur of assent.

Mr Hardacre crossed to a chunky plastic box on the wall, which had once been white but was now grimed and smeared with black fingerprints. The box had a single switch in its centre, and thick black wires snaked out of the top of it, leading to the ceiling of the tunnel, along the length of which, Tess noticed, were a series of dimly illuminated light bulbs. Mr Hardacre switched off the lamp on his miner's helmet and then looked around at the group and smiled, evidently relishing the moment.

"Ready?" he said, and before anyone could answer he pressed his finger down on the switch.

There was a loud click, like a bone snapping, and the world vanished. Around her, Tess heard a brief, shrill chorus of alarmed squeals, which then seemed to abruptly cut off, leaving a silence and a darkness that felt skin-tight, constrictive. For a few seconds Tess was convinced that she could no longer move;

she felt her throat closing up, her chest tightening. She couldn't shake the notion that she was all at once utterly alone. With an effort she raised her hand in front of her face, but she couldn't see it, she couldn't see anything.

She didn't realise she was holding her breath, waiting for something to happen, until she heard a scuffle of movement to her left. Then, for the third time in twenty minutes, Matthew Bellings cried out, his familiar, teeth-grating mewl of protest echoing jaggedly in the confined space. Immediately the light clicked back on and the world was restored. Blinking, somewhat dazed, Tess looked around her.

The children were standing in little groups, all except for Matthew. He was standing alone, in their midst but isolated. Tess focused on him, and her heart gave a sudden lurch. Matthew's face was scored with streaks of blackness. It was as if the darkness had not allowed him fully to return, as if it had eaten part of him away.

But of course that was nonsense. The black streaks were not darkness; they were simply dirt. Clearly someone had stepped up behind Matthew when the lights were out and had smeared begrimed hands across his cheeks. The question was –

"Who did this?" Yvonne snapped, stepping forward.

Tess's colleague was quivering with rage, pointing at Matthew but sweeping her burning gaze around the rest of the class. The children stared back at her silently or looked down at the floor.

"What did Mr Hardacre tell you?" she continued. And when again she was met with silence, she shouted, "Well?"

"He told us to stand still so there wouldn't be any accidents, miss," replied Julie Steele, whose dark fringe half-obscured her chubby face.

"Yes he did, Julie. So why did one of you decide to be an idiot and do the exact opposite?"

Again, silence. Angrily Yvonne said, "Right, well there's only one way to resolve this. Everyone hold out your hands."

There was a shuffling, a collective glancing around, and then hands appeared, palms up, for inspection. Tess looked from one pair to the next, her gaze skittering. As far as she could see, they were all white, unsullied.

But not all the children had complied with Yvonne's instructions. At the back of the largest group, partly concealed by their classmates, were two crouching, whispering figures. They appeared to be facing each other, holding hands. And then Tess realised that they were not *holding* hands, but that one was *cleaning* the hands of the other.

"You two," she shouted, pointing, striding across.

Two guilty heads snapped up. Beneath the yellow bulbs of their hard hats, Tess recognised the faces of Jason Hayes and Francesca Parks.

Yvonne had joined her now. With her curly red hair streaming from beneath her own hard hat, she looked faintly ridiculous, but no one was laughing.

"Come here!" she hissed, her furiously sibilant voice echoing around the cavern.

Jason and Francesca shuffled forward. Francesca was holding a begrimed Wet Wipe.

"Jason Hayes, show me your hands," Yvonne ordered.

Jason hesitated, but the expression on his face was almost resigned. Slowly he turned over his hands, revealing his palms. Despite Francesca's ministrations they were still mostly black.

And so, a split-second later, was everything else.

Just as they had a couple of minutes before, the lights in the tunnel suddenly went out. This time, caught unawares, the screams from some of the children were louder, edged with panic. There was shuffling movement and someone called out; from the sounds they made, either they or someone else appeared to stumble and fall. Yvonne's furious voice rose above the melee:

"Everyone just *stand still!* Mr Hardacre, what's going on?"

Tess heard the click-click, click-click of their guide testing the light switch.

"Must be a power cut," he said. "Hang on a sec."

There was a smaller click and suddenly a thin beam of white light cut through the blackness. It was the lamp on Mr Hardacre's helmet. The beam bobbed and shivered, playing across the walls and the faces of the children as he moved his head.

"No need to panic," he said. "We'll just get back on the train. I'll soon have us out of here."

"Miss?" said a voice in the darkness.

Tess turned, but the children were little more than shadowy shapes.

"What is it?" she asked.

"Jason's gone, miss," the voice said, and now Tess recognised it as belonging to Francesca Parks. "He's not here."

"What do you mean gone?" snapped Yvonne.

"I don't know, miss," said Francesca. "He was standing right next to me. But when the light came back on, he'd... disappeared."

Yvonne huffed. "Oh, this is ridiculous. What is that little idiot playing at?"

"Matthew Bellings has gone too, miss," one of the boys said.

Tess felt as though the situation was spiralling out of control. "What?" she said. "Are you sure?"

"Yes, miss. He was right there." A shadowy shape raised an arm, pointing at the spot where Matthew had been standing a few seconds before.

"Matthew?" Tess called, looking around. "Jason?"

There was no response. Tess and Yvonne looked at each other. Tess saw a flicker of fear in her colleague's eyes.

"Let's get the other children on the train," Yvonne said. "Count them to make sure we haven't lost anyone else."

They did it as quickly as the darkness would allow, while Mr Hardacre did a quick recce of the tunnels leading off from the central cavern, shining his helmet-mounted light down each one and calling the boys' names.

Finally he returned, shaking his head. "I'll put a call through to the main office," he said. "Find out what –"

"*Listen*," said Tess.

"What –" Yvonne began, but Tess held up a hand for silence.

"I heard something… There it is again!"

From somewhere ahead of them and to their left came a scraping, a shuffling, as if someone or something was emerging from a burrow, scrabbling towards the light. Mr Hardacre walked slowly forwards, placing his feet with care on the uneven ground, the beam of light from his helmet sweeping across the cavern walls.

Several of the children gasped as something suddenly tumbled out of one of the side tunnels. Tess saw white hands clawing at the ground, eyes flashing as a face turned towards them.

"Matthew!" she shouted and ran forward, ignoring Mr Hardacre's warning about minding her footing.

Matthew was on his hands and knees, shivering with fear, his eyes wide and staring. His face was black with dirt. His mouth was hanging open, and as Tess approached him a string of drool fell from his lips and spattered on the ground.

She dropped to her knees, gathered him up in her arms. He flinched and then relaxed, clutching at her as though craving her warmth.

"Matthew," she said softly. "What happened? Do you know where Jason is?"

Matthew looked up at her. He was clearly dazed, confused.

"He called me Michael," he whispered.

"Who did?" asked Tess. "Jason, you mean?"

Matthew shook his head. "He called me Michael. He thought… he said…"

Suddenly his face crumpled and he began to sob.

As Tess hugged him tight, trying to comfort him, Hardacre slipped past her, into the tunnel. Yvonne, bringing up the rear, panting a little, crouched down beside her. Before Yvonne could say anything, Tess gently transferred Matthew into her colleague's arms and muttered, "Look after him."

She stood up shakily. She could still see the white light from

Hardacre's lamp shimmering across the walls of the side tunnel – and then he turned a corner and all at once they were plunged into blackness again.

Tess stepped forward, feeling her way into the tunnel. She moved sideways, crab-like, her hands sliding along the rocky walls, her feet probing ahead. With every step she couldn't help but imagine a precipice in front of her, a gaping abyss. She told herself she was being foolish, but she couldn't shake the idea from her mind.

Then she rounded a corner and suddenly saw thin slivers of ice-white light limning the jags and crevices of the tunnel ahead.

"Mr Hardacre, wait!" she called and hurried towards him.

She flinched as he turned towards her, the light from his lamp flashing across her vision, blinding her.

"What are you doing here?" he said almost angrily. "You should have stayed in the cavern with the children."

"Yvonne's with them," Tess said. "Jason is one of my pupils. I couldn't just wait around in the darkness, doing nothing."

Hardacre made an exasperated sound, but he said, "Come on then. But be careful."

They moved on down the tunnel, Hardacre leading the way, his lamp light sliding across the glossy walls. Down here the world was stark and primal. A world of rock and silence, of harsh white and deep black, nothing in between.

"How deep does this tunnel go?" Tess whispered.

Hardacre's shoulders hunched in a shrug. "A mile maybe."

"Will it –" Tess began, but then she stopped.

There was a figure crouching in the tunnel ahead.

It was on its haunches, bent forward, its back to them. It was naked, its forehead resting against the rocky wall. It reminded Tess of a child playing hide-and-seek, counting to a hundred before standing up and shouting, "Coming, ready or not."

Hardacre had halted. Tess stepped up beside him.

"Jason?" she said.

The figure didn't respond. Tess slipped by Hardacre, moving towards it.

"Be careful, miss," Hardacre said.

"It's all right," Tess replied, though her stomach was crawling with nerves. "There's nothing to be frightened of."

She was within arm's reach of the figure now. She could see the nubs of its vertebrae, the white skin streaked blackly with grime.

"Jason," she said again, and reached out to touch the figure's shoulder. It was freezing cold.

Unbalanced by her touch, the figure rocked backwards. It tumbled over like a turtle on to its back, still in a crouching position, its hands crossed in front of its belly, its knees drawn up.

When she saw what had been done to Jason's face, Tess screamed. She screamed and screamed, the sound echoing off the walls. For ever afterwards she would see the image in her mind. She would see black dirt spilling from the gaping cavern of Jason's mouth and tumbling from his empty eye sockets like thick dark tears.

IN THE COLOSSEUM

Stephen Volk

When you're travelling on the Underground do you ever feel that you are being watched? Well, we all know there are innumerable CCTV cameras everywhere these days, but who exactly is on the other side of the lens? Stephen Volk's answer to this question takes us deep into a world of terrifying excess and violence, using the London Underground as his stage. Volk's tale is extraordinarily savage, but it makes a valid point about the pleasure we all take from watching. And just what do we demand for our entertainment?

GUEST DID THAT imported, ubiquitous thing now of accompanying his handshake with back-slapping, hugging men to his chest in a gesture of bonding and comradeship. They barely noticed that he discarded them mid-conversation, so pleased were they that they'd earned his attention at all. But his gaze rested only lightly, and he moved through the crowd outside the viewing theatre with the smiling ease of a basking shark, navigating effortlessly through the television critics and reviewers. He was in his element.

I stood with my back to the wall, away from the action. Merely the picture editor. Nobody wanted to talk to me, and that was fine. That's how I liked it, as I sipped my half-glass of white wine. I wanted to get away. It wasn't my idea of fun, a gathering like this, thrown in a room with a bunch of vile strangers. I would never have come in the first place, except Guest wanted me to, and he was a client. You kept your client happy. If you wanted to work again, that is.

The screening hadn't gone badly. You can never really tell, though. The journalists never applaud, there's usually a few seconds of embarrassed shuffling and they make for the drinks, or just leave. Guest was never fazed by this. He treated the whole thing as an occasion, a party at which the viewing of our programme in the basement cinema of the Soho Hotel was almost incidental. Totally incidental, in fact.

I watched his floating presence dominating the room as PR women with endless legs handed out flashily-produced documents containing the requisite information on the making of the series, ready-made stories that could be virtually cut-and-pasted into the pages of a magazine or supplement with minimum effort on the part of the columnist or feature writer.

It was the latest reality show, re-formatted from Japan, and to some people it mattered. To their readers, it mattered. It wasn't significant whether it mattered to them, the journalists. That was irrelevant. They were the messengers. And like any threatened species they were naturally keen on asserting their power. Which was where Guest's talent came in. He made them feel that it wasn't a war, just a courtship. He made them feel there was nothing to criticise, and everything to enjoy.

That wasn't his only skill. Far from it.

Beyond being able to expertly negotiate the choppy waters of the television industry, Simon Guest knew his stuff. I'll give him that. He'd been a hands-on producer before climbing the greasy pole. He knew what he was looking at, which most of them didn't. Most of them just exercised their jaws because they could. Put this back in, take that back out, then a week later, the exact reverse. Guest never did. He stuck by every decision and remembered it, meticulously, even when juggling six or seven different episodes farmed out to different editors. Not that he made anybody's life easy.

When he was in the edit suite it would be like mainlining his stream of consciousness, and difficult to keep up. More jeopardy. Don't cut there, stay on her face. More of the reaction shot. Don't cut. Lose it. Tighten it. Chop it. He had no sense of panic, ever – but every sense that a cut could be improved, by a frame, by a pixel. I'd watch his face and he'd hardly blink, his eyes glazed as he imbibed the image. And – cut! Bang on the requirement of the commercial break. Extraordinary.

But, even in the beginning, none of this made me admire him. He was clever, and successful, but arid. For all his clipped manners and hail-fellow-well-met, I always felt he was passing through this world as a visitor, refusing to be engaged with anything but his own ego, casting us all for a secret purpose with those shiny, bulging, judgemental eyes. I'd feel the tension in my shoulders tighten when he came in to see a cut, trailing sycophants as all execs did. I'd quite often have to go to the toilet and throw up, and when he left the room afterwards I always imagined the temperature rise slightly.

All of which makes him sound charismatic, which was exactly his reputation. A cunt, but charismatic.

It wasn't unknown for him to phone an editor at 2 AM and want to go back in the cutting room. "Sleep is for amateurs," he'd say. Also it was rumoured he had a habit. Often I'd see him sniffing like he had a heavy cold or take himself to the loo and come back tweaking his nose. Legend has it, he was found in the gent's at Groucho's with a weather girl sucking him off.

Bruschetta circulated and the hubbub of voices grew louder, thanks to copious amounts of alcohol. I was cornered by a freelance journo who did feature articles for the *Radio Times*. She was drilling me with questions about the programme, pen hovering over a notebook. "You'll have to ask Simon," I said, sensing her invading my personal space. "Simon will tell you that. Simon knows all about it."

Her glass looked precarious in her fingers. She gave me her card. Leaned against the wall next to me. Each eye blinked slightly out of sync with the other.

"I like that aftershave. Where did you get it?"

"It was a gift from my wife," I said.

I thought she was going to take her business card back, but she didn't. She looked like she needed that wall.

I wondered what time it was but didn't want to look at my watch in case somebody saw. One of Guest's underlings, a guy called Max, announced that we all had to move to the upstairs bar, where we were requested to keep imbibing to our heart's content at the production company's expense. With a slightly sick feeling I realised I was obliged to stick around. On the positive side, the woman from *Radio Times* had abandoned me.

I couldn't get a signal on my iPhone so, en route to the bar, I ducked out via reception with its ten-foot Botero sculpture of a cat, giant plant pots and jazzy statements in driftwood and Perspex, into the cool night air of Dean Street.

When I got through, Dee didn't sound quite as harassed as earlier, and I could hear Rex in the background giving running commentary on his choo-choo trains. I said it was past his bed time. She said she knew that thanks, was there anything else I was ringing about? Immediately I wished I hadn't. I could hear the tension. I'd rung her that morning and he hadn't slept well which meant she hadn't. "Did he have his nap?"

"Like a log. He didn't want to wake up, then he screamed like a banshee." If she was going to say he misses his dad, I didn't want to hear that. "I'm going to take him up now. Hopefully a bath will relax him."

"Yeah. Get an early night, darling."

"I always get a nearly night. I have to." I could hear the lullaby-like music of *In The Night Garden* on the TV in the background.

"Okay, I'll call you tomorrow."

"Is that people drinking in the background?" she said. "Where are you? Aren't you back at the flat yet? Who are you with?"

"Just people. For work. I'm going to go when I finish this glass of wine."

"Oh, that's great."

"Look, I'm not enjoying this, believe me."

"Oh, absolutely."

"For crying out loud. I've told you, there could be another twelve-week job in this if these people know my face. You know how it works. There's not a lot of work round at the moment, God knows. How many editors do we know who've been out of work for the last twelve months? Times are really tough. I've got to make the most of this, Dee – and Guest likes me."

"I like you too."

"Yes but you married me."

It wasn't my fault they were down in Bristol while I had to stay in the flat in Stockwell during the week because it was too far to travel back every night, and too expensive, and totally impractical with the unpredictable hours that were needed. I had mouths to feed and the mouths to feed were theirs, but it didn't make me immune from attack.

A girl with the round, muscled shoulders of an athlete came over to me as I fetched a final drink from the bar. "Hi, you must be Marcus."

"I am. How d'you do?"

"I'm Flavia."

"I know," I said. "I've been chopping your words about."

"Chop chop," she giggled, lifting a bleached mane of hair from falling in her face. Her armpit was shaved and pale against her sun-bed tan. The gesture made her already short dress ride up her thighs even further. She was the presenter of the new show. Previously star of a popular daytime telly zoo programme. Furious copulator, by all accounts. Calves muscular enough to look good in gladiator sandals, one foot turned in. Dress skimpy and not hard to imagine the boyish body and small unencumbered breasts underneath it.

"Simon wants you to come to the party."

"What party?"

"The party. You know. *Party*."

Close to, her skin looked less flawless than it did on screen. Even under the merciless scrutiny of HD. The whites of her eyes had little veins and I could see the faint scars of teenage acne, but nothing a bit of post couldn't eradicate.

"He doesn't know." A man in a grey suit and open-necked white shirt put his hand against the small of her back. "Well there's a first time for everything." He was dressed just like Guest. A cohort. Disciple. Adept.

I was quickly introduced to others – the production manager, the marketing people. They'd all worked with Guest before. His inner circle. Pippa, Sophie, Max. The leggy PR woman, Cloelia, and his Grace Jones lookalike PA, Euterpe. His clan. Living proof of the adage: If he likes you, you'll do all right. Maybe I'd do all right too, I thought.

At around nine word went round we were moving on to a club. I couldn't make my excuses and slip away without sounding like a wimp, or, worse, making it sound like a snub, not on a personal level but on a work level too. It was one night, I told myself. Only one night to do this. What difference would one night make?

The club was one of those dingy, unkempt ones like Black's, where dim lighting covered a multitude of sins. I watched Guest and Flavia with another woman I hadn't noticed before, possibly a Sunday newspaper columnist or TV pundit. The woman perpetually lolled. She took off one of her earrings because it was hurting her and carried it around. The remaining one hung from her other lobe, as if the weight of it were all it took to unbalance her.

I caught the arm of one of the PR girls. "Sorry. I've really got to go now. Will you tell Simon thanks for the party?"

"Party?" She chuckled. "This isn't the party," she said, her eyes dancing.

I was confused.

"Where is it then?"

"He doesn't know. He really doesn't know," said Max, overhearing.

"Marcus is a party virgin," said Flavia. "Aren't you, Marcus?"
They laughed.

At which point Guest raised his hands in the air and clapped, then left the room. With the uniform movement of a flock of birds the group, his tight cabal, spilled into the street, following him. Girls in posh frocks and teeter-trotters. Hangers-on. Suits. Some of them draining their glasses, some taking their glasses with them, holding them aloft like beacons to light the way down Broadwick Street and Poland Street, where none of the shops were open and even the restaurants were closing up.

"Where are we going?" I asked.

Nobody answered. Max walked backwards, tapping the side of his nose. Flavia and Euterpe linked arms, giggling and hopping and skipping in step. Guest strode ahead in his immaculate suit like a bizarre shepherd. We staggered past the top end of Carnaby Street and the London Palladium with its posters for *Sister Act* and a youth with gelled hair urinating in an emergency exit. A daisy-chain of others, similarly styled in clubbing gear, wailed their painful anthems, leering in football shirts full of sponsorship logos, staggering and gobbing as the pubs and bars disgorged their nocturnal detritus: Stag parties in ridiculous fancy dress, top hats, bobble caps, false boobs; hen nights with pom-poms on their antennae. Media whores in sober suits, we picked our way through the late night drinkers and general outcasts till we reached the tube station at Oxford Circus.

It was late by now. I'd lost all track of time. The Underground was almost closed. A guard stood at the concertina grilles looking at his watch.

We descended the steps into the station and I heard the grilles bang shut noisily behind us. Youngsters in flammable track suits and football tops yelled to get in, like a demented pack of animals, Stella cans in hand. Their howls echoed in the tiled bowl of the sanctuary below: *Oi! Oi! Oi mate! Oi! Oi!*

"Where are we going?"

Still nobody answered.

The turnstile opened and closed with its familiar clang each time, like a pair of mechanical jaws narrowly missing its prey.

Guest and his tribe gathered beyond, where the sign read *Bakerloo Line* and *Central Line* and the escalators led down. I swiped my Oyster card to go through to join them.

Seek assistance. I swiped it again.

Seek assistance.

Flavia and Euterpe giggled, hanging onto Guest's elbows, the man's smile of benediction hanging in the air accompanied by the ambient scrape of the down escalators.

One of the Underground guards, a black man with tribal scars on his cheeks, came over and examined my Oyster card, pressed a button, and ushered me through with brusque impatience.

"Thanks. Thank you," I mumbled.

Euterpe took off her shoes and carried them. Flavia kissed Guest on the lips. Under the artificial light the women seemed even more thin, alien, muscular, heartless. In this most plebeian of settings their Manolo Blanik shoes and expensive jewellery seemed suddenly disgusting. They looked displaced. Like an alluring, semi-nude fashion photograph cut out of Vogue and Sellotaped to a lavatory wall.

I thought we were catching the Tube somewhere. That was the plan, wasn't it? I was expecting to head down to one of the platforms.

That wasn't the plan at all.

Guest crossed the concourse and whispered to a uniformed guard, the same one who had begrudgingly let me through the turnstile.

"What's going on?" I said.

The elevators squealed. The trains rumbled far below. Flavia and Euterpe giggled again.

Guest's lips were close to the man's ear. When he turned back the man nodded. He unlocked a door and pushed it open and Guest stepped inside. The Underground guard didn't move, but continued to hold the door open, and the others followed.

Inevitably, so did I.

Of course I'd seen the room when I came down the steps. I'd

seen it many times as I entered the station on previous occasions, though you could never quite see what was inside apart from men sitting at screens and paperwork on desktops. I knew where we were instantly, though I'd only ever walked straight past it before. The room was full of computer screens, some of them cut into quadrants, showing time-coded CCTV images from various cameras placed on the platforms, others positioned to cover the escalators and corridors. We were in the security control room of Oxford Circus Underground station.

In total self-interest I was alarmed and wondered by what scheme of things this was remotely legal, and if it wasn't, what was I doing there? Nobody else seemed to be sharing my discomfort.

I noticed they were piling into more drink. Glasses had been arranged on trays awaiting us. Champagne provided. Ice buckets in readiness. All prepared in advance, obviously – by the machinations of our illustrious host. Guest popped a cork, filled glasses. They glided round from hand to hand.

I could see out of the windows into the empty concourse. There were two more Underground guards in blue coats and peaked hats standing by the up escalator. The one who had unlocked the door joined them. They were looking in my direction but doing nothing. Then one of the PR girls rolled down the Venetian blinds and we were alone.

I drank like the others. Impossible not to. I had come this far, I had to blend in. Be one of the crowd. This crowd, anyway.

At first, preoccupied with my own thoughts, I didn't realise fully what was going on.

As I smiled and drank and ate the smoked salmon canapés and cheese straws being passed around, I saw Max sitting at one of the CCTV screens watching a gaggle of hen nighters in angel wings and haloes waiting for a train, two of them so drunk that they leaned against one another like the letter A to prevent each other from falling flat on their faces. Their obese, bare legs looked even whiter in the low-res of the digital image. Their paleness flared into the lens. The diagonal of the platform edge bisected the shot, leading off into the black mouth of the tunnel. Right in front of me one of the PR girls kissed Max's neck and bit it lightly between her teeth, while on the CCTV screen one of the hen nighters pulled up her tutu and squatted, letting an unstoppable stream of urine trail off the platform. Max laughed and threw back his head. The PR girl fastened her glossy lips onto his.

I saw that on another CCTV screen a man was having an argument with his girlfriend.

"Hey look. This is a good one. Look at this twat."

The people around me gathered and leered and laughed. Guest had his arms round two of the girls and whilst their shoulder shook, he displayed only his usual self-satisfied grin.

At first it seemed innocuous, idle play; unusual, bizarre – but no more than that. Necking champagne, they tittered as they watched a rubber-legged drunk on the Bakerloo southbound platform zig-zagging, unable to stay upright. The footage was no more disturbing than anything on YouTube, and equally if not more pathetic, but everybody around me found it hilarious. A Marketing Man with Boris Johnson hair wanted to lay bets that the pisshead would end up on the live track. Guest took him up on it, silently taking two twenties out of his wallet. Someone else matched it and raised it by another twenty. Before long the stake reached five hundred, then upward. The drunk on the CCTV sat on the platform, his upper body swaying. The train entered the station, its door slid open, the drunk shambled on and Guest scooped his winnings. The assembled in the control room gave a round of applause.

Someone topped up my glass.

I could hear the distant sheet thunder of the trains passing through the station deep below our feet, not so much sound as a low inaudible bass I could feel vibrating through my body like slow, creeping nausea. It was the soundtrack of the night.

In parody of two gay men kissing on another CCTV screen, Guest kissed Max on the lips, to more spontaneous applause and a few wolf whistles. A silver salver was raised to reveal several lines of white powder, eagerly snorted up with silver straws. Again, it was impossible to abstain. The gay men parted from each other unwillingly. The older one seemed an intellectual type, stylishly wrapped in a French scarf and wearing expensive designer glasses. The other a good twenty years younger, with a curtain of peroxide hair covering his eyes.

Flavia rubbed her teeth with a finger as she laughed, uncontrollably it seemed, sucking up the coke like sherbert. The glass rim tinkled against her incisors as she drank. The whites of her eyes had become grey and I wondered if mine had done the same.

On CCTV the gay men kissed again, on the cheek this time as the train pulled in, and they held each other at arm's length then by the fingertips. The peroxide one got on and sat down. The older one blew him a kiss.

Everyone in the control room went "Ahhhhhhh."

The boy blew one back in return. I hadn't noticed two punkish girls getting off the train until I saw them walking towards the exit sign. Then suddenly, as the train disappeared, they turned and ran up behind the older gay man and one of them snatched his shoulder bag.

The Marketing Man made a clucking noise and leaned closer, planting a kiss on the screen.

The punk girls were away but the gay man wasn't having it. He was after them. And he could move. They were young but they were drunk or on something – that's why they needed the bag, the money in it, for a fix. They were unhealthy and he wasn't, and surprise slowed them up further. In a few seconds he'd caught up – right under the camera now – and was yanking the bag back off them, really had hold of it now and wasn't about to let go. While this tug of war was going on the other punk girl kicked him hard in the side of the knee. His leg bent unnaturally, broken like a stick, he fell. She kept on kicking with her Doc Marten boots, kicking away his hands as he tried to shield himself then grabbing those hands and hauling them back as the first girl kicked him between the legs then took a few paces run-up before delivering a drop-kick to his face.

"Wow."

"Fuck."

"Jesus Christ."

Blood and teeth flecked the platform.

Max punched the air as if celebrating some kind of skilful goal.

The Marketing Man hunched over his clenched fists and did a little dance, saliva shining on his lower lip.

She kept on kicking the gay man, the other punkish girl joining in on the other side. The man's jaw seemed to jump out of its socket and realign itself. Then they stamped on his chest and stomach.

As the others whooped and squealed and jumped up and down, Flavia was bent over the desk, with her face close to the CCTV screen. I watched Guest, revelling in the festivities, caressing the roundness of her buttocks and slide his hand slowly up her skirt. She didn't mind in the slightest. I saw her smile reflected in the CCTV screen as she eased herself slightly, parting her thighs so that his fingers could go right in.

On the screen the gay man lay wriggling on the platform, crawling round in a pool of his own blood.

Everyone formed a scrimmage around the video display, jostling for prime position.

In another time-coded quadrant the punk girls were travelling on the up escalator, screaming at each other now, a heated argument quickly becoming a shouting match. I saw a knife in the hand of one of them and this one was leaping down the up escalator now, in a blur of pixels, back the way they'd come.

My eyes flashed back to the other CCTV screen, to see the girl arriving on the platform again, strutting belligerently, then starting to stab the gay man, still prone and helpless, in the chest.

I looked around me, light-headed with the champagne and cocaine, and everyone was giggling and laughing, still.

Guest had unzipped his trousers and was against Flavia's rump, pushing hard. He held the straps of her dress like reins and when he yanked them her breasts shook loosely under her. She was propped on her elbows on the security paperwork, her cheek pressed against the CCTV screen where the punkish girl's knife was gutting the gay man, slashing at his throat and face in a random and unabated frenzy.

Many of the other CCTV screens in the room were also alive with nocturnal activity. On some deeper level underground, a gang of teenagers were running and shouting – their voices mercifully muted from where we stood and all the more horrifying for that. In the control room, in front of this image, one of the PR girls ran her fingers through a TV exec's chest hair, then stroked the erection clearly visible in his trousers.

On another CCTV screen a surge of football supporters spilled off a train onto the Central Line platform, chanting and waving their upheld scarves at the camera. Jeering and howling the calls and taunts of their tribe.

More hen nighters, in mini-skirts and antlers arrived elsewhere in the labyrinth, T-shirts emblazoned *Carrie's Hen Night*.

A few feet away from me, an ex-public schoolboy in a too-tight suit was French-kissing Euterpe, who had one nipple exposed, hard and black as sucker of a toy arrow, between his pudgy fingers.

On another semi-pixellated screen, skinhead stag nighters in Viking helmets broke out in a fight, throwing punches and karate kicks at each other indiscriminately. In front of this, the girl who had sucked Max's neck unzipped him, fetched out his penis and sat across it. I could see the muscles in her inner thighs tighten and relax as she rose and dropped, her thin, stiff arms pushing against his chest.

Flavia's saliva had started to stain her own CCTV screen like a smear on a windscreen. Her eyes were closed, her mascara running and her lips plumped with immense arousal. Her hot breath created clouds on the glass over the image of the punk girl jumping up and down beside the gay man's corpse, standing on it like a champion on an Olympic podium, then running up to the CCTV camera and waving the blood-soaked knife into its lens.

The TV journalist started rubbing my crotch, delineating my cock with her finger and thumb. I was standing against the wall and couldn't get away. I thought I could look away – from the people around me, from the CCTV screens – but I couldn't even do that.

One of the hen nighters stood on a remote platform in the bowels of the earth. She was on her mobile, texting, not realising the message can't be sent so far underground. Probably too drunk to think straight. Tucking a stray curl of hair behind her joke-shop antlers. The rest of the hen nighters on the Tube train are beckoning her, but she isn't looking. She doesn't see until the train doors have closed and it's moving off and they're gesticulating and she's left on the platform all by herself, staring to sob in inebriated panic.

With casual aplomb, Guest removed his prick from Flavia, massaging it unhurriedly with indifference to who was present as he lounged back in one of the swivel chairs.

His PA, Euterpe, had stripped naked and lay along the desktop in front of a bank of the CCTV screens, the spill of light from the monitor units highlighting her ebony skin. She poured champagne into her vagina, the bubbles mingling with the curls of her pubic hair, before Pippa (or was it Sophie?) buried her face there, to the delight and encouragement of several male colleagues. By then a Consultant and someone from Policy were sucking eagerly at her breasts like overgrown offspring.

Guest pressed his glans against the CCTV screen on which the hen nighter was weeping and everybody laughed and applauded, naked or semi-naked by now.

I tried to tear my eyes from the scene. She was no longer alone. At the far end of the platform I saw four men running towards her. She turned and saw them and screamed but they were already on top of her. The first knife was at her throat, forcing her down to her knees, then on all fours. The second knife cut away her skirt and her knickers.

The TV journalist unzipped my trousers, sank down on her knees and accommodated me in her mouth. Meanwhile in the penumbra of my vision Guest himself passed around the scene like a conscientious *maitre d'* inspecting the enjoyment of his customers, trailing a finger over this reclining nude, that buttock, this breast, pausing only to kiss lust-fattened lips or flicker his tongue against a proffered clitoris.

One of the men pulled down his jeans and jabbed inside the hen nighter until her entire body shook. Everything in her shape resisted him. She slid along the platform but they hauled her up again. She left a trail of blood from a cut across her cheek. Attacking her like a dog on heat, the first man carved into her back with the edge of his blade as he raped her, while the one at the front held her face tenderly and made baby expressions at her, before yanking out chunks of her hair like clods of earth.

The image on the CCTV burned into me as the heat spread up from the TV journalist's incendiary lips.

Guest now had the woman with one earring bent over the CCTV screens. She was touching the glass with her snakelike tongue. Her dress was lifted to expose her large rump and no underwear. Guest was fisting her up the anus, jerking her forward so that her face was rubbing against the CCTV screen every time he thrusted. He was French-kissing one of the PR girls at the same time as a man's hand – not his own – was wanking him off.

The hen nighter sagged yet again, barely conscious. The third man, who had been watching until now, picked up her joke-shop antlers and put them on, then applied himself to the part of her anatomy his friend had just relinquished.

The room was spinning round my head and nothing would stop it.

The apes on the CCTV howled and jeered mutely.

The animals roared and ran and fought and spilled blood.

When they let go and the hen nighter's frame collapsed onto

the platform, the last man sat over it like a scalp hunter and sawed at the back of her neck.

I tugged the TV journalist's hair, yanking her sharply off me and held her head still as I spurted my semen onto her cheek. I dragged her to her feet and kissed her lips hard, smearing my spunk down onto her breasts, then squeezing those breasts till she cried out, pushed me back, panting, and moved away. I moved quickly after her. I lifted her skirt and put two fingers up her vulva as deep as they could go. Ramming them in till she grunted then I lifted her onto the CCTV bench, yanked her knees up, and entered her.

I shouted as I came again, and felt hot breath on my neck and knew it was Guest. Guest's lips. Guest's fingers round my penis now, extracting me. Prolonging me. Keeping hold of me.

Guest's voice in my ear: "You're one of us now."

THE CHILL OF the night air hit me. I stood there for a moment just thankful that I was taking it in. I looked back through the grille, down the steps at the dark silhouettes of the Underground guards in their long coats and peaked hats, beyond them a patrol of cleaners in overalls setting about their subterranean work, taking the down escalators for the precious hours before the throng of commuters descended to weave their sorry way to work. I buttoned my shirt and backed away from the station entrance in a semi-trance.

I walked down Oxford Street. I'm not sure where I walked after that. The air was thick with the cacophony of West End clubland, the screams of drunk women teetering and tottering, showing all they've got, the coarse laughter of boys on the prowl and on heat, night clubs spewing out denizens of the dark in search of a shag and a high...

A homeless guy grabbed my arm. "Mate. Mate!"

I shook him off. I was infected enough already. I was touched enough for a lifetime. I wanted to scrub myself clean. I wasn't anybody's mate anymore.

I hailed a taxi, desperate to get home to some reminder I had a proper life. A life before this. This madness. This nightmare. I managed to pay the taxi driver and get to the front door before it hit me, all of it hit me, and I was sick, spewing up onto the pavement as if I was giving up all of me, everything that was inside because nothing on the outside was left. I was empty. Gone.

THERE WAS NOTHING in the *Evening Standard* the next day, or in any of the papers – as I knew would be the case – and I never saw Guest again. I was approached to edit his next series but I said I was already booked. I was asked to do the one after that, but I used the same excuse. Nobody, I think, gets asked a third time.

I followed his career in the pages of *Broadcast*, the industry magazine. He was occasionally given a comment piece or interviewed as the managing director of this production company or that, or this media organization or consultancy, or this worldwide broadcast conglomerate. He eventually gravitated to the States. Eventually went on to make history programmes for the Discovery channel. Made shows that earned him Emmys, BAFTAS, Golden Globes. I saw photographs of him in a tuxedo, delivering keynote speeches at television festivals and media conferences. I was fairly confident that wherever he found himself it would be in some other city – Paris, New York, Boston – where there was an underground system. I think wherever his travelling circus of sycophants and hangers-on went, they took their entertainment with them. Or found a way to provide it.

I'm editing another cookery show now. Lose this. Cut that. Do that in voice over. More jeopardy. Let's see what Clara thinks. Let's see what Ian thinks. Let's see what Donald thinks. Once I said, "What if Donald doesn't think anything?" It was a joke, but nobody laughed, and neither did I.

I don't even care about leaving the business any more. I work. I get paid. I do what I'm told. I made up my mind it didn't hurt any more whether it was close up or medium shot, slo-mo tagliatelle in a pan or a speeded-up shot of clouds scudding through the sky.

I wept in front of Dee once. Didn't tell her the reason. I told her it was stress, and that was fine. I didn't tell her it was Oxford Circus. I didn't tell her it was entertainment.

I thought I'd grow to be interested in Rex as he got older but that hasn't happened. I carry him. I play with him. I do what's expected of me, but sometimes I wish he wasn't there. Sometimes I wish Dee wasn't there. Sometimes I wish nobody was there.

Sometimes I feel sick. I've been to the doctor but there's nothing wrong with me. I ask why I feel sick all the time, there must be something wrong with me, and the doctor says she doesn't know, it could be many things.

Sometimes I see drunks in bars or late at night and men in football shirts. Hairless skins dense with the woad of tattoos. I don't meet their eyes if I can help it. I wonder about their lives past midnight, underground. I wonder how he finds them, recruits them, does what he does.

Sometimes Dee tells me to wake up. Tells me I'm staring into space. Staring at the TV, but not really watching. Asks me what I'm thinking. I say I'm not thinking anything.

When I cry and I masturbate I am alone. And when I masturbate I don't think of her, I think of the hen nighter on the CCTV screen in the seconds before she died. I think of her blood and I think of my fingers wet inside the TV journalist in the control room and Guest's purple, engorged cock-head against the CCTV screen.

It was years ago.

It feels like yesterday. It feels like now.

Now, I find myself not going back home early of a Friday night. I make excuses. Not even very good ones. Often I could get the three o'clock train but I don't. I say I'm working late, up against a deadline. I lie.

If I close my eyes right now I can smell and hear the Tube. The escalators. The announcements. I can feel my heart rate quicken. They excite me. It's the only thing that excites me anymore. I can't go home any more unless I've been on the tube. It used to be half an hour. Now it's more like two. I just like being down there. The flash of the *Seek Assistance* signal. The clang of the turnstile. The smell of the trains' brake fluid, acrid and electrical.

It's like foreplay.

It's like slipping back into a dream.

Nothing is healthy. Everything is sick.

We see panther-like women newsreaders telling us stuff but all we want to do is fuck them. Mess up their perfect hair and make-up and rip their perfect clothes.

Lose it. Cut. More jeopardy. Tighten it.

The only thing worth preserving is honesty, even if that honesty is the honesty of the swamp. The mud and dirt that is human beings.

Seek Assistance.

I travel under London. I don't need to see a pretty face any more, or a woman standing alone and vulnerable, just smell the odours and feel the ambience of the glimmering rails and shiny white tiles.

When I stand on the platforms I look at where the CCTV cameras are, where they are positioned, how they're angled, imagine what they'll take in. I think of who is watching. What they are doing. What they are thinking. Who they are judging. Whether they are laughing. Whether they are fucking.

I travel the Tube for hours now.

Two hours every morning before work. Three, maybe four hours at night.

Just sitting. Just moving. People around me. A man opposite reading his *Time Out*. Somebody else reading the Koran. A woman next to me, her bare arm brushing against my sleeve with the motion of the train.

I don't want to go home any more.

I want to be seen. I want to be watched.

I want to be alive.

THE ROUNDS

Ramsey Campbell

I can remember very clearly the first time that Ramsey Campbell scared me. I would have been around thirteen or fourteen years old and I was reading his story 'The Trick' in Waking Nightmares. *The last line of that tale actually froze me with fear. There's something about the way Ramsey builds up his short stories that is like no other writer I know. His use of language and imagery is almost unique in horror and he's easily one of the most respected and influential writers we have. It was a great honour then, when Ramsey agreed to contribute to* The End of The Line, *and it's wonderful to be able to bring to you a brand new story by a true master.* 'The Rounds' *demonstrates Ramsey at his very best and it will stay in your head long after you have read it.*

As THE TRAIN arrives at James Street one of the women behind me in the carriage murmurs "They're talking about us again."

"What's somebody saying this time?" her friend protests, but I miss the answer in the midst of a recorded warning not to leave luggage unattended. The amplified voice seems to herd commuters off the underground platform onto the train, and an Asian woman in a headscarf black enough for a funeral takes a seat at the far end of the carriage. Perhaps she's a lawyer from the courts at the top of James Street, since she's carrying a briefcase. The voice falls silent as the train heads into the tunnel.

There's just a solitary track on the loop under Liverpool, where the tunnel shrinks to half its previous width. Lights embedded in the walls flash out of the dark every few seconds like some kind of signal. In about a minute more passengers board at Moorfields; it's the start of the rush hour. I'm at the nearest doors well before the train pulls into Lime Street, where the Muslim woman alights further down the carriage. As I make to step onto the platform I notice she's without her briefcase.

"Excuse me," I call, but she doesn't seem to hear. Several people look up or around and then lose interest as I dash along the carriage. The case is on the floor by the seat she vacated, and I grab it before struggling between the last of the commuters boarding the train. The woman isn't on the platform. She could have used the lift, but the escalators are closer, and I sprint for the exit that leads to them.

Is she late for a main line train? By the time I reach the bank of escalators her strides have taken her almost to the top. I'd try and overtake her on the other upward escalator, but it isn't moving. "Excuse me," I shout, "you dropped this."

She turns with one hand on the banister and smiles, though the expression looks a little automatic. I'm hurrying towards her when she sails out of view. The briefcase is so shabby that I might conclude she meant to dump it if it weren't also heavy with documents. I assume that's what the contents are, but the lock is jammed; it's so distorted that someone might already have tried to force it – perhaps she has lost the key. I admit I'm glad to find her waiting beyond the escalator, this side of the ticket barrier. "Oh, thank you," she says and makes her smile rueful. "I don't know what I could have been thinking of."

I'm at least equally ashamed of having thought she might be up to no good. It shows how prejudiced we've all grown, how inclined to think in today's stereotypes. I pass her the briefcase with both hands, and she grasps the scruffy handle as she shows her ticket at the barrier. I flash my pass and am following her along the passage to the escalators that lead up to the main station when my breast pocket emits a series of piercing clanks that put me in mind of a faulty pacemaker.

I read the message on my mobile as the escalator lifts me into the glare of sunlight through the glass roof. Have to cancel, it says. No train. Beneath the huge cautionary voice of the station there's the babble of a crowd that's hurrying to the platforms while at least as many people stream out onto the concourse. The Muslim woman has disappeared among them. I pocket the mobile without sending a response and tramp down the descending escalator. As I display my pass the ticket collector says "You look familiar."

"I expect there's plenty more like me."

I'd say that was as witty as her quip, but she doesn't bother laughing. She seems to feel it's her duty to ask "Weren't you here just now?"

"If you say so."

"Did you forget something?"

"That's not me. I thought I was meeting someone but I'm not after all."

"You want to be sure what's happening another time."

The pointless exchange has delayed me so much that as I step on the underground escalator I hear a squeal of wheels – the arrival of the train I meant to catch. I clutch at the unsynchronised banisters and dash down two sinking steps at a time, to reach the platform just as the train sets about shutting its doors. With a leap that leaves me feeling rejuvenated I jam my foot between the nearest pair, which flinch apart, raising an alarm that all the others take up. "I've still got it," I declare as I board the train.

Nobody seems interested. One man lowers his head as though his tweed hat is weighing it down. A younger man is leafing through a cardboard folder full of documents, and a girl is lost in the world of her personal stereo, while a woman in a coat patterned like a chessboard frowns at a Mtogo poster as if she thinks an African restaurant has no right to advertise on the train. I find a seat near the doors as the train heads for Central Station, where it swaps commuters for commuters before following the loop back to James Street. Just one passenger alights there, hurrying behind the crowd on the platform. She's the Muslim with the briefcase.

She must have used the lift at Lime Street while I was held up at the barrier. I've a reason to have caught the first train back, but what's hers? However prejudiced it makes me feel, I can't help lurching to my feet and forcing my way onto the platform. She's already past the nearest exit – she isn't even on the stairs to which it leads. If I find she's returning to the courts, where she could perfectly well have left some item, I hope I'll be cured of making suspicious assumptions. If she sees me I'll be more embarrassed still. I sprint up the boxed-in stairs and reach the top just in time to see her leaving the enclosed bridge across the underground tracks. She isn't bound for the outside world. She's on her way down to the platform for the trains around the loop.

I hear a train approaching, and her running down to meet it. I can't see her as I dash down the steps, and she isn't on the platform scattered with commuters. I'm opposite the last carriage of the train. I could try to reach the driver or attract their attention, but what would I say? All I know is that if the woman plans to abandon the briefcase again, we should all be safe until she's well away from it. The thought sends me onto the train.

This time I don't trigger the alarm, and the train moves off at once. The carriage is crowded, but I can see every head, and there's no sign of a headscarf. Suppose she's so fanatical that she would take it off to be less obvious? I struggle through the crowd, peering at every face and at the floor beside and between and especially under the seats. All the people in the aisle would make a briefcase easier to hide, but it seems the woman wasn't in this carriage, or at least she hasn't left the case here. I haul open the door between the carriages, to see a man leaning against the next door. He's so bulky that he blocks the view into the other carriage, and he doesn't budge when I knock on the window. I make to shove the door at him, and then I'm overwhelmed by a blaze of light. It isn't an explosion, even if my innards wince. The train has emerged from the tunnel.

We're at Moorfields. The doors open to the platform, but I'm nowhere near any of them. When I push at the one between the carriages the man with his wide flabby shoulders against it doesn't shift an inch. More people squeeze onto the train, and I'm near to panicking. As it moves off I crane back to stare through a window at the platform. A woman is striding fast along a passage to the escalators. She's the headscarved Mohammedan, and she doesn't have her briefcase.

My guts clench like a helpless fist, and a sour taste surges into my mouth. Until this moment I can't really have believed my own suspicions – I might as well have been enacting a scene from a cheap thriller based on the news. As the tunnel closes around the carriage I kick the connecting door and pound on it with both fists. When the hulking man turns his big stupid head to stare at me I flash my pass, too quickly for him to take issue with it. "Let me through," I shout and mime as well.

Even he must realise we all need to be concerned about security, though he makes it clear that he's doing me a favour by stepping aside. I brush past him and shoulder my way through the swaying crowd. The lights on the walls of the tunnel are hurtling towards me like the future. There's a bag of shopping between two seats, and there's another carrier bag on the floor, but where's the briefcase? Is it even in this carriage? How much distance may the woman want to put between herself and the case, or how little? I'm nearly at the first set of doors, and I'm shamefully tempted to make my escape, but we're still in the tunnel. The train lurches as if it has been derailed, and its hollow roar seems to grow louder. I seize the metal pole above the partition that separates the seats from the crowded space in front of a pair of doors. The carriage steadies, and as I grasp there was no explosion I see a briefcase on the floor, almost hidden by the legs of passengers. "Sir," I say urgently, "is that your case?"

The man who's closest to it glances down and then just as indifferently at my face. "Nothing to do with me."

His neighbours shake their heads, and I stoop to retrieve the case. I recognise it at once – recognise the warped lock, which I'm beginning to think might have been deliberately forced out of shape so that nobody can open it. I close my fist around the ragged handle and lift the case.

At once light flares all around me. I'm back at Lime Street. All along the carriage matrix signs spell it out, and a woman's amplified voice pronounces the words for anyone who can't read. As I make for the doors I'm frantically trying to decide where to take the briefcase. The train is coasting to a halt, and I'm still trapped by all the bodies pressing close around me, when someone taps me on the shoulder hard enough for a knock on a door. "That yours?" a man says in my ear.

"It isn't," I declare and struggle around to face him. He's a cleaner in a yellow jerkin. Usually the cleaners don't collect the rubbish from the trains during the rush hour, and his appearance is as unexpected as it's reassuring – even the Union Jack badge just visible on the lapel of his jacket. "It was left before," I murmur for only him to hear. "I think –"

"We saw," he says just as low and reaches for the briefcase. "Give it here."

However grateful I am to let it go, I want to be sure he understands. "You saw who left it," I mutter.

"We know all about those."

This could be prejudice symbolised by the badge. Under the circumstances I can't be choosy, and I hand him the briefcase. "Be careful with it," I whisper. "Whatever's inside –"

"It's seen to, granddad," he says and steps onto the platform.

As he strides towards the nearest exit a young woman offers me a seat. Perhaps I look shaken by having to deal with the briefcase, unless she heard what the cleaner called me. I sink onto the seat, but I can't begin to relax until the train leaves the station and is safely in the tunnel. "Thank God that's over," I say aloud.

I oughtn't to have spoken. At least nobody seems to want to enquire into my remark. One man clasps his hands and bows his head as if to dazzle everyone with the shine of his bald scalp. A girl in a sweater striped like a wasp stares out of the window at the repetition of the lights. A young businessman reads a magazine, and the woman next to him might almost be hypnotised by the swaying of her earrings, which are shaped like inverted question marks although she doesn't look remotely Spanish. More passengers manage to find room when we reach Central Station, and soon the voice of the train reads out the illuminated announcement about James Street. In a very few moments I'll be out of the loop at last. Just one person leaves the train and heads for the exit. He's wearing a yellow jerkin, and he's carrying a briefcase.

He's the man who spoke to me. It needn't be the same case, except that I can see the warped lock. Didn't he understand my warning? How could he risk bringing the case back on the train? The explanation makes my nerves yank me to my feet. "It's him as well," I gasp. "He's part of it."

Nobody appears to want to understand or to let me off the train. I have to shout in one man's ear before he gives an inch, followed by hardly any more as I struggle past him. I've barely staggered onto the platform when the train shuts its doors. I could shout to the driver, but if anyone else hears me, won't that cause a panic or worse? My heart thumps like a frenzied drum as I dash up the steps to the underground bridge.

I can't see the man in the yellow jerkin or the briefcase. Has he used one of the lifts up to street level? I could – there are always staff at the top – but that might take longer than it's safe to take. There's a more immediate way of communicating with the staff, and I sprint across the bridge to leap down two steps at a time to the other platform.

Passengers are waiting for a train around the loop, but I can't see what I'm afraid to see. An intercom is embedded in the wall. A blue button offers **Information**, but I jab the green one that says **Emergency**. My heart deals me a couple of irregular thumps that I hear as well as feel before the grille above the buttons speaks. "Hello?"

"I'm at James Street." Lurching close to the grille, I cup my hands around my mouth to murmur "I think –"

"Can't hear you."

"You won't want anybody else hearing." All the same, the man's voice is coarse with static, and suppose mine is even more distorted? I press the sides of my hands around the grille and shove my mouth closer. "Someone's up to something down here," I say as loud as I dare. "They keep trying to leave a case on the train."

"Who does?"

"I think they're Muslims, or they may not be. Maybe they're people who're against Muslims and trying to make it look as if it's them." The speaker has begun to remind me of a grille in the door of a cell. I strain my eyes as far to the side as their aching muscles will drag them. I can't see the man or the briefcase, but everyone nearby seems to be watching me until they look away. I'm the last person they ought to suspect, and they wouldn't find my behaviour odd if they knew I was acting on their behalf. "The one who's got the case now," I say urgently, "he's one of your cleaners or he's pretending to be."

"Where are you saying he is?"

"He just got off the train at James Street. I'm not sure where he went." I have to raise my voice to compete with the sounds of the latest train. Most of the people around me converge on the doors, and I'm so confused by nervousness that for a moment I think I'm about to miss the train. Of course I don't want to return to the loop, and I'm about to demand how the railway will be dealing with my information when a man darts off the stairs and onto the train.

He's wearing an unobtrusively dark suit. It's no longer hidden by the yellow jerkin, and I might not have recognised him except for the flag pinned to his lapel and the briefcase in his hand. "He's here," I shout, and my hands sprawl away from the grille. "He's got back on the train."

The only response from the grille is a blurred metallic clatter. I didn't say that the man has the case, and now I'm sure it's too late. My instincts send me to the train before I have a chance to think, and I dodge between the closing doors. "Let me through," I say at once.

I didn't have time to reach the carriage the man boarded. Nobody ahead of me seems to believe my mission is urgent. I have to thrust my pass over people's shoulders to flash it in their faces, just long enough to leave them with an impression of officialdom. I'm crawling with sweat from the closeness of so many bodies, whose softness feels horribly vulnerable, ready to be blown apart. The carriage seems little better than airless, and I feel walled in by the tunnel, not to mention my own scarcely rational decision to pursue the man onto the train. Now I'm at the door to the next carriage, and someone is lounging against it. As I pound on the glass my heart mimics the rhythm. At last the loafer turns his sluggish apathetic head. He stares at my pass and then at me as if I might be a patient posing as a nurse, and then he slouches aside just far enough to let me sidle around the door.

I can't see the man with the briefcase. His badge is too small to show up in the crowd, and what else is there to distinguish him? Mousy hair, bland nondescript face, dark suit – none of these stands out. My heart counts the seconds like a clock or some more lethal mechanism as I force my way along the carriage. I peer at the floor but see only people's legs – bones that could shatter in a moment, flesh and muscles that would fill the air. I'm nearly at the first set of doors, and I crane around the partition behind the seats. There indeed is the briefcase.

I feel as though I've rehearsed the moment. I stoop and grab the handle, and I'm lifting the case when the train shudders in the midst of a burst of light. I'm almost used to that, because I know it means we've reached Moorfields. I still haven't located the man with the flag in his lapel, but it can't matter just now. The moment the door opens I struggle through the crowd and its reinforcements onto the platform. Where can I take the briefcase? I'm fleeing to the nearest exit when a hand grasps my shoulder. "Where do you think you're going with that?" says a voice.

It belongs to a tall man in an unobtrusively expensive suit. The lines on his high forehead and the hint of grey in his cropped black hair may be raising his apparent age, but he seems reassuringly official. "Where's safe?" I blurt.

"I'm asking what you're doing with it," he says and keeps hold of my shoulder.

"Trying to get rid of it, to dispose of it, I mean. Someone deliberately left it on the train, and not just once either. Don't you know what that means?" I'm so desperate that I shake the case at him, and it emits an ominous metallic rattle. "Just let me –"

"You made the call."

I don't see how this can be an accusation, and so I say "It was me, yes."

"Thank you, Mr Conrad."

I'm bemused by this, even though his grip on my shoulder has begun to feel more appreciative than custodial. "How do you know my name?"

"We know everything we have to know."

His eyes have grown so professionally blank that I say "You're not with the railway, are you?"

"We're responsible for this kind of situation. That's all I can tell you." He lets go of my shoulder and repeats, "Thank you, Mr Conrad."

Even when he holds out his hand I don't immediately see he's asking for the briefcase. Its reappearances have left me wary, and I say "I wonder if you've got some identification."

"Don't you think we would have?" he says and produces a wallet almost as thin as a wafer. It contains a single card with his name and his likeness and some abbreviated information. "Is that good enough for you?" he wants to know.

"Thank you, Mr Joseph," I say and hand over the briefcase.

He doesn't move away at once. He has to know what he's about, which is why I didn't panic when he lingered over questioning me – he would hardly have been putting himself at risk. There may be a trace of doubt in my eyes, since he says

"Are you sure that settles it? Would you like to be there when it's disposed of?"

"I'm sure." Indeed, I'm growing anxious for him and the case to be gone. "You're the authority," I tell him. "It's in safe hands now."

As he heads for the nearest stairway I hear a train. I'm eager to board, and more eager for it to leave any danger behind. The doors close as I find a seat and give in to expressing relief – shaking my head, mopping my brow, letting out a loud sigh that shudders with my heartbeat. "I've really done it this time," I declare.

Nobody responds except for glancing at me as if I might be a mental patient on the loose. I don't care what they think of me; I know I've kept them safe. A young man in a business suit returns to reading a comic book, and a girl gazes at her extravagantly large wristwatch, which shows seven minutes to six. A woman who pushed her thin spectacles high with a forefinger lets them subside, and a man lifts one foot after the other to rub the toecaps of his shoes even shinier on his trouser cuffs. None of the passengers might be able to do any of this without me. The idea accompanies me around the loop, past Lime Street and Central Station, and prompts me to stare along the James Street platform. I see nobody with a briefcase, but the absence isn't quite reassuring enough. As the doors start to close I jump off the train and run up the stairs to the underground bridge.

I still seem to have a task. When a train appears I stay on the platform until the doors begin to close, but I can't see anyone suspicious. As soon as I step aboard a girl gives me a seat, and everything seems settled as the train sets off around the loop. A bald man with a tweed hat on his lap gazes at the polished toecaps of his shoes before turning over his newspaper. A bespectacled woman in a checked overcoat and with queries dangling from her earlobes is reading another copy of the paper. A young man dressed for business takes a comic book from among the documents in a cardboard folder, and a young woman in a waspishly striped sweater pushes a headphone away from one ear while she consults her considerable wristwatch. As blackness closes around the train I see the time is seven minutes to six.

I could imagine the lights on the tunnel walls are signalling to me, and I search for some distraction inside the carriage. The headline on the front page of the bald man's newspaper says ISLAMIC PANIC, but I'm not sure if that's the name of a terrorist group. The bespectacled woman's paper has its letters page facing me. One letter is entitled NO ASYLUM, which seems to be the slogan of a party called Pure Brit, and the correspondent has suggested that the party is planting bombs so as to blame Muslims and provoke a backlash against immigrants. I grow aware of a voice too small to belong to any of the passengers. It isn't in my head; it's on the young woman's headphones – a recorded radio phone-in, where somebody is arguing that the bombs are the work not of Muslims or their foes but the first stages of a plan by the secret service to force the country to accept dictatorship. Another caller on the phone-in accuses the man who was credited with trying to save his fellow passengers of having planted the bomb himself. All these idle theories make me feel as if nothing is to be trusted, and I focus my attention on the young man's comic book. The cover shows a boffin grimacing in disbelief while he tells his colleagues "It's not that kind of time bomb. It's a bomb that destroys time. It'll blow the past to bits."

"It's nothing like that." The idea has gone too far, and I can't keep quiet any longer, especially since I've seen the truth at last. I can hear the women murmuring behind me like nurses, and I should have listened to them sooner. "That's right, someone's talking about us again," I tell everyone. "But don't you see, if they can keep changing it we can change it too."

Nobody appears to want to listen. They're all gazing at the floor, even those who've turned towards me. "It needn't be what any of them say happened to us," I insist – I feel as if a voice is speaking through me. "It needn't even be what did."

Everyone is staring at the floor beside me. I look at last and see the briefcase. "We don't have to be what people say just because of where we are," I vow as I take hold of the handle. A thunderous rumble swells in my ears, and brightness flares in my eyes, but it's on the wall of the tunnel. I mustn't be distracted by the absence of my shadow – of anyone's. I have to get my task right this time, and then we can head for the light, out of the tunnel.

MISSED CONNECTION

Michael Marshall Smith

You may be more familiar with Michael Marshall Smith as Michael Marshall, author of such high-octane thrillers as Bad Things *and* The Straw Men, *but it's with the addition of the 'Smith' that he moves into the territories of horror and SF. Michael's horror stories show a broad range of styles and themes, whether it be the shock of revulsion in 'More Tomorrow' or the quiet beauty of the award-winning 'The Man Who Drew Cats,' and if any writer can be termed a polymath then it is truly he. If you've never read any Smith before, then you're in for a treat. This tale has the quality of a waking nightmare, a panic dream that seems like it will never end…*

LAWSON WAS REGRETTING the decision to go shopping before he'd even bought a ticket for the Tube. All but one of the time-and-labour-saving automatic ticket dispensers was either closed or unable to give change, and it was all he could do not to let out yelps of irritable despair at the inability of those in front of him to understand the process of getting the machine to yield up its wares. The station seemed to be unusually full of squalling children and jabbering mad people, and the flu he'd thought in decline was thriving in the damp of the winter afternoon. He was beginning to feel like death cooled down, and the expedition had barely started.

His ticket finally obtained, he took the steps down to the Victoria line, where a discouraging number of people were already gathered. He'd realised before venturing out of the house that going into central London the Saturday before Christmas was a bad idea; but several weeks of late nights at the office – with no time to take lunch-breaks – meant virtually none of his nearest and dearest had yet been ticked off the present list. The fact that so many other people from Finsbury Park alone were going in at the same time boded very ill for the state of London proper. He had his route planned, however, and knew exactly which shops he was going to. Essential. Simply meandering about on a day like today was a recipe for disaster. You had to go in, buy what you wanted, and go on to the next one. Then hurry home immediately, at least an hour ahead of the general exodus. Only way to do it.

Feeling rather like a commander in the field maximising his chances of surviving a difficult and potentially dangerous mission, Lawson walked to the far right end of the platform, until he was up against the wall by the side of the tunnel. Experience had shown that when people came onto a platform they either stood exactly where the entrance put them, or walked about twenty yards either side. Few bothered to walk *all* the way to the end: thus it was in the very end carriages that one stood the greatest chance of not having one's lungs imploded in the crush. Commuter-savvy: one of the few skills one acquired by living in London.

With what Lawson had come, with suspicion, to recognise as the Victoria Line's characteristic efficiency, a Tube pulled into the station within less than a minute. It wasn't especially crowded, but – he thought as he climbed into the *particularly* non-full last carriage – it could have been. Actual results were not the point. The point was that the Tube, fearsome and irritating though it was, could be understood as a system.

Once understood, mastered.

Settling into one of the seats near the double doors, he ran over the rather vague present ideas he had for his mother and sister. They were the difficult ones; everyone else's had been decided months ago. Neither was easy to buy for: his mother because she seemed to have just about everything she wanted; his sister because Lawson had no idea what she thought or felt. He tried to remember if she'd expressed an interest in something in particular (or indeed anything at all) during the past year, but found himself unable to concentrate, the problem continually slipping away from him.

The carriage was hot and humid, and his flu made Lawson feel dislocated and strange, as if he wasn't engaging with what was around him. It was a feeling he associated with being drunk, a state he disliked. It was all the more disconcerting because his mind at the same time felt quite sharp and alert. Throughout the last week at work he had felt like this, which had worried him. It was all too possible to forget something, to fail to get to grips with a problem and realise its significance, whilst still apparently being in control. Whitehead, the young smoothie who ran Lawson's office, would keep coming in and reminding him to do things. He did this all the time, even when he knew Lawson was on top of his work. Lawson had found it difficult to remember if he'd been told before, or if he'd actually done the things he had to. He normally worked on the principle that if Whitehead didn't start chivying him about something, it wasn't a problem. But what if he *had* hassled him already, and he'd forgotten about it? It was all rather unsettling.

As it made its way into central London the Tube began to get more and more crowded, and during a two minute pause in a tunnel, Lawson elected to get off at the next stop. Not only was Warren Street actually rather convenient, at the top of Tottenham Court Road, it was a station which comparatively few of the masses now blocking the aisles would be familiar with.

When the Tube eventually started moving again he stood up and made his way to the doors, so as not to be obstructed when the time came to disembark. Lawson of course knew which side of the Tube to go to, the one that would open onto the platform on this particular station; and so when it pulled into Warren Street all he had to do was step lightly off.

He was gratified to notice that no-one left the carriage with him. Even the Tube driver appeared to realise that the station would not be a popular choice on a pre-Christmas afternoon: the carriage doors seemed to shut and the Tube to whip out of the station almost before Lawson's feet had reached the platform.

Shouldering his bag into a more comfortable position, he turned right and started to walk. He didn't get very far, however, before running straight into a wall. Confused, he looked up. He was standing at the extreme right hand side of the platform (as one saw it from the train), against the wall next to the tunnel.

Turning slowly, Lawson looked around.

Behind him were the tracks, to the right the wall, and extending out to his left was the platform. The Exit signs pointed to his left. As they should. Shaking his head, Lawson walked down the platform.

After a few yards he realised the source of his confusion, and stopped. The way out should have been to the right.

Puzzled, he turned to look back at the platform. He'd got on the last carriage to the right of the platform at Finsbury Park. When the tube got to Warren Street, he should still have been in the last carriage to the right. Instead, he'd got out at the far *left* of the platform.

Walking through the archway into the area that funneled passengers from the two opposite platforms towards the escalator, Lawson struggled to get his mind around the problem, sure that there was a straightforward explanation, but unable for the life of him to work out what it was. One possibility was that the Tube had somehow pulled much further through the platform than usual, pulling his carriage up to the lefthand side of the platform instead of the right. Unfortunately this was also impossible. It would mean that all the people who had got on to the left of him at Finsbury Park would have been pulled through into the tunnel past the platform, unable to get off. And where had all the carriages behind his come from? People who got onto them at Warren Street would be unable to get off at other stations, which was bound to be rather unsatisfactory.

Not that other people were exactly a feature of the station. He'd been right to choose it, as no-one else at all had got off there, and the way to the escalators was empty. Smiling, sniffing, and consigning the problem to his 'Strange things that have happened to me on the Tube' file (which was pretty small), Lawson got onto the escalator.

Halfway up he noticed that the down escalator was working too: that *both of them* were functional at the same time. That is, that people could use escalators to go both up and down *simultaneously*. Now that *was* an incident for the 'Strange things etc' file. The down escalator had been broken for so long that to see them both working at once was like an optical illusion. Part of what had irritated him so much about the broken escalator was that he'd never seen anyone working on it. This presumably was the explanation – they beavered away at night.

Reaching the top, Lawson scanned the posters for anything new or interesting as he made his way to the next set of escalators. While there was nothing particularly interesting, there was certainly plenty that was new. Side-by-side with the escalator-fixers the billboard stickers had obviously put in a hard night's work. He recognised none of the adverts that festooned the walls.

His temporary goodwill towards Underground engineers faded rapidly as he reached seeing distance of the next set of escalators. Both were roped off. And roped off, he noticed as he drew nearer down the cylindrical corridor, with an irrevocability that seemed to speak of the despair of the engineers that the escalators would ever work again, at least in their lifetimes.

Shoulders slumping, Lawson stopped a few yards short. His flu had brought attendant aches in his back, and the thought of struggling up about a million stairs was not a pleasant one. Why couldn't the damn things have waited another day to stop working? They'd been fine yesterday, when he'd manfully made his way in to work; but now he was on his own time, they had to grind to a halt.

He stared at the escalators bleakly, trying to galvanise himself into moving in search of an alternative route up, and wandered up to their foot. Where he noticed two odd things. The first was that the stationary escalator was filthy. The sides were covered with dust, as were the handrails, normally rubbed smooth by the grip of countless hands. Not only that, but the steps themselves were liberally strewn with rubbish: cans, wrappers and yellowing newspaper. It seemed hard to believe that even a particularly riotous pre-Christmas evening could have generated this level of debris.

More disconcerting still, the top of the escalator seemed to disappear into darkness. Instead of the familiar reflected daylight from the outside of the station – not to mention the lights which normally lined the roof of the ascending tunnel – the escalator seemed lit only by the area in which he stood, this glow fading into complete darkness about two thirds of the way up the shaft.

Lawson swore with exasperation. Clearly some mishap had befallen the escalator, and the way was closed. Everyone else had known this, which was why he had been the only person to alight from the Victoria Line at this station. Perhaps there had been an announcement on the radio, or one on the train which he'd missed?

Where did the back stairs for the station start? Not here, clearly. Mind still sluggishly working at the enigma of his confusing entrance onto the platform, Lawson peered around, a little surprised that he was still alone. He had a vague memory of stairs leading off a corridor near one of the Northern Line Platforms. The irritating thing was that the people in his carriage who hadn't had the Tube-sense to get off here were probably already at Oxford Circus and surging into the shops.

There was nothing for it but to make his way to the Northern Line and get out that way. As he walked, blinking and rubbing his eyes against a headache, he looked again at the posters that covered the walls. They seemed to fuel his flu-engendered dislocation, telling him of drinks he'd never heard of and shows he didn't realise were on. He'd had no idea they changed all the posters in a station at once: perhaps it was some new edict. As he approached the corner which would bring him to the steps down to the Northern Line he listened to the flat echoes of the noise his heels made, and still he saw no-one else walking the tunnels.

He turned the corner onto something so unexpected that he stopped dead in his tracks. In front of him were the steps which he knew led down onto the southbound platform of the Northern Line. They did not lead down into the usual shuffling melee of irritable shoppers, however.

They led down into total darkness.

Lawson was so confused that he glanced at his watch, as if to check that night had not fallen without his realising. To his surprise, his watch wasn't there. Or rather it was, but strapped to his right wrist instead of his left, breaking the habit of fifty years.

He must have been very vague *indeed* that morning, to have done such a thing. It was only after confirming it was still early afternoon that he realised how little sense checking the time had made. He knew what damned time it was. He stared down the steps into the darkness, feeling a little perturbed. Why should the platform be dark? What was going on? He was suddenly glad he had checked his watch after all, and did so again, needing confirmation that he hadn't somehow got completely mixed up. For an instant, everything about being at the station, from arriving at the far left of the platform through the roped-off escalator to this, seemed altogether odd, a sequence of related events. He felt only precariously tethered to reality, and as if there was something that he was missing. Almost as if Whitehead were hovering just behind him; as though he'd forgotten or misunderstood something important.

Finally the rational side of his mind, which was well-developed and used to being dominant, stepped in.

For some reason the Northern Line was not available at this station. To ram that fact home to passengers in passing Tubes, they'd turned the lights off. Or there was a lighting failure in some parts of the station, or a general electricity problem. Hence the dysfunctional escalator, perhaps. Either way, it was not worthy of 'holding the front page'. Just a little strange. Lawson remembered what it had been like when, for a number of years, Stepney Green Station had been shut. Passing though the dimly-lit station had given him a similar feeling, of the eeriness of something familiar looking disused.

Warren Street was not a disused station, however, and all that this proved was that he ought to listen to the radio in the mornings. He'd already wasted enough time. What he should do was find the steps and get out of this disaster of a Tube station. Yes, and then compose a letter of complaint to London Underground. It simply wasn't good enough, abandoning people in a station in this state. Feeling invigorated with a sense of indignation, Lawson started to descend the steps.

He hadn't realised just how black it would be, just how complete the darkness is underground. By the time he'd progressed a few yards to the bottom of the steps he was in limbo, unable to discern any features ahead of him whatsoever. Although he was reasonably confident that the stairs were accessible from this platform somewhere, he had no real idea how far along they were. If he went down the wrong corridor, he could search for ages and not find them, all the time getting further away from any area that he had a rough mental picture of.

After about twenty careful yards he stopped. This was no bloody good. He was in total darkness, with no idea of how far, or indeed in which direction, he should go. The harder he tried to remember, the more the undifferentiated blackness pressed in upon him. He could recall less and less which corridor the stairs came off, and whether, once in the right corridor, there were multiple choices of sub-corridor, and which of those he should take. The route ahead – which would have been so simple with light, or perhaps even *without* it if he hadn't been so worked up – had begun to fragment in his mind, left and right merging into one.

He had lost confidence in the whole idea of the stairs.

The possibility of going down onto the line occurred to him. It wouldn't be that far to walk: Goodge Street was only a few hundred yards further down Tottenham Court Road, and there he would be back into light and sanity. Even the thought of being suffocated in a press of Italian shoppers and German tourists was beginning to seem attractive.

Lawson wiped his forehead with his sleeve, feeling hot and extremely bothered. He couldn't go down the tunnel. Not only would it involve further traipsing off into total darkness with no clear sense of where he was going, but what if a train came along? He had no idea how wide the tunnel was once it got out of the station, or how much room for manoeuvre there was between it and a passing Tube. He had no interest in the idea of being the fall-guy in an enactment of the old joke about the light at the end of the tunnel being an oncoming train.

He backed up slowly, turned around, and shuffled back the way he'd come. He'd go back up to the escalators and think about it there. There was probably some simple solution that he couldn't think of because he was feeling put upon, and not entirely well. Once he was back in the light again everything would seem clearer.

When he reached the stairs he immediately felt more confident, and trotted up, relieved that here at least the lights were still working. The clacking of his heels, unnerving only minutes before, was now reassuring in its direction and purpose. Well, purpose, at least. Back at the foot of the escalators, Lawson drew to a halt and took stock. Clearly things were significantly out of line. The Northern Line, if not shut, was certainly not operating a full service. The Victoria Line was, or at least had been: Lawson toyed with the idea of checking to see if the lights were still on down there. He decided that it was not germane to his purpose, and also that he'd rather not know if they weren't.

Either way, there was clearly a problem with Warren Street, and given that, it was fairly logical that they should have shut down parts of the station. It was *not* logical that they should have dumped him at the wrong end of a platform in a station which appeared to be shut. After more than ten minutes, he realised, he had still seen no other passengers.

He could feel that parts of the problem were resolvable, their solutions tugging distantly at his mind, and felt that his inability to grab hold of some central dilemma and solve it was important. But he had no clear idea why he felt that, or of what the central dilemma was, so it wasn't much help. Instead he turned his mind to the more immediate problem of how to get himself to the point where he was just another Christmas shopper, i.e. out onto the bloody street.

There appeared to be only one possible solution. The escalator. Although broken and submerged under debris, it was a straightforward route up to the entrance, and unlike the stairs, he would be starting only one level down from the street. The question of why the entrance should appear to be so dark was a little worrying, but one that could safely be postponed, and which he would have to deal with whatever way he managed to get up there.

Lifting one rope of the barrier and pushing the other down, Lawson slid between the two. Tentatively putting one foot on the bottom step, he tested it to make sure that whatever was wrong with the escalator wasn't something that was going to make scaling it hazardous. It felt reassuringly solid.

The next few steps were slightly more problematic, as Lawson had to dislodge a number of cans before he could even get his foot on the steps properly. By the time he was about half-way up, it was quite hard going against all the rubbish, and he was in semi-darkness. Something brushed against his foot and he kicked it away vigorously: from the harsh flapping sound it made he realised it had been only newspaper. It was as if someone had upended a skipful of rubbish down the escalator. Perhaps the cleaning services had an accident with yesterday evening's haul, and it had ended up cascading down the escalator, recreating the impression of years of detritus. Feeling rather tired and depressed, his hands grimy with dust from the rails, Lawson put his head down and grimly plowed his way towards the top.

By the time he felt the gradient on the handrail begin to level off, he couldn't see anything. The sliver of light from the level below was spent on an area far down the ascending tunnel's ceiling, and was no help at the top. This was a shame, because Lawson felt that he could do with some help. Something was very wrong.

The entrance to Warren Street station is a roughly rectangular area, about twenty metres by ten, open on two sides to the street, with the ticket window and machines over to the left. Not only was the area Lawson found himself in pitch darkness, but, the flat short echoes told him, it only extended about three feet. This made no sense at all, and Lawson felt panic rising within him.

Then the lights at the bottom of the escalators went out.

Lawson gripped the rail at the top of the escalator. He refused to look back down the dark shaft, and instead concentrated on trying to come to terms with what was in front of him; or in the short term, trying to stay in a state where he had some chance of doing so.

They'd blocked off the escalator. Of course: that was it. There'd been some problem, and they'd boarded up the way to the escalator to stop people trying to go that way. Lawson felt his panic subside, until it was humming reasonably comfortably at the level of mild hysteria. If they'd blocked off the escalator at entrance level, the station must be shut: there was no other way down or up. Except the stairs, and they led down to or up from what was currently a closed platform.

So, apart from the fact that he'd been dumped here at the wrong end of the platform, everything was explicable. The station was closed, the light had been on at the level below purely because they'd been working on some problem, and they'd now turned it off again not realising that some hapless passenger, abandoned here by oversight, was trying to get out.

It all made sense, more or less.

Slushing his feet forward through what felt like cardboard boxes, hands held out in front, Lawson reached for the boarding. It felt smooth, almost varnished. He knocked on it, trying to get a sense of how thick the wood was. The sound was short and sharp. He banged harder with the heel of his palm, and succeeded only in hurting his wrist. There was no give in the wood at all, and no sound from the road outside the station. Whoever had boarded up the escalator had made a proper British job of it.

His fingers came upon a regular edge. The surface sloped inwards for about half an inch before reaching another edge, where the wood stuck out again. Puzzled, Lawson brought his hands together in the depression and ran them out in different directions along it. After about a foot each way, they reached corners, and the recess changed direction and ran upwards instead. This continued for several feet up the board, until Lawson was having to stretch. Then the two sides came inwards again until his hands were touching once more. There was a big rectangle in the boarding. Two, in fact three, he discovered, sliding his hands out to either side.

To Lawson, whose panic was once more on the rise, this meant nothing at all, except... mouth gaping slightly, he fumbled in his pockets for the book of matches he felt sure must be lurking there. When you've smoked for forty years you don't get caught without matches, however badly you've got flu and never mind how much they hurt your throat. He found a dog-eared bundle of cardboard and pulled it out, fingers finding about eight or nine bent matches. He was rather disappointed, but not very surprised, to find that his hands were trembling as he struck what felt like the least mangled of them. Nothing happened. He tried again, and the match sprang alight, spitting burning sulphur over his fingers and into the darkness.

"It's bloody panelling," he said, quietly, and the match went out.

Lawson stood still for a moment, not bothering to hurry to light another match. The after-image of what he had seen was still fading on his retinas. In front of him was a wood-panelled wall, which made a corner two feet to his left and continued until it was flush up against the top of the escalator. It looked for all the world like the corner of the sitting room in some gentlemans' club. That explained why the boarding had felt so solid, so unlike a thin and temporary barrier.

It was good to have an explanation.

It was just unfortunate that it was extremely bizarre.

Lawson let himself topple slowly forward, until his forehead rested against the smooth wood. So long as it had been explicable, he'd been alright. He'd always been game for a laugh. Not much that could throw *him* off balance. Lights being off, platforms being shut, he could deal with. He laughed in the face of them.

This was different. This was back to being left at the wrong end of an ordinary Tube platform. The two were part of the same world, and it wasn't a world that he felt he could make any headway in. The whole of the world, *this* world, was standing behind him, mutely making him feel that he'd forgotten something; that he'd misunderstood, that he'd done something wrong. And he still had no idea what it was.

But he could find out. If one had a problem, the first thing one did was break it down into its constituent parts. You dealt with those which needed to be solved first, and then soldiered on until the whole became clear. Ultimately one should be able to step outside the particular and see the general problem, and start tackling that. And the general problem that Lawson very much wanted to have solved as soon as possible was *getting out of the station.*

He pushed himself upright again and retrieved the matches from his pocket. Fumbling one alight, he looked around. As the match guttered and spat he thought he saw something to his right, some difference in the otherwise perfect regularity of the panelling. The right hand wall was not flush with the side of the escalator, but recessed about two feet beyond it. Before spending another match, he shuffled over to it to see if he could determine what it was by touch.

At first all he could feel was the contours of another panel. But as he moved his hands outwards, his fingers found notches in the wood either side, a notch that could be traced both up and down. Slightly further in, down low on the left hand side, there was a small wooden handle. It was a exit. There was a way out.

Mentally steadying himself, Lawson prepared to open the door, a match poised. The knob turned rather stiffly, but with a click the door was soon open. He pulled it a few inches, then paused to light the match, foot hooked around the bottom of the door to pull it open further once he was ready. In the insubstantial light of the flaring match he drew his foot towards him, pulling the door ajar with some effort: the hinges were very stiff and let out small rusty squeaks.

When it was open a couple of feet he stopped. Conscious that his supply of light was limited, and feeling, he imagined, rather like someone playing a computer game who, having attained some new level, is forced to play it by ear with some rapidity, Lawson quickly took in what was behind the door.

A small, squarish chamber, about two feet to a side, panelled in the same dark wood on two sides. On the left, however, there appeared to be some steps.

Pain in his fingertips.

First casting a glance behind him into the darkness, Lawson walked carefully forward into the chamber. He could climb steps in the dark. There was no point wasting another match. He put a tentative foot on the first, and, reassured by its wooden solidity, walked up several, using the banisters that stuck out from the still paneled walls on either side. This ascent was at least straightforward, with no rubbish to impede his progress.

He took a few more steps, slowly, anxious not to run smack into the door he felt must come soon. Then he stopped.

The escalator at Warren Street ended at street level. You walked off it, through the barriers, and then straight out onto the street. He put his hand out into the darkness. Nothing. He took another step up. Still nothing. Hand out in front of him, fingers splayed, Lawson took a few more steps. He must be going up some back route which lead to an area a few feet above street level. A staff area of some kind, perhaps. Quite apart from the issue of what part of the station he was now headed into, Lawson was nervous of continuing when it felt like he could be wandering blindly off the edge of a cliff. He found the matches again and struck one, peering forwards.

What he saw was not a door, or even the foot of a door, but steps.

He tilted his head backwards slowly, assuming the door would appear by about 10°. It didn't, just more steps. Holding the match, which appeared to be the one good one in the book, higher above his head, he looked further and further up until he was looking up at 45°. The light of the flame glowed warm against the dark wood of the staircase, reflecting orange round the walls far up the staircase. He could see about thirty yards, and all he could see was steps.

When the match eventually burned out, Lawson abruptly sat down. What he had seen had looked like a passage from a stereotypical nightmare in a film, except he wasn't being pursued, and the staircase hadn't got longer. It simply was that long to start off with. Longer, in fact, because had the light penetrated anywhere near the end, then highlights of the end door would have shown in the flickering light: the light wouldn't simply have faded out into darkness. And he wasn't asleep, sadly. He was awake. He was awake and on his way up a staircase that led, at a conservative estimate, to a point at least twenty yards above Warren Street Station's roof.

Lawson got to his feet again, and resumed his climb. There didn't seem to be much else that he could do.

When he'd climbed ninety steps, and thus about thirty yards, he slowed down, and continued with one hand out in front of him. He could have lit a match to see how far he had to go, but feared that the result would only depress him.

It was a couple of increasingly tiring minutes before the changing echo of his feet on the stairs warned him that he was coming to the end.

Another door.

Lawson didn't have an accurate sense of how high he'd climbed, but estimated it to be at least the height of a third storey. Trying to remember the buildings around the station, whether any of them were high enough for him to have somehow been diverted into their upper floors, he turned the handle of the door. Like its predecessor, it was stiff, further compounding Lawson's impression that whatever back stairway he was on, it hadn't been used in a long, long time.

He found himself in a smallish room, dimly lit from some external light source, the direction of which it was impossible to determine. Piled high with haphazardly jumbled furniture, it looked like a loft. Somehow, as he had begun to suspect, he must have managed to climb into the attic of one of the buildings around the station.

At the opposite side of the room there was another door. Lawson headed for it gratefully, for it had to be the way to another, descending staircase, which would lead down through the building. He wasn't sure how he was going to explain to anyone he might meet what he was doing in the building's attic, but rather pitied the fate of anyone who tried to give him a hard time about it – most particularly if they were an employee of the London Underground.

The door led through into another room, larger than the first, but equally full of disused furniture and other miscellaneous objects. Lawson edged his way along one of the walls until he came to a narrow panelled corridor off the room. This led towards another door. He was slightly puzzled to see that the few steps led up, rather than down, to the door, but reasoned that the interior design of lofts was seldom straightforward.

The door looked solid, clearly a portal to a different area of the building he was in. Reaching for the knob, Lawson had a horrible suspicion that it would be locked.

It wasn't. The handle turned easily and the door, though stiff as all the others had been, opened.

Onto the street.

Moving very slowly, mouth a stupid O of astonishment, Lawson stepped out onto the pavement. A minute ago, all he'd wanted was to be safely out into the street. But not this way. Not when he should be forty metres up in the air.

And not when the street was like this.

Lawson looked at his watch. It was four o'clock. More than that, it was four o'clock on a Saturday afternoon just before Christmas, and he was on Tottenham Court Road. So where, he pleaded silently, looking up and down the street, was everyone else?

The road was utterly devoid of people. Also of cars, either moving or stationary. He looked left, where the Euston Road, usually a passable facsimile of the Indianapolis 500, lay quiet and empty. Walking a few yards to the curb he stared to the right, down towards Centre Point and the hub of Christmas shopping madness. No-one. No-one at all.

Behind him there was a sharp bang. He turned quickly: the door he had just emerged from had swung shut, and was now virtually indistinguishable from the wall. The ground floor windows were boarded up, the first floor whitewashed. The building housed the kind of disused shop front that springs up every now and then on Tottenham Court Road when an electrical retailer folds; rapidly to become a temporary sell-through DVD shop and then eventually another electrical goods outlet. It bore no resemblance at all to Warren Street station, although it occupied the corner where the station should be.

Lawson walked down the street, trying to make sense of what

he was seeing. Unexpected people were one thing. Unexpected buildings were rather different.

He turned and backed slowly across the road, something that should have been impossible without risking death by taxi-cab. The building didn't look any more right from the other side. And neither, he realised, did the one he was now standing next to. It should have been Maples, a large and rather ugly department store. It *was* still Maples, in fact, as a large sign proclaimed, but the building looked different: the design anonymous, as if from some unknown and especially bland school of sixties architecture. It was entirely deserted inside, the shelves empty.

Walking down the street towards Centre Point, Lawson surveyed the buildings and shops with disquiet. Were *they* different? He'd never studied them properly before, and so could not swear to what they'd been like; but felt sure that they had changed somehow, become more amorphous, interchangeable.

And where were all the bloody people?

Suddenly galvanised, Lawson began striding quickly down the street. A little way along the road there was an area he knew better, including a shop where he'd recently bought a CD player. He'd recognise that, if nothing else. As he walked, he listened once more to the sound of his feet, the only noise there was to be heard.

After about four minutes' fast walking he slowed, looking carefully at the shops. His inner milometer told him that the road should be around there somewhere – and that the CD shop should be next to it, in a colonnade of recessed shop fronts.

He came to the corner he was expecting and then stopped, unsure. The building on the corner looked different, newer than he was expecting. Or older. Different, anyway. It felt, he realised, like going down a familiar road in a different direction to usual. He had always found that if he drove or walked the 'wrong' way down such a route, everything looked very different. It was hard to reconcile the two views, to merge them into one place seen from different perspectives. However much your mind tried to force the environment to assume its customary flavour, reality and recollection tugged in different directions.

The colonnade was there, in the sense that the front of the shops were further back from the main road than most. But as Lawson crossed the side road and drew closer, he saw that the shops themselves were all interchangeable, undifferentiated. The building could have been anything. And the windows were not full of matt black stereos and surprisingly small camcorders.

They were empty. All of them.

For the first time genuinely frightened, Lawson stared at the windows. This was the place, he was sure, but everything had changed. In desperation he trotted several yards past the building, to the next corner. He turned around, until he was facing back up the way he had come. He had been coming down the road: now he was facing *up* the road. Maybe it would look different that way; perhaps he would be able to see what the difference really was.

Lawson walked up the road as slowly as he could. The shop he was searching for should now be on the left, and Maples in the distance was now on the right.

It *did* look different. The view had changed, but not enough. The buildings were still all wrong, the street was still empty and unnaturally quiet.

Two different sides. Left and right.

Lawson stopped dead in his tracks, with a terrible cold feeling of falling.

Suddenly he knew what he'd done wrong, where his mistake had been. When the train had stopped at Warren Street, when he'd got off at the wrong end of the platform, it was because the platform was *on a different side* to the one he'd got on at. At Finsbury Park he got on at the far right, on the right hand side of the train. At Warren Street, the platform must be to the *left* of the train. Befuddled with crowds and flu, he'd lost track of left and right in the symmetrical carriage, and had got off expecting to be on the right of the world. When in fact he was on the left.

All his attempts to explain what had happened, his logic, had been based on coming up the road the wrong way. He'd come at the world from the wrong side. But it shouldn't actually *be* different, surely, just a different view of the same thing. To place yourself, all you had to know was which side you were coming from. He knew now: surely everything should fall back into place?

Slowly, Lawson turned to face the street that was empty on a Saturday afternoon before Christmas; the familiar but different buildings; the quiet.

SIDING 13

James Lovegrove

Congestion is that most modern of horrors, whether it be on the motorway or – as it is here – on the London Underground. We all know the horrible, sweaty, panic-inducing claustrophobia that is to be experienced on an overcrowded rush-hour train. And James Lovegrove clearly knows that horror too, for 'Siding 13' takes us to the heart of a packed Tube train, and leaves us there, trapped amongst the commuters. And the journey has only just begun...

WHEN THE TRAIN pulled up, it was very nearly full, and Marcus very nearly didn't get on. There would be another along in four minutes, if the destination boards' promises were accurate. He could wait.

Except, he couldn't. Not really. His appointment at the Whaam! Comics offices was for nine thirty sharp, and Marcus didn't dare risk being late. He'd planned to arrive quarter of an hour early, to be on the safe side, and didn't want his margin for error diminished by so much as a minute, let alone four.

Besides, there was an exceptionally pretty girl strap-hanging just inside the carriage entrance. She decided him. He could put up with a little squashing and discomfort, on the off-chance that he might get to talk to her.

He pushed on board, lugging his portfolio with him, just as the doors started to close. The train jerked into motion, then smoothly gained speed. Soon it was purring along its raised track on a causeway overlooking the Greater London suburbscape of roofs and gardens.

Marcus was not a commuter and therefore unaccustomed to travelling in packed Tube trains. All around him were the weary, grim-set faces of men and women who put up with standing-room-only journeys as a matter of course. They had their methods of escape: iPods, newspapers, paperbacks, urgent texting, the odd phone call. They were resigned to being livestock in trucks, led off daily to the ritual slaughter of work.

The pretty girl gave him a brief, incurious glance. Marcus kept staring at her sidelong until she looked at him again, at which point he quickly switched his attention to a rusty gasometer passing by outside. Two-way contact had been established. The channels were open. Good.

The train decelerated into the next station. More people boarded. The recorded announcement invited passengers to move down inside the carriage please, let the other passengers on. There wasn't much space to move down into, but everyone obliged nonetheless, shufflingly. Marcus was now pressed against the pretty girl, shoulder to shoulder. He held himself rigid, keeping their physical proximity to a minimum, in order to show her he wasn't that kind of man, the kind who took advantage or was overbearing, and definitely not the pervy, rubbing-up kind. He embraced his portfolio to his chest, the better to safeguard it and the valuables inside.

The train lumbered off again.

At the next stop yet more people clambered on, squeezing in. There were grunts of disquiet, growls of dismay. Someone exclaimed, "Ridiculous!", and several tongues tutted and *tsk*ed. Marcus was now wedged firmly between the girl and a very fat banker type who had his copy of the *Financial Times* rolled like a cosh and was running a bleary eye over columns of market data. He smelled strongly of aftershave and faintly of whisky.

Marcus loaned the girl a knowing, wry look, as if to say, *This is crazy, isn't it? Why do we put ourselves through this?*

She returned the look, with the added interest of a half smile.

"What's in there?" she said, nodding at his portfolio.

"Samples."

"Hope they're going to be OK in all this."

"Me too."

Not long after came the hoped-for "Samples of what?"

"Artwork," Marcus said.

"You're an artist?"

Normally it was a question that carried a substratum of *Oh, poor you*, but not in this instance, thank heaven.

"Yeah, I am. For my sins."

"What sort?"

"Well... " He had honed his next words carefully, over years of experience. "I do commercial stuff to make a living – design, illustration, that sort of thing. But really what I'm into is sequential art."

"Which is... animation?"

"Sort of. Not quite. Graphic novels."

"Ah."

Oh.

"Isn't that," she said, "comics?"

"That's another name for it." Marcus was aware that ears around them were tuning in. The conversation was interesting to others, a curio, a distraction. He prayed he wasn't about to crash and burn, publicly. "I'm heading off for a job interview right now, as a matter of fact. For an assignment. With the British arm of a major American publisher."

"To do comics."

"Yeah. I've, er, I've self-published a couple of titles, and done some webcomics too, but this is the next step up. They like the look of what I've done, and I'm hoping to sign some kind of deal today. It'll probably be work-for-hire at first, doing stories based on one of their pre-existing superhero characters. If all goes well, I'll soon be able to start pitching creator-owned concepts to them."

Her expression told him he was speaking a foreign language.

"For children, I suppose," she said.

"Actually... " Marcus began, and then he thought, *Fuck it, why bother?* He could rehearse the whole comics-aren't-just-for-kids-any-more argument, outline the case for sequential art as a mature modern storytelling medium, cite all the contemporary classics (*Maus*, *Watchmen*, *Palestine*, *Persepolis*), sing the praises of the greats such as Herriman, McCay, Eisner, Miller, Moore – but it would be futile. She wouldn't care. Once again he had bumped up against the unbreachable wall that divided those who understood about comics from those who did not.

"Sometimes," he finished lamely. "For children."

"I hate superheroes," the girl said, an afterthought.

So did Marcus. But he would draw superheroes for Whaam! Comics if that was what Whaam! Comics wanted. He would draw them any fucking thing they asked him to. He was that desperate to get a foot in the door.

The train squealed to a halt at another station. It had reached the outskirts of built-up London. The city looked down on it now, not the other way round. This was the last aboveground stop on the line. From here, the track would take a downward incline then flatten out at sewer level. Technically the Tube was the Tube wherever you were on the network, but practically it never felt like the Tube unless you were underground, rolling through tunnels.

No one alighted. Yet more people got on. They pushed and shoved and elbowed their way into the carriage. They were catching this train and nothing was going to stop them.

Those already on board protested, telling them to stay on the platform, wait for the next train. The pleas fell on deaf ears.

There were still people trying to get on when the "*Please stand clear of the closing doors*" message sounded. The doors ground shut, then reopened, all of them, because someone somewhere had got a foot or an umbrella or a briefcase stuck. They shut again, sealing everyone in, and the train hauled itself onward.

There was no room to move. No room to breathe. Bodies were pressed against bodies, with every cubic centimetre of space between them accounted for. It would have been a groper's paradise, if any groper had been capable of moving his hands to grope. Marcus and the girl were studiously avoiding one another's gazes now. The feel of her flesh, warm against his, served only to thicken his embarrassment. He was pillowed, too, by the flabby belly of the fat banker, with the man's alcohol-tinged breath gusting against the nape of his neck.

His precious samples were getting bent out of shape, but there was nothing he could do about it. The cardboard portfolio wasn't sturdy enough to protect them. Maybe he should have just brought the artwork with him on a memory stick, but he never felt it had the same impact on a computer screen as it did on a full-size printout. Comics art was meant to be seen on paper. Besides, there was no telling how the Whaam! Comics editor had his monitor set. The colours and contrast could be all wrong. On paper, the drawings were exactly as Marcus wanted them, right down to the finest gradation of tint and tone. With luck, the samples would survive. He would flatten them and smooth them out as best he could, once he was off this damn train.

Gaining speed, the train sank below ground level. Brick walls rose, then engulfed it. Daylight vanished, and there was only the sulphur-yellow glow of the carriage's overhead incandescents. The shimmer of wheels on rails, confined, became a rumble.

Soon enough the next station loomed. Marcus anticipated relief. It was officially In Town, where workplaces were. Surely now there'd be some people disembarking.

But no, apparently not. A woman tried to get out, declaring that she'd had enough of this nonsense, she would board the next train. But she couldn't make good on her statement of intent. She couldn't force her way towards the doors. She demanded to be allowed through, then begged, but nobody budged. Nobody could. In the end, with a mewl of dissatisfaction, she abandoned her attempt. A stiffly worded letter of complaint, she said, would be coming London Transport's way. She sounded on the brink of tears.

Meanwhile, even more people were getting on. It didn't seem feasible, but they were. The platform was crowded, bodies jostling against the train windows. They were milling, grimacing, fighting to reach the doors and insert themselves into the already crammed-to-capacity carriage. Somehow, amazingly, many of them managed it, in spite of the frantic and even angry objections emanating from within.

"Get back! Get bloody back!"

"You can't fit in! There isn't *room*!"

"We're barely able to breathe here, can't you see that?"

Placid as ever, the recorded voice instructed passengers to move down inside the carriage. Several passengers answered back, as if a real person had been speaking: "We can't, you ruddy idiot!"

The doors almost shut, bounced open, almost shut, bounced open, and finally shut. The train groaned off heavily. You could hear its engine straining under the burden of pulling such an excessive amount of weight.

Inside the carriage there were muffled shrieks, anxious cries, low moans. The woman who had tried and failed to leave was having a full-blown panic attack, wide-eyed, hyperventilating, intoning the phrase "I have to get off. I have to get off." Someone told her to shut up and stop being such a baby, and someone else told the first someone to put a sock in it, couldn't they see she was terrified?

The train plunged on through thundering darkness. The fat banker behind Marcus had started to pant very hard and was making strange noises at the back of his throat. Marcus himself felt as though he was wrapped up like a mummy. He couldn't move a muscle. His ribs seemed to be creaking. His feet scarcely touched the floor any more. He thought of sardines in a tin, but the image didn't match the reality. At least in a sardine tin there was that briny oil all around the fish. Here, the passengers didn't even have that. There was no blessing of lubrication. They were corned beef in a can.

The train slowed, and people sighed, just that little bit hopeful, expecting a station.

But it wasn't a station. The train simply came to a standstill, as Tube trains sometimes did, for no good reason, in the middle of a tunnel. A minute passed. Then another. The air was foetid, stifling. There didn't seem to be nearly enough oxygen in it. Mouths gasped and gaped, goldfish-fashion. Marcus fought hard to rein in the fear that was stamping around inside him, threatening to bolt. The train was stuck. They would never get out of here. They were trapped for ever, coffined, interred in London's bowels.

Then, at last, with agonising slowness, the train was on the move again. A station slid into view. Once more, the platform was crowded, a pawing, jockeying throng. As the doors opened, passengers yelled warnings and threats.

"Don't! Don't! We need to get off!"

"Don't fucking get on! Stay where you are!"

"Please! There's too many of us already! No more!"

"You try to get on, I'll fucking deck you!"

But they were ignored, and the pressure of bodies pushing in from outside proved greater than the pressure of bodies trying to push out from inside. The number of passengers in the carriage, unbelievably, increased. People were climbing over one another. They were squeezing themselves into the gap between heads and ceiling. They were slithering over shoulders and lodging themselves horizontally on top of the vertical passengers. It was like some insane act of weaving, human threads in a loom.

The screams were dreadful, yet the incomers didn't pause to wonder why. It didn't occur to them that they themselves were the cause, or even that they might well be contributing screams of their own shortly. There was one overriding imperative in their heads. It was what they had been conditioned to do by years of commuting: catch the train, don't miss the train, don't be late for work, ever, no matter what the circumstances.

Eventually the doors closed and the train set off with its jam-packed, suffocating cargo – driver apparently oblivious. Marcus's portfolio was crushed beyond redemption now, but he no longer cared. His only concern was getting through this, surviving. Keep breathing. Keep breathing.

Then the fat banker started choking wetly, horribly. Seconds later, he vomited down Marcus's neck. The smell made Marcus retch and nearly vomit too. He craned his head round, ready to express his disgust and demand an apology.

The man didn't look the slightest bit rueful. In fact, he didn't look anything apart from puzzled and somewhat vacant. His eyes were unfocused, face pale and sweat-sheened. His breath came in hiccups.

Marcus had never seen anyone having a heart attack before, not in real life, but instinct told him that that was what was happening here.

Querulously, he called out, "Doctor? Is there a doctor here? A nurse? Anyone? I think this man's dying."

He was hardly expecting a reply, and anyway, even if there *had* been someone with medical expertise present, what the hell could they have done?

"Listen, it's going to be all right," he soothed the fat banker. "Just hold on. You're going to be fine."

But the man had glazed over. His plump, vomit-flecked lips mouthed soundlessly. His *FT* was mashed onto his cheek, leaving an inky mirror-imprint of figures there. Marcus looked into his eyes as the light left them. The banker's head sagged, coming to rest against Marcus's ear.

Other people started gagging on the stench of vomit. Someone's bladder voided. Armpits reeked with fear. The carriage had become a gas chamber of foul odours.

And Marcus was standing next to a dead man. Worse. Not just standing. Being enfolded by the fleshy corpse, more intimately than if they were lovers.

He didn't want to give in. Didn't want to scream.

But he just had to. Couldn't help it.

And the train hurtled on, wheels squealing, a gorged metal boa constrictor.

Stations came and went. Nothing changed. If anyone got off, it wasn't noticeable. If anyone got on, it could scarcely make matters worse. Stranger's hair was tangled with stranger's hair. The air was a thick as treacle and as humid as a sweltering day in Florida. The exceptionally pretty girl now had a face that was a mask of drowning horror. Her mascara streaked her cheeks. Her lipstick was smeared like blood.

The screaming had petered out, more or less. There was just a numb, bovine hush. Now and then somebody might whimper, or let out a small, despairing wail. Otherwise, nothing. Being terrified used up too much of yourself. Better to concentrate on inhaling the next gulp of breath. Take it heartbeat by heartbeat. Hope this nightmare might end.

A station flickered by. Halt. Then on. It had been Marcus's destination, near Soho, deep in central London, the station nearest to Whaam! Comics UK HQ. He'd missed his stop – and, in all likelihood, his appointment. He would have laughed – hollowly – had he been able to expand his ribcage to do so.

More time passed, and more stations. Marcus wasn't sure but he got the impression that two or three more passengers had died. Collapsed, certainly, passed out, unconscious, still held upright by the others around them.

Then, a long while later, came a station which had no name. Nothing on its white-tiled walls except the London Underground logo, and this blank, unadorned by lettering.

Here, the train came to a stop and didn't start up again. The platform was empty. In the fevered nether reaches of his mind Marcus wondered whether this was some special location designed for just such an emergency – the unloading of a stuffed Tube train. London Transport officials would arrive shortly, a team of them, accompanied by paramedics, and they would painstakingly unpick the tangle of commuters and unpack the bodies like artefacts from a vacuum-sealed carton. He imagined there had been similar incidents like this in the past. As a work-from-home freelancer, he had scant experience to draw on, but maybe it was commonplace, an open secret among the community of regular Tube users. Once in a while a train became hopelessly overfilled, but happily there was an official procedure in place. An expert response crew was scrambled, and the matter resolved.

But nobody came. The platform remained empty. Marcus realised he had lost all sensation from the chest down. His shirt collar crackled, glued to his neck by dried puke.

He was close to blacking out when, dimly, he heard footfalls approaching. They echoed along the platform – three, maybe four sets of metal-tipped soles, tap-tapping.

Men in uniform. They resembled the average Underground employee, except that their jackets seemed darker blue and crisper, their caps that little bit shinier and more ostentatiously peaked, and the badges on the caps larger, more silvery, more intricate. Their bearing, too, was different. They held themselves tall, and walked with their hands behind their backs, with authority.

They patrolled the length of the train, inspecting. Their footfalls faded, then returned.

When they came to a halt, it was not far from the carriage window nearest Marcus.

"Doors!" one of them, the seniormost, yelled. He had a hawkish nose and deep-set, penetrating eyes.

The doors duly rolled apart.

"Oh dear," the senior man said. "Oh dear, dear, dear. Right old proper sausaging this is. Not even one of 'em popping out when the train's opened up."

"What should we do, Commandant Beck?" said one of his subordinates.

"Do? There's not much we can do, Hutchinson. We're looking at complete passenger lock-in here. This train is as compacted as my lower intestine after a week in France eating baguettes. Not even syrup of figs is going to flush out this lot. I haven't seen a sausaging this bad since the great Bakerloo Line blockage of oh-two."

"We could have a go at yanking some of them out, couldn't we?"

"I doubt it. Not without breaking limbs, or worse. No, the crowbar hasn't been made that could pry these poor sods free."

"You mean... ?"

"Yes, Hutchinson," said Commandant Beck, with a slow, vague nod. "It's a Siding Thirteen job, I'm sorry to say."

"Oh Lordy. Siding Thirteen."

"Yes. Garbutt? Make the call, would you, there's a fellow."

Another of the subordinates fished out a walkie-talkie and said, "Shepherd Unit calling Central Signalling. Authorising implementation of crisis protocol codename Tangent, repeat crisis protocol codename Tangent. Arrange points redirection to Siding Thirteen from our location, with immediate effect. Thank you, Central Signalling. Shepherd Unit out."

Meanwhile, Commandant Beck happened to catch Marcus's gaze through a chink in the twisted, immobile jigsaw of passengers.

"It'll be all right, sonny," he said through the window. "Don't you fret. Just sit tight. Everything'll sort itself out, you'll see."

But his smile didn't reassure Marcus at all. And Marcus had himself used the same tone of voice when comforting the dying banker.

The doors closed. Cumbersomely the train began to depart.

Commandant Beck swivelled his head to keep the eye contact going with Marcus. At the last moment, before he was lost from sight, Beck winked.

The next portion of the journey was short. Or long. Marcus couldn't decide which. Dark and dusty tunnels, and finally a gradual, subsiding glide into a dim-lit, close-walled zone where there was a single sign. Marcus could only just make out the writing.

SIDING 13, it said.

The train, a half-dozen carriages solid with hundreds of half-dead human beings, came to a complete rest, bumping softly into buffers. The engine chuntered, whirred, then fell quiet.

The recorded voice said, *"This train terminates here. This train terminates here. All change."*

But the doors stayed shut.

And then the lights went out.

Permanently.

DIVING DEEP

Gary McMahon

The thing that I like about Gary's writing is that he'll take an idea and run with it, and keep on running until he is in the far distance and you wonder what on earth he's going to bring you back. With the brief for The End of The Line *I did say to authors that they didn't have to set their stories on the real Underground or Metro. They could entirely invent an underground transport system if they so desired. And that is exactly what Gary has done in 'Diving Deep.' This is a peculiar story, and while it has something of the grandeur and cosmic terror of Lovecraft, there is also a quiet melancholy here, a sense of travelling within oneself, while charting the depths of the unknown.*

i

FOR YEARS HE had woken in the darkest hours after experiencing the same dream. Limitless dark, endless space: a vast emptiness all around him, stretching way beyond anything he had ever known.

He still had the dream now, even here, in the ice-crusted wastes of Antarctica, but he had finally come to understand it, almost to make peace with it. For now he knew that the void he dreamt of was not an external phenomenon; it was not *out there*, apart from him. It was *inside*: the empty and fathomless gulf that sat deep within him, at his invisible centre, into which everything of worth would eventually fall...

* * *

ii

THE FOOTAGE WAS unclear, but the picture had enough resolution that they could make out the tunnel walls. They were smooth, cylindrical, and too geometrically perfect to be considered a natural occurrence. No, this shaft in the ice was not a fluke of nature.

"This can't be right." Farris stared at the small monitor, frowning slightly in order to improve his vision. "I mean, that ice cap has been there for millions of years. Not a living soul has been down there until we arrived. So how the hell can this even be real?"

Behind him, someone coughed lightly, and he became aware of the sound of feet shuffling nervously.

"You're right, of course," said a smooth, deep, thoughtful voice. "No person has ever been down in that water until now."

Farris turned around and stared at Professor Redman. The thin old man was sitting on the edge of a folding table, absently stroking a beard that was almost as white as the snow. His eyes, behind the thick glass of his spectacles, shone like ice-chips in the dimly-lit room.

"The ice cap had not been penetrated until we brought our equipment here. However, the fact remains that this tunnel – if that's what it is – could only have been made by unnatural means. It's been bored into the ice."

Someone laughed softly; perhaps it was the same person who had coughed.

Professor Redman continued, undaunted. "That's the only explanation for the geometrically regular shape of the penetration. If I could get inside there and take some accurate measurements, I'd like to bet the house that the diameter of the tunnel barely fluctuates along its length. Do you know what kind of machine tolerances that would involve? My guess is that even our most sophisticated drilling apparatus would be unable to manage such a feat of engineering."

The room went silent. Not even the anonymous laugher made a sound. Every eye was focused on the monitor, and the sight they had puzzled over three times now. The slow, shuddering progress along the circular shaft, the way the water seemed filled with shadows, and finally, seconds before the picture went black, the way those shadows seemed to suggest some kind of markings on the smooth sides just up ahead.

That was when the camera-mounted submersible had failed, and the power went out. Nobody knew why it had stopped filming, and they had been unable to retrieve the machine. It was lost, and the best explanation the electricians and other tech guys could offer was that there had been some sort of atmospheric interference which had interrupted the signal and killed the power supply.

Atmospheric interference. Under two metres of frozen polar ice cap and another fifteen metres of clear, icy water. Farris had never heard anything so lame.

The meeting broke up not long after that, the small group of men – scientists and divers alike – drifting out into the snow. Farris was one of the first to leave the prefabricated hut, feeling the lure of emptiness. Outside, layered in winter clothing, he stared out at the whiteness and embraced it, then took it inside. He had come here for this, and now that he had it he struggled to find anything of worth in it.

As he lumbered across the hard-packed snow and ice of the compound, his boots crunching and his breath misting before his face, he glanced over at a training exercise taking place far off to his left. Four or five newcomers joined at the waist by ropes, with buckets over their heads to cut off their view and replicate snow blindness. In a snowstorm, they would be able to see nothing, to hear only the wailing of the wind. One of the buckets had a face painted on it; the team called it Boris. The man wearing Boris had wandered off from the group, his line playing out so far that he had abandoned the others. In terms of the training exercise, he was already dead.

Farris continued on his way, heading for the bunk house. He was tired. His limbs ached. The cold was cutting through his clothing.

He knew that Redman was following him. He could not hear the man, yet felt his presence not far behind. He veered away from the bunk house and headed instead towards the canteen, where if he hurried he would catch the end of the breakfast serving. He had not eaten since last night, well before his early morning dive, and he knew that if he slept without taking on any sustenance his dreams would be troubled.

"*Fa –*" Redman's voice almost reached him, but the wind snatched it away. He could have turned around and acknowledged the man, but he knew why he was being pursued. He didn't want to think about it, not on an empty stomach. Perhaps with a few rashers of bacon and some hot coffee inside him he would be more willing to listen.

He had time to grab a plate of leftover scraps and a mug of black java before Redman entered the canteen. Farris made his way across the quiet room and sat at a table against the wall. Redman filled a mug from the coffee machine and followed him, his eyes unblinking behind his glasses and his posture languid.

"May I join you?" The man's voice was smooth and educated; he sounded like a schoolteacher.

"Sure." Farris didn't look up. He ate his bacon and watched the steam rising from his mug. It made strange shapes in the air, like dancing figures.

"I need you to go down again. I won't mess around. You're the best diver on the team, and I need you to go into that shaft."

Finally he looked up, and stared into Redman's eyes. The old man licked his lips, and then took a sip of coffee.

"Why me?" It was a fair question.

"Like I said, you're the best. You've already been down there. Also… well, you don't give a damn about anything, so two dives in less than twenty-four hours is something that won't faze you."

Farris grinned. "At least you're honest – I'll give you that, you old bastard."

Redman shook his head. "I hate to ask, you know I do. But

this is important. That shaft – well, you know what I'm saying. You saw it yourself. It isn't natural."

A chair scraped across the timber floor. Somebody sang softly, under their breath. A door slammed. "I'll do it," said Farris, still staring at Redman, at his ice-blue eyes held captive behind glass. "I don't have a good enough reason not to."

iii

FARRIS HAD NEVER believed in anything, least of all in himself. It was something he had come to terms with out here, in the icy wastes; reflected in the harsh white terrain he often saw the stark contours of his own face, and the vision did not bother him. Whatever was inside him, it was out here too, a massive open space containing... nothing. Absolutely nothing. He felt connected to the Antarctic landscape in a way that he had not felt with his environment back at home, and the connection was a comfort. It meant that he was not, as his ex-wife had once claimed, dead inside. It signalled that he was merely different: his needs and desires where not like those of other men.

They stood outside the small tent, watching the horizon. The glare of the sun burnished the snow and ice, making it gleam. It was a beautiful sight, but also an intimidating one. Farris could never quite get used to the sense of awe he felt whenever he watched the sunlight kiss the shocking white landscape. It was like looking at the surface of an alien world. He barely felt the cold. One old girlfriend had told him it was because he didn't have a heart.

"Let's get you suited up and in the water." Redman glanced at him, as if checking that Farris were still up to the task. Farris nodded, and then ducked inside the tent. Redman did not follow.

Inside the tent two of Farris's colleagues helped him into his dry suit. They worked in silence; their eyes did not make contact with his. The thick neoprene suit was rather inflexible, so it was a struggle to get the thing on. Farris writhed as the suit encased him, and as always he felt a vague flicker of doubt as his body was consumed by the material and his head was covered by the thick hood. The three-finger dry gloves slid easily over his hands, and already he felt insulated body heat pressing like warm stones against his palms. He blinked as one of the men covered his face with a full-face diving mask – Farris's mask of choice when he was diving in these extreme temperatures.

"Ready?" The man's voice was distant, muffled, and he repeated the question. Farris nodded and gave the traditional hand signal to indicate that he was okay – a clear circle formed by forefinger and thumb.

They attached the rope to his harness, and he gave it a couple of tugs to test that it was secure. The signals they used were by now second nature. He had memorized them long ago, and they were never far from his mind.

One pull = *OK?* or *Yes I am OK*.

Two pulls = *Stay put* or *I am stationary*.

Three pulls = *Go down* or *I am going down*.

Four pulls = *Come up* or *I am coming up*.

Continuous pulls = *Emergency: bringing you to the surface* or *Emergency: bring me to the surface*.

Farris shuffled over to the access hole and stared down into the cold, unwelcoming water. It looked black, like ink. His dream returned to him: all that emptiness, like the huge empty space beneath his feet, under the water. To anyone else it might be terrifying... but to Farris it was strangely beautiful, and calming. He was not a man who knew fear.

The hole was the same one they'd used that morning, and it had been kept clear of new-forming ice. A small petrol chainsaw lay on the ground nearby, alongside an ice pick. Farris checked his regulator, and confirmed once again that the air was flowing freely. He peered at the pressure gauge, knowing fine well that the tank was full. It was just something he did, part of his routine. The constant checking. The disbelief, even in himself.

Then, finally, he looked up, just in time to see Redman enter the canvas enclosure. Farris gave the signal, and then turned his back on the hole. He counted to three and stepped backwards into the water.

As the water closed over his head, easing him under, he caught sight of the stand-by diver and the rope tender – the latter was playing out the line, concentrating on his hands. For some reason Farris had the sudden thought that these might be the last people he ever saw. Then all he could see was bubbles, and a rushing darkness that was sucking him down.

He turned around and began his dive, heading towards the vertical hunk of ice where they had discovered the shaft. It was located at the base of what everyone was calling an iceberg but was in reality a free-standing block which had erupted through the secondary layer of ice located far below the main cap. This lower surface formed a large flat expanse which sloped away after a few hundred metres, dipping sharply into a restless blackness.

The water was brilliantly clear: visibility was usually good down here as the ice cap protected the water from the wind and the elements, and once any sediment stirred up by the dive had settled the water was clean. Strange glowing anemones and neon jelly fish prowled the area, and where the ice dipped away there was only a clawing darkness. Farris skirted a narrow shelf of ice, inspecting the undulating denizens of this weird world, and marvelling, as always, at their simple, uncluttered beauty.

The block of ice lay just up ahead. He glanced up, at the underside of the ice cap, and imagined that he saw blocky shadows moving across the surface. This was an optical illusion of course, yet it never failed to unnerve him. The safety line trailed unhindered behind him, the water was still and clear... everything was calm and peaceful. The conditions, he thought, were perfect – even better than they had been early that morning, when he had made his first dive of the day.

There was a flurry of activity as one of the stand-by divers entered the water, following him down with his line trailing like a thin umbilical through the glassy depths. This other guy – Sanderson: one of the best – would stay close to the surface and keep his distance, yet he would be alert to any sign of danger. Farris watched as Sanderson skimmed through the water, taking photos as he went. The underwater flash looked weird, like bursts of undersea lightning.

Here we go, he thought as he approached the thing he'd returned here to investigate. The block of ice towered alongside him, attached by fat frozen fingers to the underside of the cap. He pitched downwards, heading for its wide base, and immediately saw the shaft. Even at this distance it looked strange. A perfect circle, as if bored into the ice by machines. Like a concrete manhole chamber missing its lid. He had been amazed the first time he'd seen it, but now he was merely intrigued. *How quickly we get used to the inexplicable*, was his thought as he headed down.

Down.

Down.

I don't want to go in, he thought. Then: *it's waiting for me.* His heart shuddered. What did that even mean? What was waiting for him? He put the thought down to the Fear. It always happened, sooner or later, to divers under these extreme conditions: the intense loneliness, the eerily clear water, the sense of so much unexplored territory around and below you. It all added up to the Fear. Farris had never before encountered the sensation, but had been told about it many times. Perhaps it was now his turn to experience a state of mind that had ruined so many other divers.

Before long he was floating for the second time in less than twenty-four hours at the entrance to the horizontal shaft. It was situated three feet off the slanted white surface, and was less than half a metre in diameter – just the right size for a grown man of his dimensions to squeeze inside. Now where had that thought come from? It was as if the shaft was meant for him, as if it had been designed to facilitate his access.

Don't be so fucking stupid.

Again, he felt what he assumed was fear. It was new to him, this feeling.

The safety line went taut. One pull: *are you OK?* He gave a response, indicating that, yes, he was fine. But he wasn't, was he? He wasn't fine at all. Something was niggling at him, telling him to return to the surface. The void within him was reaching out to the emptiness inside the shaft.

Just another unwelcome thought. If he carried on like this, he'd spook himself for sure. If he kept this up he'd head for the surface screaming, just like he'd seen another diver do six months ago, when the Fear had overcome him and he had lost his mind, claiming that he had seen his dead mother down there, sitting on the ice floor and smiling through a white veil of bubbles.

But, no. Farris had never been afraid of anything, and he wasn't about to start now. Instead of playing mind games with himself, he needed to focus. Just get the job done, take the overtime pay, and drink himself silly tonight back at the base.

His brief was to enter the shaft only to the point where the last submersible had malfunctioned. A distance of approximately two metres: three at the most. Just stick his head and shoulders in there, have a quick look around for the camera, and then come back out. He glanced behind him, and saw that Sanderson wasn't too far away, kicking around near the surface. Sanderson gave him the OK sign, and Farris returned it.

Then, before he could change his mind, he turned about-face and swam into the shaft.

iv

THE WALLS OF the shaft were perfectly smooth, like glass. They even shone strangely, as if illuminated from somewhere behind. Farris kicked on inside, peering into the tunnel. It seemed to stretch on indeterminately, way beyond the point where he could see clearly. His shoulders barely touched the sides, but he was all too aware of the enclosed space. It was tight down there, yet still somehow he felt strangely calm. Just up ahead he could see the motionless submersible. It looked damaged, as if from a collision.

Farris reached out and touched the tunnel walls. They were soft, and gave slightly beneath his padded fingers. *Like skin*, he thought. Suddenly he no longer felt so at ease. He stopped moving forward and reached back for the rope line. He wanted out; this was getting too weird, even for him.

His hand could not find the rope. It was no longer there.

Resisting the urge to lose control, and drawing upon his years of training and experience, Farris started to manoeuvre his body backwards along the tunnel. He moved perhaps an inch, and then became jammed, wedged in place. The walls – previously wide enough to allow him access – had closed in a fraction, just enough to ensure that he could not move back out.

Farris pushed, trying to force his way out, but he could not move. All he could do was go forward, deeper into the tunnel. He should have been afraid – he knew that – but for some reason he was not. All he felt was the compulsion to continue onward, towards whatever lay up ahead. Like a shark, he sensed that forward motion was the only way out of this. If he stopped, he might die.

The decision now made, Farris inched forward, brushing against the smooth, soft walls, and almost hyper-aware that they were closing in fractionally behind him, forming a sort of funnel as he passed through. It felt like he was being swallowed. He was surprised at how easily his mind accepted this – along with the fact that with each scrap of ground he gained, he travelled even farther from the access hole, and from possible help.

I should be shitting myself. Anyone else would be terrified.

But he wasn't. He was anxious, yes, and could feel the adrenalin as it pumped through his system, but this was not any kind of fear he had heard of. Perhaps he had simply gone insane.

The tunnel ahead of him remained regular; the diameter of the perfect circle was unchanged. At a distance that he could not estimate, it seemed to widen, forming a sort of chamber, but the closer he moved towards that part of the tunnel the farther away it seemed. Shortly he began to realise that there were markings on the walls, like the ones suggested in the footage. Characters etched into the ice. He had not noticed them before because they were shallow, and of the same white colour as the rest of the ice. At first he had thought that it was merely an illusion caused by the water swirling around him or the shadows he cast, and then he registered that the water was perfectly still. His passing made no visible impact upon the medium in which he swam; it was like moving through air instead of fluid.

He reached out a gloved hand to touch the markings, but because of the padding he could not feel them. They were strange, utterly imponderable. Then, suddenly, another shaft appeared in the wall up ahead of him and slightly to his left. Yet another appeared directly overhead. Then more, penetrating the main tunnel at what seemed like regular intervals.

The tunnel was dotted with these other, secondary tunnels of varying shapes and sizes. Some of them were too small for him to fit through, and yet others were easily large enough for him to have changed course and entered. It occurred to him to follow one of them, but he remembered that he had a limited supply of air. He could not see the gauge because of his position and the lack of space around him, but he knew that he did not have long left... twenty minutes? Half an hour? He could not be sure; time in here was meaningless.

So he kept moving forward, in the hope that he might reach that distant widening in the tunnel, and that it might lead to another way out. He was no longer even sure in what direction he was moving: he could be going horizontally, vertically, or even swimming up and down gentle slopes.

Soon paranoia began to seep into him – possibly the result of a lack of oxygen. He felt claustrophobic. Voices from his past entered his head. His wife: *You never loved anyone, least of all yourself.* His late mother: *Why can't you just be like everyone else?* His old diving instructor, who had died of a heart attack five years ago: *One day you'll get lost down there, and you'll never find a way back to the surface.*

Finally Farris felt real fear. He knew what it was by its difference to anything he had ever felt before, and realised that, despite what he had always thought, there is always something to be afraid of. Farris had never believed in anything, but now he believed in this: a series of tunnels under the ice, like some nightmare transport system for the lost and the faithless.

The other tunnels bisecting his own (and wasn't it exactly that: *his own?*) were now more numerous, and he imagined other creatures travelling through them, like so many passengers shuttled through subterranean chutes. The purpose of this system of tunnels eluded him, but he knew that there was one – nothing this perfect, or complex, could have been created by accident.

The widening was finally drawing closer. For the first time, he felt that he was closing in on the spot where the walls opened out to form a sort of oval cavern. The markings here were less clear, as if they were older than the rest. They could be words or numbers, or something like primitive cave drawings. The only thing Farris felt certain of was the fact that they were alien – not in terms of outer space or saucer-eyed Martian visitors; just something inhuman and inscrutable. Something truly not of this world.

Just as the tunnel walls pulled back from him, as the area ahead opened up and became what he now thought of as an ante-chamber, he saw the doorway. That was what it looked like: a large, perfectly circular doorway. Its diameter matched his height, and as he approached it he once again felt as if everything here had been designed with him – or someone exactly like him – in mind. The tunnel that was a perfect fit; the way the soft ice walls had lulled him, speaking to something present in his blood; and now the appearance of this gaping entrance to... well, to what?

He should have run out of air by now, but he could not bring himself to check the pressure gauge. If he was breathing without air, then so be it. The whole situation was beyond comprehension, and the only way to deal with it was to go with it – to follow it through to the end. He slowly turned and looked back the way he had come. The tube through which he had swum was now barely the size of a coin: it had tightened as he passed into this larger, wider area, cutting off the way back for good.

Turning once again to face the doorway, he moved towards it and saw that beyond the cavity lay only darkness. A still and silent blackness: Infinite space. Illimitable dark; deeper than outer space, blacker than sin. The void gaped before him, as if it had been waiting here for millennia, patiently expecting his arrival. It was a vast universe of undersea night; an infinite emptiness which called to the smaller emptiness within him.

Without thought, without fear (for that was gone now; indeed all feeling had left him), he stepped through and pushed his body out into the clutching black space. Finally he realised that he was no longer on earth: the knowledge came to him all at once, and he was not alarmed. He was interested. He was nowhere, yet he was also everywhere. There was the sense of immensity: that feeling one gets in a small boat on the open sea, where there is nothing around but more of the same, mile upon mile of nothingness. Perhaps even stretching as far as forever.

It isn't natural. His thoughts were a blur. *This place has been formed. It's been constructed, created by an intelligence that I am too small to understand.*

As he drifted away from the circular doorway, Farris became aware of numerous shapes moving past him. He could not see them; he could only sense their presence, like ghosts. None of them were human; some of them were not even shapes at all, just thoughts or dreams as faint and intangible as gaseous bursts from a factory chimney.

There came a sudden rush of images, a mental onslaught he was unable to fight: *a lobster, a huge flickering light bulb, a green triangle, his ex-wife's slashed forearm, a pool of crude oil reflecting light, blood spilled in water, rain on glass, an erect penis, a rotting vulva flowering like a corrupt jungle plant, a prolapsed anus, a bunch of lilies, an opening mouth, a tight line of stitches in a dead man's scalp, a dirty wooden table, two dusty chairs, a pile of burning books, rotten fruit on an orchard floor, a sunrise, the sky shuddering from the jets of a rocket taking flight, a closing door, a falling star, a room without end...*

He was surrounded by these unknowable beings, but none of them was remotely like him, or even like the others. But just as Farris had done, they had journeyed here of their own free will, in answer to some obscure calling which had begun to sound somewhere deep within them the day that they were born.

The blackness shifted like layers of sheets on an unseen bed. It was alive and it was curious. It had waited so long, and come so far just to meet him. Geometrical objects shimmered into being inside his head, were peeled like strange fruit, fell away. Nothing was real. Everything was truth. None of it mattered. It all meant so much.

Then, momentarily, his thoughts once more became coherent: *what if this is a way station, an interchange, connected by those tunnels? Linking places beyond the bounds of my physical reality... what if on every planet in the cosmos, in every single dimension of time and space, there is a circular shaft just like the one I entered? These hatches remain dormant for entire lifetimes, waiting for the exact right being to stumble by.*

The thoughts crowded his head like eager beasts, each one fighting for a place. He listened to them all, unconcerned by the madness of his theory.

Like those weird plants in the Amazon jungle, designed to attract a single species of insect from the millions upon millions that exist on the planet, these things are just waiting. Waiting for a consciousness with the correct configuration of criteria to arrive and trigger this reaction. And then... and then... after all that time, the system starts to operate, shunting us towards this holding area.

His hands waved before his eyes, shockingly white now that they were bereft of the protective gloves. He realised that somehow his face mask had come undone or perhaps even been removed, but still he was breathing. He was alive. He was breathing the darkness like amniotic fluid. The gap inside him – the one that he now knew had always been waiting to be filled – curled inward, like a fist closing around his bones, his heart, and the soul he had never believed in.

There was pain, but it was bearable. It was endurable.

His fellow travellers jostled for position, tilting and rotating their impossible proportions as they flowed around him like impatient commuters moving towards destinations unknown. Then something else – something vast and old and patient – stirred amongst them, slowly inspecting its catch.

Just as his lungs began to burst from the swollen blackness, an awful realisation dawned upon him, and Farris finally understood what was waiting for him in the dark.

v

...AND HE STILL has the dream now, even here, floating and waiting beneath and utterly beyond the ice-crusted wastes of Antarctica, but he has finally come to understand it, almost to make peace with it. For now he knows that the void he dreams of is not an external phenomenon; it is not out there, apart from him. It is inside: the empty and fathomless gulf that sits deep within him, at his invisible centre, into which everything of worth must eventually fall.

CRAZY TRAIN

Natasha Rhodes

Natasha Rhodes is pretty fuckin' metal (pardon my Anglo Saxon). She lives in LA, has a boyfriend in a heavy metal band and works at a rock club. This is something that is bound to affect your writing, but in a good way. When I asked Natasha to contribute to The End of The Line *I told her I wanted something set in this sleazy world of screaming guitars, big hair and fragile egos, and that's exactly what she delivered. Amazingly, for a city beset by earthquakes, LA really does have an Underground system. I've even been on it myself. However, I witnessed nothing quite so terrifying or just plain wrong as the journey on the Crazy Train that you will find herein. Hang on tight, it's gonna get bumpy...*

MY STORY BEGINS where most others would've ended – with me, Micky James, lying dead in the gutter on Sunset Strip, exactly one week before I was due to become famous for releasing the best-selling album of all time.

Drugs pushed me over the edge, they said, although I'd be hard-pressed to tell you exactly which of the colorful cocktail of uppers, downers, painkillers and barbiturates had triggered me to make the fateful decision to end my life.

The gun had helped too.

Some do-gooder had called the cops, not because they knew me or cared, but because it was the 'Right Thing To Do.' The cops weren't here yet, of course. That was pretty typical for Los Angeles, where a single, simple suicide was not nearly as exciting to the forces of law as the all-guns-a-blazing shootout happening between Mom and Pop over custody of Little Johnny in the diner a street away.

So this was it, then. No crime-scene tape for me to guard the privacy of my innards. No long-suffering beat cop to stop kids from taking photos of my brain and posting them to their friends on the internet. Tourists crept as close to my mortal remains as they dared, pretending to be shocked but secretly feeling quite pleased to have a story to tell, to have proof that LA was as dangerous as the tabloids would have them believe. Some of them even posed next to my body for pictures.

After a while a black crow strolled over and started casually pecking at part of my left cerebrum, drawing gasps of horrified delight.

Minutes passed and nothing more exciting happened. The crowds began to drift away. The cops had more important work to do, it seemed, and I'd still be dead in an hour.

One tourist remained, a young girl dressed in the typical mix of black torn netting and leather straps that passed for Goth fashion in Hollywood these days. She approached me, looking pale and interesting in the late October moonlight. She rubbed her white bony arms and looked down at me, her eyes as bright and shiny as my blood.

"I won't ask," she said. Her voice was soft and husky, like Snow White on three packs a day. "Want a ciggie?"

"Do I look like I want to smoke?" I asked her, then frowned. The girl shrugged, careless as a child.

"I would, if I'd just done what you've just done."

Behind my prone, bleeding body the back door opened to the famous rock club I'd chosen to kill myself outside of. A wail of overdriven guitars escaped as a stressed-looking bouncer came storming out. He slammed the door behind him and started to light a joint, then recoiled as he saw what he'd just stepped in.

"Fuckin' LA, man."

He shot me a single disgusted look before stepping over me to stand in a nearby doorway, scraping his boot on the doorstep.

"Am I dead?" I asked the girl. My face felt curiously numb. My ears were still ringing from the blast. There was no pain yet, just an aching echo in one ear from the noise of the gunshot. I hadn't figured on such a tiny pistol being so loud. I was amazed that I could still move, still think and feel and rationalize. I hadn't counted on that. In fact I hadn't counted on anything much beyond pulling the trigger.

"You're not dead. Would I bother talking to you if you were dead?" said the girl.

"No…"

"Then you're not dead. Here, take this. A smoke'll do you good."

I frowned again, then reached up a blood-stained hand and took a cigarette from the pack she offered me. I wiped blood out of my eyes, lifted an exploratory finger to touch the right side of my face. There was a gaping hole in my right temple big enough to fit an egg through. The skin around the hole felt rubbery beneath my fingertips, and when I pressed inward gently my skull made a little grinding noise, like a cracked eggshell still held together by the inner membranes. *Great. I couldn't even pull a trigger right.* The reconstructive surgery bill was going to be huge.

"You know, Frank Starr died about fifty yards away from here," said the girl. She was rummaging in her bag now, digging for her lighter.

"Who?"

"Lead singer, Four Horseman. Out riding his motorbike, got nailed by a drunk driver. Just across the road there."

"Well." I couldn't think of anything else to say. "That's not fun."

"Not for him, no. Guy was wearing a helmet. Didn't do him no good, speed he was going at. His band broke up the day he died."

"I'm sorry."

"Don't be. He looked a bit like you. Not as short, though. And his face was less…" She waved a finger vaguely at the hole in the side of my head.

"Shot up?"

"I was going to say Jewish, but no. Are you in a band?"

I raised my head with difficulty, glanced down at myself. I was still wearing the sweat-soaked leather pants I'd worn to our last gig, about three hours previously. My mother would never forgive me. "How could you tell?"

Her eyes lit up. "Guitarist?"

"Bassist."

She lost interest and rummaged in her bag some more. I wondered again why women always bought such tiny purses and then filled them to overflowing. Why not just get a nice big bag and fit it with a light and some handy side-pockets?

I sighed. "Is there something I can do for you?"

The girl shook her head, extracted a silver Zippo lighter from the depths of her bag. She sat down on the curb next to me and ran her gloved fingers through her hair. She had long black hair, backcombed and sticking up like a porcupine's quills. I thought she looked rather silly.

She flicked her silver lighter open and held the flame out to me to light my cigarette, then lit her own. Smoke curled up from between her silver-ringed fingers.

"Well. This has been a happy little chat." She glanced at me sideways and gave a Mona Lisa smile that did strange things to my insides. "Wanna come to a show with me?"

"Right now?"

A shrug.

"You're kidding, right?"

"You're a musician. Musicians like shows. They meet people there. Bookers and whatnot. Replacement drummers. You bring business cards?"

"To my own suicide? Are you joking?"

"I never joke about business cards. This is LA. Even the bums have business cards."

I shook my head as I lay there squelching in the gutter. An icy tide of goosebumps swum over me. I was going into shock.

Something warm and wet was hanging over my left eye. I gingerly pushed it aside. It flopped back down again, followed by a trickle of clear fluid. I shuddered, grimacing.

"Shouldn't I be going to hospital now? I mean, where's the ambulance?"

"You call one?"

"No, but..."

"You don't need an ambulance. You're fine. Bullet just grazed you. You're lucky."

"You call this hole in my head a graze?"

"What are you talking about? There's no hole. You're fine."

I looked down at the gutter. The piece of what I'd thought was my brain was gone. Had I imagined it or had the crow eaten it? I reached up again and gingerly touched my head, exploring. I located a long, stinging scrape across my left temple, but there seemed to be no other damage. My cranium was intact. I must have imagined the hole in my head, half-crazed with the after-effects of the drugs I'd taken.

"You need to come see this show with me. *Everyone's* gonna be there. Here, let me clean you up."

She pulled the warm, wet something off my left eye and showed it to me. It was just a dead autumn leaf.

"See? You're fine."

"But..."

The girl offered me her hand. It was a very nice hand. She had a tattoo of a winged rose on the base of her thumb, matching her rose-red lips, and a blue diamond ring on her pinky. The diamond was fantastically blue, the color of infinity.

It matched her eyes, I noticed.

She did that thing with the smile again. Something in my chest leapt, and I felt myself blush.

"Come on, trooper," she said. "Show starts in ten."

It took me several goes to sit up, grumbling and wincing. My head felt lighter than it had before, and I had the disconcerting, vertiginous feeling of the midnight wind whistling over the exposed scrape in my skull. It felt oddly like an ice-cream headache. I lurched to my feet after several attempts and stood there trembling and swaying, blood running freely down the side of my face.

I clutched at a nearby lamppost as an icy vertigo descended on me. I fought the urge to throw up, then gave in and was violently sick into the gutter.

When I was done I felt much better. There was no pain and the bleeding seemed to have stopped. I giggled and shook my head, dazed.

I was alive.

And better still, an attractive girl had just asked me out on a date.

Things were looking up already.

"Who's playing?" I asked.

The girl just looked at me and smiled. "It's a secret. We gotta hurry, though. Train leaves in ten."

"Train? We're miles from Union Station. We'll never make it."

"Not the regular train. The subway."

"Subway?" I started to smile. "This is LA. There's no subway in this part of town. We have earthquakes…"

The girl smiled, and took my hand, entwining her fingers with mine. Her hand was very warm.

"Not while I'm around." she said.

"So aren't you going to ask me why I did it?" I asked, as we hurried down the concrete steps that led to LA's underground system. Hot air streamed into my face, hinting at warmth and movement far below. I looked around me as we descended. I'd lived in this city for almost a decade and I'd had no idea that all this time we had a functional metro beneath Hollywood. It was surreal.

"Should I ask?" she said.

"I just botched my own suicide. Seems like a natural topic of conversation."

The girl paused on the first-level concourse and peered in through the darkened window of the tiny tattoo parlor sandwiched between two vacant art boutiques. A faded sign stuck to the door with curling tape announced that Miss Esmeralda was not in.

I leaned closer, peering in. The glass near the handle was broken, the lock twisted open. A strange black substance was smeared on the glass above it. Beneath was a deep set of claw marks, which raked across the inside of the glass.

"Break-in." The girl's voice was cool, almost bored. "I reported this shit a week ago. Cops still haven't shown up. Fuck LA."

She cupped her hands to the dusty glass and peered in. My eye fell on a half-hidden tattoo beneath the hem of her black lacy top – a music note with two crossed black scythes behind it.

"Esmeralda?" I asked, on a hunch.

The girl became very still, then turned and narrowed her eyes at me. I folded my arms and beamed at her.

"I think it's a lovely name."

She turned her back on me and rummaged in her purse again, pulling out an envelope. She slit the top with a fingernail and pulled out two tickets which she tucked inside her corset. I noticed her hand was trembling slightly. "Call me Merry, please. Or I'll be after you with a gun."

"Look, it's really not that bad–"

"Let me guess," she said, wheeling around and fixing me with a hard look. "You decided to kill yourself because you had a dumb argument with your band over the best way to promote your new album?"

"No," I lied, wondering how she knew.

"You're a terrible liar. How old are you?"

"Twenty seven. Today's actually my birthday."

"Figures. Jimi Hendrix, Janis Joplin, Jim Morrison, Brian Jones and Kurt Cobain all died at age twenty-seven."

"Does that make me famous, like them?"

"No. That just makes you dead. Like them. Come on."

She darted off down a set of steps which disappeared into a brightly lit tunnel.

I started to follow her then paused, my attention caught by a band poster taped to the wall, advertising a heavy metal show. *Damageplan Live in Ohio, Columbus*, I read. It was dated tonight. Had to be a misprint. I felt a stab of sadness. I'd never gotten to see the original lineup of Damageplan. Guitarist Dimebag Darrell had been murdered onstage during a performance back in 2004, shot by a crazed fan.

I ran a thoughtful hand over the poster, slid a thumbnail under the bottom corner. This was a lucky find. I was surprised nobody had stolen it by now. The poster would look great in my bedroom.

As I started to peel the poster off the wall, something warm dripped onto my hand. I looked down. It was blood. Fear crawled across my temples as I reached up and gingerly pressed my hand over the throbbing scrape in my scalp.

I frowned. There was no wound. The skin was smooth, unbroken. I ran my fingers along my hairline, inspected my hand.

It was bloodless. There was no scrape.

This was getting freaky. Either I'd somehow healed a serious head-wound in under eight minutes, or I'd just imagined that I'd shot myself. Maybe I'd passed out after overdosing and had hallucinated the rest.

I had to find Merry and find out.

I sighed and followed her into the darkness.

I JOGGED DOWN a long set of concrete steps and came out onto a wide, deserted concourse beside the train tracks. There was no sign of Merry. My footsteps rang loud on the tiled floor as I paused and looked around, panting lightly. I was out of shape and my left heel was starting to throb. Steel-heeled cowboy boots may look cool on stage, but they're a bitch to chase after a pretty girl in.

"Merry?"

"*Merry,*" the tunnel called back.

It was deathly quiet down here. The curving walls of the tunnel were covered with band posters advertising various shows, venues and festivals, all of which seemed to be out of date. I ran to the end of the platform, where I could see a set of stairs leading downwards. I could've sworn I heard Merry's voice drifting up from the bottom.

I hurried down to meet her. The steps were steep and I almost slipped a couple of times in my haste. The posters continued on the walls down here. There were dozens upon dozens of them, going back into history as I descended.

One in particular caught my attention.

"Huh," I said, pausing.

The poster showed four long-haired musicians dressed in flamboyant seventies attire, perched on the hood of a car. Beneath them was a horse-skull set on crossbones, backed by a set of white wings.

'The Four Horsemen,' I read. The lead singer actually did look a little bit like me, although I had a much better nose.

I continued on downwards. The posters hit the 1960s, then the 1950s, going from glossy color to basic black and white, and finally pen-and-ink, as though they'd been hand-drawn.

I finally reached the bottom of the steps and came out onto a wide, deserted concourse beside a set of rusted tracks, lit with old-fashioned sodium lights. The walls were plastered with faded old band posters and fliers in a haphazard mish-mash of overlapping styles, and genres.

They all had one thing in common, although it took me a moment to get it. Each and every poster featured a band with at least one member who had died young, or under unusual circumstances.

I drifted along the wall then paused, my attention caught by a home-made poster.

"Buddy Holly and the Crickets performing live at the Surf Ballroom, Clear Lake, Iowa," I read. "Feb 2nd, 1959."

"Plane crash," said a smooth voice. I turned. Merry was standing right behind me, so close I could feel the warmth of her body. She beamed at me, her smile wide and somehow unnerving. "They got sick of touring on crappy busses that broke down in minus twenty-five degree weather. Chartered the plane so the show could go on. It mysteriously crashed the next day, killing everyone aboard."

"What is this shit?" I asked, rubbing my chilly arms. "Some kind of memorial?"

Merry just shrugged, giving me a strange smile. I turned to look at her. She had discarded her mesh club wear and was now wearing a long black dress, a little outdated, cut to accentuate her stunning curves. She was, I decided, quite possibly the most beautiful woman I'd ever seen in my life.

She put a cool hand on my arm. "Ready?"

"For what?"

Merry leaned forwards as though on impulse and kissed me. Her lips were soft as rose petals, and when she pulled away it took me a moment to remember how to breathe.

"To see the greatest show on Earth."

A hot wind blew down the tunnel, followed by a stab of white light. The light grew, haloing Merry with an intense white luminescence. Brakes squealed as a vast silver subway train hurtled towards us at a crazy speed and braked to a smoking, shuddering stop.

We stepped back behind the yellow-painted line as the lights in the carriage briefly dimmed. The hydraulics hissed as the doors slid open.

"*All aboard!*" shouted a disembodied voice over the station PA.

Merry winked at me, then swept on board. I hesitated for a long moment before following her, jumping as the doors slammed shut behind me.

*　*　*

THE INTERIOR OF the subway car was hot, packed, smelly, claustrophobic. I discretely held my breath as I jockeyed my way through the crowd to find a seat. The broken lights in the second half of the carriage crackled and flickered. I stepped on more than one foot as I followed Merry through the crush. I couldn't help but watch the way her hips swayed as she walked, the way her silken black hair caressed her bare shoulders, the way –

"Here, you just stepped on my foot," said a voice with a light British accent.

"Sorry. It was either your foot or his."

I glanced behind me. A tall man with a wild tangle of blonde hair stood at the back of the carriage. He was scruffily dressed in torn jeans with silver studs. His faded black T-shirt bore a picture of a leopard backed by a single, stylized streak of white lightning. He looked vaguely familiar. I noticed the calluses on his fingers as he gripped the safety rail and smiled.

"Guitar player?"

"I was," he said.

"You gave up? How come?" I hunted around for a seat. They were all taken. I swore as the train started up with a rude jolt.

"I never gave up," he said. "I just made a mistake. I was tired. Coulda happened to anybody…"

"Don't give up, buddy," I said, patting him on the arm. "There's always a good gig to be found if you know where to look. Hey, maybe I can help you. You got a business card?"

"No."

"Me neither."

I offered my hand.

"Micky."

"Steve."

His hand was cold. I saw that Merry had found a seat on the other side of the carriage, next to a wiry man with a neatly-trimmed moustache. She poked her tongue out at me and turned away with a funny little smile. I sighed and turned back to my new friend.

"You know what sucks about this town?" I said, as the train picked up speed. "The music. There's no rock scene out here any more. As far as I'm concerned, rock is dead in LA."

"It's not dead. It's just sleeping."

"Sleeping my ass." I grabbed on tight to the handrail as the train jolted around a corner. The driver was going way too fast. "Nobody wants to listen to rock nowadays. The kids are all into that new crap, what's it called? Emo? Screamo? Whatever. You know what they call Van Halen now? *Classic rock*. Sounds like something your granny would listen to. Heartbreaking."

"Tell me about it," said Steve. "The other day I saw this kid outside the Rainbow wearing a Motley Crüe T-shirt. He had blonde hair and leather pants. I asked him if he wanted to be like Vince Neil when he grew up. He said, 'Vince who?'" Steve shook his head in sorrow.

I rolled my eyes in condolence, then nearly fell again as the train squealed to a stop. The carriage door grumbled open and a single passenger got on, a rail-thin man with tangled blonde hair and haunted, red-rimmed eyes. He looked around, selected a seat and stared at its occupier until the man moved.

I frowned at the newcomer.

"Hey," I said. "Isn't that...?"

"Don't stare, dude," said Steve. He leaned in front of me, blocking my view. "He doesn't like that."

"But..." I was lost for words. "Jesus Christ, are you sure that's not..."

The skinny man flinched and shot me a haunted look. Steve shook his head and gently turned me around.

"Not a good choice of words, mate. He doesn't like that song any more. He don't like any reminders."

"What song?" I leaned forward, standing on my tip-toes to try and see past Steve. The skinny man turned away from me and stared out the window with his arms firmly folded. "If that's not who I think it is, he's an amazing look-alike. The best I've ever seen." I turned back to Steve. "I still can't believe the dude's dead."

"Who's dead?" The skinny man's voice was like a whip.

"Oh," said Steve. "Now you've gone and done it."

"Done what?"

"I'm not dead!"

"I didn't say you were. But you're a great look-alike. You even dress like him. And you," I turned to look at Steve critically. "I swear I've seen you play somewhere before."

Steve and the skinny guy exchanged pained looks.

I suddenly got it, and relaxed. I turned back to Merry, who was watching me from the other side of the car.

"Hey!" I called to her, beaming. "I get it!"

"Get what?"

"The show." I turned back to Steve and the guy who looked the spitting image of Layne Staley from Alice in Chains. "Okay guys, you can drop the act now. You're busted. This is gonna be great!"

"What will?" asked Steve.

"Tributes," I said happily, rummaging in my pocket for my camera. "I love tribute bands. If you half close your eyes and stand at the back, it's just like seeing the real thing. Plus its five bucks at the door instead of coughing up two-hundred-bucks-plus-booking-fee to appease the almighty Ticket-Bastard."

Light filled the car as we flashed through a station and I recognized more familiar faces in the carriage. I raised my camera in delight and lined up a shot.

The black-haired, tough-looking guy pinned in my crosshairs gave a lazy curl of his lip and raised a middle finger as I snapped away, the chains on his leather jacket jangling.

Two seats down, a small, doleful-looking guy with shaggy curtains of brown hair and a small sad moustache obliged me with a horned-hand salute before going back to his book. He was the spitting image of John Bonham.

The long-haired guy sitting next to him shifted, as though feeling my eyes on him.

"Cliff Burton," I breathed, glancing around the train in

excitement for the rest of the guys. I'd kill for a photo with the whole tribute band, and go as far as a flesh-wound for a picture with just him. Metallica had been a huge influence on me growing up.

"Tell me," Steve's hand was on my shoulder, a strange look on his face. "Do you know who I am?"

I looked down at his T-shirt and suddenly it clicked.

"Steve Clark." I smiled, readying my camera. "Def Leppard. I *knew* you looked familiar. I know every word to *Pyromania*. What's your tribute band called?"

"Tribute? Oh dear. She didn't tell you, did she?"

"Tell me what?"

I saw Steve glance at Merry, who shook her head vigorously. I waved her over. She got up with reluctance. I noticed that everyone she passed flattened themselves back against the carriage walls in an effort to avoid her.

I handed her the camera as she reached me, threw one arm around Steve and jacked up my biggest, cheesiest grin.

"The guys at work are gonna die when they see this. All huge Leppard fans."

"Micky," said Merry. "We should talk."

"Afterwards. Just one shot."

"Fine." Merry raised the camera and snapped a picture without even looking through the viewfinder. All eyes were on me.

"Lady, that's not cool," said a man who looked just like Jimi Hendrix.

Ignoring him, I snatched the camera back from Merry and pressed the playback button eagerly.

"I always pull this face in photos, it's like a boiled monkey," I grinned, waiting for the camera to display my shot. "I don't even know I'm doing it till I – *urgh!*"

The camera hit the floor, bounced a few times. A bored-looking Bon Scott look-alike helpfully retrieved it and passed it back to me.

I took it, my hands trembling. I didn't want to look.

I looked.

The shot showed a scene out of a horror movie. What could only be described as the remains of a human being grinned up at the camera, one skeletal hand grasping the carriage's safety rail, the rotted remains of Steve's clothes hanging from his decayed body. A few wisps of blonde hair hung from the bare bone of his skull.

And next to him...

I pressed my hand to my mouth and swayed forward, my head swimming violently.

Merry took the camera and slipped it into her pocket.

"I'm sorry," she said. "I should've told you."

"Should've told me?" I was breathing heavily, black stars of shock dancing before my eyes. "How could you have *not* told me?"

"Because I wanted you to come to the show with me."

"But..."

I contemplated going mad, or passing out. Instead I turned and stabbed a finger at a man who looked suspiciously like Marc Bolan.

"You. Pretty boy. You're a bass player. That means you got a mirror on you somewhere, right?"

"Steady on, mate," said the man. But he pulled a small gilded clamshell mirror out of his pocket and handed it over. I flipped it open, shot Merry a dirty look, and held it up.

"Oh, dear," I said faintly.

The upper left side of my face was just simply... missing. A flat expanse of broken white bone jutted obscenely out of the area where my nose was supposed to be, connecting the broken underside of my lower jaw with the coy pink curls of the upper-right hemisphere of my brainstem. The bleeding had stopped and dried blood crusted the empty concave back of my left eye-socket. I looked like one of those plastic pull-apart models of the human brain you see in doctors' waiting rooms.

The mirror smashed on the floor. I stepped away from it, trembling violently.

"Told you not to look," said Jimi.

"I need a drink," I said.

"I'm sorry, Micky," said Merry. "I tried to tell you."

"Tell me what?" I was getting angry now. "Get me out of here. I want to go home."

"But what about the gig? They're all playing a show, just for you. It'll be the performance of a lifetime."

"I don't want to go to your dumb show!"

"Micky, please…"

"Who are you?" I turned to face the rest of the carriage. Everyone was staring at me by now. "I don't know you! I don't know any of you!"

"But we always play a show when someone new joins the club," said Jimi.

The train's lights flickered as it slammed around another curve. A piercing shriek of brakes came from outside. Giant showers of blue sparks fountained up against the windows, lighting up the darkened carriage.

"Micky, I know you're upset," Merry said, reaching out for me. "But it's okay. You *belong* here. With me."

I glanced back at her, then spun around in horror, pressed back against the locked door. Merry's face was crawling with worms. Her eyes were two blown-out sockets, her lips bruised and cracked from drug use. A badge pinned on her outfit read *Ask Me About Our Band Tattoos*.

That did it. I took off down the car like a rocket, jumping over outstretched feet and scattered guitar cases. I hit the door at the end and grasped the handle, wrenching it open. A tornado of rushing black air slapped me in the face. The subway train was going impossibly fast. I saw the track whipping past under my feet. There was no driver. The train just ended. There was nowhere else to go but back. As I stared out into the rushing void, a strange sound became audible above the scream of the wind, like crickets sizzling on an open grill.

I looked up and gasped.

The mouth of the tunnel rushing towards us in the distance was on fire. And beyond that was a deep, bright, white nothingness. I could hear cheers and whistles, as though a large crowd awaited us.

An ice-cold hand fell on my shoulder. I spun around with a cry.

Merry was standing behind me. She was whole and human again, her rose-red lips glittering in the low light, her long black hair whipping in the wind. Her eyes were a sea-green, glittering with unshed tears.

She turned as a skeletal figure approached us both. A beam of light flickered over him from the red stop sign we'd just blown past. I saw with a certain amount of disbelief that it was Buddy Holly, or what was left of him.

"You," he said, fleshless lips pursed in anger. The command in his voice was evident even in death. He turned to me, the lines of his decaying face hard. "Get *her* out of here."

"Why?" I asked. "What did she do?"

"Everything. She is the death of us all. Rock didn't die. *She's* killing it. One star at a time."

"Merry, what's he talking about?"

Merry smiled, although her eyes were cold. "Do you know what it feels like to hate something so much, you want to destroy anything and anyone who keeps it alive?"

"What do you mean?"

"Tell him," snapped Buddy.

Merry's eyes slid shut. She sighted. Finally, she turned and looked at me.

"I was there the night Frankie Carr died," she said softly. "I was the bartender at the Viper Room, up on sunset Strip. I made my drinks extra-strong that night, just for fun. I served the man who killed poor Frankie, made sure he drank enough to do the job right." She sniffed. "Serves him right for not tipping me."

"That's not all you did," muttered Buddy. "Go on."

"Columbus, Ohio, 2004," said Merry, turning to stare hard at Buddy. "I was working in the tattoo shop the night Nathan Gale came in. Nerdy little man, big thick glasses. He was ranting about that godforsaken band Damageplan, as he always was."

She smiled, gazing at me.

"It was the work of a moment to plant the idea of killing the founder of the band that he claimed was stealing his thoughts and laughing at him. Such sensible advice, and from such a beautiful woman... how could a paranoid schizophrenic resist?"

Her lips twisted, her face mocking. "Dimebag was a legend. Now he *is* a legend."

"You're completely mad," I told her. "Next thing you're going to tell me you shot Kurt Cobain."

"I didn't need to," said Merry. "All I had to do was introduce him to a little friend of mine. Her name is heroin."

She laughed as though she'd just made a joke.

I backed away, shaking my head. Merry followed me with a cruel little smile, jockeying me toward the open door. The train was rushing faster and faster now. I could no longer feel its wheels on the tracks. The light in the carriage was almost unbearably bright as we screamed towards the tunnel of light.

"You're insane," I told her. But a little twist in my gut told me that she might not be.

She shrugged, turned elegantly sideways.

"And you were completely sane when you pulled the trigger?"

"Go to hell."

"I have been to hell, and it is not as bad as what lies above."

"You're talking about heaven?" I shook my head. "If there's no rock in heaven, count me out."

She gave me a strange look. "Consider it done. You must come with me now."

I threw a look at the rushing tracks. "Screw that."

The train jolted violently as it went around a corner, throwing everyone to the side. The lights went out and Merry was bathed in the blue glow of the endlessly sparking brakes.

Finally I saw her for what she really was.

Merry was an angel. She must have been pretty, once. Her pale, heart-shaped face was delicate as the finest china, her rose-red lips as plump as furled petals.

But there her beauty ended. Her body was a ruin, hunched over and bent in on itself. Her twig-like arms were curled to her chest; her fingers ran over each other ceaselessly like excited spiders. The giant feathered wings that spread open behind her were rotten and mildewed, her flight muscles wilted from decades of disuse.

"What are you?" I whispered.

"Your salvation." She smiled, revealing rotting, needle-like teeth. "I was born perfect, you see. I was a perfect form, in perfect silence. Then came The Word. He said that it was Good, so I didn't argue. None of us argued. But the silence was broken. The purity had been destroyed. I always resented him for that.

"So I lay low and watched as they came, filling the perfect darkness with their light, polluting the air with their noise, their stink. Then came the music, the infernal banging of drums, the eternal chanting and dancing and laughing."

She shuddered, a tremor running through her body to the tips of her wings.

"I knew then what my Purpose was. Each of us has only one Purpose. Mine was to stop that hellish racket. Whatever it took. So I waited. I watched and I studied and I waited for the perfect time. But the music kept on coming. The human race wouldn't give up their new toy. So I stayed. I have been here since the beginning, learning the ways of those who seek to make waves, to pioneer, to lead the uprising. Steering them gently down the path to self-destruction."

She turned away, staring out of the window.

"I cannot take credit for all of them, naturally. The sounds-alikes, the corporate teen-puppets, the manufactured idols of today I do not touch. There is no need. He who does not make waves will never be intentionally sunk. But those who seek to break ground, to redefine music, to start something worth starting... those people are my targets. I stand behind them all, whispering in their ears, pulling their strings in the way that only a pretty girl can. Now and forever."

"I don't believe a word you just said, lady. And those wings are obviously fake."

Merry just smiled.

"Believe what you like. But coincidentally, you were right."

"About what?"

"About your band, Micky." She slinked towards me, seductively licking her lips. I backed away. "You're due to become famous in a week, as you rightly guessed. But not for the reason you planned. Do you know why your band is about to become so well-known throughout the world?"

"Er, because we just wrote the best album in history?" I puffed up my chest proudly. "We spent eight whole weeks writing it. It's a masterpiece."

"I hate to break it to you, kiddo. Your album stinks. But in terms of publicity, boy, have you just hit the jackpot."

"What are you talking about?"

Merry moved closer until all I could see of her were her eyes, blue as the bottomless icy ocean.

"I *mean,* when you took all those drugs and had the brilliant idea of killing yourself to promote your album... did you know that every other member of your band was planning to do the exact same thing?"

I stared at her, dumbfounded.

"Sweetheart, you became the first band in the history of rock to have four simultaneous suicides. Same night, same method. You'll all share the same funeral at the Hollywood Cemetery. The media will go nuts."

"You're lying."

"You don't have to believe it. You just have to look."

Merry swept back her arm like a circus ringmaster. In the

carriage, three horribly familiar young teens with fresh head-wounds looked up from their jamming session and waved sheepishly to me, blood running down their faces.

I stared at them, then staggered suddenly, pain slicing through me. I looked down in shock. My legs were turning to dust, the skin flaking away to reveal bare bone underneath.

My band was dead.

And somewhere, I was dying, too...

Merry turned to face me, running a long-nailed finger down my cheek. "My dear, think carefully. When did you make the decision to kill yourself?"

My mind snapped back to that moment when, a few short hours ago, I'd seen the girl in the Kurt Cobain T-shirt. She'd been in the front row. Wherever I moved on the stage, she'd always been magically in front of me. I remembered staring at Kurt's tragic black and white dead face, stretched tight over her wonderful plump breasts, grinning and distorted by the speedball of heroine and coke I'd taken just before the show. Wishing that my face had been on that shirt. Kurt had the best publicity gimmick in the world, I'd decided, in my drugged-out stupor. That lucky bastard.

Right then and there I'd started planning how to make it happen.

"It was you," I whispered. "You did this to me."

Merry giggled, gave a little bow. Back in the carriage a legion of dead musicians stared back at me, arms folded, unmoving as statues.

"Are you really an angel?" I asked, through gritted teeth.

"That's up to God to decide."

I clenched my fists at my side. "When was the last time you flew?"

With that, I grabbed Merry in a headlock and leaned backwards, pulling us both out through the open door of the moving train.

Merry's hand lashed out and caught the side of the doorway as we fell. We halted, suspended halfway down towards the tracks. The rushing wind whipped her long black hair up into a maelstrom, blinding me. Her cobwebbed angel-wings beat frantically as she sought to pull herself upright, hissing and shrieking.

"Help me!" I cried.

Faces appeared, staring out of the door above us. Hideous faces, rotted and decayed, their milky eyes staring out of bony sockets, accusing. The tallest, a young black man in a soft boating hat, stretched his skinless lips into a grin and winked at me. He wore only a long jacket, and just one shoe. Despite his advanced state of decay I recognized him as Sam Cooke, the King of Soul. I knew from my music-history class that Sam had been killed in a drunken gunfight with a hotel manager, after having his clothing and wallet stolen by his date whilst staying at the hotel.

I'd bet my last dollar that I knew who his 'date' had been that night.

With a curt nod to me, Sam seized Merry's hand and tore it off the edge of the door. He effortlessly held her dangling and screaming over the rushing black void.

"You goin' out too, buddy?" he called to me.

"Can I die?" I shouted, my gaze fixed on the rushing tracks below.

"You can't die, good sir. You're already dead."

I braced both feet on the side of the train, my arms still locked around Merry's neck. The bright tunnel was nearly upon us, rushing towards us like a giant fiery mouth. "Then Mr. Cooke, take it away!"

Sam Cooke shrugged, then released his grip on Merry's arm, sending us both tumbling under the train.

The last thing I saw before the crushing blackness closed in on me was Freddie Mercury standing in the doorway of the train, blowing me a kiss.

Then everything faded to black.

CONSCIOUSNESS SURFACED, SLOWLY.

"Bugger me backwards. He's coming around," said a voice.

I sat up with a jolt, panicking, to the obvious dismay of the medical technician fussing over me. My heart was pounding and I was freezing cold. There were tubes in my nose, an IV drip in my arm. I could taste blood in my mouth and my eyeballs itched.

"I'm alive?" I asked, as the EMT pressed me gently but firmly back into the stretcher.

"You're going to be fine. Don't you worry about anything."

My hand hurt. I told the EMT, who rolled his eyes.

"Just don't worry about it. We'll be at the hospital soon."

I raised my thumping head, looked down at my hand. A bloodstained bandage swathed my right wrist. My arm seemed curiously short. I tried to move my fingers. Nothing. I couldn't even feel them. My wrist itched like crazy. I tried to move, to shake the bandage off to see what lay underneath.

"Easy, kid." The EMT pushed me back down onto the gurney again, strapped me down at the ambulance bumped up the road. "You don't want to look at that hand."

"Why? What's wrong with it?"

"I gotta ask. That gun you had. What'd you pay for them rounds, five cents each?" The EMT shook his head in derision. "You're just lucky that your girlfriend was with you to stop the bleeding. Pretty lady she was. Very persuasive. You'd be dead if it weren't for her. That's just what you get if you use bargain-bin rounds in a cheap pistol. It's called a backfire, son."

The EMT shrugged and turned away, busied himself with a blue clip-folder of notes. "Just tell me you're not a concert pianist."

"Bassist."

"Thank Christ for that. You'll get by."

Tears welled in my eyes.

"Cheer up. Could've been much worse."

"How, exactly?"

"You could've been like *those* guys. They bought the two-dollar rounds. Their guns worked just fine."

He nodded to three body bags heaped up at the back of the

ambulance. I didn't have to ask to know who was in them.

I sank back onto my pillow, staring sightlessly at nothing.

"By the way… we have one final stop before we take you to the hospital." The EMT drew the curtains around me, whistling cheerfully. "There's been a shooting, a real bad one. Four kids killed backstage at a heavy metal show."

"*Four* kids?" I glanced uneasily at the three body bags. "Which venue?" A terrible feeling of foreboding filled me. I tried to pull myself upright, tugged at the straps that held me down. The straps were done up very tightly.

"You know. That famous rock joint up on Sunset. Apparently, a brawl erupted after one of the band members forgot to mail their debut album in to the record label that wanted to pick them up. Totally missed the submission deadline," said the EMT, looking at me strangely. "Fancy that."

I looked around me, panicking. The back of the ambulance was completely sealed off from the driver's cab. I noticed for the first time that I was lying on a thick black body bag, lying partially unzipped around me.

The EMT tutted under his breath, then reached up to adjust his face mask. He carefully smoothed a lock of long, silken black hair back underneath his hygiene helmet, then fished a pink handbag out from under the gurney. He pulled out a black mesh top, a tube of rose-red lipstick, a bloodstained handgun in a see-through crime-scene bag, then finally a CD.

"History is written by the critics, kid," he said, smiling strangely. "Didn't you know that?"

He held up the CD in front of my horrified gaze. It was labeled with the words THE FOUR COMETS – DEMO, in my handwriting.

"Hey!" I cried. "That's my…"

THE BANG WAS later attributed to a blown-out tire. The original police report from the concert venue was lost. All four members of the heavy metal band the Four Comets were reported DOA at their time of arrival at the hospital. Their demo album was never found.

And somewhere, deep underground, the band played on...

ALL DEAD YEARS

Joel Lane

Joel Lane is a gentleman and a scholar. He's something of an authority on genre fiction and perhaps the one person who has clued me into more great writers than anybody else I know. Joel is also one of my favourite short story writers. While there's something of the sensibility of the great weird tale to Joel's horror fiction, there's also something that's undeniably, well, Joel. A delicacy with prose, an assuredness with words that will guide you into darkness with a steady step; a certain poetry and turn of phrase that will both unbalance you and make you realise there is more to what you are reading than you first thought. 'All Dead Years' talks of a fear of the Underground, but also a fear of something far worse than that which can be found below...

WHEN SHE SAW the case notes, Val's first reaction was *At least she's trying to get help.* She was tired of middle-class Londoners seven-sevening about public transport while taking car crashes for granted. Here was someone admitting to an irrational fear of the Underground instead of blaming it on terrorism. That meant there might be a chance of treating the phobia. Val noted that the patient had been on Prozac for a year and it wasn't helping. Therapy was the last resort, as usual.

The initial meeting for assessment was hard work. Helen was so withdrawn she barely agreed at first to what was in her case notes. She was a petite woman in her forties, a few years older than Val, and must have been quite pretty before chronic anxiety had taken the life from her face. Fear of the

Underground had forced her to give up her job at the British Museum and work from home, writing public information materials on art history. It had mostly shut down her social and personal life as well. A question about current relationships was met only with a rapid shake of the head.

After nearly an hour, Helen began to describe her symptoms: "As soon as I go underground, I start to feel sick. Like I can't breathe. There are dead things in the walls. If I get onto the Tube I can smell the decay, hear the water dripping, I can't stand it. I have to get out before the journey starts."

Val had expected her to talk about fear of terrorism, or fire, or being mugged – but those manifest fears didn't seem to be part of it. The latent content was right at the surface. Which meant the cause would probably be harder to reach. Helen couldn't speak directly about her state of mind: "It's not a fear, it's already there. Waiting for me."

"You mean it's real?" Val said. Helen nodded, biting her lip. "Where do you think the Tube will take you?"

Helen looked down. Very quietly, she said: "When I look at the Underground map, I can see the real map." She wouldn't be drawn on what that meant, and hardly said anything more. But when Val ended the session by saying that she hoped they'd be able to work together and find some answers, a flicker of hope enlivened the older woman's dull face.

That moment stayed with Val when she left the clinic to get some lunch. It was an overcast day in late spring, the sun's heat filtering through a layer of metallic cloud. Old women and mothers with prams picked their way over the uneven pavement. Val sat on a low wall, drinking a bottle of flavoured mineral water. Her eyes trawled the sky for a trace of sunlight.

OVER A SERIES of weekly appointments, Val tried to peel off the psychic bandages from whatever wound Helen was covering up. You had to be careful in a case like this: any real progress towards understanding would be experienced by the patient as a threatening loss of control. It had to be balanced with work at the symptom level, using what Val thought of as 'acronym therapies' (NLP and the like) to disinfect the bandages.

Not that the first three sessions revealed much. Helen's childhood seemed to have been happy, and she was still on good terms with her parents. As an only child she'd been a little over-protected, and she'd had a few wild years after leaving home – including a phase as the mistress of an older man – before settling down in her current academic lifestyle. The fear had come on rather suddenly, and at first she'd valued her work and social life too much to consider moving away from London. But now the fear had taken so much away from her that, if the therapy didn't work, she thought leaving might be the only option.

It wasn't until the fourth session that Helen mentioned Paris. Val was encouraging her to relive her last panic attack on the London Underground, when she'd blacked out and woken up in the station attendant's office. Her purse and wristwatch had been stolen on the Tube. "I woke up and didn't know where I was. Thought I was back in Paris. I called out for Don but he wasn't there."

"Who's Don?"

"That prick." Val hadn't heard her swear before. "The older man. We used to go away together for weekends. Or stay at his summer house in Dorset. In the winter, when no-one was around. His wife didn't know he was there. We had a couple of days in Paris once. I thought I was back in the Underground, trying to run away from him." She looked at the clock on the wall. "Time's nearly up."

"Doesn't matter," Val said. "I think you should tell me about it."

Helen turned and looked straight at her. There was a trapped energy in her face, words looking for a voice. But it was a couple of minutes before she spoke.

"That trip to Paris, in midweek. He kept telling me the only way I could grasp the mystery of love was to submit to it utterly. He was big on mysticism, and I was young and smitten enough to believe it, or persuade myself I could. We spent the first day walking around Montmartre, all those trees and stone staircases, it was like another world. And then... well, we didn't get much sleep. So the next day I was in a bit of a daze. He wanted to go to the Catacombes. I wasn't keen, but he came out with some grand statement about how it was the true face of the city. Made me feel I was ignorant if I didn't go.

"There weren't many people down there. Living I mean. It was cold and damp. A mile of tunnels, lined with bones. They had to clear the cemeteries to make way for new bodies. The remains all ended up there. A wall of femurs, a wall of tibias, a wall of skulls. It made me feel sick. But Don was really excited. He said 'This is the truth of humanity – this is the end and the beginning,' and more crap of that nature. There was a side tunnel being repaired, and I let him drag me into it. We climbed over a wooden barrier. There was a smell of disinfectant.

"I didn't think he was really going to do it, but he pushed me against the wall of bones and put his hand up my skirt. I wouldn't let him. There were cheekbones and teeth pressing into my back. I tried to argue, but he gripped my throat. Then I blacked out. When I woke up, he was sprinkling mineral water over my face from a bottle. He said he was sorry, but the way he said it meant he was disappointed in me. I didn't think he did anything to me while I was unconscious, but at the time I wasn't sure. I was bruised already.

"Later, we were on the Underground. It was more bare than in London: there were huge stone-walled cavities without tiles or pictures. When I looked at the window I could see rows of skulls reflected in the glass. Don put his hand on my arm. It felt like bone. Suddenly I couldn't breathe. I pulled away and started running, from carriage to carriage, just trying to get away from him, but then I came to the end and stood there until he found me, just as the train came into a station. I'd wet myself. He didn't say anything. Just took my hand and led me off the train. I think if I'd tried to hold back, he'd have broken my arm."

Helen was crying. Val passed her a tissue. "Did you leave him after that?" she asked.

"Should have done. Instead, I went to stay at his house in Exeter. I'm not ready to talk about that. We were already finished. I shouldn't have gone there. Do you think I'm... sick? Do you think I'm a child?"

"You're a human being. Bad times are part of that. I don't much like the sound of this... ex-boyfriend of yours. Even now, he's got you blaming yourself for the way he treated you." Val tried to keep her voice level, but she was surprised by the depth of her own anger. Then she glanced at the clock. "OK, we'd better wind this up. Are you going to be OK, Helen?"

"Don't worry." Her face was very pale, though. Val saw her out, then sat in the reception area for a few minutes before preparing for the next session. The building's air-conditioning was on its last legs, and she imagined she could feel the sun's heat coming through the walls. Her throat was dry. All the phones were ringing. She closed her eyes and thought of rain.

IN THE FOLLOWING sessions, Helen was reluctant to talk about her last visit to Don's house. "It was miserable," she said in response to Val's prompting. "We couldn't stand each other. He'd turned jealous, like he had any right. And the house was making me ill. It was full of dead things. Why do you want me to talk about it? Some things are best just to forget. My two years with Don – waiting for him, then feeling worse when he was there – those are dead years. Why let him back into my head?"

"What do you mean, the house was full of dead things?"

"Insects. Birds." Helen crossed her arms over her chest. "Can we talk about something else?"

Val made a note to return to the topic later. But no opportunity seemed to arise. Helen wanted to focus on overcoming the fear. She felt it was important for her to travel on the Underground again. Val tried to work with her in the usual way, helping her to identify and challenge her fears.

But at the end of an hour of working carefully through the realities of the Tube network, separating the real dangers from the unreal ones, Helen said: "Just one thing. Not being afraid will enable me to get on the Tube. But how will it help me when the train gets to its real destination?"

Another time, Val talked her through the Paris episode and suggested that her uncertainty about what had happened during her blackout had led to a sense of being contaminated, and hence to feelings of guilt. Helen agreed with that, and seemed much calmer afterwards. But Val wondered if her relief hadn't just come from being offered an answer she could accept.

They met by chance at the Victoria and Albert Museum, which was showing a collection of pre-Raphaelite sketches. Val wouldn't normally have any social contact with a patient – but she felt it would be wrong to brush Helen off when getting out at all was a struggle for her. The older woman had come on the bus, but her fear of subways had made it a slow journey. They were both impressed by the quiet eroticism of the drawings. An entire wall was given over to Rossetti's sketches for his famous Proserpine image. Helen muttered: "Looks like she wishes she'd spat instead of swallowing." Val was surprised to feel herself blush.

In the café, over a pot of Earl Grey tea, they discussed the Tube. Helen had a realistic knowledge of the routes that coexisted with her map of despair. "The Piccadilly line to Green Park, then the Victoria line to Seven Sisters. Less than half an hour. Except I'd never get there."

"I'll come with you if you like," Val said. "Make sure you're safe." Helen shook her head. "OK, I'll give you my mobile number. Call me when you get to the Tube station. We can talk then, even if you can't get a signal below ground. If you start to panic, get out and phone me again."

Helen paused, then nodded. "All right. I'll call in ten minutes." She picked up her embroidered leather handbag, gave Val a nervous wave, and left. Val finished her tea. She wasn't sure the signal would reach the café, so she walked outside and sat on a bench. It was a blazing hot day, and the air reeked of traffic fumes and pigeon shit. The trees were wilting, turning yellow ahead of time.

After nearly half an hour, her phone rang. But all she could hear was a faint hollow sound like wind in a tunnel. A voice was caught up in it, repeating something. Just when she thought the words were becoming clear, the line went dead. Val tried to get the number, but it hadn't registered. She waited a few more minutes, then went home.

Helen called her an hour later. "Sorry, I couldn't face it. Caught the bus."

"I wish you'd let me know," Val said. "I've been worried."

"Sorry. I was embarrassed. I was just trying to make myself use the Tube. But if I did, you'd never see me again."

"Helen, it doesn't matter whether you use the Tube or not. I'm trying to help you overcome your fear, not put yourself at risk. You should use it when you're ready to, not before."

The older woman laughed softly. "You still don't understand. If I don't go down into the Underground, this summer will last forever."

AFTER THAT, THE sessions seemed to lose momentum. Helen was more relaxed, but her delusions seemed if anything to have hardened into a fatalistic stance. They began to talk about other things – art, films, myths – and Val found herself opening up more, sharing a little of her anger and bewilderment at the tide of ignorance that was sweeping away the ideals she'd once assumed would shape the future. "We're returning to the past and calling that *modernisation*. You wait, the next government will send children to workhouses. Time's running backwards."

Helen's joke about the summer never ending wasn't mentioned

again between them, but it was the driest and warmest autumn Val could remember. When had it last rained? The heat was pushing up the violence rate, making her uneasy if she came home late and had to face the Croydon streets after dark. After a series of stomach upsets, she gave up on tap water altogether. Every Tube journey meant running a gauntlet of sweaty bodies and hostile stares. She could smell decay in the tunnels, though that could have been Helen's fear infecting her.

The therapy courses normally lasted a year, but Val decided they'd probably achieved all they could. She'd leave the door open for Helen to contact her in the event of any crisis, and maybe they could keep in touch as friends too. Maybe Helen saw something in her face, because the first thing she said in the next session was: "I need your help. Will you come with me?"

"On the Tube? I said I would."

Helen shook her head. "No, not there. I need you to go back with me. To Don's second home."

Afterwards, Val wasn't sure why she'd said yes. Perhaps there was a greater depth of friendship between them than she'd thought. One of Val's past lovers had been violently jealous, and she respected Helen's struggle to deal with what had clearly been a bad experience. But also, she realised, this might be the only way she could learn the truth.

Nine days later, they caught the train from London Paddington to Exeter. A recent fire had scorched miles of farmland, turning wheatfields into black crusts above which cinders flapped and circled. Though the windows didn't open, Val could smell the reek of charred soil.

They spent most of the journey talking about their university days. It felt strange to remember a time when the future had seemed limitless – though for both of them, the final year had been one of claustrophobic routine. "It's amazing how mature you think you are at that age," Helen said. "But it's all ideas and words, not experience. Being a student is the only time when learning doesn't mark you."

Not far from Exeter, the train went into a tunnel. At once, Helen froze. Her eyes scoured the darkness beyond the window. Val could hear a rustling sound, like rats or birds in a forest, all around them. The sour taste of pollution flooded her mouth. Then the train re-emerged into the afternoon sunlight. Helen's face was dead white, coated with sweat. Silently, Val gripped her hand.

They booked in at a small hotel near the railway station, had a light lunch and walked out to the estuary. The long summer had reduced the Exe to a grey tongue of water in a dry, cracked mouth. "Whenever Don brought me here," Helen said, "I used to think of that line from Swinburne: *Even the weariest river/ Winds somewhere safe to sea.* But it doesn't look weary any more. It just looks dead."

Val followed her a couple of miles upriver, then away from the Exe and through a patch of woodland. From a distance, she could see the blackened hulk of a ruined house. A few charred roof-beams were still in place. "It's been like that for twenty years," Helen said. "No-one repairs it or knocks it down. He keeps it the same, to remind me."

Behind the ruined house, the garden was shielded by a ten-foot fence – most of which had withstood the storms of two decades, but a falling tree had ripped through one section. Helen pointed to the gap. She didn't seem in any mood for discussion. The dead tree and the fence-slats seemed to have blended into a rotting floor that it took some effort to negotiate.

The abandoned garden was less overgrown than might have been expected. The long, dry summer had withered the trees and stunted the dense weeds. It was like walking through a faded sepia photograph of a wilderness. Still, brambles caught at Val's feet and clumps of moss almost made her slip and fall into the brittle undergrowth. She was glad she'd chosen her more sensible shoes.

Near a willow tree whose roots bulged in the soil like veins, a low rockery was covered with moss and lichen. Helen started tugging at the rocks, pulling them free and dropping them by her feet. "Help me," she said. "Some things you can't do on your own." Val joined in, throwing the flinty chunks of stone to one side. Soon they had exposed a mound of crumbly black soil. Its closeness to the estuary gave it a brackish odour. Helen paused and wiped her face. Then, with a dreamlike slowness, she opened her backpack and took out two implements: a small coal-shovel and a rock hammer. She gave Val a tired smile and said: "If anyone asks, I'm looking for fossils in the estuary."

Val watched Helen dig in the mound for a while. She wasn't keen to help, this close to finding what she suspected was there. *Why the hammer?* she thought, and didn't like the answer that came to mind. About a foot down into the soil, Helen reached some kind of cavity. She worked along its length, opening up a trench several feet long and a foot deep. Its walls were smooth and rounded. Helen stopped and looked up at the flawless blue sky. Her face was twisted with pain. "The ground couldn't hold him," she said quietly.

THEY DIDN'T STAY at the hotel. Helen wanted to go straight back to London. She wouldn't talk about what they'd seen. When the train went through a tunnel, she closed her eyes and wrapped her arms tight around herself. Val felt at a loss. This had gone beyond what she could manage.

When they reached Paddington Station, Helen suggested they get a drink. Over a glass of chilled wine, she gave Val a playful smile. "I'll take up your offer to come with me on the Tube," she said. "From here it's the Bakerloo line to Oxford Circus, then the Victoria line to Seven Sisters."

"All right then." Maybe it wasn't too late to help.

As they passed through the ticket gates, down the escalator and along the pale tunnels, Helen didn't really seem to be afraid. Her expression was a kind of amused defiance, like a bad girl in a 1940s *film noir*. Val half expected her to light a cigarette. When the train blazed into the tunnel, Helen stepped onto it without a backward glance.

It had obviously been another painfully hot day in London. The half-dozen people in the carriage looked worn out, even sick. No doubt the bad smell was affecting them. Was there a dead rat under one of the seats? It must have been there for a while, because they'd tried to cover it up with some cloying perfume – violets maybe, or roses, something out of season.

No-one got out of the carriage at Edgeware Road, but three men got on. They must have come from some kind of workshop, because their skin looked dusty and their clothes were smeared with tar. They were either gesticulating or using a basic sign language Val hadn't seen before – either way, they were silent.

Before the next station, the train stopped in a tunnel and the lights went out. "Fuck," Val said. Helen laughed, but not in amusement. A moth flew past, its wingtip brushing Val's cheek. The odour of decay was getting worse. Just as Val was about to scream, the train began to rumble forward in the dark.

When its doors opened, they were not at Victoria. It seemed to be outdoors, though Val couldn't see the sky. How had the night come on so fast? The ground beneath her feet was more like bare rock than concrete. The wind blowing from the tunnel carried a faint smell of rotting fruit. From a long way away, Val could hear voices. Whether they were chanting or crying, she wasn't sure. She reached out to Helen, and their hands clasped as they walked away from the platform. The light was so faint it was hard to be sure you were seeing anything at all. The shapes they passed could have been people waiting, or pillars, or dead trees. Val felt a dry flake touch her face, then another. She thought they were ashes until one caught on her lips and she recognised the scent of a rose petal.

The ground beneath their feet was softer now. Val could see faint lights in the distance. There was a moisture in the air, a scent of rank soil. Then the unmistakeable whisper of running water. Had they come to the Thames? Val thought she could see many people kneeling on the bank, reaching down to the current. Beside her, Helen was breathing hard. "Where is he?" she said. Val knelt beside her and immersed her hands in the dark water. It felt colder than any unfrozen water should be, but as immaterial as mist. She tried to splash it onto her face, but her hands came up dry. And when she looked around, she realised she was alone. She got up and walked along the bank, but no-one else was there. Nor was there any bridge. But surely, if she walked far enough, the river would come to an end.

DOWN

Christopher Fowler

Christopher Fowler is a writer whose work is very much linked to London, the city he lives in and the city he loves. Who better, then, to ask to contribute to a collection of Underground horror stories? Christopher's style is deceptively simple, drawing the reader into the narrative easily, but his themes are undoubtedly complex. Here we have a ghost story that explores London Underground's past and the souls who inhabit those dark, echoing tunnels. But this isn't a story aimed to terrify you, instead there is something deeply moving about this tale of the Tube's forgotten.

HONOR OAK RESERVOIR is underneath a golf course in Peckham, Thornhill reminds himself as he walks. It's the biggest subterranean vault he's ever visited, an inverted cathedral that's the largest reservoir in Europe, with four great chambers that hold 256 million litres of water, a great heart made of orange brick ceaselessly pumping life into the metropolis. He would have liked to work on the new Brixton extension at Honor Oak but there wasn't a position, so he's back here in the Tube tunnels beneath King's Cross, moving through the dead dusty air, looking for circuit faults. He comes down every night at midnight and goes up at 4:00am; that doesn't sound hard but there are meetings before and sometimes after, and while you're down you're on the move the whole time.

Looking back, he can see the unmistakable silhouette of Sandwich hopping nimbly across the rails. Sandwich's real name is Lando – he was named after a character in a Star Wars film, and hates it – his mates call him Sandwich because no-one has ever seen him eat, even though he's the size of a bear.

Thornhill has been down for three years now, and likes the job. The perks are good, his fellow workers are a nice bunch and he gets regular health check-ups chucked in for free. They're all outsiders, of course, men and women who work down here, because they've joined a veritable foreign legion of employees who go below to forget.

But he doesn't forget. He goes down in order to remember.

"Early nineteen thirties," calls Sandwich in that peculiarly high voice of his, "Holborn Kingsway tram station. E/3 class double deckers. Wouldn't have minded driving them." Everyone down here is a bit of an expert on some aspect of the transport system. Some of them could bore for England.

"Why didn't you become a driver?" Thornhill calls back.

"Couldn't pass the eye test," Sandwich explains. "Short-sighted. When I was a kid I always wanted to drive the 1938 red Tube stock, varnished wood interiors, red and green finish, shovel lampshades. They've still got a few on the Isle of Wight."

"That figures."

"When they brought in the '67 Victoria Line carriages I reckon it took most of the fun away, anyway." After that, drivers only had to press two buttons, one to operate the doors and one to start the train. Driving a train now was not much more than an exercise in staying awake.

"You've got an N3 up ahead," calls Sandwich. "First stop." They're heading south on the Kennington branch of the Northern Line between King's Cross and Euston, checking all the junction boxes, looking for an intermittent fault that's showing up on the grid as an irregular power loss – inconsistent and too brief to disrupt service but a break all the same. Usually there's four of them working together, but tonight the other crew have been sent up to Highbury & Islington where one of the cleaners has found debris on the line. They've gone to see if any overhead cabling staples have come loose; it could be dangerous if they've fallen on the rails.

Thornhill is in boots and the orange boiler suit that makes him look like a Guantanamo Bay inmate. He raises his cage-lamp and aims the light on his helmet in the direction of the box, fixed on the wall at head-height where the main tunnel meets one of the side tubes leading away from the now-defunct Thameslink station on Pentonville Road. Such side-tunnels are rarely filled and capped. Most get used for equipment storage. Many just remain empty, and a few which run parallel to the main lines are kept clear in case of emergency, a euphemism for terrorist acts, and even the Underground staff don't know exactly where these are located.

Digging his key from his tool-satchel, he unlocks the lid of the box and peers inside. Two rows of green LEDs tell him that all contacts are working perfectly. He's pretty sure that an intermittent fault would register as a flickering light or a red, in which case he'd simply replace the connector. "Clear," he tells Sandwich. "How many more on this run?"

"Eighteen," says Sandwich, checking his chart. "They go all the way down to Goodge Street."

"That's going to take us all night. What if it's something we can't fix?"

"Then someone will have to come down with specialist equipment and run a day-test on the line," says Sandwich, who has caught up with him.

"Do you know where all the boxes are?"

"They're all on the main southbound, except the ones between Euston and Warren Street." Sandwich hands him a sheet with a diagram overlaid on their section of the tube map. He taps his thumb on the remaining pages thoughtfully. "We could still finish on time if we split up," he suggests. Crews are always supposed to operate in pairs, just in case one gets injured or suffers an attack of nerves. It doesn't happen very often; the LU workers know the dangers and are a pretty careful lot. Sandwich knows that if they take half the line each they can be back before four, and no-one will be any the wiser so long as they clock off together before the power is turned back on at 4:15am.

"I guess that would be okay," says Thornhill somewhat hesitantly, knowing he will be in breach of contract by agreeing. Sandwich has spent his entire working life so far down here. The tunnels hold no terrors for him.

"You all right?" asks Sandwich. "Only when you didn't come in last week…"

"I told you, I had a cold," Thornhill quickly explains.

"I thought maybe – the cut on your hand."

Thornhill hides his bandaged knuckles behind his back, self-conscious. "That's nothing. I'd had a few. I get a bit angry sometimes."

Sandwich is thinking it through, picking at the thought like a scab. "Because Thornhill's not actually your name, is it? I only noticed because you left your mobile in the office and saw that it's registered in a different name. I know it's none of my business –"

"You're right," snaps Thornhill, "it is none of your business."

"I mean, we all come down for different reasons. But there's a reason why there are checks in place, you know? I'm not talking about terrorism or nothing like that."

"I think I know what you're talking about."

"You didn't get the Honor Oak job, so you came back down here." It wasn't a question.

"I didn't mind where I went, so long as it was underground."

"Fine." Sandwich knows better than to ask why. As he says, everyone has their reasons. "Look, I'll go down to Tottenham Court Road and start from that end, you work from here and we should meet up at Warren Street by about three thirty." Without waiting for a reply, Sandwich nips over the rails to the far side of the tunnel and sets off, whistling something that sounds like 'It's A Long Way To Tipperary'. Moments later, Thornhill finds himself quite alone.

He has never worked alone down here before, but he's always

known that the practice went on among the more experienced crews. He isn't frightened – quite the reverse – but it still feels strange. Sandwich is a nice guy, a bit of a sad case since his girlfriend left him, but he never stops talking, never stops prying and asking questions, and the endless to-and-fro of vapid conversation never gives Thornhill time to be alone with his thoughts. Which is a pity, because there's still a lot to think about.

The faint swaying light from Sandwich's helmet in the tunnel ahead disappears, but there's still not total darkness. Somewhere further on to the left, in the curve of the ceiling, there is a grating that allows in a nimbus of pale luminescence.

He reaches the second junction box at a point where the main line meets a smaller service tunnel, and stops within the circle of darkness to listen. He can feel a cool breeze lifting the hairs at the base of his neck. The tunnels are beset by these dark zephyrs that eddy and swirl where tunnels meet. You can faintly hear the passing air, but nobody knows where it comes from or why it disappears as suddenly as it starts. Before the 1970s, an army of women used to enter the system after the last train had run. They were called Fluffers, and their job was to remove all the dust-balls, flakes of skin and human hair that had gathered in the tunnels. People always leave traces of themselves.

Improved ventilation has removed the need for the Fluffers now, so that the only human beings who venture down here after the Tubes finish running are the ones making electrical repairs or inspecting water damage. Most of the deeper stations have problems with underground wells, rivers, streams and conduits that periodically back up, and it's not a good idea to have water dripping onto electrical equipment.

The LEDs in the second box form two unbroken emerald lines. The fault lies further on, so he'll have to go deeper. All of the tunnels heading south descend toward the Thames, which is why the passages are fitted with flood gates. Thornhill can feel the temperature dropping as he sets off once more, passing beneath the dull glow of the grating, turning into the next great brick curve. The steel lines glint coldly in the beam of his lamp. Nests of mice, tiny brown bundles of fur that look as if they belong in country wheatfields instead of the London Underground system, turn black bead-eyes timidly up at him before scampering for cover. He approaches another tunnel entrance, D117 according to his diagram, and wonders if it's the one that was used as emergency headquarters for the wartime Railway Executive Committee. He's read a lot about the Tube system since – he's read a lot. He can see there's no track leading inside, and the dust has settled thick and undisturbed, far removed from commuters and cleaners.

And there, standing in the tunnel entrance, swaying very slightly, is a young man of about fifteen or sixteen, his outline barely discernable. "Can you help me?" he asks very politely, but in the kind of cockney accent Thornhill associates with old British films. He shines his torch on the lad's face, and is surprised to see that despite a neat short-back-and-sides haircut he is covered in dried mud. He wears a dirty collarless white shirt, braces and brown flannel trousers with thick turn-ups. The trousers are wet to the knees, as if he has been wading through water. "Sir? Can you help me?" he asks again.

"What are you doing down here?" asks Thornhill, surprised to find himself unalone.

"I ought to be out of London," he says apologetically. "You know, like the poster."

"What poster?"

"There's a drawing, a cartoon like, of a warden giving a boy a right telling off. *You ought not to be in London.* The Ministry of Health evacuation scheme. We didn't go. My old man thought it was for cowards."

"I'm sorry, I'm not with you."

"Where am I?"

"Euston interchange. I mean – you're underneath Euston Station. How did you get here?"

"Came up from Balham," says the lad, dusting his sleeves.

"Cor, you should have seen the mess down there. A right old state. It bounced clear down the steps and into the northbound tunnel before it went off – buried the whole length of the platform in gravel, blew out the walls, ruptured the water mains and flooded the platform three feet deep. You should have heard the screaming. Hundred and eleven."

"What?"

"Hundred and eleven dead so far. We was sheltering down there, six hundred of us kipping like sardines. The girl two down from me had both her legs blown clean off. The escalators came down, then there was another bang and we looked up through the dust – we couldn't hardly see anything – and there was only a bloody bus, gone and driven right into the crater. I think the driver got out all right."

"How did you get out?" Thornhill asks, puzzled.

"Well, we didn't." The boy shakes his head in sleepy wonderment. His eyelids close and open again. There's dust on them.

"Do you need to get up top?"

"Can't. Staying down here now. But I thought you might know if I'm going the right way for Bromley-By-Bow. I've got relatives over there. Be near them, like."

Thornhill knows he should feel absurd giving directions to a dead man, but tonight it seems like a perfectly natural thing to do. When he's finished explaining the route, his companion smiles wanly and sets off once more with a little backward wave. Thornhill stands and watches until his form has faded into the dry black air of the tunnel. He admires the lad's determination.

The next junction box proves impossible to open. A past leak has calcified the lock, so he is forced to chip away with the end of a screwdriver for twenty minutes before he can unlatch it, and the wasted time sets him back. The connections are all functioning, though, so he closes it and continues downward.

Sometimes the desiccated air sets off an ache behind his eyes, but tonight he feels fine, rather light-headed and slow, as if he is sinking into a dream. He runs the tips of his fingers along the curving wall, over the sooty fat trunks of cables, heading toward the next box. It's darker now, no overhead light seeping in from anywhere, and the breeze is moaning faintly at his back. That's when he notices the sound of another man, deliberate footfalls planted behind his own. He turns and waits, staring into the dark until it pixilates into the fractured vision of a migraine.

He doesn't like this one.

"Oi, didn't you hear me?" the man calls, his voice an angry slur. Thornhill waits until he is approached, then steps back against the concave tunnel wall. Now he sees the reason for the man's strange speech; he has no lower jaw. His tongue hangs straight down, dry and useless, looking like a leather luggage tag. He's dressed in a purple velvet jacket, tall and bony-featured, also missing his right ear and eye – they don't look bad, just scabbed over - but he's dribbling unstoppably as he shuffles closer, something Thornhill finds personal and vaguely embarrassing. "D'you work down here?" the man demands to know, seemingly oblivious to his terrible injuries.

Thornhill can smell strong alcohol on his breath. "Yes," he admits, "but I'm not a doctor. I can't help you." He assumes they'll only approach if they want something.

"I'd had a drink, of course I had, but it's the others you should be talking to." He's very animated for a dead man.

"What others?"

"They were on the platform with me. Last train of the night from Bank Station, we'd all been drinking at the Christmas bash. I didn't slip."

"You mean one of them pushed you?"

"I don't know, probably. Yeah, I mean yes they did." It sounds like he's had plenty of time to convince himself.

"When was this?" Thornhill asks, starting to understand the nature of his visions.

"December 18th 1976," says the man, shoveling his tongue

back up into his mouth without much success. "I hate it down here. I want to kill my mates for doing this, for pushing me. Yeah I was drunk, but I wouldn't have slipped. I want to go home."

"Where is home?"

"West Harrow."

"You'll need to follow the Metropolitan line from King's Cross," says Thornhill. "Go back in that direction." For a moment he thinks the man will take a swing at him, but then the poor creature turns around, almost overbalancing, and slams his hand into the wall, cracking three fingers. Then he heads away without another word. Something is leaking from his ragged jeans. Presumably he slid from the platform and went under the incoming train. What a state to be in.

Thornhill had always half-expected this day to come. He had thought – hoped – that perhaps he would see them, but had not expected them to speak, or be able to hear him. His heart is beating faster and he feels even more light-headed. He wonders if he is having some form of nervous breakdown, alone here in the tunnels, going quietly mad while the rest of the crews plug leaks and check the tracks for debris.

He knows he should probably turn back and hand the remainder of the task to someone else, but he hates to leave a job unfinished, and besides –

For some unearthly reason he finds himself crying. Once the tears start, it's very hard to make them stop. He forces himself to think about the intermittent fault, checks the diagram and heads down beyond the Euston interchange in the direction of Warren Street. Plenty of tunnels around him now, gaping black mouths like bellowing monsters, who knows where they all lead? Some of them aren't even marked on his map, as if they're hiding secrets. They snake deep inside the soil of the city, burrowing beneath London in a dark carnival of stone arteries, providing homes to who-knows-what, the dead below mimicking the living above.

It feels like he's been walking for hours. His boots are too tight and his legs are tired. He has checked eight boxes and found nothing wrong. Coming up to the ninth he starts to wonder if there really is a fault, or whether one of the controllers has simply misread a meter. But beneath this consideration is excitement and fear running like a fast-flowing river, the knowledge that everything he has dared to believe is being proved true.

According to his watch it's already 3:00am, and he has yet to locate the fault.

Something small and light brushes against his hair in the blackness, making him start. He swipes his right ear, batting it away, but there is another feather-shred flitting past, and another. And he can smell something now; the odour of cooking meat, as if he might enter the next tunnel bend and find a hamburger stand waiting to serve him. The specks touching his face and neck become more frequent. He grabs at one and rubs it between his fingers in the light of his helmet-torch. It is a smut, a drifting cinder. He sniffs it and knows at once that it is incinerated material of some kind, and his stomach shifts. He turns off the cage-lamp and his helmet-torch, and stands motionless in the pitch blackness, looking ahead.

Sure enough, there's a parabola of flickering light around the corner.

It takes him several minutes to pass beyond the wide bend in the tunnel, and here the rails are tricky to negotiate because they pass through several sets of greased points. At first he thinks there are dozens of mattresses lying across the floor, but as he gets closer he realizes there are bodies wedged between the rails. Some are burning softly from within, like dying embers in grates.

At the far end he can see a wall of twisted grey metal torn apart and fused with the surrounding brickwork, fires burning brightly inside. The exploded train carriage entirely blocks the tunnel. Even the trunking, the bundles of thick cables that form necklace loops along the tunnel walls, have been severed by the force of the explosion. Heading this way, ghostly in the pulsing firelight, hands upon each other's shoulders like Bruegel's parable of the blind leading the blind, the commuters seek a way to the surface, but as he approaches they disappear in whisps of burning dust. After all, they are the living, and have no place here among the dying and the dead.

Passing between the fallen bodies, ignoring the groans and the smell of roasting flesh, he walks on toward the source of the heat, knowing that it will disperse along with this apocalyptic vision. A temporal memory sealed beneath the streets in shafts of stone, forever trapped in the terrible moment of a July afternoon, the seventh day of the seventh month in 2005, when a terrorist bomb stole the lives of thirty seven passengers and injured seven hundred more. The dead must stay down here forever. Only the living may surface.

The present can't exist for long with the past, and so the wreckage disperses, the blinded wavering chain of survivors, each placing the next foot before the last with patience and determination, crumbles along its length and disappears, leaving only acrid dispersing smoke and the melancholy hubbub of departing spirits.

Thornhill stands alone once more. What shocks him most is not the scale of destruction but the sheer caprice of it all. He imagines a thousand families asking the same question he has asked over and over; why did it happen to us? Why were we singled out for tragedy? But of course to provide an answer one needs to understand the workings of life itself. And life must remain unknowable for the human spirit to survive.

Beyond the crash site the tunnel is clear. He can see the eleventh junction box in the halo of his torch. He unlocks the door and, with difficulty, pulls it open.

There it is, right there, the fault. A winking crimson light on the second row, beyond which there are no more greens. Feeling in his tool-bag he locates a connector, snaps off the plastic end, flips the old one out and replaces it. Then he resets the switch and watches as the lines complete themselves. Job done.

He's running late. He'll have to move faster if he wants to reach Warren Street in time to catch Sandwich. He'd like to linger back here. He senses the others are drawn upwards, if not exactly toward the light then at least to a point where the layer between the living and the dead is thinnest. But he can't afford to keep Sandwich waiting.

One thing puzzles him. There has been nothing before this night, no sign that they might appear around him, no reason why they should all turn up now. Perhaps he wasn't ready before.

He's ready now.

He once read that those who die by the hand of another are the easiest to see. At the far end of the scale are those who die natural deaths – they can never return. But what about the ones whose departures are simply accidental? What does it take to see them?

The temperature is dipping lower and the air is slightly damper. He fancies he can smell the river, but at least four stations stand between him and the Thames. The tunnel twists to the right, then to the left. He is passing close to the southbound Victoria line and descending fast. That's when he understands, of course. Finally knows what he is doing. He's known all along but denial is a powerful drug that can erase almost any other feeling. He reaches the Victorian line subjunction and descends via the service tunnel to the lower line.

Time is getting short, but he dare not run; there are transverse pipes that can trap your boot and twist it. After three years of travelling through this subterranean maze he always knows exactly where he is. Right now he is branching off beneath Tottenham Court Road, moving in the direction of Warren Street. Above him are a pair of pubs, a shabby terrace of shops and houses that lead to Fitzroy Square. He remembers how the square looked when he was working nearby on an electrical installation in a bank; the pavements were all dug up. One had a hole running all the way down to the Underground line.

Down.

It comes to him in a flash. The answer has always been right in front of him, but the time had never been right until now. He finally understands, and is ready. He looks at his watch. 4:23am. The power is back on throughout the Underground system. Sandwich will be up by now, angrily wondering where he is.

Thornhill looks down at the rails. Without hesitation he steps up on them and hops from one to the other, as if crossing the track to the far side of the tunnel. Halfway across he stops, balancing on the third rail. Slowly and deliberately he plants his right foot down on the ground. He has a strange sensation, unpleasant but momentary. It leaves him with a feeling of transformation, of departure and arrival. Then he continues to the opposite wall and waits.

It isn't long before she appears on the other side of the line, outlined against the wet black brick. She has round brown eyes, dark hair cropped in a French bob, a checkered skirt, a navy blue sweater and knee socks, just as he remembered. So like her mother. She looks over and gravely acknowledges him.

He loves the way children do that, the way they look when they're counting and concentrating, taking everything at face value, being very serious. "Hello," he says.

"Where's Mummy?"

"She couldn't be here, Amy. She had to go far away. She lives in another country now. But I'm here."

"I thought you weren't coming."

"I didn't know what to do, but I'm here now."

"It's boring. All the tunnels looks the same. I can't find Jasper."

"Jasper wasn't with you when – Jasper was back at the house." Jasper is Amy's teddy bear. On the day she had accompanied him to his job, he had made her leave it at home. *There's no room for Jasper and your bike in the car*, he had told her. If only he had made her leave the bike behind instead.

She had not been allowed to enter the bank's hard-hat area, and had gone to cycle in the little green park, the one at the centre of Fitzroy Square. He remembered thinking there was something wrong and running out into the street. Her bicycle lay on its side, next to the workman's hole. She had dropped something – a pendant from her bracelet, just a cheap little thing – it had fallen in, and she had gone to pick it up. At first he couldn't see her. It didn't seem possible she could have fallen so far.

"Where have you been?" Amy asks.

"I've been working down here, looking for you."

"But I've been here all the time." Her tone is reproachful.

"I know, sweetie, I just couldn't reach you. If my boss knew I'd taken the job just to find you, he wouldn't have let me come down tonight."

"Are you going to stay?"

His heart swells to bursting as he rushes back toward her. "Yes, of course I am. That's why I'm here." He takes her hand and it feels just as it did when she was alive, warm and dry. Her touch completes him. "Where would you like to go?"

"I don't want to go any further down." She tips her head on one side, considering the question carefully. "Up perhaps. Can we go up?"

"I don't know," he admits. "We can try."

Sweeping her into his arms, he holds her close, letting her warmth envelop him. He sets off with his lost daughter, heading back up the tunnel, toward the world that will always be just above, and only slightly out of reach.

ABOUT THE AUTHORS

Jasper Bark is a novelist, children's author and script writer who is beyond help. His many cult novels, including the acclaimed *Way of the Barefoot Zombie*, will attest to this. More shockingly his children's books, such as *Inventions – Leonardo Da Vinci* and the on-going *Battle Cries* series have been translated into nine different languages and are used in schools throughout the country to improve literacy and corrupt innocent minds. He has written scripts for animation and comic characters as diverse as *Spiderman* and *Shaun the Sheep* and appears to be unstoppable in the face of garlic, silver bullets and even kryptonite.

Simon Bestwick lives in mournfully resigned bachelorhood (or more precisely, Lancashire) and is the author of two short story collections, *A Hazy Shade Of Winter* (Ash-Tree Press) and *Pictures Of The Dark* (Gray Friar Press), and a novel, *Tide Of Souls* (Abaddon Books). His novella, *The Narrows,* was shortlisted for the 2009 British Fantasy Awards and reprinted in Ellen Datlow's *Best Horror Of The Year*. Recent publications include another novella, *Angels Of The Silences* (Pendragon Press), and a short story, 'Winter's End' in the Gray Friar Press anthology, *Where The Heart Is*. He likes folk, blues, rock and jazz music, films that have not been directed by Michael Bay, books, long walks over hills, real ale, single malt whisky and admiring beautiful women from afar. Having quit smoking he now has to exercise regularly, but consoles himself that if he fails he'll at least be a shoo-in for this year's Jabba The Hutt look-alike competition.

Pat Cadigan is the author of fifteen books, which include two non-fiction movie books, and *Avatars*, a novel for young adults. She has twice won the Arthur C. Clarke Award for her novels *Synners* and *Fools*, and her work has been translated into over a dozen languages. Born in New York, she grew up in Massachusetts, and spent most of her adult life in the Kansas City area, where she wrote for Hallmark Cards for ten years before quitting to write books full-time. She now lives in North London with her husband, the Original Chris Fowler, and her son Rob Fenner. They all use the Underground.

The *Oxford Companion to English Literature* describes **Ramsey Campbell** as 'Britain's most respected living horror writer'. He has been given more awards than any other writer in the field, including the Grand Master Award of the World Horror Convention, the Lifetime Achievement Award of the Horror Writers Association and the Living Legend Award of the International Horror Guild. Among his novels are *The Face That Must Die*, *Incarnate*, *Midnight Sun*, *The Count of Eleven*, *Silent Children*, *The Darkest Part of the Woods*, *The Overnight*, *Secret Story*, *The Grin of the Dark*, *Thieving Fear*, *Creatures of the Pool* and *The Seven Days of Cain*. Forthcoming is *Ghosts Know*. His collections include *Waking Nightmares*, *Alone with the Horrors*, *Ghosts and Grisly Things*, *Told by the Dead* and *Just Behind You*, and his non-fiction is collected as *Ramsey Campbell, Probably*. His novels *The Nameless* and *Pact of the Fathers* have been filmed in Spain. His regular columns appear in *Prism*, *All Hallows*, *Dead Reckonings* and *Video Watchdog*. He is the President of the British Fantasy Society and of the Society of Fantastic Films. Ramsey Campbell lives on Merseyside with his wife Jenny. His pleasures include classical music, good food and wine, and whatever's in that pipe. His web site is at www.ramseycampbell.com

Al Ewing is a comics writer and novelist who has mostly worked for *2000 AD* and the *Judge Dredd Megazine*, where he co-created *Zombo*, *Damnation Station*, *Tempest* and *Dead*

Signal, as well as doing work on *Judge Dredd*. As a novelist, he's written *El Sombra, I, Zombie, Death Got No Mercy* and *Gods Of Manhattan* for Abaddon Books. He moved to York from London eight years ago after circumstances he doesn't talk about. York is very small and cosy and you can walk everywhere. It's the last place in the world anyone would build a Tube system. He's sleeping much better these days, thank you.

Christopher Fowler was born in Greenwich, London. He is the award-winning author of thirty novels and ten short story collections, and author of the popular Bryant & May mysteries. He has fulfilled several schoolboy fantasies, releasing a terrible Christmas pop single, becoming a male model, posing as the villain in a Batman graphic novel, running a night club, appearing in the Pan Books of Horror and standing in for James Bond. His work divides into black comedy, horror, mystery and tales unclassifiable enough to have publishers tearing their hair out. After living in France and the USA he is now married and lives in King's Cross, London.

Joel Lane lives in Birmingham and works as a journalist. His work in the supernatural horror genre includes three collections of short stories, *The Earth Wire, The Lost District* and *The Terrible Changes*; a novella, *The Witnesses are Gone*; and a chapbook, *Black Country*. His articles on weird fiction writers have appeared in *Wormwood* and elsewhere. Joel has also written two mainstream novels, *From Blue to Black* and *The Blue Mask*; and two collections of poetry, *The Edge of the Screen* and *Trouble in the Heartland*. A third poetry collection, *The Autumn Myth*, is forthcoming. Joel has edited an anthology of subterranean horror stories, *Beneath the Ground*, and co-edited (with Steve Bishop) the crime fiction anthology *Birmingham Noir*. He and Allyson Bird have co-edited an anthology of anti-fascist and anti-racist stories in the weird and speculative fiction genres, *Never Again*, due out this autumn.

Rebecca Levene has neither shame nor pride. She likes writing and rarely says no when someone asks her to do some. This might explain how she's come to write a children's adaptation of *The Three Musketeers*, a *Beginner's Guide to Poker*, an extremely sweary video game and an erotic romance. She's currently working on the third volume of her series of supernatural thrillers. The first two – *Cold Warriors* and *Ghost Dance* – are available from all good bookshops.

James Lovegrove was born on Christmas Eve 1965 and is the author of more than 30 books. His novels include *The Hope*, *Days*, *Untied Kingdom*, *Provender Gleed*, and the Pantheon Triptych (*The Age Of Ra*, *The Age Of Zeus* and *The Age Of Odin*). In addition he has sold around 40 short stories, most of them gathered in two collections, *Imagined Slights* and *Diversifications*. He has written a fantasy series for teenagers, *The Clouded World*, under the pseudonym Jay Amory, and has also produced a dozen shorter books for readers with reading difficulties, including the series *The 5 Lords Of Pain*. He has been shortlisted for numerous awards, including the Arthur C. Clarke Award and the John W. Campbell Memorial Award, and his work has been translated into 15 languages. His journalism has appeared in magazines as diverse as *Literary Review*, *Interzone*, and *MindGames*, and he is a regular reviewer of books for the *Financial Times*. He currently lives with his wife, two sons and a cat in Eastbourne, a town famously genteel and favoured by the elderly, but in spite of that he isn't planning to retire just yet.

Gary McMahon's fiction has appeared in magazines and anthologies in the UK and US and has been reprinted in both *The Mammoth Book of Best New Horror* and *The Year's Best Fantasy and Horror*. He is the British-Fantasy-Award-nominated author of *Rough Cut*, *All Your Gods Are Dead*, *Dirty Prayers*, *How to Make Monsters*, *Rain Dogs*, *Different Skins*, *Pieces* *of Midnight, Hungry Hearts,* and has edited an anthology of original novelettes titled *We Fade to Grey.* Forthcoming are several reprints in 'Best of' anthologies, the novels *Pretty Little Dead Things* and *Dead Bad Things* from Angry Robot/Osprey and *The Concrete Grove* trilogy from Solaris.

Graham Joyce has said of **Paul Meloy** that 'he is one of the best writers of short stories in Britain' and, indeed, Paul has won the British Fantasy Award for his short fiction, much of which has been collected in the acclaimed *Islington Crocodiles* (TTA Press.) When he's not dreaming up dark and surreal worlds he works as a psychiatric nurse.

Mark Morris became a full-time writer in 1988 on the Enterprise Allowance Scheme, and a year later saw the release of his first novel, *Toady.* He has since published a further sixteen novels, among which are *Stitch, The Immaculate, The Secret of Anatomy, Fiddleback, The Deluge* and four books in the popular *Doctor Who* range. His short stories, novellas, articles and reviews have appeared in a wide variety of anthologies and magazines, and he is editor of the highly-acclaimed *Cinema Macabre,* a book of fifty horror movie essays by genre luminaries, for which he won the 2007 British Fantasy Award. His most recently published or forthcoming work includes a novella entitled *It Sustains* for Earthling Publications, a *Torchwood* novel entitled *Bay of the Dead,* several *Doctor Who* audios for Big Finish Productions, a follow-up volume to *Cinema Macabre* entitled *Cinema Futura* and a new short story collection, *Long Shadows, Nightmare Light.*

Adam L.G. Nevill and is a writer of supernatural horror, including the novels *Banquet for the Damned* (PS Publishing, 2004, Virgin 2008) and *Apartment 16* (Pan, 2010). His next novel, *Beast,* is published in May 2011 by Pan Macmillan. He lives in London and can be contacted through www.adamlgnevill.com

John Llewellyn Probert has been described by *Black Static* magazine as 'arguably the most dapper man in horror fiction'. He is the author of five short story collections, the most recent of which are *Wicked Delights* (Atomic Fez) and *Against the Darkness* (Screaming Dreams). He won the Children of the Night award for his first book *The Faculty of Terror* (Gray Friar Press). You can find out about all of these and more at www.johnlprobert.com, where there are also some pictures of him to help the fashion-conscious reader decide if *Black Static* was right.

Michael Marshall Smith is a novelist and screenwriter. Under this name he has published over seventy short stories and three novels — *Only Forward*, *Spares* and *One of Us* — winning the Philip K. Dick, International Horror Guild, August Derleth and British Fantasy Awards, as well as the Prix Bob Morane in France. Writing as Michael Marshall, he has published five internationally-bestselling thrillers, including *The Straw Men*, *The Intruders* and *Bad Things*, and 2009 saw the publication of *The Servants*, under the name M. M. Smith. His new Michael Marshall novel *The Breakers* will be published in 2011. He lives in North London with his wife, son, and two cats. He can be found online at www.michaelmarshallsmith.com

Natasha Rhodes is the British-born author of a disturbing number of horror and fantasy novels, including *Blade: Trinity*, *A Nightmare on Elm Street: Perchance To Dream*, and *Final Destination: The Movie 1* and *2*. Her most recent novel series stars supernatural crime fighter Kayla Steele, the first three books of which, *Dante's Girl*, *The Last Angel* and *Circus Of Sins* have been published internationally to occasional critical acclaim. She lives in Hollywood and makes a living filming rock bands and celebrities on the infamous Sunset Strip. She would write a book about her experiences if she thought anyone would believe her.

The winner of two British Fantasy Awards, **Nicholas Royle** is the author of a short story collection, *Mortality*, two novellas – *The Appetite* and *The Enigma of Departure* – and five novels, including *Counterparts*, *The Director's Cut* and *Antwerp*. Recent stories have appeared in *Riptide*, *Shoestring*, *Last Drink Bird Head*, *Black Static*, *Stilled Lives* and *The New Uncanny*. He teaches creative writing at Manchester Metropolitan University and reviews fiction for the *Independent*. He runs Nightjar Press, which specialises in publishing original short stories as signed, limited-edition chapbooks. He hopes to have a new novel and collection out in 2011, as well as an anthology of Gothic bird stories, *Something Terrible, Something Lovely*, a title borrowed from William Sansom, which will be published by Two Ravens Press.

Stephen Volk was creator and lead writer of ITV1's award-winning paranormal drama series *Afterlife* starring Lesley Sharp and Andrew Lincoln, and the notorious BBC TV 'Halloween hoax' *Ghostwatch*, which spooked the nation, hit the headlines, and caused questions to be raised in Parliament. His latest feature film, *The Awakening*, stars Rebecca Hall, Dominic West and Imelda Staunton and his other credits include Ken Russell's *Gothic,* starring Gabriel Byrne and Natasha Richardson; *The Guardian*, directed by William Friedkin; and Channel 4's *Shockers*. He also won a BAFTA for the short film *The Deadness of Dad* starring Rhys Ifans. His first collection, *Dark Corners*, was published by Gray Friar Press, from which his story '31/10' was nominated for both a British Fantasy and a HWA Bram Stoker Award. More recently, his novella *Vardoger* earned him a nomination for both a Shirley Jackson and a British Fantasy Award. His stories have also appeared in *Year's Best Fantasy and Horror*, *Best British Mysteries* and *Best New Horror*, and he writes a regular comment piece for the magazine *Black Static*. More details on his website: www.stephenvolk.net

Conrad Williams is the author of the novels *Head Injures*, *London Revenant* (a novel which is predominantly set in the capital's underground rail network), *The Unblemished*, *One*, *Decay Inevitable*, *Blonde on a Stick* and, forthcoming from Solaris, *Loss of Separation*. He has also written four novellas and over 80 short stories, some of which are collected in *Use Once then Destroy*. He is a past recipient of the International Horror Guild Award, and the British Fantasy Award. Having lived in London for 13 years, a slave to the Northern Line, the Bakerloo Line and the Piccadilly Line, he now lives in Manchester with his wife and three sons, and is a thoroughly overground kind of guy. The last short 'underground' story he wrote was 'O Caritas', which appeared in The *Solaris Book of New Fantasy*, edited by George Mann.